12 ROSE STREET

Other Joanne Kilbourn Mysteries
by Gail Bowen

The Gifted
Kaleidoscope
The Nesting Dolls
The Brutal Heart
The Endless Knot
The Last Good Day
The Glass Coffin
Burying Ariel
Verdict in Blood
A Killing Spring
A Colder Kind of Death
The Wandering Soul Murders
Murder at the Mendel
Deadly Appearances

12 ROSE STREET

A JOANNE KILBOURN MYSTERY

GAIL
BOWEN

McCLELLAND & STEWART

Library and Archives Canada Cataloguing in Publication information available upon request

ISBN 978-0-7710-2400-9
eBook ISBN 978-0-7710-2402-3

Published simultaneously in the United States of America by McClelland & Stewart, a division of Random House of Canada Limited.

Library of Congress Control Number available upon request

This is a work of fiction. Characters, corporations, institutions, and organizations in this novel either are the product of the author's imagination or, if real, are used fictitiously without any intent to describe their actual conduct.

Lyrics on page 155 from "I'm a Pirate," by Mark Summers. The song is published online at www.talklikeapirate.com/juniorpirates.html.

Cover design: Leah Springate
Cover image: © Peeter Viisimaa/Vetta/Getty Images

Printed and bound in the USA

McClelland & Stewart,
a division of Random House of Canada Limited,
a Penguin Random House Company
www.penguinrandomhouse.ca

1   2   3   4   5   19   18   17   16   15

Penguin
Random
House

For my husband, Ted,
with thanks for helping me pass Old English forty-six
summers ago

CHAPTER

1

When Brock Poitras moved into our building, my husband, Zack, our soon to be sixteen-year-old daughter, Taylor, and I had been living in Regina's Warehouse District for a little over a year. I took my early morning run with our dogs, but our area can be dodgy and Zack was relieved when Brock, who had been a wide receiver for the Saskatchewan Roughriders, began joining me. Brock and I never talked much when we ran, and Labour Day morning was no exception. After we exchanged greetings, Brock took our mastiff Pantera's leash, I tightened my hold on our bouvier Willie's, and we set off.

Rose Street was about halfway along our usual route, and whenever we turned onto it I felt as though we entered another world. Demolition had cleared the way for progress in our part of the neighbourhood, but Rose Street remained a grim Dickensian landscape of condemned warehouses, abandoned shops, and once-tidy pre-war bungalows that had crumbled into slum dwellings. Brock had grown up on Rose Street. As much as anyone could be, he was inured to the ugly realities of life in the heart of North Central. I was not, and whenever we ran there my nerves were tight.

That morning trouble was not long in coming. When we were midway down the block, the front door of the storey-and-a-half on our left burst open. A woman and a man were screaming curses at each other. Within seconds, the man picked the woman up, slammed her body from the porch onto the concrete front walk, and ran back inside. Brock and I halted in our tracks. Startled at the break in routine, the dogs tensed and turned to us for direction.

The porch was at least two metres above the walk, and I was certain the impact must have broken the woman's bones, but, still cursing, she scrambled back onto her feet. Brock took Willie's leash and fished in his pocket with his free hand for his phone. "I'll call 911," he said. I moved towards the woman.

She was really just a girl – late teens, Aboriginal, and high on something that was making her manic. She was flailing her arms, and she couldn't stop talking. "I'm sixteen weeks' pregnant," she said, whirling to face me. "Sixteen fucking weeks. I've got three kids, and that asshole boyfriend of mine is still making me work the street. I told him he should fucking get a job. I'm sixteen weeks' pregnant. I don't want strangers jamming their cocks in there. It's not good for the baby. Sixteen weeks." She held out her hands imploringly, then her eyes opened wide and she bent double and clutched her abdomen. "What the fuck?" she said.

"Hang on," I said. "There's an ambulance on its way."

She had beautiful, long-fingered hands. She reached towards the crotch of her jeans and when her fingers came back bloody, she began to keen. "Sixteen weeks," she moaned. "Sixteen fucking weeks." Her eyes met mine. "Do you think I lost the kid?"

"I don't know. The EMT workers will take you to the hospital," I said. "There'll be people there to care for you. My name is Joanne."

"I'm Angela," she said, and her voice was dead.

"Angela, is there someone to take care of your children?"

"Just Eddie," she said. She grimaced with pain. "Everybody told me he was a son-of-a-bitch bastard. I shoulda listened."

The ambulance arrived, and the police were right behind it. Brock and I gave our statements and told the police that, as far as we knew, Angela's boyfriend was still inside and three children were with him. The police took our contact information and strode towards the house.

The EMT workers were loading Angela into the ambulance. I couldn't leave without checking on her. The manic phase had passed. She was drained. Her skin had a yellowish tinge and her lips were bloodless. When she spotted me, she raised her hand in a kind of salutation. "See you around, Joanne," she said.

"Angela, I'm so sorry."

Something in my words ignited her. Angela's tone was scathing. "So you're sorry, and everything's all right again," she said. "Everything's fixed. Joanne, you seem like a nice lady, but you're fucking clueless. Nothing's ever fixed for people like me."

The EMT workers closed the doors and I turned to see an old Aboriginal woman wearing trousers, a hunting jacket, and men's bedroom slippers come out of the house across the street from Angela's. The stuccoed two-storey at 12 Rose Street had caught my eye on earlier runs – first because it was seemingly in good repair and second because it was painted an eye-scorching shade of mustard yellow. The old woman found a place on the sidewalk beside Brock. As the ambulance disappeared around the corner, she clicked her teeth. *"But as for the murders and the sexually immoral, their portion will be in the lake that burns with fire and sulphur . . . Revelation 21:8."* Her eyes, black as pitch, fixed themselves on me. "The Bible isn't talking about that girl.

She's blameless – so are the other ones who are forced to commit indecent acts. The lake of fire and sulphur burns for the evil ones, the ones who break innocent bodies and steal souls." Her words still hanging in the air, the woman turned and went back inside.

Brock and I waited until Angela's children had been led out of the house at Number 15. They were very young, and when a female officer approached them, they went with her willingly. Clearly they knew the drill. After the children were safely inside an unmarked car, two officers brought out Angela's boyfriend, Eddie. He was shirtless – a thin, pale, heavily tattooed young man sporting low-slung jeans, a blond ponytail, and an expression of abject remorse. As the officers shepherded him into the back seat of the squad car, Eddie was co-operative. He, too, knew the drill. Acquiescence and a show of penitence now would hold him in good stead when he appeared in court.

We finished our run in silence. The brutality we had witnessed had shaken us both. Before Brock got off the elevator in our building, he handed Pantera's leash to me. "I wasn't close enough to hear exactly what went on," he said.

"Her name is Angela. She was pregnant," I said. "And I'm pretty certain she lost her baby."

His face was stony. "That may not have been the worst outcome," he said.

Zack was at the breakfast table with the morning paper when the dogs and I came in. "How was your run?"

"Fine," I said. I swallowed my urge to tell Zack about Angela. "The weather should be great for the opening."

"Speaking of . . ." he said, holding out the morning paper. "Check this out."

A photo of Zack and Brock was on the front page. "Nice-looking dudes," I said. "What did they do?"

"Read the story," he said. "It's a very favourable account of what the Racette-Hunter Training and Recreation Community Centre will mean for this city."

I skimmed the article. "Absolutely glowing," I said. "As are you. And you deserve to glow."

For over a year, Zack and Brock had been putting in punishing hours to make the Racette-Hunter Centre a reality, and today was its official opening. The centre had begun as the dream of Zack's friend, the late Leland Hunter, a developer who believed that through mentoring and on-the-job training the people of the deeply troubled community of North Central Regina could salvage their lives and change our city. After Leland's death, his widow, Margot Hunter, asked Zack to take over the Racette-Hunter project. She hadn't had to ask twice.

A year of swimming in the murky waters of civic politics and dealing with obstructionists on city council had politicized my husband. Now he was running for mayor and Brock Poitras was running for council from Ward 6, our ward in North Central.

I was managing both Zack's campaign and Brock's, and we were counting on the opening of Racette-Hunter to give them a much-needed boost. Civic elections don't engender much interest. Our opponents were a mayor running for his fourth term and an equally entrenched city council – all of whom had seemingly bottomless war chests.

Zack and Brock both had impressive resumés, but both were dragging some heavy baggage. As a trial lawyer, Zack had been ruthless and single-minded. When it was necessary, he got blood on his hands, and the colleagues he eviscerated in court had long memories. Zack had been a paraplegic since he was run over by a drunk driver at the age of seven. He was forty-nine when he and I married. Until then, believing that his chances of making it to a ripe old age were minimal, Zack had lived like an eighteen-year-old with a death wish: hard drinking, gambling, fast cars, and many, many affairs, not all of which ended amicably.

As a husband, lover, friend, stepfather, and grandfather, Zack was everything I could wish for. As a candidate for public office, he was a challenge. The number of skeletons in his closet was daunting, and every day I awoke waiting for another one to topple out.

By any criteria, Brock Poitras was an extraordinary man. He'd grown up in North Central. He came from a single-parent home, he was Aboriginal, and he was gay.

Brock's brains and his talent as an athlete protected him against the hopelessness that makes so many inner-city kids vulnerable to gang membership, drugs, alcohol, and crime. When a torn meniscus ended his football career, Brock earned an MBA.

From the day Zack recruited Brock to be second-in-command of the Racette-Hunter working team, Brock was Zack's go-to guy. Zack likened their relationship to the trust that exists between a quarterback and his best wide receiver. Brock was a natural for the permanent position of executive director of Racette-Hunter, and when Zack and Margot offered him the job, Brock didn't hesitate.

I poured myself a large mug of coffee – it was going to be a big day for us all. I hadn't planned to tell Zack about the incident on Rose Street until later, but he knew me too well. He wheeled his chair close and took my hand. "What's wrong?" he said. Zack listened intently until I was through, then he held out his arms and I folded into them. When, finally, we broke apart, I was almost ready to face the day.

Zack, Taylor, and I arrived at the Racette-Hunter parking lot at the same time as Margot, her eighteen-year-old stepson,

Declan, and Margot and Leland's nine-month-old daughter, Lexi. We were all wearing the forest-green sweatshirts with the Racette-Hunter logo that identified volunteers. Declan gave us the once-over. "We look like the world's lamest softball team," he said. We all laughed, but the truth was we did feel like a team. In fact, we felt like a family. There were only two condos on the top floor of our building on Halifax Street: the Hunters lived in one, and our family lived in the other. But our connection went far beyond physical proximity.

Margot and Zack had been law partners, and sometime sparring partners, for two decades, and after a lengthy period of friendship, Taylor and Declan were on the cusp of romance. After Leland's death, Margot and I grew close. I had been her labour coach, and Zack and I had both been with her when Lexi was born. Not long after Lexi was safely launched into the world, Margot, who was from a big close family, began considering having a second child. I was her sounding board as, lawyer-like, she marshalled the arguments for and against enlarging her family as a forty-four-year-old single mother. From the outset it was clear that Margot wanted another child, and I was pleased but not surprised when she announced that she'd decided to have another baby right away.

Margot and Leland had been truly in love, and Margot found it difficult to think about sex with a casual partner. After deliberation she decided on donor insemination and she was now happily pregnant. Her baby boy was due on Valentine's Day. In a week Declan was starting his first year at the University of Toronto. We were all moving along, and on that bright morning it felt right that our two families were together to celebrate a project that mattered so much to us all.

Brock and Margot had decided to keep the formalities of the opening to a minimum. The noon ribbon-cutting was a photo op only. The speeches would come at suppertime, and they would be brief. The focus of the day was exploration and fun. Tour guides recruited from North Central would show off the buildings and talk about the programs. The swimming pool and the basketball courts would get a workout, and there would be plenty of old-fashioned outdoor games for the kids.

The centre was comprised of eight two-storey buildings linked to form an octagon. The space enclosed by the octagon was known as "the green," and by eleven o'clock Brock, Zack, and I were on it watching Zack's and my granddaughters, Madeleine and Lena, run together in a three-legged race. They were halfway across the green when someone in the crowd to my left caught Zack's eyes. "You won't believe who's coming our way," he said.

Brock and I turned to follow his gaze. "Cronus," I said. "Wow. What's he doing here?"

Zack shrugged. "Nobody has a bigger investment in North Central than Cronus."

I gave Zack a sidelong glance. "He does pretty much own it, doesn't he?"

Cronus was a slumlord. He held the deeds for dozens of the neighbourhood's overcrowded, rat-infested houses, and his motto as a landlord was "maximum income, minimum maintenance." Cronus was also known to be into rough sex – always consensual, he was quick to point out. When a girlfriend who shared Cronus's pleasure in spanking, hair-pulling, and limb-twisting ended up dead, Cronus landed in the prisoner's box. Zack had successfully defended him, and Cronus continued to be grateful. In addition to paying Zack a hefty fee, Cronus had offered him his top revenue-earning property. Zack demurred, but Cronus promised Zack that someday he would reward him. It was an assurance that unnerved me.

That sunny morning, Cronus approached with his hand extended. He offered it to me first. I took it but only after steeling myself. Cronus gave me the creeps. It wasn't just his occupation or his enthusiasm for rock-'em sock-'em sex. It was the man himself. He was always immaculately dressed. That day he was wearing a custom-tailored white summer suit that would have done Gatsby or Mick Jagger proud. The workmanship was artful, but all the tailors in Hong Kong couldn't disguise the fact that Cronus was a snake. His shaved head was bullety; his eyes were hooded. He had a habit of flicking his tongue before he spoke. His hand was unnervingly cold and smooth, and I was relieved when he released mine.

The three-legged race was over. Madeleine and Lena had come in fourth and were standing in line to receive their ribbons. Zack pointed out the girls to Cronus. "Those brilliant athletes are our granddaughters," he said.

Cronus's gaze was cool and assessing. "How old are they?"

Zack's smile faded. "Madeleine is eight and Lena is seven." He moved his chair closer to Cronus. "What are you doing here?" he said. "Watching children at play isn't exactly your scene."

Cronus nodded his bullety head. "True," he said. His eyes travelled over the green. "When I was a kid, our neighbour took me to her church's Sunday school picnic. All I remember is lining up and waiting while some lady with a great rack and a face like a bloodhound gave each of us an egg on a spoon. When we all had our eggs and spoons, she counted to three. Then she yelled, 'Run for Jesus.'"

Cronus seemed lost in nostalgia; Brock nudged him towards the present. "Did you win?"

Cronus nodded. "My prize was a plastic bookmark with a mustard seed stuck on it. A piece of shit. I gave it to the girl I accidentally tripped at the finish line."

Madeleine and Lena sprinted over to show us their ribbons. Zack took their photos and introduced them to

Cronus. The girls' personalities had long ago declared themselves. Madeleine – like her mother, Mieka; my eldest son,
Peter; and me – was fair-haired, green-eyed, earthbound, and
risk-averse. Lena had the black Irish good looks and mercu-
rial temper of my younger son, Angus, and my late husband,
Ian. As different as they were, the girls were unusually close.
When the whistle blew to announce the next race, they
handed us their ribbons and took off. Cronus watched as
they lined up, and then turned to face Brock and Zack.

"I've heard a rumour that you should be aware of,"
Cronus said. "There's a plan to abduct one of the kids here
today."

Simultaneously, Zack and I looked towards our granddaughters. The foot race had begun. Madeleine was a strong
runner and she was out in front. Lena lagged behind the
pack. When she spotted us watching, she stopped to wave.

"Tell the little one she'll never win if she takes her eyes
off the prize," Cronus said.

"I'll tell her," Zack said. "Cronus, did whoever passed
this rumour along to you say that any child in particular has
been targeted?"

Cronus was watching the race as avidly as if he'd bet
money on it. "My source says that they just want to take a
kid – any kid."

My heart was pounding. "Why?"

"Come on, Joanne. A smart broad like you can figure this
out." Cronus's tone was sharp. "Not everybody wishes Zack
and Johnny Football here well. People are impressed by the
way they've managed to stickhandle the R-H Centre into
being. They're starting to believe that Zack and Johnny
Football have the stones to run the city. But a turnover at
City Hall is not good news for the groups who've had our
current mayor and city council by the short and curlies
since the day they were elected."

"And if a child were abducted at the opening," Brock said, "the centre would be screwed from day one, and Zack and I could wave goodbye to our chances of being elected."

Cronus nodded. "You guys have been making a lot of promises. Racette-Hunter is Zack's baby and you're the director. If you can't keep a neighbourhood kid from being snatched at a picnic, people are going to think twice before they trust you to run this city." He turned towards me and narrowed his eyes. "You should be watching the race, Joanne. Madeleine is about to win."

Obediently, I turned in time to see our granddaughter cross the finish line. Lena and a little red-headed girl had given up and were strolling along chatting.

Zack moved closer to Cronus. "Do you know who's behind this?"

"I have some thoughts," Cronus said.

"Have you shared your thoughts with the police?" Brock asked.

Cronus's expression was withering. "You grew up in this city. How long did it take you to start believing that cops were your friends? And you were a poster boy for all that cultural sensitivity shit. The authorities *do* need to be involved. That's why I'm standing here talking to you. But keep my name out of it."

"We can do that," Brock said. "But so far all you've given us is a rumour. We need more – a lot more."

Zack's voice was deep and gentle. "Cronus, it took courage for you to tell us about the planned abduction, and believe me, I'm grateful. But knowing something terrible is about to happen isn't enough. We have to stop it."

No one spoke. Zack, Brock, and I watched as Cronus scuffed the grass with the toe of his white summer shoe. He was weighing his options. It was a big decision, and as the seconds ticked by, my pulse picked up speed. When I felt my blood pressure spike, I moved in front of Cronus, so close that our faces were just inches apart. "The future of Racette-Hunter is on the line," I said. "That means that the future of this neighbourhood is on the line. More importantly, a child's life could be at stake. If there's any way you can short-circuit this plan, you have to do it."

The warm September air was alive with the sounds of life in the city: a dog barking, a car alarm blaring, the siren tinkle of an ice-cream truck's bell, a boy calling out a friend's name with growing frustration – Riley, Ri-ley, RI-ley! RI-LEEE!!! The world was going on around us, but like lovers, Cronus and I were focused wholly on each other. Close up I could see the marks of life on Cronus's face: a surgical scar above his left upper lip and another on the right side of his nose, a slight pouching in the skin under his polar blue eyes, a droop in the flesh beneath his chin. Cronus's examination of my face was equally intense. Finally, his face relaxed and a small smile played on his lips. He had reached a decision. "What the hell," he said. "We only live once. Might as well make it count. Right, Joanne?"

"Right," I said.

Cronus's next words were a surprise. "I need you to take a picture of Brock, Zack, and me together." He reached into his leather shoulder bag, found his phone, and handed it to me. Then he crouched beside Zack's chair and motioned Brock to squat next to him. When everyone was in position, Cronus said, "You guys put your arms around my shoulders and smile. I want a photo that shows that the three of us are good buddies."

I took enough shots to make certain I had one that met Cronus's criterion and handed him the camera. He gave me the thumbs-up and showed the photo to Zack and Brock. "That should do the job," he said.

Zack was frowning. "So what is the job?"

Cronus flicked his tongue. "I'm sending off this photo of the three of us with a message." He started to tap out the message, but his fingers wouldn't cooperate. He flexed them, then began again. It was a laborious process. He typed slowly – repeating a series of numbers out loud as he entered them: "2-5-1-0-0-6." Task completed, Cronus dropped his phone into his bag, withdrew a large manila envelope, and handed it to Zack. "Here's my contribution to your campaign. I'm a cash-and-carry guy, so keep an eye on it."

"I will." Zack extended his hand to Cronus. "Thanks for everything."

"Hey, it's my city too," Cronus said.

"Yeah, and what you just did for this city was major," Zack said.

Cronus shrugged. "I had a silver bullet and I used it. It was no big deal." He shook hands with Zack and Brock and then he held out his arms me. I was surprised at the gesture, but I embraced him warmly. When we stepped apart, Cronus's face was soft. "That was nice," he said.

The three of us watched silently as Cronus made his way back across the green. Surrounded by laughing kids, he was a lonely and enigmatic figure. "Any ideas about what that little exercise with our photo was all about?" Zack said.

I shook my head. "You heard the man," I said. "That photo is the silver bullet."

Zack pulled out his phone. "I have faith in Cronus," he said. "But even silver bullets have been known to miss the mark. I'm calling Debbie."

"Tell her to meet us here," I said. "The kids' activities are all taking place on the green. If Debbie is going to secure the space, she'll need to be familiar with it."

Debbie Haczkewicz was in charge of the Regina Police Service's Major Crimes Section. Enduring friendships between police officers and trial lawyers are few and far between, but Debbie and Zack went way back. Fearless, dogged, and passionate about their work, they were kindred spirits. As soon as Zack began talking to Debbie, Brock left to find Margot, and I phoned my daughter, Mieka. She and her friend Kerry Benjoe were in charge of the children's activities, so I asked them to round up Declan, Taylor, and the other volunteers who were helping with the kids' games and meet us on the north side of the green.

After I hung up, I turned to Zack. "I guess now we just wait."

"We have our own security here today," Zack said. "And we have volunteers from the neighbourhood. No shortage of bodies – just a question of how to deploy them." Zack shifted his chair so he could take in the area. "Logistically, we're in good shape."

Shelley Gregg, the architect who designed the Racette-Hunter Centre, believed that kids who lived in a neighbourhood where they could never safely run free needed a space where they could play without fear. The eight buildings that housed the classrooms and the recreation facilities all had large windows overlooking the green. The windows were there to let in more than light. Racette-Hunter offered people a place where they could change their lives. Changing a life is difficult work. Seeing the kids every day was intended, in Cronus's phrase, to help people keep their eye on the prize.

By the time Debbie Haczkewicz arrived, Lexi Hunter was perched on Brock's shoulders watching Declan, Taylor, and the other volunteers spread out a dozen rainbow parachutes. The scene had the bright innocence of a Grandma Moses painting, but Debbie's presence was a grim reminder of the cloud that hung over the children squealing with delight under the billowing silk.

As Mieka and Kerry Benjoe went through the security precautions that were in place, Debbie took notes. The children were all wearing numbered red wristbands with the R-H logo.

Adults who brought children to the centre were wearing matching numbered bands. No child would be allowed to leave the R-H Centre with an adult whose wristband did not match the child's. The kids were on the buddy system and every fifteen minutes, a volunteer blew a whistle and hollered, "Buddies." The action didn't resume until every child had been paired. The children had been told to check the photo IDs worn by the adults to whom they could go if they were lost or scared.

Debbie nodded when the two women finished their report. "So as long as the children stay in this space, they're safe," she said.

Zack picked up on the edge in Debbie's voice. "But there's no guarantee the children will stay in this space," he said.

"None," Brock said. "In theory, they're all to be under adult supervision at all times, but kids are unpredictable. They dash ahead. They see a friend and wander off. The question now is whether we should go public with this."

Since her husband's death, Margot had been determined to make Racette-Hunter a reality. We all knew hers would be the deciding voice in the decision and our heads turned her way. "We don't go public," she said. "If we do, we might as well shut the doors to R-H right now. We've done everything we can to make this facility safe. All we can do now is build on what we have. We can coordinate our security with the police. We can text safety reminders to our volunteers. We can be vigilant, and we can pray."

Brock took Lexi from his shoulders and lifted her into the air. She giggled gleefully as he began to pump her up and down. "Margot's right," he said. "Let's just get through the day."

Brock's words were clearly intended to bring the meeting to a close. Mieka and Kerry took the hint, said their goodbyes, and headed back to where volunteers were now distributing pails of ping-pong balls to each of the parachute groups. The game they were about to play had been around since Mieka was little. The kids had to work together to make the parachute rise and fall so the ping-pong balls would pop up in the air. It was a team-builder. Given Cronus's news, it seemed an inspired choice.

We all watched as Mieka and Kerry headed towards the parachute games, but when Debbie started to leave, Margot and Brock exchanged a quick glance and called her back. They summoned Zack and me as well.

Brock moved closer to Margot. "You or me?" he said.

"Me," Margot said. "Debbie, Brock and I may be able to shed light on these threats. After my daughter was born, I decided to try to have a second child with donated sperm. Another pregnancy at my age was a big decision, and I couldn't afford a misstep, so I boned up on genetics. The upshot of my reading was that I decided against an anonymous donor. I wanted someone I knew and respected. I asked Brock. He agreed, and I'm now three months' pregnant." Zack's eyes met mine. Margot had never intimated that her donor was someone she knew.

Brock gave Lexi one final pump up and down and then nestled her in his arms. "As a gay man, I'd always figured that a child wouldn't be part of my life," he said. "The prospect of being a biological father was a gift. I talked it over with my partner, Michael, and he agreed. And then he changed his mind. My guess is that Graham Meighen changed it for him."

"What's Graham Meighen got to do with this?" I said. Meighen was a prominent developer in Regina who had always opposed the centre. He was also a vocal supporter of the current mayor, Scott Ridgeway.

"When Michael moved to Regina, Meighen took him under his wing," Brock said. "Graham was very welcoming to me too until I became director of Racette-Hunter, then the big chill hit. When I decided to run for council, Meighen and his friends announced they were supporting my opponent, Duane Trotter, and told Michael that he had to choose sides."

"They made Michael choose?" I was incredulous. "I can't imagine high rollers like Meighen being involved in that kind of schoolyard stuff. Do those guys take blood oaths too?"

"Whatever they do, it's the tie that binds," Brock said. "Michael and I had been together two years. I thought I knew him, but he went with Meighen's group."

"People have a way of surprising us," Debbie said curtly. "What's Michael's surname?"

"Goetz. Dr. Michael Goetz. He's a psychiatrist."

Zack turned to Debbie. "Dr. Goetz is responsible for all those shiny billboards Brock's opponent is putting up all over North Central."

"Michael's always prepared to pay for what he wants," Brock said. "I can deal with billboards. And I can deal with the crap that's making the rounds about my private life. I've been accused of pretty well everything, and I'm still walking around."

Lexi had fallen asleep in Brock's arms. He turned to Margot. "Should I put Lexi in her stroller? She may not understand the words we're saying, but she picks up on tones."

Margot nodded. "See if you can slide her in there without waking her."

Wide receivers are fast and agile. Brock had Lexi settled in her stroller in seconds. When she saw Lexi was content, Margot turned back to us. "Brock's concerned about my reputation," she said. "There's a rumour going around that any man who wants a job at Peyben has to perform stud service for the boss."

The anger rose in my throat. "The logical source of that one would appear to be Dr. Goetz."

Brock lowered his eyes. "There aren't any other possibilities," he said. "Margot and Michael and I were the only ones who knew that I'm the father of her baby."

Margot did her best to raise a more palatable possibility. "It's possible Michael confided in someone," she said. "People talk. Someone else could be spreading the rumour."

Debbie had a way of cutting through emotion. "Let's get back to the problem at hand," she said. "Spreading an ugly rumour during an election campaign is not a crime. Conspiring to abduct a child from a public gathering is. Do you think Dr. Goetz is capable of making that leap?"

"I honestly don't know," Brock said. "In the last year, Michael has done a number of things that I didn't believe he was capable of."

"Such as . . . ?" Debbie asked.

Brock's laugh was short. "Such as breaking off with me and going back to his old boyfriend Slater Doyle."

"The breakup was a surprise?" Debbie asked.

"It was a body blow," Brock said. "We were fine – enjoying our life together, making plans for the future – and then Michael started questioning everything about our relationship. It was as if he was trying to find a reason to leave."

"And he found one," Debbie said.

"He did. I don't want to go into it, but what Michael did didn't make any sense. Certainly going back to Slater Doyle didn't make any sense. Slater is destructive and unethical and Michael knows it."

"Brock's right about Slater Doyle," Zack said. "He was a lawyer, but he was disbarred for dipping into clients' trust funds and falsifying his firm's trust ledgers to cover his tracks."

"Now he's running Scott Ridgeway's re-election campaign," Brock said. "And he's managed to get Michael involved with Duane Trotter's campaign. And that's another thing that doesn't make sense. It's hard for me to be objective, but Trotter has done nothing for the people of Ward 6. He's a lackey for the developers and the only reason he wins is because Ward 6 has such a dismal turnout at the polls. Trotter's backers have deep pockets and that means all his campaign has to do is put up billboards in high-traffic areas, spend a bundle on media, then get out their core vote."

"Who is their core vote?" Debbie asked.

"Not to put too fine a point on it," Brock said, "they're people who hate Aboriginals. Michael and I lived together happily for over two years. I know him. He's not a bigot. He cares enough about at-risk kids to publish journal articles with concrete recommendations about how to save them. Now he's backing a candidate who lards his speeches with code words like 'hard-working,' 'community-minded,' 'law-abiding,' 'contributing members of society,' 'givers not takers.' The phrases seem perfectly innocuous, but his supporters know that Trotter is drawing a line. On one side are people like them; on the other are people like me."

"Dog whistle politics," I said. "Slimy but highly effective."

Lexi stirred in her sleep, and Margot knelt down to soothe her. Debbie lowered her voice. "Brock, this is a delicate situation. Nothing has happened yet. All we have is a rumoured threat that, in all likelihood, is groundless. Dr. Goetz is well liked in this city. I've never dealt with him personally, but his reputation is solid." Debbie raised her hand in a halt sign. "Of course, none of that matters if he's party to a conspiracy."

On the green, the parachute popcorn game had reached a fever pitch. Kids were starting to scream and the parachutes were flapping violently. Mieka and the other volunteers were moving among the children, collecting the ping-pong balls and explaining the rules for a quieter game.

As he watched the scene, Brock's broad back was to us. Finally, he turned to face Debbie. "I hate this," he said. "But you should talk to Michael. He's aware of how much the R-H Centre means to me, and for reasons I don't understand, he seems determined to undermine me."

Debbie had been taking notes. She stopped and looked at Brock. "You think Dr. Goetz is capable of becoming involved in a plan to abduct a child."

"Michael would never hurt a child, but if the plan is originating with the Ridgeway–Trotter campaign, Michael is probably aware of it."

Debbie closed her notebook. "In that case, I'd better pay him a call."

After Debbie left, Margot took hold of the handles of Lexi's stroller. "Time to get back to business," she said. "Anybody care to join me in welcoming people to the R-H Centre?"

And so with tight smiles and anxious eyes, we greeted the community. Those of us who knew about the possibility of an abduction were waiting for the other shoe to drop. It didn't take long.

Dinner was going to be a combination barbecue–corn roast on the green. In the days when my late husband, Ian, and I had been involved in party politics, I had organized a dozen such dinners. The meal for the R-H opening followed a pattern I knew by heart. The poultry association donated three hundred split broilers and the grills and personnel to cook the chickens. Local supermarkets donated corn, and neighbourhood families brought casseroles, salads, buns, pickles and pies, cakes and cookies.

People were lining up with their plates when a young volunteer ran over to me. She was out of breath and agitated. "There's a man over there who says he needs to find Brock Poitras. I told him that I didn't know where Brock was, but he didn't believe me. He's very angry."

"I'll handle it," I said. I followed her. A man was standing in front of a large sign that read WELCOME. He was a tall, lithe blond with severe brown eyes, an ironic twist to his mouth, and a sharply cleft chin. He introduced himself as

Michael Goetz. I offered my hand. "I'm Joanne Shreve," I said. "They're just about to serve dinner, so things are a bit chaotic, but I'll find Brock."

Dr. Goetz didn't take my hand, but my offer to help seemed to disarm him. I'd noticed Zack over by the barbecue watching the man from the poultry association grill his chickens. "My husband is just over there," I said, pointing. "He'll know where Brock is."

"I have no desire to talk to your husband," Michael Goetz said. "Just come back with the information."

"Fair enough," I said. I went to Zack and told him about Dr. Goetz.

"He sounds like an asshole," Zack said.

"I wasn't charmed by him," I said. "But this is between him and Brock, so if you tell me where Brock is, you and I can get out of the line of fire and fill our plates."

"Not that easy," Zack said. "Brock took Margot and the baby back to the condo. Apparently, Lexi's diaper failed to do the job. She was certainly pungent. Anyway, Brock offered to help with the cleanup."

"Why do I think that explanation isn't going to calm Dr. Goetz?"

"Do you want me to talk to him?" Zack said.

"God, no," I said. "That would just make everything worse. I'll break the news."

"What are you going to tell him?"

"The truth," I said.

Zack chortled. "That's a novel approach."

"Maybe," I said, "but it makes sense. There's no reason to lie. Michael Goetz ended his relationship with Brock. Brock's free to go anywhere he wants with whomever he wants."

As I approached Michael Goetz, I could feel the anger radiating from his body. He was fighting for control, but he was losing the battle. His fists were balled and the pulse in his neck was throbbing. His greeting was a challenge. "Well?" he said.

"Brock isn't here," I said.

"Where is he?"

I gazed across the green. The line for the barbecue was moving smoothly. People had been asked to bring blankets to sit on and they were returning to them with their plates and getting ready to enjoy dinner. Babies were crawling around. Little kids were running between the islands made by the blankets. It was a pastoral scene.

"On a mission of mercy," I said, trying to lighten the mood. "Margot's daughter had a three-alarm diaper, and Brock went back with her to the condo to give Lexi a quick bath."

Dr. Goetz was coldly furious. "Charming," he said. "But Brock's always ready to help the widow Hunter in every possible way."

"Meaning?"

"I'm sure he's fucking her."

"I think you'd better leave," I said.

"Because you don't want to hear the truth?"

"I know the truth. Margot is pregnant. Brock was her sperm donor."

Michael Goetz's laugh was harsh. "The original plan was for a procedure called intrauterine insemination. A catheter is used to place washed sperm directly into the uterus. But Brock and the widow Hunter chose to insert Brock's sperm into her vagina with his penis."

When I saw the hurt in his eyes, I knew he was telling the truth.

"I'm sorry," I said.

Dr. Goetz's smile was a rictus. "So am I," he said. "For the record, I'm not the son of a bitch Brock believes I am. I'm just a guy who's caught in a trap. First I'm forced to leave the man I love. Now I've got the cops at my door asking if I'm involved in some kind of plot to wreck the opening here today."

"Are you?"

He looked away.

"You knew about the plan, didn't you?" I said.

Michael Goetz raised his chin defiantly. "Indirectly. There was nothing I could do to stop it." Before I could pursue the point, he turned on his heel and walked away.

When I found Zack again, he handed me a plate of food. "The potato salad was going fast," he said. "So I am selflessly donating my share to you."

"You're a giver," I said.

Zack frowned. "You don't look like a woman who's just about to chow down on a double portion of potato salad."

"My encounter with Michael Goetz was disturbing," I said. "He seems like he's falling apart, Zack."

"I gather he's made a number of lousy decisions lately."

"Michael said he was forced to leave the man he loved."

Zack ripped off a chicken leg. "That's bullshit. The guy's a psychiatrist. He must have a few insights."

"None that are doing him any good," I said. "Oh, and something else. According to Michael Goetz, Brock and Margot got pregnant the old-fashioned way."

"Brock's gay," Zack said.

"He and Margot both wanted a child. Obviously, they worked out the technicalities." I took a forkful of potato salad. "Cumin," I said. "I love potluck. There are always surprises."

"So did the good doctor have anything more to say?"

"Just that the police have been to see him."

Zack bit into his chicken and nodded approvingly. "The chicken man knows his stuff." He snagged a tomato from my plate. "I'll bet having the cops show up at his door was a shock for Goetz."

"I'm sure it was," I said. "Zack, I know Michael Goetz treated Brock badly, but I felt sorry for him today."

"You have a tender heart," Zack said. "But at the moment, we have more pressing concerns than Michael Goetz. The fireworks start in an hour. They last thirty minutes. If we make it through the fireworks, we're home free."

My nerves twanged. "Bite your tongue," I said. "Ninety minutes can be a lifetime. I'm not going to exhale until every single child here is safely on the way home."

CHAPTER

2

The truck with the fireworks had arrived on the green and the sun was beginning to set when the speeches began.

The program opened with a prayer from Ernest Beauvais, the elder who had been with the Racette-Hunter working team since it began a year and a half earlier. A temporary stage had been set up on the north end of the green for the speeches. As Ernest approached the microphone and his deep bass rumbled out the prayer he used to start all our meetings, I relaxed. Ernest spoke in Cree, but I knew what he was saying. "Great Spirit – Grant us strength and dignity to walk a new trail."

Margot was the first speaker, and from the moment she stepped onto the stage holding her freshly bathed nine-month-old daughter, the crowd loved her. She spoke briefly and movingly about our collective responsibility to the next generation and the role Racette-Hunter hoped to play in giving all the children and adults in our city a chance to realize their potential. The audience was rapt.

Then Margot introduced the mayor, and it was immediately clear that something was wrong. Scott Ridgeway always bounded on stage to show that he was pleased as punch to be wherever he happened to be. That night, he hung back. Finally, an exasperated Slater Doyle all but frog-marched the mayor up the accessibility ramp and pushed him towards the microphone.

I had seen Scott Ridgeway many times. A bland blond with a cheerleader's smile and a fondness for generalities, he was always smooth, but that evening he looked terrified. He started his speech, lost his train of thought, then froze and stared at the audience. After what seemed like an eternity, Slater Doyle went to the microphone, said the mayor was under the weather, and ushered Ridgeway smartly off the stage. Milo O'Brien, a recent addition to our campaign team, tapped Zack's shoulder. "Looks like the classroom monitor is going to puke. It's your turn, big man." Zack moved swiftly, wheeling up the ramp in his all-terrain chair, adjusting the microphone, and starting in.

Zack's speech was electric. He pivoted in his chair, displaying it like someone in an infomercial, all the while talking about the features that had allowed him to move over the rough terrain of the construction site during the building of Racette-Hunter. Zack explained that he was now able to get around the centre in his everyday wheelchair, but there was a time when he needed extra help navigating. He ended by saying that at some point in their lives, everybody needs help getting where they want to go, and Racette-Hunter was there to offer that help. "My wheelchair," he said, "is made by a company called Renegade. Their motto is 'Blaze your own trail.' That's what Racette-Hunter will allow you to do."

"Nice job," muttered Milo. "That wheelchair shtick was fucking inspired." Then he went back to tweeting.

I'd met Milo when Ginny Monaghan, a woman I admired, ran in my federal riding. Ginny lost the election, but I'd been impressed with Milo. Beating Ridgeway was going to be tough, and Milo was exactly what we needed – a political strategist who loved the game, had no politics of his own, and believed that all that mattered was winning. Our campaign was fuelled by the desire to change the system. Milo would tell anyone who asked that he didn't give a shit about changing the system, but he did give a shit about winning, and the odds here appealed to him. With his constant texting and tweeting, his machine-gun rat-a-tat-tat phone conversations, and his continuous intake of Crispy Crunch bars, he drove Zack crazy, but the moment Milo came on the scene my spirits soared, and until the last ballot was counted, I was prepared to treat him like spun glass.

Brock Poitras came to the microphone next.

He spoke not as a candidate but as the director of the Racette-Hunter Centre. His speech was short and personal. Brock said that some might believe that growing up in North Central as the gay Aboriginal son of a single mother meant he had not just three but four strikes against him. Yet today, he had an exciting and fulfilled life. His message was simple: realizing your potential isn't always easy, but it is possible.

Margot's expression as she watched Brock speak was thoughtful. "Jo, what are Zack and Brock's chances of winning?"

"It's early times," I said.

"Meaning their chances aren't good."

"In a clean campaign, they'd have a decent chance."

"But this isn't going to be a clean campaign."

I wrapped my arms around myself. The temperature was dropping. "They've already hit us with that ugly rumour about you demanding stud service from potential employees. Now there's a possible attempt to abduct a child. I've spent most of my adult life in politics, but I don't understand what's going on here. All I know is that an ordinary civic election feels like it's becoming a very high-stakes game.

You don't get a bottom feeder like Slater Doyle to run your campaign unless you're prepared to break kneecaps."

Margot was cool. "Graham Meighen has had his way in this town for a long time. A new broom sweeps clean and that's the last thing Meighen and his cronies at Lancaster Development want. He'll be slick about it, but he'll do whatever he has to do."

"I didn't realize you knew Graham Meighen that well."

"I don't, but I've seen him in action. Meighen was the first of Leland's colleagues to call on me the day Leland died. He offered condolences and then, in a very courtly manner, cautioned me against making any business decisions until the first grief had passed."

I smiled. "Looking out for your best interests," I said.

"Which, amazingly, coincided with his best interests," Margot said. "Graham wanted to make certain I didn't accept anyone's offer to buy Peyben until he had time to put together an offer I couldn't refuse."

"But you did refuse."

"Of course. Leland spent a lifetime building Peyben, and he didn't trust Graham Meighen. That said, Graham's performance as the concerned friend was smooth as silk. When the occasion demands charm, Graham knows how to turn it on."

Onstage, Brock was wrapping things up. He thanked everyone for coming, reminded people to keep a close eye on their children during the fireworks display, and said he hoped to see many of the crowd the next morning when the R-H Centre would be open for business. Elder Beauvais said a closing prayer and it was time for the big show.

Fireworks displays have never lost their allure for me – the smell of bug spray, the blankets spread on the grass, the sleepy kids fighting to stay awake, the flash, the whistle, the chorus of oohs and ahs as the sky explodes with showers of stars that disappear as they drop to earth – summer enchantment. Like every child who's ever held a sparkler, Madeleine and Lena tried to write their names in the darkness with their glowing wands. When they ran out of sparklers, the girls lay on their blanket and watched in silent wonder as comets and rockets exploded in flashes of light. Faces illuminated by the light show, Taylor and Declan exchanged the age-old whisperings of the young in each other's arms. Fireworks and September love – the evening should have been the perfect coda to summer, but my eyes kept sweeping over the children around us. Indistinguishable in the darkness, they darted from blanket to blanket like fireflies. I prayed they would be more difficult to capture.

Finally, it was time for the spectacular last blasts of sound and colour. Rockets soared, and volleys of red, green, and yellow swept the inky sky. Blue stars burst to scatter white, green, and gold glitter. Fountains of silver and gold hissed through the air, and finally a comet erupted from the ground and bloomed into a giant red chrysanthemum.

As its petals faded and fell to earth, leaving nothing but a hint of smoke in the air and a memory of magic, people began to collect their children, fold their blankets, and say their goodbyes. We said ours too. Declan and Taylor went back to our condo on Halifax Street in his car. The days till Declan left for university were dwindling to a precious few, and he and Taylor seemed determined to make the most of the time they had left. And Tuesday was the first day of school for Madeleine and Lena. Faced with serious wardrobe decisions that needed to be settled before bedtime, our granddaughters raced towards Mieka's van.

It was finally time to exhale. When we got back to the condo, the terrace door was open, and Zack and I went out to say goodnight to our daughter and Declan. They were curled up together on a chaise longue, and Zack harrumphed like a dad in a 1950s sitcom. Embracing Taylor's passage into womanhood was proving difficult for him.

I smiled at the kids. "If you need anything, you know where we are."

"Right inside the door," Zack thundered.

The apartment was cool, so I turned on the fireplace and pulled a chair close to the warmth. "We survived the day," I said. "We've earned some quality time with Old Pulteney."

Zack wheeled to the sideboard, poured us each two fingers of single malt, placed our glasses on the tray he'd balanced on his lap, and wheeled back. I took my drink, held it up to the light from the fireplace, and swirled the amber liquid. "You told me once that to enjoy this fully, we need at least a half-hour free of stress before we take our first sip," I said.

"Let's waive that rule," Zack said. He raised his glass. "To getting through the day," he said, "and to Cronus, who made getting through the day possible."

We sipped our Scotch. "Zack, do you think there really was a plot to kidnap a child?"

Zack nodded. "I do. My guess is the child wouldn't have been hurt – just spirited away for long enough to make head-lines and discredit Racette-Hunter. Then he or she would have been returned to the bosom of his or her family."

"So no harm done except for the damage to Racette-Hunter."

"Which would have been irreparable," Zack said.

"Zack, if the photo Cronus sent of him with you and Brock was the silver bullet, we have to find out who he sent it to and why it worked."

"I'll talk to him tomorrow," Zack said.

"Don't wait till tomorrow," I said. "Somebody wants to destroy Racette-Hunter and torpedo Brock's campaign and ours. You and I will both sleep better if we know what we're up against."

Zack picked up his cell, made the call, but quickly broke the connection. "Cronus's cell is turned off. He's probably in the midst of an enchanted evening of spanking, biting, and hair-pulling."

"Cronus may have saved our bacon day today," I said. "He's earned a romantic interlude."

We both slept well, and when I rolled over the next morning, saw the familiar contours of Zack's body beside me and watched the play of shadows on the wall, I savoured the moment. There hadn't been much peace in our lives lately. When Zack's cell shrilled, I reached across to answer it before it awakened him, but he was too fast for me.

He listened, then swore softly. "Where are you exactly?" he said. "Okay, I'll be there in ten minutes."

He reached for my hand. "Cronus is dead," he said. "A beat cop found his body lying on the hood of his Porsche. Cronus listed me as next of kin so they want me to identify the body."

A block of ice seemed to form around my heart. "Where is he?" I said.

"In the parking lot behind the Sahara Club."

"Do the police know what he was doing there?"

"Cronus lives in the condo over the club," Zack said. "You and I had an open invitation to join him at the Sahara for dinner. I never took him up on it."

Zack's tone was remorseful, so I was brisk. "We can talk about that later," I said. "Right now let's just do what we have to do. I'll call Brock, tell him about Cronus, and ask him to walk the dogs."

"Jo, you don't have to come."

I rubbed his shoulder. "My grandmother always told me that a burden shared is a burden halved," I said. "Let's get going."

———

The Sahara Club was on Dewdney Avenue in a strip called "nightclub row," six blocks from where we lived. The area was sketchy. Most of the clubs occupied the main floor of buildings that had been abandoned in the 1960s when businesses started moving to the malls that were springing up on the city's outskirts like mushrooms after a three-day rain.

There weren't many scenic routes in our neighbourhood, and sometimes when Zack and I went for a wander after dinner, we'd head for nightclub row. For the most part, the clubs were charmless, gritty places with dead bulbs in the neon letters that proclaimed the club's name and windows with yellowed signs announcing daily specials for cocktails that no one had ordered since the 1970s. In summer, the doors to the clubs were open and the music of bands that were either on their way up or on their way out blared into the street. Kids too young to be in a bar would be dancing on the sidewalk, high or drunk but harmless. Life in the Warehouse District.

The Sahara Club was an anomaly. For one thing, it was not a club. It was and is a steakhouse and piano bar. For another, in a neighbourhood of buildings that have been allowed to deteriorate, the Sahara has been carefully maintained. In winter, the steps and sidewalk are always shovelled; in summer, the flowers in the window boxes flourish; in all seasons, the legs of the neon camels marching on the sign over the club's entrance move with the precision of the Rockettes.

The camels always made Zack and me smile, so our after-dinner meanderings often brought us to the sidewalk outside the Sahara. When the weather was pretty, the windows would be open, and we could smell the steaks sizzling and hear a pianist playing tunes that had the cool elegance of Cole Porter or Johnny Mercer. We'd always intended to go in one day.

That morning the side street that led to the parking lot was choked with police vehicles, but there was a parking space in front of the club and we took it. Zack's wheelchair is a dynamite calling card and the first constable we talked to waved us in. Yellow crime scene tape marked boundaries we weren't allowed to cross, but because Zack was there to identify the victim, the constable escorted us straight to Debbie Haczkewicz. She was watching the police photographer as he took photos of Cronus from every angle.

The body had not been moved. Cronus, still in his Gatsby suit, was on his back on the hood of his white Porsche, staring sightlessly at the dark September sky. Numb, I gazed at his battered body. His face was almost unrecognizable. His nose was broken; his eyes were swollen; the cuts on his skull, face, and lips had bled copiously. His beautiful white suit was blood-soaked and filthy with imprints of the boots that had kicked and stomped on him. Later we would learn that Cronus died of an occlusion of the carotid arteries and jugular veins. In layperson's terms, he died from manual strangulation. It would have been an agonizing death.

Zack took a deep breath. "I can make it official, Deb," he said. "That's Cronus."

Debbie made a note of the information. "Is Cronus his given name or his surname?"

"It's both. He was born Ronald Mewhort Junior, but after he and his father had a falling out, Ronald Junior had his name changed legally. Cronus was the Titan who came to power by castrating his father."

Debbie raised an eyebrow. "I'll bet that showed Dad. Zack, do you have any idea why Cronus would have identified you as next of kin?"

"No."

"Do you have any idea why someone would have killed him?"

"Yes." Zack turned his wheelchair to face Debbie. "Deb, I didn't tell you this yesterday because Cronus asked me to keep his name out of it, and I saw no reason to violate his confidence. Cronus was the one who told me about the kidnapping plot. After he warned me, he had Joanne take a photo of him with Brock Poitras and me, and he sent the photo to someone immediately. He included a message – a series of numbers. The numbers were 2, 5, 1, 0, 0, 6. He didn't say why the numbers were significant, but he did say the combination of the photo and the numbers were the silver bullet that would put an end to the plot."

As Zack talked I could feel Debbie's adrenaline pumping. This was a solid lead. "So Cronus may have been killed because he warned you about the possibility of a kidnapping," she said.

"That would be my guess," Zack said. The sun was coming up. The pale light of dawn revealed the full extent of the cruelty that had been inflicted on Cronus's body. My knees were weak and when I gripped Zack's chair to steady myself, he shot me a quick anxious look. "Debbie, I've told you everything I know," he said. "Find Cronus's phone. There'll be some answers there. In the meantime, Joanne and I have to get our bearings and we have to eat something. If you want to talk, you know where to find us, but right now we need to go home."

Debbie waved us off absently. Her mind was already grappling with the information Zack had given her. We were silent as we threaded our way through the officers working the crime scene and headed for our Volvo. I slid into the passenger seat and watched as Zack transferred his body from his chair to the car, dismantled the chair, and stowed it in the back seat. When he was through, Zack held out his arms to me. I leaned into him, breathed the familiar scent of his skin, felt his warmth, and wept.

When we got home, the dogs had been fed and watered, the coffee was on, and Brock was sitting at the butcher-block table. He stood. "I thought I'd stick around and see if there's anything I can do."

Zack's smile was faint. "Maybe make the last twenty-four hours go away."

"That bad," Brock said.

Zack nodded. "Cronus was either killed by gang members or by someone who wants to make his death appear to be gang-related. The beating he took was beyond brutal. And he'd been stomped."

Brock's gaze was steady. "The gang signature," he said. "But you don't think Cronus was killed by a gang."

Zack shook his head. "No. I think Cronus was killed by whoever received that picture of the three of us. If the cops can find Cronus's phone, they'll be on their way to solving this."

Brock's laugh was rueful. "And where do you suppose that phone is at this moment?"

"Probably at the bottom of a landfill," Zack said. "But we're going to have to let the cops handle this."

"Right," I said. "We have a campaign to run. You and Brock are booked to have breakfast with the Builders' Association. The election is only eight weeks from today."

"I'll remind the builders of that," Zack said. "I'll also remind them that if there's a new administration they'd be wise to get in on the ground floor."

"Donate now, and reap the benefits later," I said.

"It's a quid pro quo world," Zack said.

"Isn't that what we're trying to change?" I said.

Brock was matter-of-fact. "We can't change anything unless we win the election," he said. "It's time to suit up and get in the game."

———

After Brock went down to his condo on the third floor to dress for the breakfast meeting, Zack and I showered and readied ourselves for the day. Zack chose a light grey pin-stripe dress suit, a pale blue shirt, and a blue paisley tie. As I bent to straighten his tie, I said, "You look like a *GQ* cover boy. How are you feeling – really?"

"Like homemade shit," he said. "How about you?"

"The same," I said. I gazed at our still-unmade bed long-ingly. "I would like nothing better than to burrow under those covers with you and stay there forever – safe and warm and away from the world."

Zack chuckled. "You know what Grace Slick said: 'No matter how big or soft your bed is, you still have to get out of it.'"

"Jefferson Airplane had answers for all of life's large ques-tions," I said. I looked at my watch. "Come in and sit down with Taylor and me while we eat. You don't have to be downtown for another hour and Taylor always makes you feel better."

It was impossible not to get a contact high from sitting next to Taylor at breakfast that morning. She was not a girl given to fizzing with emotion. She had inherited serious talent as a visual artist from her birth mother, Sally Love, and knowl-edgeable collectors were already quietly buying up her work. When she talked about the art she made, Taylor was mature and thoughtful, but as gifted as she was, Taylor was still two months' shy of her sixteenth birthday. That bright September day she was starting Grade Eleven at Luther College High School. She would be with her friends again, and when she turned sixteen she'd be starting driver education. As she anti-cipated the year ahead, Taylor's words tumbled over one another. Except for Declan being away at university, it was, she assured us, going to be the best year ever.

Seeing Taylor's joy made an unbearable morning almost bearable. Still, when Declan came to drive Taylor to school, I knew that Zack and I were both relieved that we could give in to our sadness. Twenty-four hours earlier Cronus had been alive, as full of plans as we all were. Now he was lying on a slab in the morgue. I couldn't shake the image of Cronus's body splayed like a hunter's trophy on the hood of his car. The shadows under Zack's eyes suggested that he hadn't been able to shake the memory either.

When the door closed behind Taylor, I went over and rubbed Zack's shoulders. "Your muscles are tight."

"They're going to have to stay tight," Zack said. "I've got a couple of phone calls to make, and Brock's on his way up."

"Go make your calls. I'll keep Brock company."

When Brock arrived, I gestured to the living room. "Come inside. Zack's going to be a few minutes, and I need to talk to you."

Brock followed me into the living room and we sat in the reading chairs in front of the window. "I'm guessing this is about Michael," he said.

"It is. Brock, Michael told me yesterday afternoon that he knew about the plan to kidnap a child but there was nothing he could do to stop it. You have to talk to him and find out what's going on. He's in over his head. He told me that he was *forced* to leave you."

"By who?"

"He didn't say, but he did tell me that you and Margot had intercourse. He implied that you're still involved sexually."

Brock made no effort to hide his frustration. "Michael knows that's not true. He knows that I'm gay, not bisexual. Margot and I tried the medical route for three months. Nothing happened. Margot is forty-four. She felt time was running out. Intercourse was a last resort. We had intercourse three times. I didn't tell Michael that Margot and I had sex until her OB/GYN confirmed the pregnancy. At first the news didn't seem to bother him. Then out of nowhere there was this big explosion, and he told me the relationship was over." Brock placed his massive hands, fingers spread, on his knees. For a beat he just stared at them. Finally he said, "If it had been Zack, would you have wanted him to tell you?"

As I turned the question over in my mind, the only sound in the room was the ticking of the grandmother clock. When the silence between Brock and me grew uncomfortable, I said, "I'm sure Zack would have done exactly what you did, and I'm sure I would have been as hurt and confused as Michael is."

"But you would have stayed with Zack."

"Absolutely," I said. "There are a lot of years ahead and I want to spend them with him."

Brock's gaze was level. "That's how I feel about Michael."

"Then talk to him," I said.

"I'll try," Brock said. "But I'm not optimistic. These days, Michael is not the man I knew."

After Brock and Zack left, I put the dogs in the Volvo and drove over to Mieka's. It was 8:20, and the girls left for school at 8:45. Plenty of time for photos. When I saw Madeleine and Lena, I remembered a *New Yorker* cartoon I had put up on the fridge one September. A little girl is staring with loathing at the clothing laid out on her bed. The caption read "That outfit just screams 'first day of school.'"

Our granddaughters were dressed in matching black watch tartan skirts, white turtlenecks, and dark green tights. Their bangs were trimmed; their hair was neatly braided; their faces shone. By the end of the week, they'd be wearing T-shirts and shorts; if they were lucky they would have found socks that matched. Their hair would have the wild abandon of hair that had been washed before bed, dried fitfully and slept upon, and unless Mieka caught them before they went out the door, there would be a smear of jam on at least one girl's face.

But today was the day the girls posed on the front steps for the family album, the way Mieka, her brothers, and, later, Taylor, had posed on other first days of school. The house in which Mieka now lived had been mine before I married Zack. When her marriage foundered and Mieka and her daughters moved back to Regina, we all agreed it would be best for Mieka to buy the house that held so many memories for us all.

Zack, Taylor, and I had decided to start afresh in the first house we would live in as a family. The three of us had a lot of fun poring over paint chips and quibbling about furnishings and drapes. Two hours after our New Year's Day wedding, Zack and I moved into our newly retrofitted house. We brought our daughter, our dogs, Taylor's cats, and our clothes. Everything else was left behind. The house Mieka and her girls shared was substantially the same as the house in which I'd raised my children.

As I snapped pictures of Madeleine and Lena with my phone and sent them off to Zack, my mind was crowded with memories. Like my own children years before, the girls were beyond excited. Equipped with new backpacks, pens, notebooks, pencils, and erasers, they were ready for a great adventure, and they couldn't wait for it to begin.

When the yellow school bus came, they raced towards the street. Standing on the porch, Mieka and I could hear the shouts of kids welcoming them. After we waved them off, Mieka waited until the bus disappeared, then she turned to me. "Something's wrong," she said.

I nodded. "Do you remember Zack's client, Cronus?"

"The creepy slumlord? He's pretty hard to forget."

"He was murdered last night. Cronus was the one who alerted us to the possibility that a child would be abducted at the opening."

Mieka's hand rose to her throat. "Oh God. When nothing happened yesterday, I thought we were in the clear. I assumed the warning was just a hoax."

"We thought everything was okay too, then this morning Debbie Haczkewicz called to ask Zack to identify Cronus's body. He'd been tortured and stomped on. Whoever killed him had left him lying face up on the hood of his car, so we'd know what they were capable of."

Mieka put her arms around me. "Come inside, Mum. Let me get you some tea."

"I'm okay," I said. "I was going to take the dogs for a run along the levee."

"Give yourself some time," Mieka said. "You look a little wobbly. Why don't you get the dogs out of the car. They can run around in the backyard while we visit."

"Sold," I said. Mieka's backyard was familiar territory for Willie and Pantera, and they bounded after each other happily. Mieka and I usually visited in the kitchen, but that morning she shooed me into the living room. "The girls wanted the fireplace on this morning. I turned it off before they left for school, but it's still cozy in there. Put your feet up and I'll bring the tea. Daughter's orders."

Fifteen years earlier when I'd purchased the living room furniture, I had three criteria. The furniture had to be sturdy, stain-proof, and comfortable. It had cost twice as much as I'd budgeted for, but it still looked and felt good, and as I settled into the couch, I was glad I'd splurged. As Mieka had promised, the room was toasty and I was pleasantly drowsy by the time she came in with the tray of tea things. Mieka and I both believed that tea should be served in china cups and saucers, the thinner the better, and that morning she had chosen my favourite Aynsley for the Earl Grey. The tray also held a plate of buttered scones and a bowl of sliced peaches.

"You're spoiling me," I said.

Mieka poured the tea. "You've spoiled me a few thousand times. Besides, you look as if you could use some TLC."

I sipped my tea. "I'm fine. There's just been too much lately. Until yesterday I was climbing the walls trying to get the campaign on track, and Zack was climbing the walls because it didn't look as if there was any way Racette-Hunter would open its doors on Labour Day. Then we had the abduction threat. When that was put to bed, Cronus was murdered. Now the campaign has to switch into high gear. I feel as if someone is pelting me with stones."

Mieka's cell rang. She looked at the screen. "I'd better take this. It's from April's Place."

April's Place was a café/play centre that Mieka and her business partner, Lisa Wallace, had opened in North Central. It was the twin of UpSlideDown, the original centre they had opened in the Cathedral District four years earlier. UpSlideDown was an uncomplicated gold mine. April's Place was proving to be neither.

Mieka listened intently to the conversation. "Okay, I'll be right there," she said.

She broke the connection and groaned. "After three days on the job, our new manager just resigned. Mum, I hate to leave you, but I really have to stay on top of this."

I sat up. "I'm fine, Mieka. I have food to eat, tea to drink, and I'll bring the dogs in to keep me company. I'll lock up when I leave."

Mieka bent down and embraced me. "I worry about you," she said.

"Don't. Take care of the problem at April's Place and let me luxuriate in a morning off."

After Mieka left, I poured myself a second cup of tea and gazed at the impossibly delicate cup that held the Earl Grey. My marriage to my late husband, Ian, had taken place in the time of cup-and-saucer showers. The cup in my hands had a narrative that I'd always found difficult to unravel. The focal point of the cup is a dark-haired Victorian lady in a full-length blue gown with a rose peplum. She appears to be doing nothing but enjoying the tranquility of her world, but the setting of her world is perplexing. A fragment of a building that appears to be the Palace of Westminster in London is prominent. Big Ben is easy to identify, but the river that flows past the palace is seemingly the Yellow River of China, and the illustrations on the teacup place the dark-haired lady in a land of Roman columns and Oriental paper lanterns. The handle of the cup is a beautifully rendered blue and yellow butterfly whose name I once knew.

I gazed at the serene lady. With the Yellow River flowing past Big Ben and all those Roman columns and paper lanterns, her life must have been complex, but she seemed to be handling it. I envied her.

I carried the tray back into the kitchen. Through the screen door I saw that rain was coming down, soft and dense – the kind of rain that would last awhile. I let the dogs in, went back to the living room, turned on the gas fireplace, stretched out on the couch, and covered myself with an afghan. The house was fragrant with the scents of memories: morning pancakes, marigolds, wet dog fur. It wasn't long before I drifted off to sleep.

My dream had no beginning and was quickly over. I was holding on to an old rubber inner tube – the kind children used to float on at the lake when I was young. In the dream, I was an adult and I wasn't floating. A rope attached the inner tube to a slick red speedboat that was moving so quickly that the inner tube to which I was clinging was periodically lifted out of the water. The ride was exhilarating but terrifying.

On the shoreline, cottages and docks sped by in a blur. People on shore were waving, but I couldn't let go of the inner tube to wave back. Finally, the red speedboat turned towards the centre of the lake, and the driver opened the motor full throttle. The water in the lake's centre was black and deep. There were weeds there that I knew could ensnare me and pull me under. I couldn't hold on any longer. I let go of the inner tube and the red speedboat kept on without me. The ride was over. I was safe. I could swim back to shore, but I was overwhelmed by an existentially deep sense of loss. When I awakened, I was still numb with grief.

I pulled the afghan close. Always sensitive to my moods, Willie moaned beside me. I reached down and stroked his head. "It's all right," I said. "It was just a dream."

If, as Carl Jung believed, dreams offer solutions to problems people are facing in their waking lives, the message in my dream was simple to interpret. All I had to do was let go of the rope that tied me to the red speedboat. But I knew that, in the curious logic of dreams, Zack was the driver of the speedboat. And I knew that, no matter what, I would never separate myself from him.

I picked up my cell and hit Zack's number on speed-dial. His voice was deep and warm. "Hey, telepathy," he said. "I was just about to call you to thank you for the pictures of the girls."

Still caught in the web of my dream, I couldn't speak. "Is everything okay?" Zack said.

"Everything's fine. I just wanted to tell you that I've loved you from the night we went to the Stone House and looked down on the valley together. I don't want a different life, Zack."

"Has something come up?

"Fear," I said. "But I'll get over it." I cleaned up the dishes and went into the hall where Mieka had taken my jacket

and the dogs' leashes. On the cobbler's bench by the door
there were some old photo albums. On special days, like the
first day of school, Mieka brought out the albums to show
Madeleine and Lena their grandfather, Ian. Mieka had idol-
ized her father, and she wanted her girls to know the kind of
man he'd been. I picked up the album on the top of the pile
and leafed through.

I had taken most of the photos. There were a few of Ian
and me together, looking impossibly young as we unwrapped
presents on Christmas morning or cross-country skied, but
most were of Ian and our children.

I had never doubted that Ian loved our kids, but he was
an absentee father. I looked at the picture of Mieka's Grade
Eight farewell ceremony. Ian and I were flanking her, as proud
parents do, but Ian had missed the bonfire for the Grade
Eights and their parents after the ceremony. There was some
crisis at the legislature, and he'd had to go back to the office.
I wondered idly if Ian's absence had hurt Mieka or if she
even remembered.

The second album was filled with photos of Ian and me in
the first heady days after we surprised Saskatchewan and
ourselves by winning the provincial election. Howard
Dowhanuik was premier and Ian had become Attorney
General and second-in-command.

The album seemed to contain another life. In the early
days, all of us connected to the new government had been
like family, but ambition, time, geography, and mortality
had separated us. Most of the people in the photos were now
just names on my Christmas card list, but there were two
with whom I'd stayed close. Our party had had a good run –
almost fifteen years in government, but like most politicians, Howard went to the dance once too often. After we
lost the election, Jill Oziowy, the ebullient redhead who had
handled the party's communications during our years in

power, stayed around for a while, but when Ian died, she left Saskatchewan and moved to Toronto to work for NationTV. She'd been in New York City or Toronto ever since. Jill had been like a member of our family and I missed her, but over the years she'd sent a number of plum assignments that required a background in politics my way, so we had stayed in touch, albeit mainly electronically.

Howard Dowhanuik and I had stayed close too. The events of the past twenty-four hours had spooked me. Logic suggested that Cronus's death was somehow connected to Zack's campaign for mayor, but I couldn't connect the dots. Howard had the old politician's passion for political gossip, and it occurred to me that he might have heard rumblings about what was going on inside Scott Ridgeway's campaign.

Howard's condo was on a cul-de-sac five blocks from Mieka's. I'd called ahead, and he was waiting at the door for me. During his college days, Howard had boxed professionally. His time in the ring and his time in politics had given him the battered wariness of an aging eagle. I reached out and touched his cheek. "You shaved for me," I said. "I'm honoured."

"You've always been worth shaving for," Howard mumbled, then, embarrassed at his display of sentiment, he shifted his focus to my car. "Why don't you bring in the dogs? Give us time for a real visit."

"Fine with me," I said. I pointed to elections signs on his lawn. One read SHREVE; the other read GINA BROWN. "Nice signs," I said. Gina Brown was running for city council in Ward 3. She was a nurse-practitioner with innovative ideas about community-centred health care and a take-no-prisoners approach that I found appealing.

When the dogs and I came into the house, Howard was already in the kitchen, pouring coffee. I picked up my mug and took a sip. The coffee was good but very strong. "This should clear away the cobwebs," I said.

"I sure as hell need something," Howard growled.

"Troubles?"

"Boredom," Howard said. "Never get old, Jo."

I put my hands over my ears. "Can't hear you," I said. "Howard, there are a dozen things you could be doing. Writing that book you've been going to write for twenty years. Volunteer work. Teaching. The university would be thrilled to have you teach that class in Canadian politics again next semester."

Howard spooned sugar into his coffee. "The kids piss me off," he said. "Strolling into class whenever the spirit moves them, texting, whining about their grades."

"Okay," I said. "So you don't want to write, you don't want to volunteer, and you don't want to teach. Howard, if you're really at loose ends, why don't you come and work on our campaign?"

"Because I don't like your husband."

"He doesn't like you either," I said. "But you wouldn't be working with Zack. You'd be working with me. I really could use some help."

Howard looked at me hard. "Are you feeling okay?"

"Just too much on my plate." I gave Howard a précis of the events of the last two days.

When I was through, Howard said, "Jesus, no wonder you look tired. Aside from joining the campaign – which I'll have to think about – is there anything I can do?"

"Yes," I said. "Tell me what you know about how involved Graham Meighen and Lancaster Development are in Scott Ridgeway's campaign."

Howard added more sugar to his coffee. "Apparently, Meighen has let it be known in the business, construction, and real estate communities that they have to win this one," he said.

"We've done polling," I said. "They're ahead."

"Yeah, but they've never had a serious opponent before. They know that Zack won't be a pushover, and they're nervous about the slate of progressives running for city council. The status quo works for these guys," Howard said. "But, Jo, they're honest citizens – at least as honest as they have to be – they wouldn't be part of a hoax that involved a threat to take a kid. And they certainly would not have had a guy murdered."

"Well somebody did," I said.

Howard narrowed his eyes at me. "This really is getting to you, isn't it?"

"It is," I said. "And if you'd seen what they did to Cronus it would be getting to you too. We're all vulnerable, Howard, and in that wheelchair, Zack is an easy target. I just wish I knew what I was up against."

Howard put his arm around my shoulder. "Whatever it is, you don't have to fight it alone," he said. "Throw in an invitation for dinner the next time you cook brisket and I'll join your campaign."

I leaned in. "Funny, I was just on my way to the butcher to order a brisket. My recipe takes two days. How about Thursday night?"

"You're on."

When I pulled up in front of Lakeview Fine Foods, my phone was ringing. It was Zack.

"Perfect timing," I said. "I was just going in to order a brisket."

"Good. I love brisket. How come we haven't had it lately?"

"Because it's been summer," I said. "Zack, I've invited Howard to have dinner with us Thursday night. I want him to join our campaign."

"I don't like him."

"He doesn't like you either. But we need him, and he needs us, so I think it's time you buried the hatchet." Zack didn't respond, so I barrelled on. "When Peter and Angus were little guys, and they were sniping at each other, I always made them sit on the couch and hug for ten minutes."

Zack chuckled. "Howard has to hug first," he said.

CHAPTER

3

That day there was a function that I would have given anything to forego. It was a memorial lunch for my friend Beverly Levy, who had died of pancreatic cancer a year earlier. She was thirty-eight years old. Before my retirement from the university the year before, Beverly had been my colleague in the political science department. The purpose of the lunch was to raise money for a scholarship in her honour. I had been very fond of Beverly and remembering her would be painful, but she had met death with a grin and a raised middle finger. The least I could do was honour her by donning my best suit and pantyhose and pumps.

The luncheon was being held in the Agra Torchinsky Salon of the Mackenzie Art Gallery. The salon was a second-floor space, ideal for receptions because of its proximity to the art but also because the floor-to-ceiling glass of its west wall brought the treed beauty of Albert Street into the room.

I arrived late and had trouble finding a parking place. I had hoped I'd be able to slip in unnoticed, but when I checked my ticket, I discovered I'd been seated with the university president, a number of the university's senior administrators, and Bev's parents. Bev's father was Graham Meighen. I'd seen her mother, Liz Meighen, often at the hospital. She rarely left her daughter's side, but until that day I'd never spoken to Graham. I wasn't looking forward to breaking bread with him, but there was no turning back. The president's table was directly in front of the podium. I manoeuvred my way through the other tables, slid into my chair, and lowered my eyes.

The program for the luncheon lay on the bread-and-butter plate. My memories of Beverly at the end were so sharp that it was startling to see the photo of her as she was before her illness. She had been passionate about the outdoors. The photo on the front of the program was of Beverly triumphant at the end of a hike along Vancouver Island's West Coast trail. The breath caught in my throat. With her spiky black hair, her brilliant azure eyes, and her athlete's body, she seemed destined to live forever. She was dead before the year was out. Liz Meighen, who was seated next to me, reached over and stroked my arm.

I glanced up and saw that her eyes, too, were filled with tears. "It's just so wrong," she said. All I could do was nod and cover her hand with my own.

We sat with our hands touching through the brief biography of Beverly and the explanation of how the university would match funds donated if the total reached a certain point. Our first opportunity to talk came during the salad course.

"I asked to have you seated at our table," Liz said. "I hope you don't mind. Bev was so fond of you."

"And I was fond of Bev. I'm sorry I didn't speak to you when I sat down, Liz. I'm a little off my game today."

"I've been off my game since Beverly's diagnosis," Liz said.

"You're still the finest woman I know," her husband said. I had seen Graham Meighen only once, and that had been at a distance at Bev's funeral. I'd remembered him as being attractive, and he was. His features were even; his hair was full and silvery; his tan was deep. Bev had told me once that her father had been on his university's wrestling team, and the power of his body was still evident. He reached across his wife, extended his hand to me, and introduced himself. "I hope you know how much your friendship meant to our daughter," he said.

My eyes stung. "She was an extraordinary person," I said. "Zack enjoyed her company too."

"So many people fall away when a friend is dealing with terminal illness," Liz said. "Zack barely knew Bev before she was diagnosed, but she looked forward to his visits. She said he never treated her as if she was sick."

"They had some spirited conversations," I said. "They're both such strong personalities, I wasn't sure they'd get along, but they did. Bev said Zack was an acquired taste."

Liz was the model of patrician civility, but for the briefest moment there was a glint of mischief in her eyes. "Graham, perhaps you and Zack should spend some time together."

Graham was smooth. "I can't imagine Zack and I acquiring a taste for each other's company, but if you think it's a good idea, Liz, we'll give it a try. We could invite the Shreves over for a barbecue."

Liz's laugh, like her daughter's, was full and throaty. "Graham, you are such a bullshitter," she said.

Graham laughed too. "It keeps you coming back," he said.

The servers came in with the entrée, a chicken breast stuffed with something and bathed in something else. Everyone at our table was a veteran of fundraising luncheons, so no one commented on the food. We ate as much as we could and pushed back our plates.

When dessert was served, it was time for a segment the program referred to as "Memories of Beverly." Graham spoke first. After he thanked everyone for coming to the luncheon, he leaned close to the microphone. His baritone was pleasantly mellow.

"From the beginning, Beverly was her own person," he said. "When she was four, she asked me where she went after she fell asleep at night. I explained that while she slept she stayed in her bed. She considered my answer, then she said, 'You're wrong, Daddy.' After she'd given the matter more thought, she said. 'You're wrong about a lot of things.'" When laughter rippled through the audience, Graham raised his hand to still it. "Oh, she wasn't finished. Beverly never let me off the hook easily. She pondered the question for at least another thirty seconds before she made her final pronouncement. 'Daddy, maybe you're wrong about everything.' And with that she wandered off to find her mother." Graham smiled at his wife, but Liz's face remained stony. He paused for a second, then carried on. "All her life, my daughter believed I was wrong about everything. But that didn't stop me from loving her and it didn't stop her from loving me." Graham's voice broke. He returned to our table, murmured apologies to the president of the university and his colleagues, brushed Liz's cheek with a kiss that she seemed not to notice, then left. In Margot's words, a smooth-as-silk performance.

As the reminiscences continued, Liz and I both kept our eyes focused on the centrepiece of vibrant multihued Gerbera daisies. Gerberas had been Bev's favourites. We were both fighting tears and our strategy seemed to be working until the last speaker came to the podium to propose a toast. Mary Sutherland had managed the university bookstore for as long as any of us could remember. Mary's toast to Beverly was brief and graceful. She closed with the Dr. Seuss line: "Don't cry because it's over, smile because it happened."

We raised our glasses to Bev, sipped, and the luncheon was over. The salon emptied quickly. It was a workday and the guests had commitments. They lined up at the tables where they could leave cheques for the scholarship and say their final farewells before leaving.

Liz and I lingered at our table for a moment, then we both picked up our things. Liz leaned across the table, plucked two gerberas from the centrepiece, handed one to me, and pressed the other inside her program. We walked downstairs in silence, crossed the lobby, and stepped through the glass doors at the gallery entrance. The rain had stopped. The sun was peering out, and the air smelled of wet leaves and grass. Liz touched my arm. "I know how busy you are, Joanne, but could you indulge me for a few minutes?"

In the year since Beverly's death, Liz's face had become permanently lined by sadness. I was weary, but turning down any request Liz made was unthinkable. "Of course," I said. "But won't Graham be waiting?"

"Graham will already be back at his office," Liz said. "He always has urgent business to take care of. Besides, what I have in mind won't take long. After Beverly and I visited the gallery we always went to the Mackenzie's Outdoor Sculpture Garden. You and I don't have to do the whole tour, but I'd like to pay a quick visit to Potter, Valadon, and Teevo."

Liz didn't have to explain the reference. Potter, Valadon, and Teevo were Joe Fafard's life-sized bronze sculptures of a bull, a cow, and a calf. The three animals stood in an informal grouping on the lawn close to Albert Street. Many a harried driver, frustrated by traffic and urban life in general, had found solace in Fafard's reminder of a simpler time.

Clearly, Liz Meighen felt a powerful connection to the animals. When we reached them, Liz went to Potter, rubbed his flank, then moved to Valadon and stroked her back. Finally, she went to Teevo, the calf, and rested her hand on his head. Her movements, as Beverly's had been, were artless and sure. "You and Bev are so much alike," I said.

There was sorrow in Liz's smile. "Nothing you could have said would please me more. I miss Beverly every second of every day. I tell myself that she was in my life for thirty-eight years, and that I should be grateful for that."

"I know. After my first husband died, I tried to hold on to the fact that we had had almost twenty good years together."

"You wanted more," Liz said simply. "So did I. I wanted Beverly's to be the last face I saw before I died." She took a deep breath and straightened her shoulders. "But it wasn't to be. This Friday is the anniversary of Bev's death. I've been keeping very much to myself this past year. I'm going to allow myself one last day of grieving and then I'm going to rejoin the world."

When I turned onto Halifax Street, I saw that Debbie Haczkewicz's grey Ford Fusion was parked in front of our building. As I waited for the gate that led to our parking garage to open, I rested my forehead against the steering wheel. Standing in the wet grass looking at the Fafard cattle, I had found a measure of peace. Whatever news Debbie brought would inevitably shatter that peace. The red speedboat's passage towards the unknown was inexorable. All I could do was hang on to the rope and hope for the best.

Debbie and Zack were at the dining room table having coffee when I came in.

"Perfect timing," Zack said. "Debbie just told me she has some intriguing information."

I kicked off my pumps, gave Zack a quick embrace, and took the chair next to Debbie's. "Shoot," I said.

Debbie raised an eyebrow. "Hold on because this one's a doozie. Cronus named Zack as his executor and sole beneficiary."

Zack leaned towards her. "You're kidding."

"No. The lawyer who handled Cronus's will called this

morning to say that since Cronus named you as next of kin, executor, and sole beneficiary, we should deal with you."

"Who's the lawyer?" Zack asked.

"Darryl Colby," Debbie said.

"The cherry on the cheesecake," Zack said. "Darryl's one of the few lawyers in town who really gets under my skin."

"It's his aftershave," I said. "It's industrial strength."

"I'll remember to conduct all my business with Mr. Colby electronically," Debbie said.

"I won't have that option." Zack rubbed his eyes. "You know, this really is sad. I barely knew Cronus. To me, he was just another case."

"Well, you obviously meant something more to him," Debbie said.

Zack's face was sombre. "I know, and I'll do everything that needs to be done. I'm assuming you won't be releasing the body for the foreseeable future."

"It will take forensics time to get everything they need – not just from Cronus's body but from his car. The Porsche is still in the parking lot behind the Sahara Club being processed: fingerprints, photographs, blood samples – all the initial stuff. We'll transport it to the police garage later this afternoon so we can give it a thorough going-over. There are a lot of question marks around this case, and we don't want to rush to judgment."

"So what do you think happened to Cronus?" Zack said.

Debbie shook her head. "I know what somebody *wants* us to think. The excessive violence and the stomping on the body suggest gang involvement. We also found a red bandana at the scene."

"Implicating Red Rage," Zack said.

"We're checking out that angle," Debbie said. "But the placement of that red bandana is a little too convenient. Gang members are proud of their scarves. They go through the stomping ceremony to win the right to wear them. I can't imagine any gang member casually dropping his scarf close to the body of someone he'd just murdered."

"Rival gangs have been known to battle," Zack said. "A member of another gang might have ripped off the bandana during a fight and held on to it so he could use it to frame Red Rage later."

"We're working on that possibility too," Debbie said. "The first step is tracing the scarf to a specific member of Red Rage. If there is DNA on the scarf other than Cronus's, and it matches the DNA of someone we have on file, we've scored – at the very least we've connected with a person who can supply a lead about what happened to the scarf."

"Will that person be able to tell you why someone killed Cronus, then placed his body on the hood of his car?" I said. My voice was bleak, and Zack reached out and took my hand.

"I doubt if they'll volunteer that information," Debbie said. "I know what you're getting at, Joanne. This whole gang angle doesn't ring true. Cronus comes to you and tells you that there's a plot to abduct a child from the opening of Racette-Hunter. Six hours later he's murdered and dumped on his car in the parking lot behind the Sahara Club. The first hours of a police investigation are always tricky. We're jumpy and if we get what we think could be a lead, it's tempting to drop everything and follow it. This case has a lot of gang markers and we'll check them out, but the fact that Cronus believed the photo he sent out was enough to thwart the kidnapping plan suggests something larger."

"I don't suppose Cronus's phone has turned up."

"Only in my dreams," Debbie said. "So we soldier on. We continue to find out everything we can about the scene, the body, and the victim's past, and hope we come up with something."

"So at this point we don't know anything," I said.

"That's right," Debbie said. "But, Joanne, I promise you we will, and when that happens, I'll let you know as much as I can."

As she stood to leave, Zack's cell rang. He grimaced and mouthed Darryl Colby's name. Debbie and I left him to it. When she and I exchanged goodbyes, Debbie's face was soft with concern. "Are you all right?"

"No," I said. "I'm scared to death."

Debbie laughed shortly. "That makes two of us," she said. And then for the first time since I'd known her she embraced me. "We'll get them," she whispered and then she was gone.

Zack was still on the phone when I went back into the living room. "Open the windows," he said. "Darryl's on his way."

I sat on the couch and peeled off my pantyhose. Zack watched appreciatively. "Don't ever do that again unless we can celebrate the moment."

"No time to celebrate now?"

"No," Zack said. "Darryl will be here in fifteen minutes."

"What's the rush?" I said.

"I have no idea. Darryl just said the matter was urgent."

"It must be urgent if Darryl's coming here. The one time he encountered Pantera was not pleasant."

Zack laughed quietly at the memory. "It was pleasant for Pantera. He got to push his snout into Darryl's ass and usher him out of the house."

"I'll put the dogs upstairs," I said. "I still shudder when I remember the size of Darryl's dry cleaning bill."

I shepherded Willie and Pantera into our room. As I changed clothing, I summoned up my memories of Darryl Colby. There were mercifully few. The first time I met him was at a bar association Christmas party. He sang "You're a Mean One, Mr. Grinch" in a big booming bass, and I told Zack that Darryl seemed like a lot of fun. Zack shuddered and said that, in the immortal words of Dr. Seuss, Darryl was as cuddly as a cactus and as charming as an eel and I'd be smart to stay away from him. Except for Darryl's memorable encounter with Pantera I'd kept my distance.

Darryl Colby was near the top of my list of people I never wanted to see standing on my doorstep, but seemingly my options were being whittled away. When he called from downstairs, I buzzed him in. His aftershave, heavy with the scent of musk, made my eyes water. He was tall, heavy-set, large-featured, and raven-haired. Before Darryl stepped over the threshold, he looked past me suspiciously.

"I shut the dogs into one of the rooms upstairs," I said.

Darryl didn't acknowledge my assurance that he was safe; in fact, he didn't acknowledge my presence at all. Zack came out to meet him, hand extended in greeting. "It was good of you to meet me here, Darryl. Can I get you something to drink?"

Darryl didn't shake Zack's hand, but he did place his order. "Double JD on the rocks," he said. I led Darryl to the dining room. He put his briefcase on the table and waited. Zack wheeled back with three glasses of bourbon on the tray on his lap. He handed the drinks around.

"Joanne will be joining us, Darryl," he said. "Obviously the information in Cronus's will affects us both and she should be here when you explain the specifics."

Darryl took a large sip from his glass. "That won't take long," he said. He removed a folder from his briefcase. "Here's the will. I've couriered Cronus's files to your office at Falconer Shreve. You have three floors of lawyers there. They won't have any difficulty handling the legal work."

Zack raised an eyebrow. "You're quitting?"

"I want to be as far away from this as possible," he said. Then he drained his glass and picked up his briefcase. "I hope you realize that Cronus has really fucked you."

"Was that his intent?" Zack said.

Darryl shook his head. "No," he said. "Cronus believed you were his one true friend."

"So why would he fuck me?"

Darryl's smile was both smug and cruel. "That's for me to know and you to find out," he said. Then he left.

When we heard the door close behind him, Zack picked up his glass. "So what do you think?"

"I think I'm glad you pour generous drinks," I said. "I'd better get dinner started. What are you in the mood for?"

"Spaghetti," Zack said. "I'll take a look at the will and whatever other goodies Darryl brought us and then I'll come and make a salad."

By the time Taylor came home from school, the spaghetti sauce was simmering but Zack was still hunched over his laptop. Our family tries to keep mealtime talk light and lively. That night Taylor carried the ball for the three of us. She'd had a very good day. She'd been invited to a sixteenth birthday party sleepover on a farm where the parents owned riding horses. Her new Latin teacher actually made Latin *interesting*, and best of all, her first-term schedule had three days with no first period classes, so she could paint at night and do homework in the morning.

In its previous incarnation, the building in which we lived had been a warehouse where women kept their winter furs. The words COLD STORAGE, written in block letters three feet high, were still visible on the building's faded cream brick. When Margot and her husband, Leland, moved into 325 Halifax Street, they planned to buy out the condo owners on the first floor and convert the space into offices for their development company, Peyben. Leland's death changed everything. The last condo owner had moved out over a year ago, but Margot was still mulling over how best to use the space on the main floor. When Taylor could no longer work in her old studio, Margot offered her the use of a large, undeveloped room on the first floor. The offer was heaven-sent. Our building was secure and Taylor's studio would be just an elevator ride away.

As a thank-you, Taylor was painting a portrait of Margot with Declan and Lexi for a Christmas gift. After we'd cleaned up, Taylor went downstairs to work on the portrait, and Zack and I took our coffee out to the terrace. The rain had washed the air, and we positioned ourselves so the sun was warm on our faces. For a few minutes we were quiet, breathing in the scent of nicotiana, revelling in the peace of a perfect September evening.

Zack broke the silence. "How was the luncheon for Bev?" he asked.

"Emotional – especially at our table. I sat between Liz and Graham Meighen."

"That can't have been easy."

"It wasn't, but I'm glad Liz and I were seated next to each other. We both needed shoring up."

"How was Graham?"

"Charming. He told a nice story about his relationship with Beverly. The punchline was that when she was four, Bev told her father she thought he was wrong about just about everything."

Zack laughed. "From the conversations I had with Beverly, I don't think her opinion changed much on that score."

"It didn't," I said. "But according to Graham, he and Bev had a loving relationship. That was news to me, but Liz didn't react."

"How is Liz?"

"She's struggling," I said. "Bev will have been dead a year this Friday. Liz is hoping that once the anniversary has passed, she'll be able to move forward." I remembered the lines sorrow had carved in Liz's gentle face. "It won't be easy."

I picked up the carafe and poured us each more coffee. "Your turn now. What's new on the Cronus situation?"

Zack tented his fingers and breathed deeply. "Let's see. I spent the last hour or so tracing Cronus's holdings in North Central. It seems you and I are big winners in the game of slum Monopoly. Among other properties, we own a good chunk of Rose Street."

"Did you happen to notice if we own Number 12?"

"Nope, but I can find out easily enough."

"Don't bother. It's so nice just to sit here and relax."

Zack sipped his coffee. "Agreed," he said. "So what's special about Number 12?"

"The day I waited for the ambulance to come for Angela, the girl whose boyfriend threw her to the pavement, an old woman who lives at Number 12 came outside and quoted the Book of Revelation – a vivid description of the lake that burns with fire and sulphur for murderers and the sexually immoral."

Zack was pensive. "And this was directed at Angela?"

"No. Angela is a sex worker, but the old woman said Angela was an innocent, and the lake was reserved for the evil ones, the ones who use the bodies of innocents and steal their souls."

Zack grimaced. "I wonder where that puts us on the continuum. Thanks to Cronus, you and I will never have to work another day in our lives, but our comfort will be financed by rent money from sex workers, addicts, alcoholics, and everybody else that polite society considers subhuman."

"And we'll be exploiting the people our campaign is promising to help."

"Yeah, and I guess that's what Darryl was alluding to when he said Cronus fucked me. Jo, I don't see how I can run for mayor when I own this real estate."

"I don't either," I said. "If we sell that property we're going to make a lot of money and change nothing. The new owners will still be gouging people to pay for rat-infested substandard housing with black mould and faulty wiring."

"And the beat goes on," Zack said. "The only way to deal with those houses is to do what Peyben is doing with The Village – tear the buildings down and start from scratch. I'm prepared to do that, but while the big machines tear down the old to make way for the new, the people who live in Cronus's houses have nowhere to go." Zack rubbed his temples. "It's going to be tough promising to change the city when I can't solve a problem in my own backyard."

"Do you want to quit the campaign?" I said.

"No," Zack said.

"Then we'll call a press conference tomorrow, explain the situation, and say that you'll improve the properties you own as much as you can without disturbing the tenants, and as mayor you'll work towards long-term solutions to the city's housing problem."

Zack grinned. "You make it sound so easy."

"We're going to take a lot of flack," I said. "But we both know how to duck." I picked up my coffee mug. "I'll call Milo and get him to set up a press conference. Let's do it on Rose Street – show that you're prepared to face the problem head on. I'll make sure Milo copies Slater Doyle on the announcement."

"So Ridgeway's people can't leak the contents of Cronus's will," Zack said admiringly. "What makes you think they'd even know?"

"I imagine Darryl Colby will find a way to get the information to them. This is Regina. Everybody knows and everybody tells. You should probably give Brock a call. I'll go over to Margot's and fill her in."

"Is this a double massage night?" Zack said.

I kissed the top of his head. "I certainly hope so," I said.

When I stepped across the hall and rang Margot's bell, Brock answered the door. In the background, I could hear the *Baby Einstein: Lullaby Classics* CD I'd committed to memory when Madeleine and Lena were born. The room was gently lit and there was a faint scent of Baby's Own soap in the air. It was a scene of such tranquility that I felt a pang at having to break the peace with my grim news.

"Margot's in the nursery rocking Lexi," Brock said. "She may be a few minutes. Lexi has her own ideas about bedtime."

"I can drop by later, " I said.

"No need," Margot said, coming in from the nursery. "Lexi is down for the count," she said. "Of course, after my daughter and I have rocked for an hour, I'm just about down for the count myself." She peered at me closely. "Is everything okay?"

"We've had a tough couple of days," I said. "And it's not over yet. Would you mind giving Zack a call and telling him Brock's here? There's something the four of us need to talk about."

When Zack arrived, Margot greeted him at the door. "So what's up?"

Zack wheeled towards the living room. "For starters," he said, "Darryl Colby popped by this afternoon. It turns out that I am Cronus's executor and sole beneficiary. Jo and I now own a sizeable portion of the slum housing in North Central."

"Holy shit," Margot breathed.

Brock's eyebrows furrowed. "So how are we going to handle this?"

Zack leaned forward. "Milo O'Brien is texting the media, inviting them to a news conference in North Central tomorrow at 9:00 a.m. Milo's giving them the broad strokes about the inheritance from Cronus, and he's copying Slater Doyle on the announcement. I'm going to promise to do everything I can to make the houses I've inherited habitable for the tenants. I'm going to say that when I'm elected mayor, my first priority will be affordable housing. Then Joanne and I are going to head for the hills."

Margot leaned forward. "Peyben can help. By the end of the week, we can have workers on the job making those houses safe and livable. We'll show that you know how to get things done."

"And drive home the fact that Zack did more in one year to establish a training and recreation centre in North Central than the city, the province, and the feds have done in decades," Brock said.

Margot was thoughtful. "I wonder if that's why Cronus named Zack as his sole heir."

"We'll never know," Zack said. "But the day he died, Cronus made a significant contribution to our campaign. When I thanked him he said, 'This is my city too.'"

Sometimes Zack's and my massage sessions ended up in making love, but most of the time they just gave us a chance to unwind and talk. That night as I poured the massage oil into my palm, Zack introduced a topic that was on my mind too.

"What do you think is going on with Margot and Brock?" he said.

I rubbed the oil into Zack's shoulders. "I think they're both lonely. They're both crazy about Lexi, they're having a child together, and they enjoy each other's company."

"No romance?"

"Brock's still wounded from the breakup with Michael Goetz," I said. "And he *is* gay."

"Brock and Margot managed to get pregnant. Or was that just a one-shot deal?"

"Actually, Brock told me it was a three-shot deal." I kneaded Zack's shoulders.

When I began to work deep circles in his muscles with my thumbs and fingertips, Zack groaned with pleasure, but his mind was still on Brock and Margot. "You don't think there's a chance they'll have a future together?" he said.

"Who knows?" I said. "Their child will always be a bond. But Margot and Brock both know what it's like to share a life with a person they love. Sooner or later, I imagine they're both going to want the whole package."

"There's a lot to be said for having the whole package."

"There is," I agreed. "Now, you're still tight. I'm going to massage your feet for a while."

"That's not very sexy. I can't feel my feet."

"I'll work my way up."

CHAPTER

4

The press conference was being held on the sidewalk in front of 12 Rose Street. I'd suggested the street because Zack and I now owned every house on the block. I hadn't mentioned Brock's and my encounter with the old woman who lived at Number 12 to Milo. He had chosen the house simply because its mustard-coloured stucco was, in his words, "so shit-bucket ugly that nobody should have to live with it."

By the time I arrived, a small crowd had already gathered. There was a solid media turnout, a sprinkling of the curious and the bored; a half-dozen kids who should have been in school, a couple of sex workers looking exhausted at the end of their shift, a man with a walker muttering obscenities to himself, two drunks, and some guys who were obviously coming down hard from a high. The old lady from Number 12 was there, again wearing her hunting jacket, trousers, and men's slippers.

There were no signs of life at the house where Angela lived. I didn't know Angela's last name, but I'd brought along a note, telling her I was thinking of her and giving her my contact information. Before the press conference began

I knocked at her door. I could hear the television blaring inside, but when no one came to the door, I dropped the note in Angela's mailbox and went back across the street.

Slater Doyle was standing a few feet away from the action, observing. As always, his mid-brown hair appeared to have been freshly barbered, the creases in his trousers were knife-edged, and the sides of his tie's Windsor knot were perfectly symmetrical. Slater suffered from photophobia so he was never without the tinted shades that served the dual purpose of protecting his eyes against the light and making it impossible for interlocutors to peer through the windows to his soul.

On the rare occasions when we had run into each other, Slater and I had always been civil, but that morning when I approached him, he turned away. I ignored the slight and stepped into his line of vision. "Glad you could make it," I said.

I expected a little banter, but Slater's tone was urgent. "What's Zack going to do with the houses?"

"Stay tuned," I said. "Now I have a question. Have the police talked to the people behind your campaign about Cronus's murder?"

It was a shot in the dark, but it hit the target. Slater tensed. "What people?" he said. "We have the same support we've had in the last three elections. No defections. No additions. Same loyal crowd of upstanding citizens."

"We're looking into that," I said. "The Shreve campaign is absolutely transparent. If you want a list of our donors and the amount of their donations, I'll send you one. Will you reciprocate?"

"No."

"Inspector Haczkewicz is confident that the police will find out why Cronus was murdered," I said.

"It was a gang thing," Slater said quickly.

"That's certainly how someone wanted it to look," I said.

Slater lowered his voice. "You have a fine family, Joanne. Despite your husband's physical limitations, you appear to be devoted to him. Your adult children have turned out well. Your daughter Taylor has a promising career and those granddaughters are adorable."

"Is that a threat?"

"No, simply a reminder that the Ridgeway campaign is going to do whatever it takes to win."

"That works both ways," I said. "Now, no more shop talk. We have company."

My son Angus, who had just started his articling year with Falconer Shreve, was walking towards us. Angus bore a striking resemblance to my late husband, and that day when I saw him – tall, handsome, dressed as young male lawyers dress, and absently touching the unruly forelock that he had inherited from his father – I felt a pang. When I started to introduce Angus, Slater Doyle cut me short.

"Angus Kilbourn," he said. "Twenty-two years old, graduated from the University of Saskatchewan College of Law last spring, worked three summers in Falconer Shreve's Calgary office, and now articling with his stepfather's firm."

Angus whistled. "The Ridgeway campaign must have one sweet database," he said.

"We like to keep track of people," Slater said and strode away.

Zack's announcement followed the lines we'd decided on the night before. He explained Cronus had named him executor and sole beneficiary and that while the housing problem in North Central required long-term solutions, Peyben workers would be on the job before the end of the week, talking to tenants in the houses Cronus had owned and arranging for the repairs that would make the houses habitable over the winter. When Zack explained that starting this month ten-ants' rents would be dedicated to repairing their homes, there was a murmur of interest.

The media didn't have to scramble for queries. Did Zack have a theory about what had happened to his benefactor? Was there a possible connection between Cronus's passion for rough sex and his death? Inevitably, someone asked whether the fact that Zack was suddenly a slumlord would hurt his campaign. The journalists were probing, but as a trial lawyer, Zack was expert at answering what he had to answer and deflecting the unanswerable. When the old woman in the hunting jacket raised her hand, Zack moved his chair to face her. "You have a question," he said gently.

"I have the word of God," she said. Her voice was deep and stirring. "Matthew 7:24–27. *Everyone who hears these words of mine and puts them into practice is like a wise man who built his house on the rock. The rain came down, the streams rose, and the winds blew and beat against that house; yet it did not fall, because it had its foundation on the rock. But everyone who hears these words of mine and does not put them into practice is like a foolish man who built his house on sand. The rain came down, the streams rose, and the winds blew and beat against that house, and it fell with a great crash.*" She folded her arms over her breast and levelled her glittering black eyes at Zack, waiting for a response.

He answered as smoothly as a man who was in the habit of reading the New Testament over breakfast. "The lesson of that passage is not lost on me," he said. He gestured towards the mustard yellow house behind him. "This house will be made safe. So will all the other houses my wife and I now own. If that means rebuilding the foundation, that will be done. These houses will have a firm foundation. They will not fall."

I glanced over at Slater Doyle. He was on his cell and he did not look happy. As far as I was concerned, Slater's discomfort was reason enough to declare the press conference a success.

The final question came from a young man from a local free newspaper called *Prairie Dog*.

"In leaving you everything he owned, Cronus obviously sent a message about his faith and trust in you," the young man said. "How did you feel about him?"

"He was a client, not a friend," Zack said. His composure broke. For a few moments he was silent. When he spoke his voice was husky with emotion. "I wish I could change that now," he said. "Thank you all for coming today." And with that, the press conference was over.

When Zack joined us, Angus clapped him on the back. "Nice stickhandling," he said. Milo, in the way of political operatives, had been standing at the back of the crowd. When he caught my eye, he made the thumbs-up sign and left for fresh adventures. The media packed up; the watchers wandered off; Angus went back to work. Zack and I were alone on the sidewalk. The sadness clung to him.

"Want to go home for a while?" I said. "Lick our wounds in private?"

"That is *so* tempting," Zack said. "But Norine called. She wants me to stop by Falconer Shreve to discuss Cronus's files."

"I'll go with you," I said.

"I'd appreciate that," Zack said. "I am not eager to be alone with my thoughts."

Success always comes with a price tag. Three years earlier when Falconer Shreve had been bursting at the seams, the firm moved from its old offices into one of the glass towers downtown. The new digs were sleek, corporate, and, to my mind, unwelcoming. The first time I saw Zack's new office, I was struck by its assertive masculinity. The walls were painted the same soft grey as the walls in our cottage, but the ambience was distinctly male. Black leather client chairs, a grey leather couch, an oversized mahogany desk; large black-and-white photos of great moments in sports: Muhammad Ali knocking out Sonny Liston; the Blue Jays' Joe Carter catching Otis Nixon's bunt for the final out in the 1992 World Series; the Roughriders' Dave Ridgeway kicking the thirty-five-yard field goal in the last seconds of the 1989 game that gave Saskatchewan the Grey Cup.

I said nothing, but Zack gradually softened the office's edges. Silver-framed family photos now had pride of place on his desk and credenza, and the walls were hung with some eye-catching Canadian art. That morning, Zack closed his office door behind us and wheeled over to a painting titled *Mozart Core* that I'd given him for his last birthday. For a few moments, he was silent, absorbing the work's exuberant splashes of pink, purple, orange, yellow, and green. "This painting always makes me feel hopeful," he said.

"You should write to Scott Plear and tell him that," I said. "Artists like to know that a piece has found a good home." I took his hand. "So is *Mozart Core* getting the job done today?"

Zack's eyes hadn't left the painting. "We may have to give it a few minutes. It's been a lousy morning. The question that kid from *Prairie Dog* asked really got to me. I wish I had been a better friend to Cronus. I wish I'd been a friend to him period."

"Cronus obviously felt you were his friend. That's going to have to be enough."

"I guess so," Zack said. "Death eliminates the possibility of a do-over."

"On the day he died, Ian and I had a fight," I said. "It wasn't anything major, just the usual. I thought he spent too much time at work and not enough time with us. Anyway, we quarrelled, and Ian left. I was angry, and I didn't say goodbye. I had to live with that memory for a long time."

Zack held out his arms to me. "We never talked about this before."

"No, and I don't want to talk about it now. I just wanted you to stop beating yourself up about Cronus. You can honour his memory by doing exactly what you're doing, so let's find Norine and get on with it."

Norine MacDonald had been with Zack since Falconer Shreve opened its doors twenty-eight years earlier. She had extraordinary organizational skills, she was smart and unflappable, and she knew what Zack wanted before he knew it himself. She was tall, stately, and elegant with the high cheekbones and the long legs characteristic of many Plains Cree. Norine had competed nationally as a long distance runner and she told me once that she'd seriously considered becoming a coach and working at the high school on her reserve. Luckily for Falconer Shreve, she chose another path.

For as long as I'd known her, Norine's wardrobe was exclusively Max Mara. Today she was wearing a single-breasted tan wool suit, a silky cream blouse, and a gold chain necklace. She looked sensational. When she saw us, her face brightened. "Good to see you both," she said. "Inspector Haczkewicz called. Darryl Colby's offices were broken into and pretty well trashed last night. Mr. Colby had couriered Cronus's files here yesterday afternoon, so whoever did it probably didn't get what he or she was looking for."

"So where are the files?"

"In Angus's already cramped office. Zack, there are a lot of boxes. Cronus was old school – paper files."

"The files are evidence," Zack said. "So I assume Debbie is sending someone over to take the files off our hands for a while."

"Yes, but when the police are finished with all that paper, someone here will have to go through it."

"Angus can be our point man," Zack said. "Digging through Cronus's paperwork will teach him things the College of Law didn't teach him. Besides, Angus is family. One day, he might be running our slum empire."

"Every mother's dream for her son," I said.

Norine glanced at her watch. "Zack, you have a meeting with the labour union people in twenty minutes. After that, you're having lunch with Annie and Warren Weber at the Scarth Club."

"Okay, Jo and I are out of here. I'll stay in touch." In the elevator, Zack turned to me. "Why don't you join us for lunch?"

"Thanks, but I'll pass. I'm going to go home and have a nap, and then get the brisket for tomorrow night started." The elevator doors opened and we headed for the street. "Zack, how close are you to Warren Weber?"

"Well, he's been a major contributor to R-H and he likes to keep track of where his money's going, so I would say we're pretty close."

"If you get a chance, ask Warren if he's heard anything about what's going on inside the Ridgeway campaign. Something's wrong. Scott Ridgeway was a zombie at the opening of R-H, and in case you haven't noticed, the mayor hasn't appeared in public since. Today Slater made obliquely threatening references to our family, and then he took off. As soon as you started talking about making the houses we own safe, Slater was on his cell, and he did not look happy."

"Sounds like there's trouble in paradise," Zack said. "I'll see if Warren's heard anything."

When we hit the street, Zack and I went our separate ways. Mieka called just as I pulled into the parking lot at Little Red Meat Wagon. "I'm at UpSlideDown," she said. "Can I buy you a cup of coffee? I'm in the mood for company."

"I'll be there in ten minutes," I said. "Your uncle Howard's coming for dinner tomorrow night. I'm just picking up the briskets."

"Briskets – plural?"

"You and the girls and your brothers are all brisket fans. Do you want to join us?"

"That would be fun," she said. "We'll talk about what I can bring when you get here."

There aren't many peaceful times at UpSlideDown, but mid-morning is as close to serenity as the play centre gets. That morning the usual contingent of mums, many of them pregnant, were sipping herbal tea and chatting while their children played in the quiet space.

When Mieka spotted me, she came over. "All is calm. All is bright," she said. "Let's seize the moment."

We sat at our usual table, close to the kitchen, where Mieka could keep an eye on the action. I noticed there were two young women whom I hadn't seen before helping out.

"Who are the new assistants?" I said.

"Kerry Benjoe's sisters. Kerry suggested we start them out here – let them pick up on the vibe, then see if they're interested in co-managing April's Place. Most of the clientele is Aboriginal and it's important for everybody to know that Aboriginal people are in charge."

I rubbed her arm. "Good call," I said.

Mieka smiled. "Good genes – yours and Dad's." She chewed her lip – always a sign of tension with her. "Dad would have been fifty-seven tomorrow."

"Is that why you had the photo albums out at your house?"

Mieka took a paper napkin from the dispenser and rubbed at a spot on the table. "Dad was so young when he died, and he missed so much. I try to make him part of our significant days."

"Like the girls' first day of school."

Mieka smiled. "You always made sure the boys and I knew the first day of school was significant."

"The only day of the year except your birthdays when you guys got to eat junk cereal," I said. "Mieka, I'm very glad that you're making sure the girls know that Ian is a part of their history."

"Part of their history, but not part of their lives," Mieka said. "As far as Madeleine and Lena are concerned, Zack is their grandfather."

"He's the only grandfather they've ever known," I said. "Zack loves the girls, and they love him. How can that be wrong?"

"It isn't wrong," Mieka said. "But it isn't right either. It's tough for any man to compete with Zack, let alone a man the girls will never know."

I could hear the sadness in her voice. "Mieka, we're not on opposite sides on this," I said.

"I know. It's just that sometimes, it seems as if I'm the only one who remembers Dad. Angus thinks Zack walks on water. Pete knows he couldn't keep his clinic open if Zack didn't cover a lot of the bills. And you . . ." She threw up her hands in exasperation.

"What about me?" I said.

"It's pretty clear that you love Zack more than you ever loved Dad. Don't forget I grew up in that house. I remember the two of you quarrelling." She raised her hand in a halt sign. "I know it didn't happen often, but I can still hear the sound of the front door slamming when Dad went off to the legislature."

"I wanted him to spend more time with us."

"I've read everything that was written about his time in government," Mieka said. "During the years that he was deputy-premier and Attorney General, he changed the province. He was doing important work."

"So was I," I said. "I was raising you and your brothers." I picked up my mug and carried it into the kitchen, and then went back to the staff bathroom. I splashed cold water on my face and breathed deeply until I felt calm enough to face my daughter. I didn't want us to part in anger.

When I came out of the kitchen, Mieka wasn't alone. There had been many surreal moments in the last few days, but this one was right up there. Mieka was still sitting at the table, but Slater Doyle had taken my place. A tiny blond girl was sitting on Mieka's lap.

As soon as he spotted me, Slater stood so abruptly that he nearly knocked over his chair. For a moment I thought he was going to bolt, but he regained his composure. "Hello again," he said.

"Twice in one day," I said. "It must be kismet."

Mieka's eyes travelled from Slater to me. "I didn't realize you two knew each other," she said. When neither of us said anything, Mieka turned to the little girl in her arms. "This is Bridie Doyle, Mum. Bridie, this is my mother, Ms. Shreve."

I held out my hand to her. "I'm very glad to meet you, Bridie," I said.

Bridie was perhaps four years old, a fairy-tale child, very delicate with white blond curly hair and a sweet smile. Her hand was almost weightless. "Thank you," she said softly.

"You're welcome," I said. I looked at Slater. "Your daughter?"

"My pride and joy," Slater said.

"I can understand why," I said. "Slater, I'm glad I ran into you again. There's something I wanted to talk to you about."

"Not in front of Bridie." Slater's hostility was evident and Mieka frowned.

"This is just campaign business. Zack's doing Jack Quinlan's radio show tomorrow, and I know the mayor is scheduled to be on it next week. Would you agree not to stack the deck with supporters?"

Slater raised an eyebrow. "Just real callers with real questions?"

"That's the idea. You and I both need to get a clear picture of where we stand."

I could see Slater weighing my proposition. "We go last," he said finally. "How do I know you won't cheat?"

"You don't," I said. "You'll have to trust me." I zipped my jacket. "I'm taking off now, Mieka. Let me know what you decide, Slater."

When Bridie slid off Mieka's knee and headed for the play area, Mieka came over and gave me a quick hug. "I'll bring a roasted vegetable salad tomorrow night. It'll be good with the brisket." She turned to Slater. "There's fresh coffee," she said. "And you're in luck. The morning glory muffins are just about to come out of the oven."

Cooking always calms me, and after I put the briskets in marinade, I made a chicken casserole that Taylor was fond of, had a hot shower, rubbed myself with lavender lotion, and took a long nap. I awoke feeling ready to tackle what lay ahead.

What lay ahead was Milo O'Brien. When he called from downstairs, I braced myself and buzzed him in. As always, Milo was wearing khakis, a black T-shirt, and a Blue Jays cap. He had his phone in one hand and a half-eaten Crispy Crunch bar in the other. "Good news," he said. "People are tweeting about the big man's press conference and the tweets are overwhelmingly positive. They like that he got out in front of the situation. They like the answer he gave to the old Bible-thumper, and they like that he's not just talking about getting the houses fixed, he's actually getting workers on the job."

Milo pulled up a stool to the kitchen table and began drumming his fingers. He had a wild, kinetic energy that kept him constantly in motion and drove Zack crazy. "Quinlan's producer called," he said. "The slumlord story is trending, so they're going to give Zack the entire second hour of the show. One small complication. Quinlan thinks the dynamic will be better if Zack's across the desk in the studio with him."

"So we fly to Saskatoon," I said.

Milo's startlingly bright blue eyes were amused. "That's right. You're a white knuckler, aren't you?"

"I'll be all right," I said.

"Good." Milo finished his chocolate bar and rolled the wrapper into a ball. "The *Leader-Post* is doing polling on the civic election today and tomorrow. We should have numbers by Friday. But even without the numbers my spidey sense tells me we're moving in the right direction. Zack's a charismatic guy."

"Milo, what do you know about Slater Doyle?"

"He's the enemy. Apart from that – nothing much. Slater knows what he's doing. He's smart – smart enough to know that his candidate may be in trouble. My guess is that Ridgeway's people are very concerned about those poll numbers."

"What do you think they'll do if we come out ahead?"

Milo shrugged. "Retaliate." He slid off the stool and headed for the door. "The plane for Saskatoon leaves at 6:55 tomorrow morning. You can get the tickets online."

"Aren't you coming?"

He shook his head. "No need, if you're going. There's stuff I can do here."

"Well, thanks for stopping by," I said.

"No problem," Milo said. He reached into the pocket of his khakis, pulled out a Crispy Crunch, and tossed it to me. "For the flight," he said.

———

Zack called just after Milo left. "How was lunch at the Scarth Club?" I said.

"Long, liquid, and pleasant," Zack said. "I must have been there a hundred times, but that place still knocks me out. I love the portraits of those pompous old farts who were the club's first presidents, and I love that motto they had carved about themselves over the salon mantlepiece: "They Builded Better Than They Knew.""

"There's something to be said for tradition," I agreed.

"Boy, is there ever," Zack said. "Warren is the fourth generation of his family to belong to the club, and he says the recipe the bartender uses to make the Old Fashioneds we had today is the same recipe that was used to make the Old Fashioneds his great-grandfather favoured, fruit salad in an Old Fashioned glass filled with ice, bourbon, and a dash of bitters."

"Sounds as if you had a couple," I said.

"I'm high on life," Zack said airily.

"Where's your car?" I said.

"In my parking space at Falconer Shreve," Zack said. "Warren's driver took us wherever we needed to go."

I laughed. "So where did you need to go?"

"Many places," Zack said.

"Do you want me to pick you up?"

"Warren and I are still making the rounds," Zack said. "The driver will deliver me to you."

"Where's Annie?"

"At the gym working on her abs." Suddenly, Zack was all business. "Jo, this long, liquid lunch of mine has been highly instructive. You asked me ask to see what Warren knew about the people behind Ridgeway."

"And . . ."

"And some of Ridgeway's major contributors are starting to ask questions about why the mayor hasn't appeared in public since he freaked at the Racette-Hunter opening, Warren's buddies may be old, but they can still smell trouble, and they're hanging on to their money."

"Milo implied Ridgeway's numbers are soft," I said. "The possibility of losing an election always dries up some funding sources."

"But Ridgeway's still ahead," Zack said. "I don't get it."

"Neither do I," I said. "It's seven weeks till the election. In politics, that's an eternity. People like Warren's friends and companies like Lancaster Development have been buying politicians for years. They're too experienced to panic because their candidate's vote is wobbly."

"Well, for some reason they *are* panicking," Zack said, "and this afternoon Warren did what he could to speed their exit. He took me around, introduced me to people who I'd assumed would be supporting Ridgeway, said the Ridgeway campaign might be headed for trouble and they should either support me or wait this one out."

"And Warren didn't elaborate on what the potential trouble was."

"No, and I didn't push it. Warren did tell me that in the past few days Graham Meighen has been hitting up Ridgeway's supporters hard for cash donations."

"That doesn't make any sense. That campaign is well financed, and since he was disbarred, Slater's been a model steward of other people's money. Since Ridgeway was first elected, Slater has never spent a dime more than he had to on an election. There's no reason for Graham Meighen to be going around town cap in hand."

"Maybe not, but Warren told me that on Wednesday, Graham Meighen approached him personally asking for a donation."

"And . . . ?"

Zack chortled. "Warren told Meighen to go to hell, that he was supporting me."

"And we missed the moment," I said. "Let's at least celebrate it. I haven't had an Old Fashioned in twenty-five years.
Why don't you pick up a jar of maraschino cherries on your
way home and we'll go crazy."

CHAPTER

5

Jill Oziowy called just as I was putting the casserole in the oven for dinner. As always her voice was vibrant. Jill set her own course, and she had a gift for taking people where she wanted them to go. "I watched the podcast of Zack's news conference this morning," she said. "It piqued my curiosity, so I pulled up our coverage of the Cronus murder. Gruesome stuff going on out there in the Queen City."

"You don't know the half of it," I said.

"Fill me in."

I gave Jill the condensed version of all that had happened from the time Cronus warned us that a child would be abducted from the R-H opening. When I finished, she said, "Sounds like a story to me."

"A story that continues to unfold," I agreed. "I hate loose ends, and there are many, many loose ends here. The problem is I don't have time to follow them up. Scott Ridgeway, our current mayor, is a lightweight. Everyone knows he's a puppet for the developers, but he's affable; he's enthusiastic about all the ceremonial stuff mayors have to do, and until the Racette-Hunter opening, he'd never met a camera or a microphone he didn't like. He was scheduled to speak that night and he froze. His campaign manager had to literally push him onstage, and when Ridgeway just stared at the audience, his campaign manager had to haul him off. The mayor has been AWOL ever since."

"No candidate disappears for two full days during a tight campaign," Jill said.

"No, and Zack just learned that Ridgeway's cash cows are getting skittish. The *Leader-Post* is doing some polling today and tomorrow, and Milo O'Brien, our political gun for hire, thinks we may be pulling ahead."

"You don't sound exactly jubilant," Jill said.

"I'm not," I said. "I'm worried."

"Come on, Jo, you've been doing politics for a long time. You're too smart to get sucker-punched."

"In an ordinary election, yes. But from the time Cronus warned us that a child would be abducted, this has not been an ordinary election. Jill, I think there's a connection between Ridgeway's campaign and Cronus's murder."

"You think they had him killed?"

"I don't know. All I know is that Cronus had me take a buddy photo of him with Zack and Brock Poitras, the candidate for city council in our ward. Cronus sent out the photo with a cryptic message – all numbers, seemingly random. Within twelve hours he was dead."

"I'm coming out there," Jill said,

"Are you serious?"

"You bet I'm serious. It's been a long time since I've done real journalism. This smells like a red meat story, and I want to be the one doing the reporting."

"This may get ugly."

"It couldn't be any uglier than what's going on here."

"Trouble in the halls of NationTV?"

"Just our biennial bloodletting."

"And you're caught in the middle?"

"I'm the target. Yet another young turk has been brought in to save the network. He wants NationTV to pull back on hard news and focus on 'lifestyle programming' so we can capture the eighteen to forty-nine demographic. Same old, same old – shorter segments, less analysis, more focus on self-help, home improvement, and fun. He's getting a lot of support from the brown-nosers upstairs. I seem to be the only one standing in his way."

"Hey, déjà-vu all over again," I said. "Remember the water-skiing squirrel?"

Jill chuckled. "God, I'd almost forgotten. Same situation. Different young turk. If that squirrel was still alive NationTV would give him his own show – prime time."

"You won that battle, and you'll win this one."

"I'm not optimistic," Jill said. "But I'm not going to oblige the network by falling on my sword. I've been a journalist for over twenty-five years. I want to leave a legacy. If this Ridgeway story is half as hot as I think it is, I'll be able to force NationTV to admit that investigative journalism has a place in network television."

"That's the Jill I know and love," I said. "And I have an idea about where you can start. You have the video of Zack's press conference. Hang on to everything that was filmed but didn't make it to air. When Zack talked about ensuring that the foundations of the Rose Street houses were firm, he was responding to a question from an old woman quoting the Bible. As soon as Zack started in, Ridgeway's campaign manager, Slater Doyle, jumped for his cell. I'd pay good money to know who he called."

"Save your money," Jill said. "I'm still on salary at NationTV, and that means I'm free to ask questions, follow leads, and keep on digging until we hit pay dirt."

"All of a sudden I can't stop smiling," I said. "Jill, I can't tell you what it will mean to me to have you here. Lately I've been feeling like Sisyphus, rolling my boulder up the hill and just standing by as it rolls back down again."

"From now on there'll be two of us to push the boulder," Jill said. "It'll be like old times. I'll call you as soon as I know what time I'll be arriving in Regina."

"Try to book a flight that will get you here in time for dinner tomorrow," I said. "Howard Dowhanuik and the kids are coming for brisket. Zack loves a full table."

"And tomorrow is Ian's birthday," Jill said. The ache in her voice was unmistakable. "Jo, I miss you all so much."

"We miss you too," I said. "But tomorrow we'll be together. And on Ian's birthday. He would have gotten a kick out of that."

The second-hour slot on *Quinlan Live* was good placement for Zack. Although the studio was in Saskatoon, the show was broadcast provincewide between 8:30 a.m. and 12:30 p.m. and rebroadcast at night. By the end of the day, much of the province had heard Jack Quinlan's voice: badgering, teasing, empathizing, pontificating, enthusing, consoling.

Quinlan's politics were as far to the right of mine as it was possible to be, but I liked him. Over the years, I'd been on *Quinlan Live* dozens of times as an academic whose views on the politics of foreign takeovers, culture, race, poverty, and a host of other issues lit up the phone lines. Jack was often outrageous, but he was always fair, and I knew he'd give Zack a chance to talk freely.

The flight to Saskatoon took only thirty-five minutes, but that was still thirty-five minutes too long for me. I didn't exhale until the plane touched down and then it was back to business. On the cab ride to Quinlan's studio overlooking the Saskatchewan River, Zack and I talked about questions that might prove problematic. With live radio the nutbar factor is always high, but the producer of *Quinlan Live* was adept at using the cut-off button.

When Zack did his pre-broadcast mike check, the board was already lit up. Quinlan turned to Zack. "Ready to rock and roll?" he said.

Zack slipped on his headphones and gave him the thumbs-up. Zack had a good radio voice: deep, intimate, and assured. His précis of his relationship with Cronus and of the effect that relationship might have on his campaign was comprehensive but concise.

And then it was the listeners' turn. Call-in shows are a landmine for candidates. As a rule, there's some judicious stagemanaging beforehand, but the agreement Slater Doyle and I reached meant that Zack was flying without a net. My pulse quickened as soon as the first caller came on and didn't slow until the hour was almost over.

The calls had broken about 60–40 in Zack's favour. Zack had spent his adult life thrusting and parrying in courtrooms, so *Quinlan Live* was a comfortable arena for him. He picked up key points in the positive comments and ran with them, tying them to planks in his platform. And, without breaking a sweat, he found the weak spot in the argument of hostile callers, picked apart their case, and dug in.

With five minutes to go in the hour, there was a treat. Peggy Kreviazuk called in and in her breathy, still-girlish voice endorsed Zack's candidacy and urged others to support him. Peggy had been a force in progressive politics in our province for close to sixty years. A regular at the weekly meetings of the Regina City Council, Peggy was one of the few people I knew who took civic politics seriously. Her integrity was beyond question, and someone in the Office of the City Clerk recognized her integrity by occasionally passing along information that Peggy could use in her questions to the mayor and council members. Two weeks earlier, when we'd bumped into each other at the farmers' market, Peggy and I had a spirited talk about the election. Peggy always turned heads. That day her wispy hair was an improbable but flattering shade of pink, and she was sporting a top printed with the *New Yorker* cartoon of Homer Simpson wearing a Che Guevara T-shirt. When she saw me, she extended her arms and gave me her standard greeting. "The struggle continues, Joanne."

I gave her my standard response. "And so do we, Peggy," I said.

When Peggy finished her encomium to Zack, the second hand of the large clock on the wall opposite Jack Quinlan was ticking towards the end of the hour. I didn't allow myself to exhale. "Time for one more call," Quinlan said. "Cassandra's on the line. So, what are your thoughts about the upcoming civic election in Regina?"

"I've been following the campaign closely," Cassandra said. Her voice seemed familiar – precise in its enunciation but with a huskiness that conveyed urgency. "You're an impressive candidate, Mr. Shreve. I've watched your career. You're a man who gets things done. You're frank about your failings. You're a person of character, and people whose judgment I trust think highly of you. I've read your platform, and what you say is correct. We live in a wealthy society. We have enough money, enough food, and enough work for everybody. Your campaign slogan is spot on. There *is* 'enough for all.' And it *is* time that we redressed the balance between the haves and the have-nots. You're clearly the better of the two mayoral candidates."

When she paused, Zack jumped in. "Thank you, Cassandra. Politics can be bruising, but I'll take a lot of bruises for a call like yours."

"I'm afraid that I'm about to inflict a bruise too," she said. I stiffened, and Zack shot me a quick look. "Suddenly it seems possible that you might win," the woman said. "It's time to end your campaign, Mr. Shreve. Ridgeway's cohorts are prepared to do whatever it takes to defeat you. There's already been one tragedy. If you stay in the race, *everyone* will suffer."

Jack Quinlan was quick off the mark. He leaned into his microphone. "These are serious allegations, Cassandra," he said. "Do you have any specifics?" It was the right question, but it came too late. Cassandra had already broken the connection.

Quinlan wound up the show, and the news came on. Quinlan opened his mike, exchanged a few words with his producer in the control room, and turned back to Zack and me. "Cassandra was a first-time caller, and she called from an unlisted number. My producer talked to her briefly before she was on-air. He said she was rational, focused, and articulate. He thought she'd be ideal."

"She chose a great nom de guerre," I said. "Cassandra had the gift of prophecy, but Apollo placed a curse on her so that none of her predictions would be believed."

When Zack and I were alone in the elevator, he pulled out his phone and started tapping away. He found what he was looking for, then handed his phone to me. "If you want to bum yourself out, check the number of Cassandra's prophecies that came true," he said.

"I'm already bummed out," I said. "Zack, I recognized Cassandra's voice. I've heard it before, but I can't place it."

"No surprise there," Zack said. "Nothing comes easy in this campaign."

I'd cooked the briskets for four hours the night before. They were in the refrigerator ready to be sliced, so I could reheat them for an hour before we ate. While I prepared them, Zack ran through his messages. After we'd both finished our tasks,

I glanced at my watch. "We have time for a swim before lunch," I said.

Zack groaned. "Wasn't Cassandra's warning enough misery for one morning?"

"Did that get to you?"

"Nah. Trial lawyers get death threats. All the same I'm going to call Debbie. Cassandra was seemingly sane and definitely knowledgeable. We have to take her warning seriously."

Getting Zack to hit the pool was never easy, but swimming kept his muscles toned and his blood pressure from spiking, so I persisted. That day after thirty minutes in the pool, I could see the tension drain from Zack's body and I could feel it drain from my own.

Milo O'Brien joined us for lunch – more accurately, he was present at the lunch table as we ate. When I offered him a salmon sandwich on rye, he blew me off, opened a fresh chocolate bar, then, foot tapping, fingers drumming, gave us a snapshot of the response to Zack's appearance on *Quinlan Live*. As erratic as Milo's behaviour was, we'd learned to trust his reading of Facebook and tweets.

And Milo's report was provocative. To my surprise, most of the messages had come from new supporters who urged Zack not to be intimidated and continue to fight the good fight. When he'd finished, Milo slid off his stool, slapped Zack on the back, said, "Hang tough, big guy," and left.

Zack watched as Milo made his exit, reaching out to beat on every surface his hand touched. "Milo is one weird dude," Zack said.

"Politics makes strange bedfellows."

"Speaking of," Zack said, "have you ever wondered whether there's a bedfellow in Milo's life?"

"Nope," I said. "Milo is smart, devoted, and loyal – that's enough for me. My guess is that having sex with Milo would be like having sex with a woodpecker – a lot of rat-a-tat-tat and not much more."

Zack and I were still musing over Milo's private life when Howard Dowhanuik called.

Howard had never mastered the art of preamble. "Do you have any idea what was going on with that last caller on *Quinlan Live*?"

"She was giving us a warning," I said.

Howard was withering. "Thanks. I would never have picked that up on my own. I'm assuming Zack's not going to heed the warning."

"You're right. He called Debbie Haczkewicz about it, but we're just going to play through. Milo O'Brien, our numbers guy, says the response on social media has been overwhelmingly positive. A lot of people who were on the fence or indifferent are supporting us now."

"Good," Howard said. "And more great news. I'm bringing dessert tonight."

"You're turning on your oven?"

"I didn't say that. I said I'm bringing dessert. Be grateful."

"I am grateful, but you'd better double your order – Mieka and her girls and Angus and Peter and Maisie are coming over. And a surprise – Jill Oziowy's coming to town."

"God, I haven't seen Jill in years," Howard said.

"You saw her at the gathering Zack and I had after our wedding."

"I didn't stick around that day. Remember?"

"I remember. You didn't approve of the groom. Anyway, it will be good to see Jill again."

"I've always been surprised that you and Jill stayed friends," Howard said.

"Why wouldn't we stay friends?"

Howard harrumphed – an invariable tip of his hand when

he didn't want to answer a question. "Just – you know – people drift," he said.

"Well, Jill and I didn't, and you and I didn't. See you at six."

Jill's plane was arriving in Regina at 5:35. Mieka lived five minutes from the airport, so she and the girls were picking Jill up and coming straight to Halifax Street.

Zack had just finished mixing a pitcher of martinis and putting on a Bill Evans CD when Mieka and the girls arrived with Jill. I'd wanted our condo to be particularly welcoming and it was. The hearty beefy fragrance of brisket filled the rooms. Taylor had set the table with linen and china in the warm hues of Tuscany: terra cotta, saffron, dark green, and pomegranate. I'd filled a drabware vase Taylor found at a flea market with sunflowers for a centrepiece.

Jill and I spent our first few minutes in a blur of hugs, half-sentences, and more hugs. Jill looked terrific, but she always did. Our local paper had done a profile of her not long after she became Ian's press secretary. The profiler had opened his piece with the sentence: "Jill Oziowy is not a conventionally pretty woman, but she is not without appeal." She had enlarged the first paragraph of the article and taped it to her office door. When I'd first met Jill, she had untamed shoulder-length carroty-red hair, freckles, startlingly gold-flecked tawny eyes, and an open smile. The freckles, the smile, and the tawny eyes were the same, but Jill's hair was now auburn and it was cut very short with a diagonal line in the bangs. Her form-fitting leather jacket was the same shade as her hair and she was wearing slim-cut black pants and fashion boots. In the early days, Jill got much of her wardrobe from Value Village, but I suspected the outfit she was wearing that night owed more to Holt Renfrew than to VV.

Jill had brought gifts: for Madeleine, Lena, and Taylor, sports shorts and pretty shrugs; for Zack, six elegant

blown-glass martini glasses with hand-etched palm fronds
and delicate stems; and for me, a six-pack of Moosehead
and a giant bag of Cheetos. My heart leapt when I saw the
beer and the garish orange-and-yellow Cheetos bag. There
had been many election nights when Jill and I sat at my
kitchen table, sipping a Moosehead and waiting with orange
sticky-crumbed fingers for early election results. On those
nights it seemed that Jill's heart and mine beat as one. We
were two women whose lives centred on Ian Kilbourn, and
in those moments we knew there was nothing we could do
to alter his political fate.

When Zack handed us our martinis in the new glasses,
I was still happily clutching the Cheetos bag. Jill came over
and hugged me again. "I'm so glad you liked my present,"
she said. "You have no idea what it means for me to be with
all of you again – especially today."

It was a perfect September evening, warm enough to sit
out on our terrace and watch the city. Angus's contribution
to the meal was a dozen chilled Corona Extras; Peter's girlfriend, Maisie Crawford, brought an antipasto platter; Mieka
brought the promised roasted vegetable salad; I'd made
latkes that simply needed to be warmed before dinner; and
Howard's mystery dessert was sitting in bakery boxes on
the sideboard. There was nothing to do but enjoy our time
together. Zack, Jill, and I had martinis; Howard and the kids
had ginger ale; and everybody else had beer. When we all
had drinks in hand, Jill raised her glass and said, "To Ian
Kilbourn – without him, none of us would be here."

Lena wrinkled her nose. "Granddad would be here," she
said. "So would Taylor and Maisie. We should say their
names too."

Jill accepted Lena's suggestion with grace. "All right," she
said. "To Ian. And to Granddad, Taylor, and Maisie."

I'd feared the evening might get mired in Auld Lang Syne,

but the present was chock full, and the future was filled with shining possibilities.

Taylor had brought up the portrait of Margot and her family for us to see. The painting was unfinished, but the canvas was alive with light and colour and the likenesses of Margot, Declan, and Lexi were already filled with life.

Jill was captivated. "That's an amazing piece," she said. "And you are how old?"

"Sixteen on November 11," Taylor said

Madeleine and Lena had fish of their own to fry. Madeleine was trying out for the basketball team, and Lena was trying out for everything, including the Pius X Liturgy Club. When I reminded Lena that she was an Anglican, she said it didn't matter; besides, the Liturgy Club got doughnuts from Tim Hortons for their meetings.

The local paper wanted to do a feature on Peter's street-front vet clinic. The clinic was located in the city's core and clients paid what they could, which was usually not much if anything. Zack subsidized the clinic, and Peter thought Zack's contribution should be part of the story, but Zack vetoed the idea, saying he didn't want to politicize a private commitment.

Talk of the campaign dominated the dinner table. Everyone, even Madeleine and Lena, had an opinion about how the race was going. When I suggested that our local NationTV might do a daily political feature from the school-yard at the girls' school, Jill was quick on the uptake. "That's not the worst idea you ever had," she said. "It might be fun to do a weekly segment from different schools around the city. Find out what kids want for their hometown."

Mieka shot Zack a significant look. "A wise grandfather would invest in a trip to Dessart with his granddaughters before they're on NationTV chatting about the choices voters face in this election."

Zack turned to Madeleine and Lena. "My policy on bribery is flexible. Choose your day, ladies. Sky's the limit."

Howard's surprise dessert turned out to be three-dozen Black and White cookies from a Jewish bakery that had just opened on Smith Street. Howard presented the cookies as if he'd invented them himself, noting the even distribution of black fondant and white fondant icing and announcing that each bite had to contain both black and white icing. The cookies were large, and the perfect bite was almost impossible to manage but we had fun trying.

Willie and Pantera were never shy about letting me know when it was time for their post-dinner run on the roof garden. That night when I picked up my jacket, Madeleine and Lena followed suit. Then, in the way of parties, everyone decided to come with us. We stepped out of the freight elevator into a cool, starry evening. The air smelled of autumn: woodsmoke, wet leaves, and the acrid scent from the heavy heads of the marigolds that still flourished in the roof's planters. The lights strung on the evergreens made the roof garden seem like fairyland.

As her daughters played a game of hide and seek whose rules only they understood, Mieka watched fondly. "This will be a great memory for them," she said. She slid her arm through Jill's. "I'm so glad you're here tonight. You've been part of our lives from the beginning. I want you to be part of the girls' lives too."

"Tonight's a start," Jill said. "While I'm here I'd like to do something special with Madeleine and Lena."

"Like that time we went tobogganing on the night of the first real snowfall?" Mieka said.

"I remember every single second of that night," Jill said. "I'd been watching the snow through your dining room window while we ate. So had your dad. When we were through eating, your mum started to clear the dishes and Ian took command. "Just leave everything. That's tobogganing snow. If we get dressed and go now, we'll be the first ones on the hill."

"The creek was frozen solid and we slid across the ice and climbed up to the bike path," Pete said.

"And as soon as he got on the bike path Dad took off," Angus said. "He wanted to be the first person on the toboggan run, and he was. He didn't even take one of us kids with him."

"Your dad *was* a kid," I said, and Jill and I exchanged a smile.

"We stayed out way past bedtime, but it was a perfect night," Mieka said.

"Not quite perfect," Jill said. "You kids probably don't remember this part, but when it was time to go, I decided to have one last ride. I struck a bump, got thrown from my toboggan, and hit my tailbone. God, did that hurt."

"I remember," I said. "Ian ran home to get the car so he could take you to the medi-clinic. And the kids and I trudged back to the house with the sleds and the dogs."

Mieka's brow furrowed. "It was still a great evening," she said.

"It was," I agreed. "But after I got you kids to bed, I had to deal with the dishes. The moral of that story is *carpe diem*, but clean up the kitchen first."

Mieka was clearly exasperated. "Mum, you just blew away the pixie dust."

Zack put his arm around me. "Mieka, your mother is the one who sprinkles the pixie dust for us all."

Jill had had a long day of travel and the next day was a work or school day so we wound down early. Zack and I saw Jill and Mieka and the girls to the door. Jill stood aside as we went through the usual round of family hugs. She seemed isolated and Mieka picked up on her aloneness. "Why don't you stay with us tonight, Jill?" she said. "You won't have to go through the hassle of checking into a hotel, and you and I can get caught up over breakfast."

Jill brightened. "I would love to help you tuck in the girls, Mieka, thank you. It would be great to be in the Kilbourn house again."

After the elevator doors closed, Zack turned to me. "That was a lot of fun," he said.

"Any evening when I get a six-pack of Moosehead and a bag of Cheetos is a triumph," I said. "Now we should probably offer our help in the kitchen."

The kitchen crew had everything under control. Angus and Peter were scrubbing pots, Taylor and Maisie were piling dishes in the dishwasher, and Howard was boxing up the rest of the cookies for us.

"You guys are terrific," I said. "My story about the mess I came home to after tobogganing wasn't a plea for help tonight, but I really do appreciate this."

"A great meal deserves a great cleanup," Maisie said.

The buzzer sounded from the lobby downstairs. I pressed the intercom. Milo O'Brien was on the other end. I shot Zack a questioning look. "He thought he'd have the *Leader-Post* polling results tonight," Zack said. "Let's see what he's got." He gave his chair a quarter-turn towards Howard. "Jo tells me you've decided to become part of our campaign. She's grateful and that means I'm grateful. If you have a minute, I'd like you to stick around for Milo's report."

"All the time in the world," Howard said. He placed his box of leftover cookies inside the microwave, out of dog range, and shook Zack's hand. The gesture was significant.

Zack and I had been married during the 10:30 Holy Eucharist service at the Cathedral. Two months before our wedding Zack had cross-examined Howard during a trial.

Zack's questioning had been brutal, and as far as Howard was concerned, I was marrying the enemy. On my wedding day the handshake Howard shared with my new husband was perfunctory. The handshake tonight seemed like the real thing, and I was pleased.

Milo and Howard had never met, and I watched Howard's face carefully as Milo bopped across the living room, drumming on every surface his fingers touched. I'd always marvelled at Howard's ability to make quick, smart assessments of people, but Milo was a cat of a different stripe, and I noticed that Howard was taking his time forming an opinion.

"So we've got the poll results," Milo said. "Out of 1,813 randomly selected voters chosen by age and gender to match the population: 36 per cent of those planning to vote say they're for Zack, 34 per cent say they're for Ridgeway, 1 per cent are for the guy who wears the tinfoil hat to keep the government from reading his brain, and 21 per cent are undecided."

"Whoa!" Zack said. "The first time we've pulled into the lead."

"Don't cream your jeans," Milo said. "A 2 per cent lead is well within the margin of error."

"But it's an uptick," Howard said. "And politics is about momentum."

"The Big Mo," Milo agreed. "Once you've got that going for you, you ride the wave."

"Right," Howard said, and he and Milo exchanged a comradely smile.

"So we just keep on doing what we're doing," Zack said.

"That's the plan," I said. "I can make you a tinfoil hat. Maybe you can pick up some votes from the people who are convinced the government is trying to read their brains."

Zack and I laughed, but Howard was gloomy. "I wish I could read Cassandra's brain," he said. "She sounded very certain of her information. Is there any way we can find out who she is?"

"Pray that my synapses connect," I said. "When Cassandra called in there was something familiar about her voice. I've been mulling it over, but I still can't figure out who she is."

Milo picked up his phone and tapped away. "I just tweeted asking for help identifying Cassandra," he said. He glanced at his phone screen. "And here's a response already. 'Lois from *The Family Guy.*' And here's another one, 'Don Cherry.'" Milo dropped his phone into his pocket. "It's going to be a long night," he said. Then he headed for the door, drumming all the way.

We offered Peter, Maisie, and Angus a nightcap, but they'd all had full days, and Howard, looking more invigorated than he had in weeks, left with them.

Zack and I said goodnight to Taylor, then went up to our room. Zack took off his tie and began unbuttoning his shirt. "Wouldn't take many days like this to make a dozen," he said. "So how do you feel about our surging vote?"

"Nervous," I said.

"Because you think the lead might disappear?"

I took off my slacks, hung them in the closet, and tossed my blouse in the laundry hamper. "No," I said. "Because I think you might suddenly be in a position to win this thing. Slater Doyle told me that Ridgeway's people would do whatever it took to defeat you. Now Cassandra has said the same thing."

"And you believe her."

"I do," I said. "When I was a little girl I used to listen to a radio show called *Maggie Muggins*. Every episode ended with Maggie saying, 'I don't know what will happen tomorrow.' Maggie was always very excited about the uncertainty, but the idea of not knowing what was ahead terrified me then and it terrifies me now."

CHAPTER

6

When Graham Meighen called early Friday morning, he went straight to the point. "Joanne, I'm calling about Liz," he said. "She's fine – at least physically, but tomorrow is the anniversary of Beverly's death, and it's already hitting her hard. All week she's been locked away in Beverly's old room, going through family photos and watching home movies. I'm calling to invite you and Zack to join us for dinner Sunday night. It will give Liz something to look forward to – at the very least it will get her out of that room. And I can promise you a memorable meal. I was fishing in the Queen Charlottes this week, and I caught some spectacular coho."

"Thanks for the invitation," I said. "I'll check with Zack and get back to you."

"With what will no doubt be a very graceful rejection," Graham said, sounding gently amused. "Joanne, I know there's enmity between us politically, but I'm asking you to put it aside for an evening. I'm at a loss about how to help Liz. She shuns me, and she doesn't want to see anybody else. Her behaviour is erratic. She's lost in her own world. To be frank, when I look at her, I can barely recognize the woman I married.

But the other day at the scholarship luncheon, when she called me a bullshitter for suggesting the four of us get together, I saw a spark of the Liz I knew. I'm hoping that if I call her bluff about the barbecue, she'll find that spark again."

I remembered the longing in Liz's voice when she told me how she had hoped that the last face she saw before she died would be Beverly's. "Our calendar's clear for Sunday night," I said. "What time would you like us?"

"Seven," Graham said. "And to put your mind at ease – the house is fully accessible. We had it retrofitted in the year before Beverly died."

"Thanks for letting me know," I said. "See you at seven on Sunday."

Predictably, Zack uttered a daisy chain of his favourite expletives when I told him about accepting the invitation. Equally predictably, he cooled off after I explained that I'd agreed to have dinner with the Meighens because Liz needed help and I didn't know what else to do.

Zack and I weren't the only members of our family who weren't looking forward to Sunday. Classes at the University of Toronto were starting on September 8 and Declan was taking the early flight to Toronto. He and Taylor had spent all of Saturday night bundled up on the roof garden talking.

Declan had promised to say goodbye before he left, and Zack had just poured our morning coffee when the kids, pale with fatigue but quietly happy, came through the door. They were hand in hand and when they joined us at the kitchen table, I saw that they were both wearing silver Celtic knot rings on their left forefingers. I took Taylor's hand in mine so I could look more closely at the ring. "That's lovely," I said.

"Declan bought the rings online," she said. "They're a way to keep close while we're apart."

Declan had loved Taylor for over two years, but until the past summer Taylor had kept their relationship fond but platonic. Now there was a romance, and there were rings – another milestone.

Taylor was dreamy during church, but she often was. Once, when I'd drawn her attention to the line "Lord keep our thoughts from wandering" from the Young People's Service in the old prayer book, Taylor had just smiled and returned to her musings.

Declan texted when he landed at Pearson, and when we were having lunch, he called to say he was in his dorm and all was well. Taylor passed along the news, put the lunch dishes in the dishwasher, and said she was going to her studio. When she was at the door, she turned and came back to Zack and me. "Don't worry about me. I'm fine. Declan and I know who we are, where we are, and where we're going."

"That's impressive," Zack said.

Taylor smiled her new secret smile. "Not really," she said. "When you know you've found the right person, every-thing else just seems to fall into place."

And with that, our not-quite sixteen-year-old daughter headed for her studio.

When I'd met Zack, he drove a white Jaguar with a vanity licence plate that said *Amicus* – friend. These days most of our travel involved kids and dogs, so like me, Zack had a station wagon, but we'd kept the Jag insured. On pretty nights, it was fun to put down the top and feel the rush of driving a slick car through the city.

Neither of us was looking forward to an evening with Graham Meighen, so Zack suggested we take the Jag so we could at least enjoy the trip. As we drove to the Meighens, Zack and I were quiet, absorbed in our own thoughts. We were both wary of Graham, but we were also aware of what the evening could mean to Liz and we were anxious not to make a misstep.

The Meighens lived in Whitmore Park, a pleasant neighbourhood of large lots and well-kept, nicely landscaped homes developed in the 1960s. Osler Place was its crown jewel. The homes there were the same vintage as their more modest neighbours, but the six houses on Osler Place were built on double lots and all were large. On our drive through the neighbourhood, I'd noticed that the number of lawn signs for Zack and for Scott Ridgeway was pretty well even. All six houses on the Meighens' street had large signs supporting the incumbent mayor. But the Meighens' lawn also sported a modest SHREVE sign.

Zack pointed it out to me. "Do you think our hosts will pull that out of the lawn as soon as we leave?"

"No. I think it'll stay put. My guess is that Liz called our headquarters and asked for the sign – part of the erratic behaviour Graham alluded to."

Zack reached into the back seat, took out the pieces of his chair, and began to assemble it. After he'd transferred his body from the car to his chair, he shrugged. "Well, let's get it over with."

Liz answered the door. She was wearing a simple red turtleneck and an ankle-length black skirt scattered with embroidered poppies. She greeted us both warmly and took our coats. For a moment she seemed unsure about what to do with them. Then she smiled and said, "The hall closet, right?" and we all laughed.

"Graham's outside fooling with the barbecue," she said. "Zack, would you mind letting him know you're here so we can have drinks. Just go through the kitchen."

"My pleasure," Zack said, and he wheeled down the hall.

Liz gestured towards the living room. "Come in here with me," she said. "We have a fire going, so it's cozy."

The walls of the room into which Liz led me were eggshell; the floor was red oak and the couches and the four easy chairs drawn around the oval coffee table in front of the fireplace were upholstered in muted lemon and bittersweet patterns. Liz and I settled into chairs that faced each other. "I'm so glad you came," she said. "There's something I want to give you." She glanced towards the arch that separated the living room from the hall to make sure we were alone, then reached under the seat of her chair and pulled out an envelope. "This is a donation to Zack's campaign," she said. "I'd hoped to be able to help with the actual work, but I'm just not up to it."

"What's the matter, Liz?"

She put her hand to her chest. "I'm losing ground," she said and her voice wavered.

We could hear Zack and Graham coming towards the living room on a wave of bonhomie. Instinctively, I slid the cheque Liz had given me under the seat of my chair. Fortunately, Graham was wholly absorbed in his role as host. "I have promised Zack the best martini he'll ever have," he said.

"I imagine he bridled at that," I said. "Zack's very proud of his martinis."

"Perhaps some day I'll have a chance to try one," Graham said. "Until then, Joanne, would you like a martini?"

"Thanks, but I'll have to pass," I said. "I'm the driver tonight."

"A glass of wine?" Graham said.

"I'll have wine with dinner," I said. "Some club soda would be great."

Graham turned to his wife. "Liz?"

"I'm not supposed to have alcohol with the new medication, am I?"

"It's fine in moderation," Graham said.

Concern pinched Liz's face. "Are you sure?"

Graham rested his hand on his wife's shoulder. "I read the instructions the pharmacist gave us twice. I'll get you a glass of Merlot."

Dinner began smoothly. The coho was indeed superb and Zack's appetite for Graham's stories about fishing in the Queen Charlottes seemed insatiable. As Zack tapped information about lodges and guides into his phone, I saw a fishing trip in my future.

There were a few awkward moments. When Graham asked Zack how he was enjoying politics, Zack was frank. "Until Labour Day I was having a lot of fun," he said. "I believe in what we're doing. I like being around people and Joanne will tell you I'm happiest when I'm at the centre of things. But Cronus's death has shaken us both."

If Graham had anything but passing knowledge of Cronus's death, he certainly didn't flinch. "Cronus was the man who was murdered," Graham said to his wife. He turned his eyes to me and they stayed there. "I didn't realize he was a friend of yours," he said.

"He wasn't," I said. "But he supported Zack's campaign and not long before he died, he did us a favour."

Graham's eyes hardened. "What kind of favour?"

"Just something political," I said.

"And he wanted nothing in return?" Graham said.

"He wanted a picture of himself with Zack and Brock Poitras, so I took one." I watched Graham's face carefully. It revealed nothing, so I pressed on. "I used Cronus's phone to take the photo and as soon as he saw it, Cronus sent it off with a message."

"Probably wanted to prove to somebody that he was playing with the big boys," Graham said mildly. "What was the message?"

"Just some random numbers," I said. "The inspector in charge of the case thinks the picture could be evidence."

Liz had been picking at her food, now she put down her knife and fork in the parallel position that indicated she had finished eating. "I really would rather not talk about death tonight," she said. "Let's change the subject."

And we did. We talked of the usual things people discuss at dinner parties: movies, books, other people. Liz and Graham seemed easy with each other and he was attentive to her without hovering.

Liz was not a cook. Graham had barbecued the salmon and their housekeeper had prepared everything else, but Liz had a dessert specialty: lemon pots de crème. After we'd cleared away the dishes from the main course, Liz brought the tray with the ramekins to the table. The pots de crème were warm and they smelled heavenly. We all murmured appreciation and dug in. The dessert was mouth-puckeringly sour. Liz's hand flew to her forehead. "I left out the white chocolate," she said. "I've made this recipe a thousand times. How could I forget the chocolate?"

"Your mind was elsewhere," I said. "It happens to me too," I said. "I usually just throw in what I forgot."

"Could we do that?" Liz's voice was small and hopeful.

"Let's give it a try," I said. The chocolate was on the counter in a measuring cup. We microwaved it and stirred some into each of the ramekins. I tasted mine. "The dessert's wonderful, Liz. Let's take it in to the men."

"Give me a minute," Liz said. She was close to tears. "Joanne, this is not an isolated incident. I've heard that extreme grief can cause dementia. I'm wondering if that's what happening to me."

"Are you seeing a doctor?"

"A psychiatrist. He keeps telling me I'm improving, but I'm not."

"Graham seems attentive. What does he think?"

"He says that if I just take my meds and keep seeing the psychiatrist, I'll be fine." The penny dropped. Liz's voice, husky with emotion and precise in its enunciation, was the voice of the woman who had called *Quinlan Live* urging Zack to withdraw from the race.

I stepped close to her and lowered my voice. "You're Cassandra, aren't you?"

Liz's eyes widened. "Leave it alone, Joanne. Please. For all our sakes, just leave it alone." And with that, she picked up the tray we had set the desserts on and hurried out of the room.

To all appearances, the evening ended smoothly. Graham said the pot de crème was even better with the melted chocolate added at the last moment, and Zack said he'd never had pots de crème but Liz's dessert was fabulous. When Zack was chatting with the Meighens in the hall, I slipped into the living room. I'd left my purse there, so I'd have a chance to retrieve the envelope Liz had given me. I found the envelope, tucked it in my bag, and was back in the hall within seconds.

Graham and Zack shook hands, and Graham urged Zack to call him if he had questions about choosing a fishing camp in the Queen Charlottes. When Liz and I embraced, I whispered, "I'll call you tomorrow." She remained silent but shook her head. When we separated, she appeared dazed. In an attempt to soothe her, I took Liz's hands in mine and squeezed them. "That was a great evening," I said. "Our turn now."

When we got in the car, Zack snapped on his seatbelt. "What the hell did you mean by 'our turn now'?"

I backed out of the driveway. "When Liz and I were together in the kitchen, I realized that she was Cassandra. I confronted her and she panicked. I thought if I suggested that the four of us get together again, Graham might not suspect anything had upset her."

"And he wouldn't realize Liz was Cassandra?" Zack said. "It's too late for that, Jo. Graham might not have heard *Quinlan Live* when it was broadcast, but my guess is he'd heard the podcast before the day was out."

"And once he recognized Liz's voice, he knew he had to discredit her. So he invited us to dinner to show that she was a wreck and he was a loving husband, Damn it, Zack, I walked right into the trap. Ian always said I was terminally naive."

"Don't beat yourself up, Jo, Graham Meighen is a socio-path. They're brilliant manipulators. Several of my legal colleagues are sociopaths and they've screwed me in court more times than I care to remember."

I gave Zack a quick look. "You really believe Graham's a sociopath?"

"He has all the signs," Zack said. "The superficial charm, the fake empathy, and that freaky ability to maintain unin-terrupted eye contact. Did you notice all those penetrating gazes he gave you when Liz screwed up the dessert."

"I noticed," I said. "I thought he was just embarrassed for her. Graham's eyes are so like Bev's – that intense blue-green. I guess I got sucked in."

"Did Bev ever seem concerned about her father?"

"No. She certainly never suggested he was pathological. She talked about Liz frequently, and always with great affec-tion, but all I can remember her saying about Graham was that he was moody and he had a short fuse when something didn't go his way. That may explain why Liz was so secre-tive about giving me a cheque for our campaign tonight."

"A cheque and a SHREVE sign on the lawn. Liz is still her own woman."

"She is," I said. "But it's an uphill battle. She's seeing a psychiatrist, and I'm sure she has friends. I just hope the support she has is enough. Tonight when we were leaving, Liz made it clear she doesn't want me to call her. Given the situation with Graham, I get it, but I don't like it."

"Neither do I," Zack said. "But Liz is at the centre of this, Jo. We have to trust her judgment."

For the next two weeks, it seemed that our campaign had found the sweet spot. Zack's numbers were rising slowly but surely. The days stayed warm and sunny, so we planned a series of suppertime wiener roasts in city parks in the various wards across the city. There were ten new and progressive candidates running for city council, and in each ward we coordinated our efforts with those of the candidate who was running against the incumbent councillor. The turnouts were good. At every event we had volunteers selling SHREVE T-shirts in Zack's favourite red, and sign-up lists for people who would knock on doors, take signs, or drive our voters to the polls on election day.

Milo was proving to be worth his weight in rubies. His online training material for volunteers was invaluable. There were general rules about conduct on the doorstep and guidelines for reporting back information electronically. Regina is a city of neighbourhoods, and Milo had created a voter profile for each of them, identifying average income and education, predominant family structure, and issues of concern. When Zack showed up for the wiener roasts, he knew exactly what kind of people he would be meeting, and he had a solid grasp of the issues that most concerned them. He was also able to establish relationships with the candidates running for council. If the fates were with us, after November's swearing in ceremony, City Hall would be a very different place.

Howard and Milo, an odd couple if ever there was one, struck up an alliance based on a common goal and a growing admiration for each other's talents. Milo's strategies for creating a solid ground game were the same ones we'd employed for years, but the databank Milo had created and the skill with which he used social media to connect with voters blew Howard away. For his part, Milo was impressed with the depth of Howard's ability to sniff out a potential problem and deal with it before it bloomed into a crisis.

For all intents and purposes, Zack was Cronus's next of kin, and he had asked that Debbie keep him informed of developments in the case. So far the investigation into Cronus's murder had eliminated some possibilities but produced very few leads. Forensics had found nothing of significance in Cronus's Porsche or in the parking lot behind the Sahara Club. The only DNA other than Cronus's found on the red bandana had been traced to a member of Red Rage named Dakota Lerat. At the time of the murder, Dakota was serving a sentence of two years less a day at the Regina Correctional Centre. He remembered that somewhere along the line, his red bandana had disappeared, but his memory of the period during which he lost the scarf was hazy. He was free-basing crack cocaine, and Dakota admitted that, at that point, scoring rock pretty well occupied his thoughts 24/7. When the police questioned him, Dakota was adamant on one point. He wanted his fucking bandana back.

The police were looking into Redd Rage's encounters with other gangs during the months before Cronus's murder, but Debbie admitted that trying to find the person who lifted Dakota's bandana was like searching for the proverbial needle in the haystack.

The investigation into the trashing of Darryl Colby's office was also proving to be an exercise in futility. There were no fingerprints. The cash on hand was left untouched. The computers and office equipment were new and expensive, but nothing was taken. It seemed logical to conclude that the intruders had been searching for Cronus's files.

Jill was running into brick walls too. The circumstances surrounding Cronus's death were murky, so Jill was following every rumour and talking to every possible source. It was time-consuming and aggravating work, but Jill was optimistic that once she found the weak spot in the campaign's protective shell, she could crack through to the truth. The combination of living in the house on Regina Avenue with which she was so familiar and tracking the rumours about who wanted Cronus dead and why Mayor Ridgeway's public appearances since Labour Day had been few and far between was proving tonic for Jill. We spoke on the phone frequently, and she sounded buoyant, but we were both busy, and our calls always seemed to get cut short. I longed for a quiet evening where we could simply sit and talk without interruption. My chance came the following Friday. Zack was speaking at a legal colleague's retirement dinner, and Taylor was away for the weekend at her friend's farm.

That morning the market had fall vegetables so perfect that they didn't need tarting up, and the dinner I'd prepared was simple and vegetarian. Jill brought wine. The weather was pretty enough for us to have our drinks on the terrace. When we stretched out on the chaises longues, Jill gazed critically at our outfits. She was wearing blue jeans, a grey-and-black-striped V-neck, and sneakers, and I was wearing blue jeans, my favourite green cashmere pullover, and sneakers. "I see we both dressed for dinner," she drawled.

"This is like the old days when Ian was out of town and you'd come over and help me get the kids to bed," I said. "It's been too long, Jill."

She sipped her Chablis thoughtfully. "It has," she agreed. She closed her eyes and sighed contentedly. "Sunshine. And my best friend and a glass of wine within arm's reach. Perfection."

"So life is good?" I said.

Jill's eyes were still closed. "Graham Meighen called today to invite me to lunch."

"How did that come about?"

"I've been gathering information on everyone connected with the Ridgeway campaign. Graham said if I had questions he'd be willing to answer them over lunch."

"Are you going to take him up on his invitation?"

"I don't know. What do you think?"

"It would be useful for us to know more about him," I said. "Zack and I had dinner with Graham and his wife last Sunday night. They lost their daughter a year ago, and Liz is struggling. Graham seemed very concerned about her."

"*Seemed*," Jill said. "You doubt that his concern was genuine?"

"It could be, but the timing of the invitation was interesting – he phoned the morning after Zack did *Quinlan Live*."

"So why is that significant?"

"Because the night we had dinner with the Meighens, I realized that Liz Meighen was Cassandra. Graham must have known it was only a matter of time until I identified Liz as the caller. I think the dinner was a pre-emptive strike. Jill, Liz Meighen is in bad shape. Sunday night she told me she was afraid she was suffering from dementia."

"And you believe Graham invited you to dinner, so you could see that his wife was *non compos mentis*. Nasty."

"Beyond nasty," I said. "Liz made it clear that I should keep my distance, and I have, but I'm concerned about her."

"If I had lunch with Graham Meighen, I could ask about his wife," Jill said. "I may be able to set your mind at ease about Liz Meighen. And . . . to be frank . . . I'm interested in meeting Graham. It's been a while since I had a bad boy in my life." Jill picked up the bottle of Chablis. "But I'll jump off that bridge when I come to it. Let's eat."

———

During dinner our conversation moved towards the changes in our lives. By any criteria Jill's life was a success. Her career at NationTV was distinguished. She had earned the respect and the friendship of her colleagues and she had been generous in mentoring young people who sought careers in broadcasting. She was good company and she had never lacked friends or lovers. Yet that night as we sat at the dining table with the candles guttering, it was evident that something was missing. "There's such peace in this house," she said finally.

"When Zack's around, he shakes things up," I said. "But I know what you mean. As we said in the 1960s, the vibes here are good."

"Because the vibe between you and Zack is good," Jill said.

"It is. Proving once again that it's never too late to find the right partner."

"It's too late for me," Jill said. There was no self-pity in her voice. She was simply stating a fact. She shook her head impatiently. "Forget it. Ask me about my stepdaughter."

I laughed. "Okay, tell me about Bryn."

"She's doing brilliantly," Jill said. "She's always loved fashion, and the fashion industry in New York loves her. She got another promotion, and she just bought a condo in Tribeca."

"A condo in Tribeca," I said. "The fashion industry in New York *must* love Bryn."

"They do, but I was the one who paid for the condo."

"Do you see Bryn often?"

Jill raised an eyebrow. "I saw her when I signed the cheque for her new digs."

"So you and she aren't close."

"Bryn doesn't need other people," Jill said. "When I married Evan, I had this crazy idea that a loving stepmother could rescue Bryn from all the shit Evan and his family had piled on her." Jill's face fell. "It didn't work. I thought I could heal the wounds, and I tried. I really did."

"Bryn had lived with Evan and his family for sixteen years," I said.

"And they had been tearing her apart from the day she was born," Jill said. "She survived by creating a Bryn-centred world, and after the wedding she made it clear there was no room in that world for me."

"I'm sorry."

"So am I," Jill said. "But c'est la vie. And Mieka and the girls are giving me a crash course in family living. Madeleine and Lena are a joy, and Mieka and I are up half the night talking. It's been a long time since I've felt that connected to somebody. When the election's over, it's going to be hard to leave."

"Then don't leave," I said. "You're not happy in Toronto. Why don't you move back here?"

"To be honest, I have been thinking about it. I just wasn't sure how you'd feel."

"Where did that come from?" I said. "I'd be overjoyed. After Ian died, you and I were both shattered. We had to make decisions. You moved away and I tried to move on. We never had a chance to really knit our lives back together. If you lived in Regina, we'd have that chance."

Jill reached across the table and touched my hand. "In that case, I'll start checking the real estate listings."

When Jill left, her face was suffused with the afterglow of good wine and open talk. I'd spoken the truth when I told Jill I'd be thrilled if she came back to Regina, but as I put our dishes in the dishwasher, my mood was less buoyant. Jill's romantic history was a troubled one. She had an unerring instinct for finding men who treated her badly. Graham Meighen had never been anything but charming in my presence, but years as a trial lawyer had made Zack a trustworthy judge of character, and he'd been sure of his ground when he assessed Graham as a sociopath. Jill was a smart, hard-edged journalist, but when I looked at her, I still saw the vulnerable girl with the big smile and the untamable red hair who came to Ian's office because she shared his principles. Remembering what some of the men she'd so casually referred to as "bad boys" had done to her, I was uneasy.

Brock seemed lost in thought when we met on the stoop for our Monday run. I handed him the dogs' leashes while I did my stretches. When I took back Willie's leash, Brock was still preoccupied. "Bad weekend on the campaign trail?" I said.

"No, actually it was a great weekend. We had to order more window signs and we're getting a lot of positive feedback. All's well on that front, but something disturbing happened."

We started down Halifax Street. "Do you want to talk about it?" I said.

"Yes, because it's something you and Zack should be aware of. I couldn't get to sleep last night, so I brought my bike down and went for a ride. I'd been riding for about ten minutes when I sensed that someone was following me. I did a couple of those manoeuvres you see in thrillers . . ."

"Doubling back on yourself, running a red?"

Brock nodded. "It sounds like a B-movie when you describe it, but whoever was driving the car, a black suv, stayed with me, and it was unnerving. I cut short my ride and headed for home. The suv followed me and it stopped in the street, motor running, while I walked my bike up the ramp into the lobby."

I felt my nerves twang. "A man on a bicycle's an easy target," I said. "So is a man in a wheelchair. Maybe you should tell the police."

"No need." Brock held out his hands. "I didn't get a licence plate number, and nothing happened to me."

"That doesn't mean nothing could," I said. "Be careful, Brock, and do me a favour, tell Zack what happened, and don't minimize the incident. I don't want either of you to drop your guard."

We had a good run. It was one of those blue and gold September days when the idea of being inside breathing recycled air was sacrilege. When we got back to Halifax Street, I turned to Brock. "What have you got scheduled for this morning?"

"Nothing," he said. "I'm keeping three mornings a week free for politicking."

"Perfect," I said. "Why don't you and I drop off the dogs and spend the morning knocking on doors. I'll bring my camera. It's time for a new brochure and we'll get some heartwarming pictures of you as a man of the people."

Ward 6 is the largest of Regina's ten wards and it has the lowest voter turnout – in the last election, 14 per cent of its eligible voters came to the polls. That morning Brock and I drove to Broders Annex, an older inner-city neighbourhood of small but generally well-kept homes with pretty gardens. The residents of Broders Annex are a mix of retired people and young couples starting out, so our chances of finding people at home and open to a chat were good. Door-knocking is my least favourite part of campaigning, but on that bright day we were lucky. Many people were working outdoors, and it was rejuvenating to stand in the midst of the jewel tones of a fall garden, talking about the beauty of asters and exchanging ideas about how Ward 6 could share in our city's growth.

It was getting close to lunchtime when we turned onto Toronto Street. A sandy-haired man who appeared to be in his seventies was raking his lawn. He was wearing a Saskatchewan Roughriders jersey. Brock and I exchanged a glance. "I think this one is for us," I said.

Brock went up and introduced himself and me. I exclaimed over the lush profusion of an autumn clematis climbing on the arch that led to the backyard. "This is such a great neighbourhood," I said.

"And we'd like to keep it that way," the man said. There was something in his voice that raised my hackles. "There's been talk of building infill housing across the street," he went on. "A lot of us are not too happy about the prospect of getting the wrong kind of neighbours."

"What kind of neighbours are the 'wrong kind'?" Brock asked mildly.

"Well, no offence," the man said. "A lot of them are Indians. Not Indians like you. You're the right kind. I remember when you played for the Riders. You've always been a credit to your people, but there are some who just don't know how to take care of things."

"There are all kinds of people who don't know how to take care of things," I said.

"True," the sandy-haired man said, "and you wouldn't want them living across the street from you, would you?"

"No," I said, "I wouldn't."

The man turned back to Brock. "Our current councillor from Ward 6 paid me a visit the other day. We exchanged ideas. Councillor Trotter is opposed to infill housing and he hinted that it's not going to happen here on Toronto Street. Where do you stand on that?"

Brock shrugged. "The city is already committed to purchasing the land in those vacant lots across the street from you and a number of other lots in the area. They've also committed to building low-income housing. All tenants in the new buildings will take a course in home maintenance as a condition of their lease."

"That's not good enough," the man snapped. "They'll still be living across the street from me. I'm voting for your opponent."

"Your choice," Brock said. "Thanks for your time."

"Wait," the sandy-haired man said. "I notice your friend has a camera. Maybe she could take a picture of you and me together and send it to me."

Brock's eyes met mine. For both of us the situation evoked the painful memory of the buddy photograph I'd taken of Cronus with Zack and Brock on Labour Day.

Brock was the first to recover. "Maybe Joanne could take a picture," he said. "Incidentally, this is Joanne Shreve. She's managing my campaign and her husband, Zack's."

The sandy-haired guy was philosophical. "A picture's a picture, no matter who takes it. Right?"

"Absolutely," Brock said. "The same way a touchdown is a touchdown, no matter who scores it. Ready when you are." He put his arm around the sandy-haired man's shoulders, and the older man put his arm around Brock's waist. I took the picture and got the man's email address so I could send it to him with a nice note.

I dropped Brock off at the Al Ritchie Family Wellness Centre, where he was having lunch with parents interested in coaching football.

The wellness centre wasn't far from the houses on Rose Street that Zack and I now owned so on impulse I decided to check them out. I was hoping I'd run into Angela, and I was in luck. She was sitting on her stoop, smoking and watching her children. The oldest, who appeared to be about three, had a rusty metal sand pail. He was trying to dig up the hard-packed dirt of the front yard with a stainless steel soup spoon. Both the other children were staring incuriously at the soup spoons they clutched in their own small hands. When I parked in front of her house, Angela stood and limped towards the front gate.

She looked gaunt and ill. "Eddie says you sent me a letter and some money," she said.

"I dropped off a note a couple of weeks ago," I said. "I included my address and phone number in case you wanted to get in touch, but there was no money in the envelope."

Her lips twitched. "Eddie found the envelope in the mailbox. He'd already opened it when he brought it into the house. He said you'd sent $500 cash, but he'd taken it because I wasn't bringing in any money these days. Then he made me watch him rip up the card and flush it down the toilet."

"Why would he do that?"

She shrugged. "Why does Eddie do anything? Anyway, thanks for thinking of me."

Suddenly the youngest child grabbed the handle of the sand pail and pulled it towards her. The boy who'd been digging for dirt hit the baby hard with his spoon. The baby howled and Angela turned and limped towards her. She scooped up the screaming baby, then bent, picked up the sand pail, and flung it against the front gate. The boy who'd been digging the dirt started to cry and other child joined in. The gate had a padlock on it.

"Angela, if you'll unlock the gate, I can give you a hand," I said. "I have kids of my own and grandkids."

She gave me a long, hard look. "And I'll bet their lives are fucking perfect." She limped up the stairs, put the howling baby on the porch, and then limped back, grabbed the other two children, and disappeared into the house.

I stood on the sidewalk staring at the sand pail lodged against the gate. Much of the paint on the pail had flaked away, but there were still enough patches of white, turquoise, ocean blue, and sandy brown to reconstruct the idyllic scene of beach life that had greeted the pail's first owner.

Like my children and my grandchildren, that child was one of the lucky ones.

———

Zack was heating up last night's borscht when I got home.
"That smells good," I said. "How was your morning?"

"Heartbreaking," Zack said. "Debbie called. They've
released Cronus's papers. They're already at Falconer Shreve,
but Debbie had two files she thought we should see delivered
here." He wheeled to the butcher-block table, picked up a file
folder, and handed it to me. "Take a look," he said.

The folder was filled with booklets and computer printouts.
The title of the brochure on top was *Living With* ALS. I riffled
through the other material. "These are all about Lou Gehrig's
disease," I said.

Zack nodded. "It was in Cronus's desk drawer."

I remembered the difficulty Cronus had typing out the
message he sent with the photo of him with Zack and Brock.
"Cronus had ALS?"

"Looks like it," Zack said grimly. "According to Debbie,
Cronus's Daytimer lists an appointment he had on August 15
with a neurologist."

I shuffled idly through the material in the folder. "And
the neurologist confirmed that Cronus had ALS?"

"He's out of the country. Debbie's office is still trying to
reach him, but apparently the pathologist who did the initial autopsy was very thorough. The relevant test results
came in yesterday. Cronus had early stage ALS."

Bright as a knife the memory of Cronus's face as he made
the decision that led to his murder flashed through my mind.
"We only live once," he'd said. "Might as well make it count."

"He knew they'd kill him," I said.

Zack shrugged. "He probably did, but he still sent out the
picture."

"He could have lived years," I said. "They would have
been difficult years, but still . . ."

"Cronus sacrificed them," Zack said. "We'll never know
what Cronus was thinking that day, but he was prepared to

die." Zack opened the second file and handed me a single sheet of paper. "These are Cronus's instructions for his farewell to the world. Check out the date."

"August 15," I said. "The day he got his diagnosis."

"And Cronus had Darryl draw up the will naming me executor and sole beneficiary right after the jury found him innocent of his girlfriend's murder. That was over a year ago. As far as Cronus knew then, he was in good health."

"So there was no urgency in leaving instructions for his funeral. But that changed on August 15." I read the directions on the single sheet of paper. They were pithy.

1. cremation

2. private funeral

3. no religious crap

4. SHORT service – Zack Shreve delivers eulogy. Frank Sinatra sings "My Way." Zack takes his wife and my ashes out for dinner at the Sahara Club, and we all go home.

The irony of choosing the Sahara Club for Cronus's farewell hit me like a slap. "Zack, given the circumstances of Cronus's death, do you think we should choose another restaurant for our meal with him?"

"Cronus always wanted us to go to the Sahara Club with him," Zack said tightly. "Why the hell didn't we go, Joanne?"

"I don't know," I said. "Look, this second-guessing is just making us more miserable. Let's go over to the couch and be close for a while."

Zack and I were still big fans of what teenagers used to call petting. After ten minutes of semi-chaste lovemaking, we were both at the heavy-breathing stage, but Zack had an afternoon of meetings, and lunch was waiting, so with reluctance, we moved to the table.

By the time we started lunch, we were both in better spirits. "So how was your morning?" Zack said.

"Perplexing," I said. "Brock and I went door-knocking together in Broders Annex and we met a man who was concerned that infill housing would mean he'd have to live across the street from Indians."

"He said this to Brock?"

"He exempted Brock because Brock was a football player and a credit to his people."

Zack turned down the gas under the borscht. "The dinosaurs still walk among us," he said.

"Indeed they do," I said. "And they vote, although not for Brock. Zack, the guy who doesn't want Indians living across the street from him, says that he's voting for Councillor Trotter because Trotter told him he doubted that infill housing would come to Toronto Street."

"Trotter can doubt all he wants, but the city's already committed to it," Zack said.

I took sour cream and fresh dill out of the fridge and began chopping the dill. "Has the city bought the land?"

"They announced the project last year. They must have made their move by now. I'll get Norine to check."

Norine called back just after lunch. Zack's face was impassive as he listened to the report, but when he hung up he was clearly both amused and amazed. "Son of a bitch," he said. "Despite the big announcement, the city never actually purchased the land. Guess who owns it?"

"Us," I said.

Zack nodded. "At the time of his death, Cronus owned twenty-six separate parcels of land in the area where the city announced they would be building low-income housing."

"That includes Toronto Street," I said.

"It does. So Trotter's information could be accurate. Apparently, Cronus was a meticulous recordkeeper. Norine's got Angus working on the files on the properties. Should be an interesting job for the scion of a slumlord. And it will be very interesting for our campaign to know why the city is dragging its feet on this."

After Zack left for his afternoon of meetings, I sat down to check my messages. I hadn't told Zack about Angela because there was nothing to tell. I had dropped in on a sad and seemingly hopeless life, stayed five minutes, and left. But the images of the children's misery and of Angela's fury as she condemned the fucking perfect lives of my family were sharp-edged. I couldn't focus on the messages on my phone screen. Finally, I gave up.

One of the initiatives at Racette-Hunter was a program called Shop Smart/Eat Healthy. There were no grocery stores in North Central, and not everyone had regular access to a vehicle. Shop Smart/Eat Healthy offered family classes about nutrition and regular excursions to big-box stores where a careful shopper could get more bang for his or her shopping buck.

With a Costco Cash Card, Angela could buy what she needed. If she was interested in Racette-Hunter's Shop Smart/ Eat Healthy program, she'd have free transportation to the store and help loading and unloading groceries. The plan was workable, but Angela was proud, and the prospect of playing Lady Bountiful swooping in with a temporary solution did not sit well with me. The cash card was an unpalatable option, but the memory of Angela's son trying to find fun with a battered sand pail and a kitchen spoon trumped my liberal guilt. I picked up my wallet and my car keys. It was time to head to Costco.

When I went to get into my Volvo I noticed that one of the tires was low, so I took Zack's Jaguar. It was a fun car to drive and I was moving at a fair clip in the right lane of the Ring Road when a black suv started coming up on my left.

It pulled even with me, then, in the blink of an eye, swung into me, bumping me into the ditch. The airbag inflated, the car rolled, the airbag began to deflate, and the Jaguar righted itself. The whole sequence was over in seconds. Stunned, I sat, still strapped into my seat. A good Samaritan ran down the bank of the ditch, leaned into the Jaguar, unsnapped my seatbelt, and told me to get out in case the car caught fire. I didn't move, so he hoisted me in his arms and carried me up the embankment to the road. He put me down carefully, then asked if I was okay. His voice, like the rest of him, was immense. He introduced himself as Boomer.

Boomer was the kind of guy you wouldn't want to meet in a dark alley – shoulder-length dirty blond hair, missing teeth, heavily tattooed arms, a barrel chest that burst out of his leather vest, torn jeans, motorcycle boots. An unlikely saviour, but he was mine and in my eyes, he was beautiful.

The Ring Road was always busy, and cars slowed to see what had happened. It wasn't long before the sirens sounded – an ambulance arrived, then the police, then a fire truck. First responders everywhere.

Later, I would discover that I had extensive bruising and a pulled shoulder muscle, but initially I was simply numb – an isolated figure watching as strangers tried determinedly to get me to talk. Everyone had questions, but I had no answers, so I clung to Boomer, my protection against the real world. I didn't call Zack. I didn't look at the Jaguar. When the EMT asked me my name, I told them it was Joanne Ellard, the birth name I hadn't used in thirty-five years.

Boomer proved to be not only my saviour but my best witness. He'd been riding his motorcycle behind me and he'd seen what happened. As the emergency medical team checked me over, Boomer's voice boomed out his narrative to the police.

Someone had checked my wallet, found my next-of-kin card, and called Zack. He arrived just as they were about to load me into the ambulance. Before handing me over to my husband, Boomer exchanged a few words with Zack. The EMT had given me something for pain, and the medication was beginning to hit. Everything suddenly seemed very far away. The last thing I remember was seeing Zack hold out his arms to Boomer, and Boomer bending to be patted on the back.

I spent Monday night under observation at Regina General Hospital. Despite my protests, Zack stayed beside me. All night I drifted in the grey zone between wakefulness and sleep. But whether I was awake or asleep, the images of the weather-beaten sand pail and of Angela limping into the house carrying her crying children were never far away.

When I awoke, Zack's chair was close and he was holding my hand. "Can I get you anything?"

"A toothbrush," I said.

Word for word this was the exchange Zack and I had the morning after we first made love, and we both smiled at the memory. Zack kissed my hand. "You and I both know where toothbrushes lead. Let's get you out of here."

Two hours later, I was home.

During the early years when my kids were in sports, I handled all injuries that didn't involve blood by buying two Freezees from the concession stand. I'd sit the injured child down, tell him or her to stay still, elevate the arm or leg, hold one of the Freezees on the injured area, and open the other Freezee and give it to the child to suck on. The treatment was based on the acronym RICE – rest, ice, compression, elevation. The therapy for my pulled shoulder muscles followed the RICE protocol except it didn't involve Freezees.

Before I left the hospital I was fitted with a cold shoulder wrap that kept my shoulder iced, compressed, and relatively immobile. Suitably trussed, all I had to do was take my anti-inflammatory painkillers and get plenty of rest. I settled in on the couch in the living room with a comforter, Lady Antonia Fraser's memoir of her life with Harold Pinter, and a pot of tea. I was determined to be a compliant patient who healed quickly. Zack offered to clear his calendar for the next few days, but I reminded him that the election was now only a month away and every day counted.

I was just nicely into the first stirrings of passion between Lady Antonia and Harold when the doorbell rang. It was Brock. I stood aside to let him in. He usually moved with the athletic looseness of a person comfortable in his own body, but that day as he walked towards the living room he was tense.

"I know you're supposed to be resting," he said. "But I had to see how you're doing." He tried a smile. "I recognize the cold shoulder wrap from my football days. Those things really do work. Anyway, we need to talk. I promise I won't stay long."

He helped as I lowered myself carefully back onto the couch, then pulled a chair over and sat beside me. His face was grave. "Joanne, I don't want to add to your anxiety, but I think we have to face the fact that whoever did this to you probably thought that Zack was driving the car."

My stomach roiled. "You're right," I said. "There aren't that many white Jags in the city and the vanity plate is a giveaway." Out of nowhere a memory came. One night before we were married, Zack and I had parked down by the creek. A police officer arrived and took great pleasure in shining his flashlight on us. As Zack was zipping up the cop suggested that the next time Mr. Shreve was feeling randy he should rent a room or at least drive a less identifiable car.

Brock was looking at me with concern. "Joanne, are you okay?"

"I'm fine. My mind just drifted there for a moment."

"I'm sorry. You should be resting. I just need to be clear about exactly what happened. Did you get out of the car at any point? If the person following the Jag saw you get out, that would change the picture."

"No, I got into the car in the underground garage. I was on my way to the east end to shop." My shoulder was aching and I adjusted my position.

Brock picked up two small rectangular pillows from the couch and placed them expertly behind my neck and shoulder. "Better?" he said.

I nodded. "Much better. Thanks. Brock, Debbie's coming over in a few minutes. Why don't you stick around and see if anything new has come up?"

"I'd like to. Maybe the three of us can start putting the pieces together."

"We live in hope," I said. "Make yourself comfortable. I'm going to curl up for a while." With that, I turned back to my tepid tea and Lady Antonia and Harold's far from tepid love affair.

After she'd given me a quick, concerned head-to-toe, Debbie moved straight to the business at hand. She took out a paper notebook, wrote Cronus's name in the middle of the page, and circled it. Then she drew spokes out from the circle and labelled each neatly: *alleged abduction conspiracy; Darryl Colby's office; the black suv.*

"You're going to have to add another spoke," Brock said. "Two nights ago I had trouble sleeping. I took my bike out for a ride. I had a strong sense that I was being followed – by a black suv. After what happened to Joanne, I'm certain we're being targeted."

Debbie added a spoke, labelled it *Brock Poitras,* and stared at the diagram. "Something's missing," she said. "In fact, a lot of 'somethings' are missing. I'll go back to Boomer. See if he remembers anything more."

I changed position and winced at the pain. "Debbie, could I have Boomer's contact information? I'd like to thank him."

Debbie touched my hand. "So would I," she said.

Zack came back for lunch. After I filled him in on the morning's activities, he frowned. "You didn't get much rest this morning. This afternoon will be different. I'm staying here to make certain you follow your doctor's orders."

I slept until four o'clock when Taylor came home, followed shortly by Mieka and the girls bringing chicken soup, the universal panacea, and my favourite, crème brûlée. The procession continued. Jill arrived with a gloriously soft, pale green cashmere robe nestled in a pretty box. The florist brought a half-dozen arrangements. Peter and Maisie came by with an armload of glossy magazines. Angus called. He was buried in Cronus's papers, but if I needed his help, all I had to do was whistle.

As we were about to sit down for dinner, Margot and Lexi arrived with a vase of Chinese lanterns. Mother and daughter were both wearing pullovers the colour of a ripe pumpkin. Just looking at them cheered me. When she heard Margot's voice, Taylor rushed in, eager for news of Declan's adjustment to university. She and Declan texted regularly and skyped daily, so it was unlikely Margot would have anything to report that Taylor didn't already know, but that didn't dampen our daughter's enthusiasm.

Zack and Taylor were cleaning up after supper when Brock came to take the dogs for their run. I was curled up on the couch again with Lady Antonia and Harold, and Brock squatted beside me. "Just checking on you," he said.

"Good because that gives me a chance to check on you too. I wish we could all just stay in this building till whoever's behind this gets caught. Cassandra's words were prophetic. We're all suffering."

Brock picked up on the resignation in my voice. "Jo, we're going to get through this."

"I know," I said. "But until we do, be careful."

By Thursday the pain in my shoulder was subsiding. I still flinched when I caught a reflection of the purplish-blue bruising covering the right side of my body, and I was still on anti-inflammatory pills, but I was off the painkillers, and my energy was returning. It was time to get back in the game.

When Angus arrived that evening with his report on Cronus's holdings, I was ready. Cronus's records may have been old school, but, according to Angus, they were meticulous. Each of Cronus's twenty-six properties had its own file – legal papers, tenant grievances, reports from Public Health Officials and the fire department; receipts for repairs; the names of every tenant and the dates of their tenancy. Complete histories, except that none of the files had a record of an offer of purchase from the city.

Stapled to the cover of each file was a small, handwritten note listing the amount Cronus had originally paid for the house and the current market value of the property. The average price Cronus had paid for his houses in the 1980s was $60,000. With the exception of one house, each of the properties Cronus owned could now be purchased for around $200,000. The exception was 12 Rose Street. In 1984, Cronus had paid $62,000 for the now mustard yellow house. In the space where the current market value of the property was listed, Cronus had printed "NOT FOR SALE AT ANY PRICE."

Cronus's memorial service was held at Speers Funeral Chapel at 5:00 p.m., on Friday, September 19. Zack had suggested postponing the ceremony until I felt better, but we'd included information about the time and place of the service in the obituary and I opted for proceeding as planned. Working on the files had piqued Angus's interest in Cronus so he was joining us.

In addition to our family, there were three mourners in the chapel. Zack whispered that the plainclothes officer in the back pew was there because the police are always interested in the guest list at the funeral of a murder victim. The presence of the other two attendees was less easily explained. Slater Doyle was there. So was the Bible-quoting woman who lived at Number 12. Neither Zack nor I had a clue about why either of them had come.

The polished mahogany table on the altar held three items: a large silver-framed photo of Cronus in his white Gatsby suit, a spray of crimson orchids, and the metal urn that Zack had chosen. The *Urn and Casket Guide* Zack had consulted identified the urn's colour as "Inferno Red." Zack was certain Cronus would have approved.

Delivering a eulogy about a slumlord who was into rough sex and had no truck with "religious crap" would have daunted most men. Zack had waded in and worked on several drafts of the speech. None satisfied him, and he finally decided he would simply read Paul Anka's lyrics to "My Way," then we would listen to the Sinatra recording.

When Zack rehearsed the lyrics at home, we both cringed at the line about how the speaker took his blows and did it his way. But Zack had an actor's voice and an actor's ability to get inside the words. That late afternoon in a generic funeral chapel empty except for six people and the Inferno Red urn that contained all that was left of Cronus, the opening lines of the song touched a chord in me.

I remembered the small smile that played on Cronus's lips when he reached his decision about using the silver bullet. "We only live once," he'd said. "Might as well make it count."

At the end, Cronus had made his life count. I'd read through the ALS pamphlets that he'd collected. He could have lived another five years. They would not have been easy years, but he would have been alive to all the quotidian joys that life offers. Instead, he had chosen the hero's option. He traded his life for something larger than himself, and he had faced the end with defiance and pride. When Zack finished and Sinatra's distinctive baritone filled the chapel, I was in tears. Zack and I listened hand in hand until the song was over. Despite Cronus's directive, I said a prayer. By the time I looked up again, Slater Doyle, the undercover officer, and the old woman were gone.

"Time to go," Zack said. Angus picked up the orchids and the photograph. Zack put the urn on his lap and led the way out of the chapel.

When we stepped outside into the sun, Zack took a hard look at my face. "Why don't we put off dinner at the Sahara Club until you're feeling better," he said.

"Good plan," I said. "I'm not quite ready to take on a slab of meat. Would you mind waiting, Angus?"

"Nope. Okay, if I come back to the condo and talk about a couple of things with Zack?"

"Fine with me," I said. "You guys and Taylor can decide what to order in. I'm going to bed. You can bring me a plate."

"You hate eating in bed," Zack said.

"I do, but a week from today is my birthday. It's also our first citywide rally, and I plan to be in fighting trim."

CHAPTER

7

The intervening week was without incident, which, given our campaign's recent history, was reason enough to celebrate. My fifty-eighth birthday started out the way the best birthdays should. Zack and I made love, and because we no longer had to follow the porcupine rule of having sex very carefully, we were adventurous. Afterwards, Zack gave me my first gift of the day, a pedicure using a deep red nail polish in a shade called "Throb." When Brock and I got back from our first mercifully foreshortened post-accident walk with the dogs, he asked me to wait on the third floor while he dashed into his condo and came out with a gift box. Inside was a gift certificate for Crocus and Ivy, my favourite everything-I-don't-need-but-long-to-have shop, and a T-shirt with the message "Keep Calm and Carry On."

"Perfect," I said. "Can I order these T-shirts by the gross?"

"I'll look into it," Brock said. "Happy Birthday, Jo."

There were surprises waiting at my place at the breakfast table. Taylor and I always exchanged wacky socks on birthdays. Over the years we'd been fiercely competitive about who could find the craziest pair. That morning as I opened the box Taylor watched my face carefully. The socks inside weren't our usual machine wash–tumble dry horrors; they were gorgeous – obviously hand-knit of brilliantly coloured wool in striking patterns.

"Taylor, these are amazing," I said. "Where did you get them?"

"I made them," she said. "I went online and found the pattern – it's Icelandic. I'd never seen anything like that combination of colours and patterns before, so I went down to Knit-Wit and bought the wool. Do you really like them?"

"I love them," I said.

Taylor sighed with relief. "Good, but just in case, I have a backup present." She handed me a gift pack of Chanel bath products.

"Perfect," I said. "I can't think of anything I would enjoy more. Now, I'm starving. Let's eat."

"Not so fast," Zack said. He wheeled into the living room and came back with a ceramic sculpture that was unmistakably Joe Fafard's work. The sculpture was of my old friend, the artist Ernest Lindner. The piece was relatively small – perhaps a foot tall. Ernest sat in his easy chair, wearing his usual overalls and blue slippers, smoking his pipe and looking, as he always did, fiercely interested. I had admired the piece from the first time I saw it, in Ernie's house decades before.

When Ernest died, I was a single parent with three children. A piece of Joe Fafard art was wildly out of my price range, but I'd always remembered this piece, and now here it was.

Zack, looking like the proverbial cat that swallowed the canary, pushed his chair close. "You're pleased with your present?"

"I'm ecstatic," I said. "How did you find it?"

"I had Darrell Bell track it down," Zack said. "A guy in Calgary owned it, and now you own it."

I examined the piece. "It's perfect," I said. "And Joe got Ernie's expression just right – he was fascinated by the human comedy. Ernie was ninety-one when he died, but he never seemed old to me. He used to say there's always something new to discover."

"Not a bad thought for a birthday," Zack said.

Jill called early to say "Happy Birthday" and apologize because she'd ordered her present online and it hadn't been delivered yet. She sounded tense, but when I asked if there was something wrong, she said she'd been burning the candle at both ends and the lack of sleep had caught up with her. I knew the feeling.

I spent the rest of the morning doing exactly what I wanted to do. During my recuperation, long, hot baths in Epsom salts had been part of my regimen. That morning I filled the tub, left the Epsom salts in the medicine cabinet, and opened the Chanel No. 5 soap and bath gel set. After my bath, I dressed and went over to Margot's to play with Lexi and check out the colours Margot had chosen for Lexi's brother's nursery and the outfits she'd already bought him. Not surprisingly, Brock had already contributed everything the well-dressed newborn needed to prove he was a Saskatchewan Roughriders fan.

Margot and I took our tea into the family room, where we watched Lexi carefully place different sizes of brightly striped balls into bowls, then dump the bowls and start again. "She loves balls," Margot said. "Look what Brock's taught her to do." Margot sat on the floor and then opened her legs in a V. Lexi crawled across the room, ball in hand, bumped down into a sitting position, imitated the V of her mother's legs, then rolled the ball to Margot, who rolled it back, and so it went until Lexi crawled over to me and handed me the ball. "Your turn," Margot said. And so Lexi and I rolled the ball back and forth in Margot's sunny family room. "I can't think of a better way to spend my birthday than this," I said.

"You deserve a good birthday," Margot said. "You've had a harrowing month, but you're through it. You look great, Jo."

"I had a very nice beginning to my day."

Margot had one of the all-time great dirty laughs. "I knew it. I could tell when you walked in the door. You and Zack are like teenagers."

"We started late. Now, I'd better get a move on. There are a few dozen details about the rally I should check on." I crawled over and scooped up Lexi, who rewarded me with a lovely gummy smile. I hugged her close. "That smile is my second best present so far," I said. Margot slipped into the family room and came back with a pastel envelope.

"It's for a year of spa days for you and friends of your choosing. Of course, I'm hoping that Lexi and I will always be on the list. It's a very selfish gift."

"That's not a selfish gift," I said. "In Milo's words, it's fucking inspired." We both laughed, but when Lexi joined in the laughter, Margot and I grimaced.

After the Racette-Hunter complex was completed, the R-H staff moved out of the old converted Noodle House that had served as their temporary offices into the new building. That left the space on Cornwall Street vacant, and Zack and Brock's campaigns rented it for their headquarters. The old Noodle House was bright and airy but small for the number of workers involved in two campaigns. People worked cheek by jowl, many sitting on exercise balls, listening to classic rock, using each other's desks and office supplies, overhearing one another's conversations and fuelling themselves on bad coffee and greasy doughnuts. But spirits were high, and whenever I swung by, it appeared that everybody was having fun getting things done.

The rally had been my idea. Our suppertime neighbour-hood hot-dog barbecues had worked well, and I wanted to build on our success. We'd rented the Pile O' Bones Club, a facility that was strategically located near the city's centre. The name of the club was an allusion to Regina's past. Before the arrival of settlers in the 1880s, First Nations hunters stacked the bones of the buffalo they killed in a pile, believing that buffalo herds would return to the area to visit the ancestral bones. The hunters named the area Oskana-Ka-asateki, or "the place where bones are piled." The explorers, fur traders, surveyors, and settlers who moved through the area, needing a name that was less Cree and more catchy, took to calling the settlement "Pile O' Bones," but Princess Louise, wife of the Governor General, decided that the new settlement deserved a more regal identity, so Pile O' Bones became Regina.

Despite a name that was a romantic allusion to our city's past, the Pile O' Bones Club was without charm. However it was also large, fully accessible, and surrounded by a patchy lawn where we could set up barbecues. We'd hired a couple of local bands, invested heavily in wieners, buns, condiments, and juice, and crossed our fingers about the weather and the turnout. The plan was for people to pick up a hot dog and a drink, enjoy the sunshine and music, then come inside, listen to Brock introduce the men and women who were running as progressives for city council, and hear Zack reiterate what was at stake in the election.

Because it was my birthday, after Zack finished firing up the troops, our kids, grandkids, and I would join him and a giant cake would be rolled out on stage. Everybody would sing "Happy Birthday." Taylor and our granddaughters would help me blow out the candles, then we'd all hit the streets and go full out to elect a new mayor.

When I dropped by Shreve–Poitras headquarters to pick up the cheques for the hall rental and the bands, the place was deserted. Our workers were already at the Pile O' Bones. I was just about to lock up and leave when Slater Doyle came through the front door.

"If you came to buy a T-shirt, you're out of luck," I said. "Looks like our volunteers have already taken them all to the rally."

Slater's expression was grave. "Is there some place we can talk privately?"

I gestured to the empty room. "Choose a chair."

"We should be somewhere where no one can walk in on us."

There was a small office at the rear of the building that was used for storage. I led Slater to it. When he closed the door behind him and leaned against it, I felt a twinge of panic.

"This won't take long," he said. "We need to talk about how you want to deal with an affair your husband had."

"There's nothing to talk about," I said. "Zack has always been open about his past. I'm not crazy about the number of women he was involved with, but I've accepted it."

"This isn't about Zack," he said. "It's about your first husband, Ian Kilbourn."

The walls of the tiny, cluttered office seemed to close in on me. I took a deep breath. "Go on," I said.

"Do you remember a woman named Valerie Smythe?" Slater asked.

"Of course," I said. "She was Ian's secretary." The image of Valerie – tall, spare, severe, and watchful – flashed through my mind. Valerie's job was taking care of Ian, and her job was her life. She was, in the phrase of the time, "the office wife."

"Ian would not have been romantically involved with Valerie Smythe," I said.

"You're right," Slater said.

"Slater, what's this all about?" I said. "Ian's been dead almost fifteen years. If there was an affair, making it public now won't affect the outcome of the election."

"Depending on what you decide today, it could," Slater said evenly.

Slater was still blocking my access to the door that led out of the room. My panic was rising. I tried to keep my tone rational. "I don't understand any of this," I said. "What could Valerie Smythe have to do with this election? After Ian died, she was just another name on my Christmas card list."

"Apparently, after you and Zack married, Valerie found your Christmas cards offensive. She felt you were rubbing it in."

"Rubbing *what* in?" I said

"Her fall from grace," Slater said. "Valerie Smythe was Roger Bouchard's executive assistant."

The penny dropped. "And Bouchard was the CEO who embezzled funds from his investment firm," I said. "Valerie was a witness for the Crown, and when Bouchard came to trial, Zack was his lawyer."

"And Zack tore Valerie to shreds on the witness stand," Slater said. "She had a breakdown afterwards. She hasn't been able to get a decent job since, and she blames Zack for ruining her reputation."

"So Valerie comes to you with some trumped-up story about Ian," I said. "Slater, I'm still not getting this."

Slater removed his tinted glasses. Unprotected, his pale grey eyes blinked against the light, but it was clear he wanted me to see his eyes as he told me. "The story isn't trumped up, Joanne. Valerie Smythe tape-recorded your husband's exploits. But why talk when we can listen?" Slater took an old compact cassette player from his jacket pocket and held it out to me. My limbs felt heavy and strange. When Slater saw that I was rooted to the spot, his tone was matey. "I know this has been a shock, Joanne. Let me help. I'll get the tape started – full volume so you don't miss anything. I'll set the scene for you. Your husband is getting a great blowjob and he's just about to ejaculate."

Within seconds I could hear Ian's voice coming from the player. He was urging his lover on, telling her where to touch, how to suck, when to lick. Finally, there was the wordless crescendo that I knew so well; the abrupt cry of ecstasy and then, after a pause, his voice still hoarse with passion. "Your turn now. I've been wanting to bury my face between your legs all day."

It was too much. I reached to grab the cassette player from Slater. Somehow I knocked it out of his hands, and it clattered to the floor where crazily, it kept on playing. I bent to pick it up, but Slater was too fast for me. He hit pause. "You need to hear the rest of this. Ian's mistress is very appreciative." Slater frowned. "You don't look well at all, Joanne. I was going to save this for a surprise, but I think you've had enough surprises. The voice you're about to hear is your best friend Jill Oziowy's."

My knees had turned to water. There was a small table covered with campaign literature next to me. I grabbed the edge of it to steady myself.

Slater hit Play and Jill's voice was in the room. She was whimpering, urging Ian to tongue her more, suck her clitoris, eat her. The sounds of Jill's bliss seemed to go on forever, but finally she sobbed, and it was over. "Oh, God, I never knew it could be this good. I love you so much."

My stomach lurched. "What are you planning to do with this?" I said finally.

"That depends on you," Slater said.

"What are my options?"

"If Zack withdraws from the race, your children will never hear this – incidentally, this is not the only tape. There are dozens more. Your husband and your best friend were insatiable. When it came to the smorgasbord of sexual delights, they were gluttons." Slater's chuckle was lascivious. "Joanne, do you really want your children to hear their father having anal sex with Jill Oziowy?"

"None of this makes sense," I said. Out of nowhere images of Jill at Ian's funeral flashed into my consciousness. I had been numb, but Jill had been wracked with grief. Several times I had reached out to console her.

Slater Doyle stared at me in silence, his grey eyes blinking against the harsh overhead light. I knew he was telling the truth. "I'm not going to ask Zack to withdraw because Ian and Jill fell into bed together a few times," I said.

"The affair lasted fifteen years, Joanne," Slater said. His voice was cool. "All the dirty details are in the tapes. There are boxes of them filed by date. Valerie Smythe is very proud of her professionalism."

"She's proud of betraying a man who trusted her?"

The look Slater gave me was pitying. "Valerie wasn't the only one in that office who betrayed a trust, Joanne. The first time Valerie Smythe covered for Ian was when you were pregnant with Mieka. Until your late husband died, keeping his affair with Jill secret was part of Valerie's job."

"So she knew exactly when Ian and Jill would be together."

"Not only that, she acquired the skills she needed to tape their encounters." Slater stepped away from the door. "You'll want to talk to Zack about this, but I'll need your decision by midnight."

I felt as if I'd been flayed alive, but I managed to keep my voice firm. "This isn't Zack's decision to make," I said. "It's mine, and I'm turning you down. The negotiations are over, Slater. It's time for you to leave." My heart was pounding. I moved close to him, so close our bodies were almost touching. "How can you live with yourself?" I said. "How can you look into your daughter's eyes knowing that some day she'll realize that you're scum?"

Slater's laugh was derisive. "Sticks and stones, Joanne. Sticks and stones. You have until midnight to reconsider. If I don't hear from you, I'll give Mieka the tapes when she opens UpSlideDown tomorrow morning. By then, Ian Kilbourn's hijinks will be all over the Internet."

Zack and I had agreed to meet outside the Pile O' Bones at 4:30 p.m. When I arrived, Zack was there waiting. The kiss I gave him was long and hard.

"Whoa," he said. "What did I do to deserve that?"

"A thousand things," I said, "starting with the fact that you're not an asshole."

Zack chuckled. "I'm assuming there's a story behind that."

"There is," I said. "But it's a story for later."

The rally was a triumph. The late-afternoon sun was warm, the crowd was large, there were enough hot dogs for everybody to have seconds, and the bands kept everyone in a good mood until the speeches started. As he introduced Zack, Brock held Lexi in his arms. Brock's red SHREVE T-shirt was XXXL and Lexi's was the smallest we had. Her nine-month-old smile was irresistible. The huge ex-Roughrider and the beautiful baby presented a great photo op and the smartphones were busy. The brief speeches by the candidates for city council were passionate and inspiring, and the audience, an overflow crowd, many of whom were also wearing SHREVE T-shirts, was wildly enthusiastic.

By the time Zack came onstage, the audience was primed. They laughed at every witticism and applauded every applause line. Zack had discovered that the shtick with which he'd ended his speech at the opening of Racette-Hunter was a crowd-pleaser. That afternoon at the Pile O' Bones, he again showed off his all-terrain wheelchair and used its features to explain how his policies as mayor would give all of Regina's citizens a chance to realize their potential. He finished with his now familiar line. "My wheelchair is made by a company called Renegade. Their motto is 'Blaze your own trail.' Every woman, man, and child in this city has the right to blaze his or her own trail."

While the crowd roared, all of our children and grandchildren and I joined Zack onstage. When I looked at their faces, reality hit me like a slap. I would have crawled through broken glass to protect them, but I was about to deliver news that would turn their lives upside down. Madeleine and Lena, standing hand-in-hand, bubbling with delight at the applause, made a bobbing bow to the crowd. Mieka grinned at me. "They're revelling in this," she said. "Actually so am I."

I put my arm around her shoulder and squeezed. Mieka had loved Ian and she adored Jill. She would be the one most wounded by the news, and there was nothing I could do to cushion the blow. When the birthday cake was brought in, the burning candles swam in front of my eyes, and my breath caught in my throat. People began singing "Happy Birthday." I moved towards the cake, and Taylor, Madeleine, and Lena helped me blow out the candles. Finally – mercifully – it was over.

As he rolled down the ramp off the stage, Zack was one happy guy. "Time to shake a few hundred hands, Ms. Shreve," he said.

"Why don't you and Brock take Taylor and the granddaughters and get started. There's something I have to talk to Mieka and the boys about." Zack gave me a questioning look but just nodded and turned his chair around.

There was a green room backstage at the Pile O' Bones. I'd shepherded many nervous politicians into it so they could have a final run-through of a speech before facing an audience. That afternoon, I led my children there and closed the door behind us. The faces of all three were glowing. They were happy because Zack's rally was a success, because I was having a good birthday and because, for the moment at least, it seemed that all was for the best in this best of all possible worlds.

I had no idea how I would find the words to tell them about Ian and Jill, but it was either me or Slater Doyle, so I simply laid out the facts as I knew them.

As I explained Ian's long-term involvement with Jill Oziowy, I kept my eyes on my children's faces. The glow faded quickly, replaced first by disbelief and then, in the case of Peter and Angus, by anger and disgust. Mieka began to cry.

"All those times he couldn't be with us, he was with Jill," Angus said.

"We don't know that," Mieka said, tears streaming. "Dad had a family. Why would he get involved with Jill?"

Peter was the gentlest of my children, but his tone was withering. "For Christ's sake, Mieka, grow up. He did it because he was horny and Jill was willing to put out."

Mieka whirled around to confront me. "Why did you have to tell us now?"

"Because Slater Doyle came to me an hour ago and gave me a choice. If Zack agreed to get out of the race, you and your brothers would never have to learn about your father and Jill. If Zack refused, Slater was going to tell you himself. Valerie Smythe, your father's secretary, made audio tapes of Ian and Jill having sex. I've heard one of them, Mieka. Listening to it was like having a knife plunged into my back. Apparently, there are many more, but I couldn't give in to blackmail. For the record, Zack didn't make the decision. I did. Zack still doesn't know about any of this."

Angus had tears in his eyes now too. He put his arms

around me. "You made the right choice," he said, and his voice cracked with emotion.

"I agree," Peter said. His face was stony, but I could see the pulse in his neck. "You had no alternative. You couldn't let Ridgeway's people blackmail us. Zack's one of the good guys."

Mieka was chewing her lower lip – always a sign of distress. "And Dad isn't? He's our father. How can you two just turn against him?"

Peter reached into his jeans pocket, fished out a tissue, and handed it to his sister. "We're not turning against him, Mieka. He turned against us. Repeatedly – for fifteen fucking years."

Someone knocked loudly on the door, no doubt eager to use the bathroom off the green room.

"We should get out of here," I said. "Why don't you three go home and try to absorb this. I know what you're going through. But I can't leave Zack alone. The media would have questions and that's not fair to him."

"I'll stay with you and Zack, Mum," Peter said quietly.

Angus brushed back his unruly forelock. "Nothing personal, Mieka. But I'm going to stay too."

Mieka mopped her eyes and blew her nose. "I'm going to take the girls home. Tell Zack I'm sorry. I just can't play the game right now."

The crowd in the hall had not thinned out. There were line-ups at the table selling SHREVE T-shirts and at the tables manned by volunteers signing up other volunteers to knock on doors, put up signs, and make sure our voters got to the polls on E-Day. Brock came over when he saw us. "Everything okay?" he asked.

"Everything's fine," I said. "Pete and Angus and I thought we'd help Zack with the handshaking."

Brock smiled at Mieka. "Had enough fun, huh?"

"Something like that," she said. "Are the girls with Zack?'

"With Zack, Taylor, Margot, and Lexi," Brock said. "They're outside, and the three young ladies are the centre of attention. They seem to be handling it well. Now if you'll excuse me, there are a couple of people here I should talk to."

We reached the door just as Jill was coming in. When she spotted us, she grinned. "I know I'm late, but I was starving, so I got in the food line and listened to the cheering on the loud-speakers." She held out her hot dog. "Worth waiting for, huh?"

Mieka and her brothers walked past Jill as if she was invisible. Jill's face fell. "Has something happened?"

"Yes. The kids just found out about you and Ian."

Jill looked confused for a moment, and then the colour drained from her face. "Oh, my God. How did that happen . . .?" Her sentence trailed off. The full horror of the situation was beginning to hit her. "Jo, we have to talk.

"I agree," I said. "But I don't want to talk here." Still hold-ing her hot dog, Jill followed as I went up the stairs to the stage and back to the green room.

After she closed the door behind her, Jill looked at me beseechingly. "Jo, you have to understand – "

"Shut up," I said. "There's nothing to understand. I may be naive, but I get this. An hour ago I listened while Slater Doyle played an audio tape Valerie Smythe made of you fel-lating Ian and him returning the favour. The quality of the recording was excellent. I felt as if I was in the room with you. And the clip I heard was just a sample. Slater told me the affair began before Mieka was born and was still going on when Ian died."

Jill's entire body was shaking. It was as if she'd been sud-denly plunged into ice water. "Jo, please – "

"Shut up," I said. "Because there's more. Slater told me that if I didn't get Zack to withdraw from the race, he'd give the tapes to my children. I had no choice. I called Mieka,

Peter, and Angus in here and told them that the father they loved was an adulterer and that all the times he was too busy to be with his family he was fucking their Auntie Jill."

"Give me a chance to make things right," she said. "I'll do anything."

"You've done enough," I said. "We're finished, Jill. Get your things out of Mieka's house. Then go away, and stay away."

I opened the door to the hall, but Jill didn't move. Her face was ashen; her eyes were dead. She was desolate – the sole survivor of a catastrophe that had claimed the world as she knew it. For a moment, my heart went out to her. But the moment didn't last. "Better eat your hot dog," I said. "It's getting cold."

When I came back into the hall, Zack was surrounded by people. Among them was Howard Dowhanuik. When he spotted me, he came over. "Where the hell have you been?" he said. "I saw you taking Jill off somewhere. You looked like a thundercloud and she looked terrified." He craned his neck to peer behind me. "Where is Jill anyway?"

I ignored the question. "Let's go outside and find a place where we can talk."

The sun was warm and the bands were good. It seemed there were people everywhere, but finally we found a spot at the back of the building.

I didn't waste time on preamble. "Did you know Jill and Ian were having an affair?"

Howard winced, but he didn't answer.

"It's a simple question," I said. "Did you know that Ian was having sex with Jill?"

Howard took a deep breath. "I knew," he said.

"Why didn't you tell me?"

Howard ran his hand over his head "There didn't seem to be any point. As soon as I found out about the affair, I talked to Ian. Over the years I must have asked him to break it off with Jill a hundred times. I told Ian he had a great wife and family and he was making the party vulnerable."

"But it didn't matter to him," I said.

"It mattered," Howard said.

"Then why didn't he end the relationship?"

Howard looked away. "Jesus, Jo, don't make me do this."

"I deserve to know," I said.

Howard's old hawk's face was carved with pain. "Yeah, you do," he said. "Ian said he couldn't walk away from Jill because he was in love with her. I'm sorry, Jo."

"So am I," I said. "But I needed to hear the words."

"How did you find out?"

"Slater Doyle told me," I said. "Remember all those speeches you and Ian made about letting the province's moral compass be our guide to governing? How could you even say the words?" Howard reached out to console me. I shook him off. "Don't," I said. "I'm hanging on by a thread, and I have a campaign to run. Just leave me alone. I need to be inside with Zack."

There was still a cluster of supporters around Zack, and when I joined him, Angus, Peter, and Taylor came over and we moved through the crowd as a family, smiling, shaking hands, urging people to sign up. It was almost seven-thirty when we watched the last vehicles leave the parking lot. As a half-ton with a load of new SHREVE lawn signs turned onto the street, Zack was clearly gratified. "Everything just clicked." He hooked his arm around my legs. "And things clicked because you made them click," he said. "Why don't we take Taylor and the boys somewhere for a burger?"

"You go ahead," I said. "My shoulder's bothering me and I'm tired. I think I'll just go home."

Zack's face filled with concern. "I'm coming with you. Your turn to get the attention. Time for serious pampering."

I waited until Taylor was tucked in reading and Zack and I were showered and in bed before I told him about my encounter with Slater Doyle. Zack listened without comment. When I told him that I'd turned down Slater's deal and that I'd already spoken to Mieka, Peter, and Angus, he drew me close. "You shouldn't have had to carry all this alone," he said.

"There was nothing you could do," I said. "And the rally was important – you didn't need distractions."

"Are you planning to talk to Jill?"

"I've already talked to her," I said. "The kids and I ran into her just after I'd finished telling them the news. When they saw her, they just kept on walking. I told Jill to get her stuff out of Mieka's house, go away, and stay away."

Zack kissed my hair. "So that's that," he said.

"Not quite," I said. "By the time I saw Howard I'd pretty much exhausted my supply of righteous indignation. I asked Howard if he knew why Ian had risked everything to keep seeing Jill."

"And . . . ?"

My eyes stung with tears but I was determined not to cry. I took a breath and plunged ahead. "Howard said that Ian told him he couldn't give up Jill because he was in love with her."

For a few minutes we lay side-by-side, silent, absorbed in our own thoughts.

"I'd do anything for you," Zack said finally. "But I have no idea where to start with this."

"Just hold me," I said. I was almost asleep when Zack murmured, "You do know that if you'd asked me to withdraw from the race, I would have."

"I know," I said. "That's why I didn't ask."

CHAPTER

8

When the phone rang the next morning at a little after seven I was lying in bed, mentally sorting through the rubble left by Slater Doyle's news. I'd told Brock I was feeling less than great and he had taken Willie and Pantera on their run. Taylor and her friends were throwing a surprise birthday breakfast for a classmate at a café near Luther, and Zack was in the kitchen making breakfast, so I was alone.

Given the scarring events of the previous day, I assumed the call was from Mieka or one of her brothers. I was wrong. My caller was Liz Meighen. Her tone was both urgent and apologetic. "Joanne, I realize this is terribly early for a phone call, but I have to see you this morning."

I was running on empty, but I was relieved to hear Liz's voice. "I've been trying to get in touch since we had dinner with you," I said. "Are you all right?"

"No," she said. "I'm not, and I need to see you."

Reflexively, I turned to prop myself up on my elbow. The pain that shot through my shoulder was sharp, and I wondered if Zack and I had been premature in our athleticism the day before. "Would it be possible for you to come here?"

I said. "I was involved in a car accident a while ago, and I'm having a bad day."

"I know about your accident," she said. "It was on the news. And I know about your late husband's affair with his press secretary. I can only imagine how hurt your children must have been to learn that their father had been involved with another woman."

I was incredulous. "How did you know about the affair, Liz? Was Graham involved in Slater Doyle's scheme to get Zack to withdraw from the race?"

"That doesn't matter," she said. "All that matters is that you know what's going on. I'll be there at ten, and, Joanne, what I tell you must remain private."

Given everything that was happening, it was impossible to stick to the house rule about keeping mealtime conversation light. When Zack handed me my scrambled eggs and toast, I took a few bites, murmured appreciatively, and waded right in.

"Liz Meighen's coming over," I said. "I tried to dissuade her, but she was determined. Zack, Liz knew about Ian and Jill."

"So Graham's involved in this."

"Apparently. Liz feels the situation is urgent."

"Do you want me to stay until she comes?"

I shook my head. "Liz wanted our meeting to be private."

The buzzer from the lobby sounded, cutting off further discussion. "That will be Milo," Zack said. "Jo, I've already filled him in on the situation with the tapes. I figured you might not want to go through all that again."

"You're right. Thanks."

Zack wheeled over, buzzed Milo in, and turned his chair back to face me. "Slater has already posted a couple of steamy tapes of Ian and Jill."

"Did you listen?"

"Yes."

"And?"

"Audio porn just doesn't do it for me."

"Let's hope the public shares your preference."

When he heard Milo's distinctive seven rhythmic raps on the door, Zack braced himself. He knew Milo was invaluable, but he found Milo's kinetic energy jarring. Zack had snorted when I'd tried to explain Milo by quoting Thoreau's words about those who hear a different drummer. Whatever the explanation, Milo certainly kept step to music he alone could hear. That day he bopped in and took his place at the kitchen table.

"Sorry about that crap Slater pulled yesterday, Joanne. I know it hurt your family, but it hasn't affected our campaign. Nobody cares about audios of a dead politician getting it on with his lady friend."

Zack narrowed his eyes. "Joanne was married to that politician, Milo – maybe try to be a little more delicate?"

Milo blew off the warning. "Joanne didn't hire me to be delicate. She hired me to get the job done. So here's what I know. Slater's extortion scheme would have worked if Joanne had caved. She didn't, so thanks to her we're still in the game. Time to lace up our skates and hit the ice." Milo pulled his laptop out of his satchel, turned it on, and tapped away. "Get ready to be the first kids on the block to see the new Ridgeway ads."

"Have you seen them?" Zack said.

"Nope, we're all virgins here. A buddy of mine at Serpent's Tooth, the company that did the post-production, thought we'd be interested in checking out the files. He gave me the password for the FTP."

Milo uploaded the files and the screen was filled with a black-and-white mug shot, side-view and front view, of a sullen Aboriginal man. A soft female voice identified the man as Bernard Iron. A rapidly scrolling list of Iron's prior offences played over his face. More black-and-white footage: this time of Zack and Iron emerging from the Regina court-house. They were both smiling. Then Iron spotted the TV camera and began shouting obscenities, snarling and shaking his fist. It was a mad dog moment and the camera captured it and froze the image. The soft female voice said, "Zachary Shreve worked every angle of the law to set this man free. Two weeks after Shreve convinced a jury Bernard Iron was innocent, Iron raped and killed a young mother. Now Zack Shreve wants to be your mayor. Can he be trusted to make decisions that will affect *your* family?"

There were three more commercials. They were standard length – thirty seconds – and the format was the same for each. The mug shots; the priors; the moment of triumph as Zack and his client left the courtroom; the soft female voice recounting the subsequent carnage wreaked by a man Zack had set free. The three of us watched silently. The commercials were devastating and we knew it.

Zack turned to me. "So what do you think we should do?"

Milo unwrapped a Crispy Crunch bar and munched. "My pal at Serpent's Tooth thought our campaign might want to reconsider the happy-happy joy-joy spots we're planning to run. They're not in the can yet, so it will be easy enough to go negative."

"No," I said. "Let's not panic. We're taping the first commercial of Zack and Mieka talking about his support for small business this afternoon at UpSlideDown. We agreed to tape one ad a day next week. Let's stick with the plan."

"So we're not going to answer this?" Zack said.

I turned to Milo. "When are the Ridgeway spots going to air?"

"October 5 and then every day till the election."

"Time is not on our side," I said. "We can't let Ridgeway's people drive our campaign, and I don't like attack ads."

"Well, I do like them," Milo said. "I like them because they work."

"Not always," I said. "Milo, see if you can book Zack on *Quinlan Live* again on Monday morning."

"Because we're going to get hit with some negative shit?"

"No, because we're going to get hit with negative ads based on a false premise. Quinlan's a lawyer. He understands that you can't find a person guilty of a crime he didn't commit because somewhere down the line he might commit another crime. He and Zack could have a nice lawyerly chat about the law."

Milo cocked an ear. "What's that I hear? Why, it's the sound of radios being turned off all over the province."

"I'm all right with that," I said. "If Zack goes on *Quinlan Live*, he'll show that he deals with problems head on and doesn't let the opposition call the shots." I checked my watch. "It's nine-thirty, you guys better get out of here. My guest might be early."

"Don't worry if you can't make it to UpSlideDown for the taping," Zack said.

"You'd better check with Mieka," I said. "If Slater dropped off the tapes, she may not be up to doing the ad."

"Slater really is a piece of work," Zack said. "We can reschedule if Mieka's not ready. I'll call you and let you know where things stand."

"Good. I don't imagine my guest is going to stay long, and I still have to find your blue Viyella shirt. Periwinkle is a good colour for TV, and you look seriously hot in that shirt."

As soon as the men left, I filled the kettle, arranged the tea things on a pretty tray, and waited. At 8:30 I called UpSlideDown. There was no answer. At 9:00 I called Mieka's cell. It rang repeatedly. When I tried her again just before 10:00, she finally picked up. "I listened to one of the tapes," she said. Her voice was cold steel. "I heard what Ian and Jill said to each other, how they *were* with each other. Fifteen years. How could they do that to us?"

"I don't know," I said. "Do you want me to come down there?"

"I'm all right."

"At least let me get Zack to tell the agency to cancel the shoot this afternoon."

"No," she said. "I told Zack I'd do the ad and I will. Zack is family, and unlike Ian, I keep my promises."

It was the first time Mieka had ever referred to her father as "Ian." It was a significant moment and a painful one. "I love you," I said, but Mieka didn't hear me. She'd already broken the connection.

Liz didn't arrive at ten. As the morning dragged on and there was no word from her, I grew increasingly uneasy. Finally, I called her cell, but it went straight to voicemail. I didn't leave a message. By quarter to twelve, I faced facts. Liz was not coming, and if I didn't get a move on, Zack wouldn't have his periwinkle shirt.

On Saturdays, there was always at least one birthday party at UpSlideDown. This weekend's party was pirate-themed, and the joint was jumping. In addition to the kids with eye patches and striped shirts, there were kids just dropping in to have fun on a rainy Saturday. Mieka already had permission from the pirate parents to have their children in a political commercial, and two volunteers from our campaign were stationed at the door getting releases from parents of the other kids.

I had learned from the assignments Jill had thrown my way over the years that TV productions have a way of disrupting everything. Because our ads were all going to be taped on location and involve ordinary citizens, we had asked the production company to be as unobtrusive as possible. That afternoon I was relieved to see that the lights and mikes were already in place, well out of harm's way. The director's instructions to the kids were straightforward and sensible. "Have fun but watch out for the cables on the floor." When I caught Zack's eye, I motioned for him to join me, and we slipped away to a storage room in the back so he could change his shirt. "So what did Liz Meighen have to say," he asked.

"Nothing," I said. "She never showed up."

"Did you call her?"

"No answer on her cell and I didn't want to try her at home. I gather the situation is fraught, and I didn't want to make matters worse."

Zack shrugged out of his dress shirt and pulled on his blue Viyella. "I love you in that shirt," I said. I buttoned the top button. "Time to get your bald spot powdered."

"What bald spot?"

"The one that covers three-quarters of your head," I said. "Let's go."

Mieka was wearing jeans and a turquoise cowl neck sweater I hadn't seen before. The production company's stylist had worked her magic. My daughter's fine dark blond hair was smoothed into a smart ponytail twist and her television makeup was flattering but not overwhelming.

I went over and hugged her. "You look beautiful," I said.

She chewed her lip. "I don't feel beautiful. I feel sick."

"You don't have to do the commercial today, Mieka."

"Tomorrow won't be any better. And I want to do this for Zack. Peter's right. Zack is one of the good guys."

The spot opened with Mieka, standing in the corner reserved for quiet play, talking about Zack's support for neighbourhood small businesses. Mieka was a nervous public speaker, but she was passionate about her subject and she did her segment in three takes. I stood behind the cameraman and watched his screen as he taped Zack with the kids. Only a fraction of the tape would be used in the final one-minute commercial, but it was wise to shoot generously, so when Captain Slappy, a children's entertainer in full pirate gear, jumped up on a table and began singing a pirate song, the cameras kept rolling. Kids always gravitated towards Zack, and as Captain Slappy sang there were two wide-eyed little boys beside his chair. Zack was a quick learner and when Captain Slappy repeated the chorus, Zack joined in.

> *I'm a pirate! That I be!*
> *I sail me ship upon the sea!*
> *I stay up late – till half past three!*
> *And that's a peg below my knee!*

When the last notes of "I'm a pirate!" faded, I leaned over and asked the director to make certain I got the footage of Zack singing his pirate song.

UpSlideDown closed at 3:30 on Saturdays, and after everyone left, the space was quiet enough for Zack to talk to the camera. When the lighting was being adjusted, Mieka took my arm. "I have to talk to you."

"We should get out of here," I said. "Those microphones are sensitive." We went back to the room where Zack had changed. The dress shirt Zack had been wearing was still draped over the back of a chair. Reflexively, I picked up the shirt and began smoothing its creases.

Mieka watched me. "I'm finished with the tapes," she said. "Do you want to listen to them?"

"No," I said.

"Good call," she said. "They're disgusting. And if that wasn't enough, all the entries are dated. It's easy to discover where Ian was when he was supposed to be with us."

I could feel my daughter's anger. "Mieka, don't do this."

"Remember the farewell ceremony we had at the end of Grade Eight? After the ceremony there was a bonfire and a barbecue for the Grade Eights and their parents. Ian had to skip it because Howard 'needed him at the legislature'?"

"I was thinking about it the other day when I saw the picture of the three of us after the ceremony."

Mieka's voice was toneless. "Ian didn't go back to the legislature to see Howard," she said. "He went back to have sex with Jill. Valerie Smythe was working late, and she heard him tell Jill that he couldn't get through the night without being inside her."

I put my arms around my daughter. For a long time we just held each other.

Neither of us said a word. There was nothing left to say.

I was watching Zack finish up his segment when I spotted Howard Dowhanuik outside the door. He was hatless and without an umbrella. Howard had never mastered the art of the inside voice, so I picked up my coat and umbrella, unlocked the door, and joined him.

"You should have come earlier," I said. "You missed Cap'n Slappy and the pirate party."

"I knew you were doing the ad here this afternoon, so I thought I'd take a chance. I figured if I came to your house you'd throw me out."

I touched his arm. "I don't blame you for what happened. You tried to put a stop to it, which is more than either Ian or Jill did."

Howard turned towards the street. People were bent against the rain, rushing to get home. I moved my umbrella to cover him. With age the flesh had fallen away from Howard's face. His profile now was as chiselled as the face on the head of a coin. "Is there anything I can do to straighten this out?" he said. "Jill's beside herself. She thinks she's lost everything."

"Did she send you?"

He nodded.

"You're wasting your time," I said. "I want Jill out of our lives. You're going to have to pick a side, Howard. Either you're with Jill or you're with me and my children."

"I've never seen you like this, Jo. You've always been so – "

"Stupid?" I said. "Yesterday I discovered that fifteen years of my life were a lie. Until Slater Doyle opened my eyes, I was certain that Ian died believing the most important people in his life were his family. I had a lot of good memories. Now all I have are questions that I don't want answered. Where was Ian all those times when he missed the kids' events? Where was he the nights I scraped his dinner into the garbage because Valerie Smythe called to say he was caught in a meeting? Where was he when I couldn't get through to him to tell him that I was in the ER with one of our kids who needed stitches or a cast or an X-ray?"

Howard had moved away from me. He was getting soaked, but he seemed oblivious to the rain "It never once occurred to me that Ian was unfaithful," I went on. "He and Jill must have thought I was such a fool – the gullible wife who's the last to know that her husband has a mistress. You must have thought I was a fool too."

Howard turned back to me, his face filled with anguish. "No one ever thought you were a fool, Jo. Ian had a great deal of respect for you."

I was livid. "*Respect!* Jesus Christ, Howard. I wasn't Ian's favourite sixth grade teacher, I was his *wife.* He was supposed to love, honour, and cherish me, and goddammit, he was supposed to be faithful."

"I'm sorry," Howard said. "I've made everything worse."

I watched as Howard walked off into the rain. His words had been a fresh wound and I was already reeling. Too much had happened. Jill and Ian, the vicious mayoral race. Liz's desperate call and then her failure to show up. When Howard turned at the corner and disappeared, I closed my umbrella, raised my face to the sky, and waited until the rain cooled my face and cleansed my thoughts.

Filming the ad took longer than I'd anticipated, and it was 6:00 p.m. by the time Zack and I got back to Halifax Street. I'd called Taylor from UpSlideDown and she'd ordered Japanese food to be delivered at 6:30. Zack made us martinis, and we kicked back to enjoy our drinks and listen to our daughter talk about the portrait she was painting of Margot and her children.

Taylor had brought out a book of paintings by Mary Cassatt, the late nineteenth-/early twentieth-century American artist whose best-known works were of mothers and children. She was particularly taken with a portrait called *The Bath*. As she pointed out Cassatt's meticulous drawing and the way she used blocks of colour to capture the intimacy between mother and child, Taylor's excitement was contagious. "I love everything about this painting," she said. "I read somewhere that Cassatt's portraits were too accurate to be flattering to her subjects, but I can't imagine this being more perfect."

"You're on safe ground with Margot, Declan, and Lexi," I said. "They don't need to be flattered. They're all very attractive."

As always we had over-ordered, but as always it didn't matter. We were all keen on leftovers. When I opened the fridge to put away the remaining sushi and tempura, I saw a florist's delivery package.

Taylor was standing behind me. "That came when I was ordering the food. I put the flowers in the fridge and forgot all about them. I'm sure they're still okay."

The flowers were from Gale's Florist. When I tore away the wrappings and saw the gerberas, the image of Bev, triumphantly alive, flashed through my mind. Bev said once that she loved gerberas because they seemed to have a lust for life. Liz could not have chosen a more graceful way to apologize for missing our meeting, and I was smiling as I opened the notecard that came with the flowers.

There was no signature, but Liz's expensive buff-coloured stationery was embossed with her monogram. The hand-writing was shaky, but the three-word message was clear: *Don't Trust Anybody.*

Taylor was watching my face as I read the card. "Is some-thing wrong?"

"I'm not sure," I said. "Taylor, would you mind putting these in water while I call and thank the friend who sent them."

When I called the Meighen home, a woman answered. When I asked for Liz, she said, "Mrs. Meighen is gone for holiday. This is the housekeeper."

"Could I speak to Mr. Meighen?"

"Call back, please. Maybe leave message," she said, then broke the connection.

I tried again. This time the phone rang six times and Liz's recorded voice asked me to leave a message. I left my name and cell number and asked that either she or Graham call me.

When I went back into the kitchen, Zack was watching Taylor decide precisely where each gerbera should be placed in the drabware vase. He wheeled close to me. "Taylor said you were calling the friend who sent the flowers. I'm taking a wild guess and assuming it was Liz Meighen explaining why she was a no-show this morning."

"Close but no cigar," I said. I handed him the note that had come with the flowers. He read it, frowned, glanced at Taylor, and said nothing. I got the message. We weren't going to discuss the situation in front of our daughter. And so we waited. Taylor had an artist's eye, and it took a while before she was satisfied with her flower arrangement, but finally she stood back, cocked her head, and gazed critically at the gerberas. "What do you think?" she said.

"Perfect," Zack said.

"I agree," I said. "Not a bloom out of place."

"Good," Taylor said. "Now I can still squeeze in a couple of hours in my studio before bed." She blew kisses our way and headed out.

As soon as the door closed, Zack turned to me. "What's going on with Liz?"

"Your guess is as good as mine," I said. "I don't buy the housekeeper's explanation that Liz is on holiday. Less than twelve hours ago, Liz was a no-show at a meeting she had been desperate to arrange. She's old school when it comes to etiquette, and she orders flowers to apologize for inconveniencing me. So far, so good, but then Liz goes to the florist to drop off a handwritten note warning me that I can't trust anybody and takes off on a vacation. It doesn't wash, Zack."

"I agree," Zack said. "It doesn't make sense, but Liz admits she hasn't been thinking clearly."

"It's possible that she asked someone else to take the note to Gale's," I said. "But given Liz's state of mind, I can't imagine she'd trust anybody else to do the job." I checked my watch. "Gale's will be closed by now," I said. "But after church, I'm going to drop by the shop and ask some questions."

CHAPTER

9

When I awoke Sunday morning, I piled my pillows against the headboard, took the sculpture of Ernest Lindner from my night table, and placed it on my lap. Looking at Ernie's face, I remembered the conversations we'd had – about art, his youth in Vienna, the summer home at Emma Lake where he did some of his best work, and always the eternal and unanswerable question of what made men and women happy. They were good memories – almost good enough to blot out the ugliness of Ian and Jill's betrayal. It would take a lot of time to redress the balance – to overcome the pain and remember the many joys of my life during the period when Ian was my husband. But I had spent the night in bed beside the man I loved and who loved me. As I ran my fingers over the surface of the ceramic Zack had given me for my birthday, I felt my strength returning.

Zack stroked my arm. "You're really pleased with that, aren't you?"

"I love it," I said. "And I love you. Zack, I'm going to do whatever it takes to get us through this."

"How about pancakes for breakfast?"

"That would be a start," I said.

———

When I got back from our very gentle run, the pancake batter was made; the griddle was hot, and Cronus's Inferno Red urn was on the sideboard. "Is Cronus joining us for breakfast?" I said.

Zack wheeled up beside me. "I was thinking more about dinner," he said. "Is tonight a good night for us to go to the Sahara Club?"

"Absolutely," I said. "I'm ready for red meat, and Taylor's always up for a steak. Angus wanted to come. I'll check with him. If he's available, I'll make a reservation."

Taylor was crucifer that day at the Cathedral, so we had to be at church early. While Taylor got robed, Zack and I had twenty minutes to wait before the service began. We both welcomed the chance to be together in a space where many turbulent hearts had found peace.

Then the church began to fill; Mieka and our granddaughters joined us and the organist struck the chord of the processional hymn.

Mieka was pale and her eyes were deeply shadowed, but her chin was high and her shoulders were squared. As they always did when they weren't serving, Madeleine and Lena took paper and markers out of their backpack and made drawings of girls with fancy hair. It was a Sunday service like every other Sunday service, and yet everything had changed. During the Lord's prayer, Mieka and I both stumbled over the line "Forgive us our trespasses as we forgive those who trespass against us."

When the service was over, the girls spotted friends and went to join them and Zack zeroed in on the dean. Mieka and I stayed in our pew and waited for Taylor. "It was good to have you beside me today," I said.

"Same here," Mieka said. "I notice we both had a problem with the line about forgiving those who trespass against us."

"We'll get there," I said.

"It's going to be a while for me," Mieka said. "Maybe I'll never get there. Last night after the kids went to bed, I boxed up all the pictures of Ian I'd put up around the house and the photo albums I was always showing the girls and took them to the garage. Jill's stuff was still in the guest room, so after I'd finished with the photos of Ian, I packed up her things. I felt sick even touching her clothes. When I was through I called Pete and Angus to come over for a beer."

"You're brothers are stoic with me," I said. "How are they really doing?"

"Angus is okay. He was young when Ian died and as we all know, Ian didn't spend much time with us. Peter's very angry. Neither of them wanted to hear the clips."

"Well, that's a blessing," I said. "What are you going to do with them?"

"I packed them with Jill's things."

"That was wise. There's no use dwelling on the past. We all have a lot to look forward to."

"I'm trying," Mieka said. "I'm taking the girls to the Science Centre this afternoon. I sent Jill a text telling her that her suitcases are in the hall and asking her to get them out of our house while we're gone. I told her to leave the key I gave her on the kitchen table."

"One step at a time," I said.

Mieka gave me a tired smile. "Right," she said. "One step at a time."

On the way home from church, we drove to Gale's Florist on 13th Avenue. Alison, the owner's daughter, was at the counter misting a bouquet of peach roses, warm as a glowing sunset.

"Those are exquisite," I said.

Alison raised a nicely arched eyebrow. "If the orders I've been sending to your address are any indication, I doubt if you're in the market for flowers."

"You're right about that," I said. "Alison, I came to ask about the gerberas that were delivered to our house yesterday."

"Is there a problem with them?"

"No, they're lovely. I just wondered about the card Liz Meighen sent. Did she bring the card into the store herself?"

"Yes."

"Did she seem all right?"

Alison stopped misting the roses. "Joanne, you and my mother have been friends for years. You know she's big on protecting our customers' privacy."

"I know, and I appreciate it. But Liz Meighen is also a friend and I'm concerned about her. She called yesterday morning and said she had to see me. We agreed on a time, but she never showed up. The message she sent with the flowers was unsettling enough to bring me here today. Do you know who Liz dealt with when she brought in the note?"

"It was me," Alison said. "And I've been worrying about her ever since. She wasn't herself. Mrs. Meighen has known me since I was ten years old, but she couldn't remember my name. She was confused and she seemed to have trouble focusing. When she left, I walked her to the door to make certain she wasn't driving."

"And she wasn't?"

"No, she had a cab waiting."

"Did she say anything about going on a trip?"

For the first time since I'd begun asking about Liz, Alison relaxed. "Oh, you know about the trip. I wasn't supposed to tell anybody."

"But she did say she was leaving town?"

"Yes. When her daughter was ill, Mrs. Meighen came in

here often. She liked to choose flowers that would lift Beverly's spirits. I hadn't seen her for ages, so yesterday I told her how good it was to see her in the shop again. She said she probably wouldn't be back for a while because she was going away. I asked where she was going, and she put her finger to her lips."

"So you don't know where she went."

"No. I just hope that wherever she is, she'll find what she needs."

Zack had functions or meetings all afternoon. It would be a long day for him, so the reservation I made at the Sahara Club was an early one. Taylor and Angus were both free for the evening, so in addition to Cronus there were four of us at dinner. Cronus's choice of the Sahara Club for his big night out was in character. The restaurant's website said it all. "The best steaks, big wines, all the while you are surrounded by a surplus of polished oak and red velour booths." The all-male wait staff was discrete, and the patrons had the self-satisfied auras of the successful. Cronus would have pronounced the Sahara Club "a classy joint."

Zack had brought the Inferno Red urn along in a roomy leather messenger bag, and after he'd ordered a bottle of Dom Perignon, he took the urn out and set it on the table. When the waiter brought our champagne, we drank a toast to Cronus and turned our attention to our menus. "Sky's the limit," Zack said. "This is Cronus's party." We ordered appetizers, then, because the Sahara was a steak house, we all scrutinized the beef options.

"That thirty-two-ounce Kobe Tomahawk looks interesting," Zack said.

"I wonder if the Sahara Club has a defibrillator on site?" I said. "I was thinking you and I might share the Chateaubriand for two."

"Sold," Zack said. "But only because, as you have pointed out once or twice, I'm a sharing kind of guy."

"I'm not," Angus said. "I'm twenty-two years old and it'll probably be a while before I get another chance to eat a steak that costs $159.95."

"Cronus would be proud," Zack said. "How about you, Taylor?"

"I'm going to have the filet mignon."

Zack motioned the server to come over and we ordered. "I have news," Taylor said. "I talked to Cole Dimitroff this afternoon. Darrell thought it would be a good idea if I talked to Cole directly."

"And?" I said.

"And I really like how he plans to use my paintings in Corydon's advertising. Since he bought *BlueBoy21* from Dr. Treadgold, Cole's had the painting at his apartment. The plan now is to hang *BlueBoy21* and *Endangered* in the head office, but all the Corydon stores will have copies of the paintings and details from the paintings will be used in their print advertising."

"So what does Corydon sell?" Angus asked.

"Very expensive clothing for men," Zack said. "They cater to a gay clientele, hence the name Corydon."

"Because . . . ?" Angus said.

"Because Andre Gide wrote a book about homosexuality titled *Corydon*," I said.

"Cool," Angus said. "So, Zack, did you get a good deal for the right to use Taylor's work?"

Taylor gave her brother a look that would have curdled milk. "Angus, *I* was the one who worked out the agreement with Cole, and I got very good terms. Thanks for asking."

"Sorry," Angus said. "I'm a dweeb, but even dweebs have their uses. I was the one who discovered that the house Mum and Zack inherited at 12 Rose Street is not for sale at any price."

Taylor's eyes widened. "It must be really special."

"It's not," I said. "It's well kept, but it's still slum housing."

"Slum housing with a strange history," Angus said. "I went through the file. Before Cronus purchased the property, it was a party house."

"What's a party house?" Taylor said.

"It's a place where people go to get drunk or shoot up or have sex or all three," Angus said. "There were pictures in the file. Mattresses on the floor. Stuffing coming out of chairs. Broken glass. Blood stains everywhere. Black mould. To his credit, Cronus cleaned it up. He still has a cleaning service in there every two weeks."

Zack was dubious. "Are you sure about that? Not many slum houses have a cleaning service."

Angus winced. "I could be wrong. I really just skimmed through the file. I'll give it a serious look tonight."

"Bring the files to the house Tuesday," I said as the appetizers arrived. "That house intrigues me, so does the woman who lives there."

Zack speared a piece of smoked salmon. "Shall we declare a moratorium on talking about our slum empire while we're eating?"

"Good idea," I said. "Thanksgiving is two weeks away. We're going to the lake from Thursday night till Monday afternoon, so all suggestions about food and fun are welcome."

The food was excellent and Taylor's news and the prospect of Thanksgiving had buoyed our spirits. Zack watched in amazement as our younger son ate the last morsel of his thirty-two-ounce steak. We had a final toast to Cronus, then Zack placed the red urn back in his messenger bag, and, full and happy, we made our way to the entrance. Angus and Taylor went ahead to get the car while Zack settled the bill.

As Zack and I waited for the credit card machine to complete the transaction, I looked back into the restaurant. The arrangement of the red velour booths gave diners privacy, and the booth in which Graham Meighen and Jill Oziowy were seated hadn't been visible from where we had been sitting. But I could see the booth and its occupants clearly from the entrance. Jill was wearing a silky low-cut black top that revealed her cleavage. As I watched, she laughed, leaned forward seductively, and touched her index finger to Graham's lips.

I tapped Zack's arm. "Check out the booth near the window on the right side of the dining room."

Zack turned his chair. "Son of a bitch," he said. "That didn't take long. I guess Jill is now officially in the Ridgeway camp."

I glanced at Jill. She and Graham were now holding hands. "How is this going to end?" I said.

Zack slipped his credit card back into his wallet and sighed. "Not well," he said. "Let's just hope the collateral damage is minimal."

CHAPTER

10

I didn't go to Saskatoon with Zack for *Quinlan Live*. I needed to check our poll numbers and identify areas that we might win if we redeployed volunteers, so after Zack and Milo left for the airport, I went straight to the Noodle House. As always, I took whatever chair was vacant, cleared a space on the table in front of me, and opened my laptop. Before I settled in with my polls and volunteer lists, I googled Graham Meighen. The portrait accompanying his executive profile was the usual head-and-shoulders shot of the flourishing businessman. He was sixty-four and there were few surprises in his biography. He was born in Storthoaks, Saskatchewan, a town that now had a population of fewer than one hundred. He had a degree in business from the University of Saskatchewan. He ran his father-in-law's construction company for years before becoming CEO of Lancaster Development. He served on a number of boards. Seemingly, he was a successful man and a wealthy one.

I was still staring at Graham Meighen's portrait when I realized the second hour of *Quinlan Live* was about to start. The Noodle House had a radio left behind from the days when the Noodle House *was* a noodle house. I turned it on and leaned back. Quinlan announced that the topic for the day was "Do attack ads work?" He introduced Zack, and then, before the lines were opened to callers, Zack and Quinlan had a lawyerly conversation about the rights of the accused to legal counsel. As Milo had predicted, the topic was dry despite Zack and Quinlan's spirited exchange, and callers soon pushed the dialogue into more fertile ground. It didn't take long for arguments about the effectiveness of attack ads to disintegrate into a simple exchange of attacks.

I hadn't talked to Milo about orchestrating our callers, but I recognized many of the voices relaying our campaign's talking points about the favouritism and lack of transparency of the Ridgeway administration, its indifference to the poor and marginalized, and its lack of a coherent policy for future sustainable development.

Our supporters pitched some low balls, but they were well within the range of robust rhetoric. The attacks on Zack were unrelentingly ugly and ad hominem. Zack was the criminal's friend, he had gang connections, his family's lavish lifestyle was financed by the dregs of society. Quinlan cut off one particularly vitriolic caller but not before she had accused Zack of being a gambler, a drinker, and a fornicator who lacked the moral strength to lead our city.

I was boiling, but Zack sounded sanguine. He thanked the caller for her time, repeated one of his favourite lines, "I have committed many sins but no crimes," and began talking about his plans for Regina.

I smiled when I heard the voice of the next caller. It was Peggy Kreviazuk, and she was in full take-no-prisoners mode. "Zack Shreve has been open about the mistakes he's made in the past," she said. "I don't approve of personal attacks, but Scott Ridgeway and our current city council are puppets of Graham Meighen and his associates at Lancaster Development. I have questions about the character and behaviour of Meighen and his crowd. This is not mudslinging. There are serious questions and we deserve serious answers.

"Three years ago the Ridgeway campaign responded to public pressure and promised immediate action on affordable housing. Last year the mayor announced the city had designated certain properties on Rose Street and other areas of Ward 6 as sites of future infill housing. I have it on good authority that the city has paid out hundreds of thousands of dollars for these properties, but the money did not go to the owner of the properties. It went into the pockets of Lancaster Development so that they could buy the Rose Street houses, tear them down, and replace them with condominiums they would sell at market value. Mr. Mayor, you have appeared only at select carefully staged events since Labour Day. Step forward and answer questions about why the taxpayers' money has ended up in Lancaster's pocket."

Graham Meighen's image was still on the screen in front of me, and Liz Meighen's warnings were stamped on my consciousness. My heart was pounding. The mayoralty race was already a high-stakes game, and Peggy had just upped the ante.

Jack Quinlan was smooth. "Those are provocative questions," he said. "Mayor Ridgeway and Mr. Meighen deserve a chance to answer them. I'd like to extend an invitation to both the mayor and Mr. Meighen to join me on *Quinlan Live* at a time and date of their choosing."

The top of the hour meant time for the news. Zack called me before the newsreader had finished the first sentence of the first story. "Jo, I know you wouldn't send out an eighty-two-year-old woman to do our dirty work, but do you think Peggy was right?"

"I have no idea," I said. "I didn't know Lancaster was planning to build condos on those properties. I certainly hadn't heard the city had given the money allocated for the infill housing to Lancaster."

"Well, it sounds like somebody knew, and that person fed the information to Peggy."

"The informant would have had to be somebody Peggy trusted," I said. "My guess is it was Jill. She knows Peggy from the old days when Ian was in government. Now she's looking for a story. And Jill and Graham have obviously spent some time together. She could have unearthed the information about the condos and decided to set the cat among the pigeons to stir things up. I'll see what I can find out. What time are you getting home?"

"With luck, before one."

"Good. We can have a swim."

"That's not much of a carrot."

"I'll sweeten the pot."

The glow I felt at the prospect of having Zack home didn't last long. I had just closed down my laptop and picked up my jacket when Howard phoned. His greeting was not cheery. "What dunderhead is responsible for handing Peggy Kreviazuk that bombshell about Lancaster's dirty dealings with the mayor's office? Anybody who knows Peggy knows she wouldn't make that information public anonymously. She might as well have painted a target on her chest."

"I know," I said. "I'm worried about that too. All I can tell you is that the information didn't come from our campaign. We don't know anything about the condos. I think Jill was the source, but I can't deal with that now. Right now, I'm going over to Peggy's to warn her about the Ridgeway campaign goons and plead with her to back off."

Peggy lived in a neat bungalow in the Cathedral District. She was outside wearing her SHREVE T-shirt and raking leaves when I pulled up. There was a SHREVE sign on her front lawn.

She pointed to the street. "Check out the signage in my neighbourhood. Not a single Ridgeway sign. I know. I check every morning."

"I wish we had a hundred volunteers like you," I said. "Which brings me to the point of my visit. Peggy, I don't want to lose you. That information you had about Lancaster is dynamite. I'm not sure going on *Quinlan Live* with it was the wisest course."

Peggy leaned on her rake. "Neither was I, but the deed is done," she said. "And Quinlan put the ball firmly in Ridgeway and Meighen's court. It's up to them to respond."

"Who told you about Lancaster?"

Peggy's expression was mischievous. "You know I can't tell you that."

"Was it Jill?"

"No, although she was here. You just missed her. She wanted to know the name of my informant too."

"Did you tell her?"

"Of course not. Jill's a friend, but she's also a journalist, and I didn't want to jeopardize my source."

"But the source is trustworthy."

"Absolutely." Peggy hesitated before speaking again. "The information came from someone in the Office of the City Clerk."

"The employee who's slipped information your way before," I said.

"Yes," she said. "And if my source's identification became known, the consequences would be serious."

"Understood," I said. "But, Peggy, if you hear anything else, just pass it along to me. There are been a few incidents that we think are associated with the Ridgeway campaign. It might be dangerous to cross them. I'll figure out a way to get the facts out without putting you in harm's way."

Peggy patted my hand. "I know you mean well, but I've always made my own decisions, and I'm not going to change now. I was born in this city, and I love it, but for the past decade and a half we've been governed by a gang of venal charlatans. It's time they were called to account."

"I agree. I just want you to be cautious. And, Peggy, be careful around Jill. She's seeing Graham Meighen."

Peggy was incredulous. "He's the CEO of Lancaster. They're what we're fighting against."

"Jill seems to have changed sides," I said tightly.

"Have you and she had a falling out?"

"Yes," I said. "And I really would rather not talk about it – not even with you."

"In that case, we'll talk about something that interests us both. Follow me into the backyard so I can show you the tulip bed I just dug."

Peggy was a serious gardener. Her plantings of perennials reflected an intimate knowledge of our city's inhospitable soil and unpredictable temperatures. In her garden as in her politics, Peggy had always fought back against implacable elements. I'd visited her backyard in all seasons. In spring and summer, it was a riot of colour and scent. But fall was in the air, and that late morning Peggy's backyard had the spare beauty of a garden being readied for winter.

The tulip bed ran the full length of Peggy's back fence. "I'm impressed," I said. "That's a lot of digging."

"And a lot of planting and mulching, but it'll be worth it when the tulips start peeking through," she said.

"It will be," I said. "What colour did you plant?"

"Every colour," Peggy said. "A good garden always has a few surprises."

I took out my phone. "Go stand by your garden," I said. "I'm going to take before-and-after pictures: one of your garden now and one when the tulips bloom."

When I had my photo, Peggy walked me to my car. "Joanne, I won't bring up the subject again, but you and Jill have been friends for a long time. Life's too short to lose someone you care about. Jill's proud. You may have to take the first step, but it will be worth it – for both of you."

Peggy's words stayed with me as I drove home. I knew she might be right, but I also knew I wasn't ready. And then out of nowhere, a memory, from the summer after Mieka was born. Jill and Ian were supposed to go out of town for a meeting, but Jill called in the morning and said she wasn't feeling well, so Ian would have to find another aide to go with him. I remember asking Jill if she had the flu, and she said she was just having a bad period.

It was a pretty day. I always took Mieka for an early walk and that morning I decided to walk down to Jill's apartment to see if there was anything she needed.

Jill was a long time answering the buzzer. When she finally opened her door, I was glad I'd come. She was still in her nightgown. She was very pale and it was clear she'd been crying. The drapes were pulled and the room was gloomy. "I need to go into the bathroom," she said. "I'm soaking through this pad." When she turned, I saw that the back of her nightgown was bloody.

Mieka had fallen asleep in her carriage, so I covered her, helped Jill to the bathroom and out of her nightgown, then got towels and a basin of water to give her a sponge bath. After I'd bathed Jill and wrapped her in a towel, she told me where I could find a fresh nightie. When I opened the dresser drawer that held Jill's lingerie, I saw two sleepers for a newborn and a baby sweater with a pattern of ducks.

I took the nightgown back to her. I told her I'd seen the baby clothes and I asked if it was possible she was having a miscarriage. She told me she'd been pregnant. She said she'd hoped to keep the baby, but the father said that was out of the question, so she'd had an abortion that morning.

The nurse had told her to expect a certain amount of blood. I checked. Jill didn't have a fever and she wasn't in pain, so I changed her sheets and helped her back into bed.

Mieka and I stayed at Jill's all day, and then I went home to make supper for the man who, in all likelihood, had impregnated her.

When I got back from Peggy's, Zack phoned to say he was on his way from the airport. I set the table, took leftover gazpacho out of the refrigerator, popped a baguette into the oven, and put out a package of Zack's favourite Boursin au poivre and a bowl of cherries and apricots I'd bought at the market on Saturday. Then, because it had been a difficult morning, I poured us each a glass of Merlot.

Zack was appreciative. "Wine, Boursin, and no swim trunks in sight." He held out his arms. "I'll do an extra twenty laps for the pleasure of just looking at you across the lunch table."

We held to our rule of not talking about the campaign while we ate. Zack had met some old friends of mine on the plane coming back to Regina, so he passed along their news; we discussed whether I should order two turkeys for Thanksgiving or just a very large turkey and a ham. The kind of inconsequential conversation that is the glue of a loving family. We took our tea into the living room and Zack settled back in his chair. "Time to get back to the real world," he said. "Did you find out who fed Peggy the questions about Lancaster?"

"Yes, I went to Peggy's this morning. She told me her contact was her informant in the Office of the City Clerk."

"So it wasn't Jill."

"No, but Jill did come to Peggy's this morning and asked for the name of the source. She might have wanted the information for Graham or it might have just been for her story. The important thing is Peggy didn't tell her. You and I are the only ones who know and we have to keep it that way."

"Fair enough. If this gets out, whoever it is could lose his or her job."

"And that can't happen. Enough people have been hurt."

Zack wheeled closer and took my hand. "Including you."

I nodded. "Including me. I'm trying hard to move ahead, but as long as Jill's around, I keep getting blindsided by memories."

"Did something happen today?"

"Nothing new. Just a nasty epiphany. When Mieka was a baby, Jill had an abortion. She was in rough shape so I stayed with her. Today it occurred to me that the father was probably Ian."

Zack touched my cheek. "If you'd known that Ian had fathered Jill's baby, would you have walked away that day?"

"No," I said. "I wouldn't walk away from any woman who was going through that."

"Then let it go," Zack said gently.

"I'm trying," I said. "But it's complicated. Jill and I share so much history. She's godmother to all my children and I was matron of honour at her wedding. So in one pan of the scales, there's all that generosity and love, and in the other there's fifteen years of betrayal. It's tough to get the balance right."

Zack kissed my hair. "You will," he said. "Give yourself a little time."

CHAPTER

11

Tuesday was the last day of September, and that morning when Angus arrived with the files on the Rose Street properties, the chill of autumn was definitely in the air. I'd made cinnamon buns, so the condo was filled with what a friend called "the scent of sentimentality." Cinnamon buns had been a favourite of Ian's, but Angus and I were not keen on remembering things past. In the twenty minutes we sat together at the butcher-block table, neither of us mentioned Ian's name.

After we'd cleared the dishes, we got to work. When Angus piled the files on top of one another, the stack was a foot high. He looked at it dubiously. "Mum, if you want to, we can go through these one by one, but I can tell you that none of them contains an offer to purchase from the city. Cronus never received a cent of city money."

"So Peggy was right," I said. "I'll bet some of the City Hall accountants pulled an all-nighter last night."

Angus pushed back his forelock. "Creative Bookkeeping 101," he said. "Zack says Cronus's motto was maximum rent, minimum upkeep. That's pretty much what the files indicate – except for the property at Number 12 Rose Street."

"What's the deal there?" I said.

"Well, a company called SPOT-LESS really does come to the house every two weeks to keep the place shipshape inside and out."

"And up goes a red flag," I said.

"It's not the only one," Angus said. "Mum, there's something really off about the history of that house. Cronus bought the property in 2000. He gutted the house, added a second floor with three bedrooms and three bathrooms, ripped up the basement, and added what looks from the plans like a big recreation room and three more bathrooms.

"When the renovations were complete, the house was rented to a company called B&D Enterprises. B&D were there for six years, and during their tenancy SPOT-LESS came at least three times a week, sometimes more. After B&D left, there were more renovations to the basement and a woman named Nell Standingready moved in."

"You've seen her," I said. "She was at the press conference we held after we learned that we'd inherited Cronus's houses. She quoted the Biblical passage about building a house on a firm foundation."

"A powerful woman and a memorable one," Angus said. "Anyway, she's lived in the house rent-free since she moved in."

"No other tenants?"

"No. Just Ms. Standingready. It's an interesting situation."

"And one worth looking into," I said.

After Angus left, I drove out to Costco to get a cash card for Angela and her kids. When I came home, I put Willie on his leash. My shoulder wasn't ready for handling both dogs, so I gave Pantera a hug, a dog biscuit, and an apology, and Willie and I headed for Rose Street, filled with resolve. It was still early, and street action was minimal: a couple of boys riding bikes that had seen better days, a man pushing a shopping cart with a dartboard poised precariously on a green garbage bag filled with empty liquor bottles, a drunk who was vomiting copiously on the sidewalk, and a mini-skirted platinum blonde with legs that wouldn't quit.

As I stood in front of Angela's house, I was beset with the same fears that had nagged me since the morning I was run off the road. If I had been in Angela's shoes, I would have loathed a woman like me whose family might not have been "fucking perfect" but who possessed all the tools they needed to make good lives. The metal sand pail was still lying on its side near the wire fence. When I spotted it, I remembered the little boy with the big spoon, and I knew that I'd passed the point of no return.

Jill had once told me that the easiest way to lure someone from their house was to begin taking pictures of it, so I positioned myself on the sidewalk, took out my phone, and started snapping away. It didn't take long for the front door of Number 15 to open. Angela came out, sat on the stoop, gave me a cursory glance, lit a cigarette, and blew a plume of smoke into the fall air. Her face was bruised and her lip was swollen. She didn't encourage communication, but the front gate was unlocked, so I joined her on the stoop. Angela had left the door open a crack and the hyperkinetic sounds of a kids' show squawked from the TV inside.

Willie sprawled on the space in front of the steps. Angela tensed. "Your dog looks like a bear," she said. "Is he okay with people?"

"He's fine," I said.

"Why are you taking pictures of the house?"

"It was just a trick to get you out here. I wanted to talk to you."

Her face grew sullen. "About what?"

"About the house across the street – the mustard-coloured one."

Angela laughed. "Were you wondering why the hell anybody would paint a house that colour?"

I smiled at her. "That question has crossed my mind. But this isn't about decorating. The man who owned the property died and he left us that house and quite a few more around here."

"Somebody told me you guys are going to fix up these shit-boxes."

"That's right."

"If I tell you what I know about Number 12 can we go to the top of the list?"

I took out my phone. "Give me your full name and your phone number, and I'll take care of it."

Angela gave me her contact information, and then she fell silent. The voices of SpongeBob and his friend Patrick drifted from the house. They were learning to use cuss words. Our granddaughters had gone through a SpongeBob phase, and I remembered the episode well.

Beside me, Angela lit a fresh cigarette. "I've been living here for four years. The only people I've ever seen in that house are the cleaners and Nell Standingready."

"Can you tell me anything about Nell Standingready?" I said.

"She's nice," Angela said. "She's nice to my kids, and she's nice to me. Some people look down on me because of the work I do, but I've got kids and I've got Eddie, so I don't have a choice. Besides, Nell's daughter, Rosalie, was a prostitute. She was in really bad shape. I heard she had a kid – poor kid, having a mother like that. There are certain things I won't do, but the word on the street was that Rosalie would do anything for a fix. I haven't seen her in years. She's probably dead. Anyway, Nell's always nice to me. When she makes bannock or hamburger soup, she always brings us some and she makes Jell-O cakes for my kids' birthdays."

"Nell doesn't have any other family?"

"Nobody ever visits her. There's a picture of a little girl in the living room, but when I asked Nell if she was the girl's Kookum, she started to cry. People have a right to their sorrows, so I never asked again."

"Your previous landlord kept files," I said. "Did you know that he was the one who paid for the cleaners?"

"No. I wondered, but I mind my own business. Not like Eddie. One day when Nell came over with some cookies she'd made for the kids, Eddie asked Nell who the fuck she thought she was having somebody else clean her house. I could see she was mad, but she didn't say anything. She just handed me the cookies and walked away. Nell really hates Eddie."

As she had watched Angela being loaded into the ambulance on Labour Day morning, Nell had said that the lake of fire and sulphur burned for the ones who broke the bodies and stole the souls of the innocents. As I looked at Angela's bruised face, I hoped that Nell was right.

I took a notebook out of my purse and wrote down the address of the Racette–Hunter Centre. "There are classes in martial arts for women at the centre," I said. "One of the classes meets every afternoon at one o'clock. There's child care, so you can bring your kids."

"A class full of women who wouldn't say shit if their mouths were full of it," she said. "I wouldn't fit in."

"You'd fit in. Most of the women in the class come from our neighbourhood and they're there to learn to protect themselves. The teacher is a woman named Linda Ironstar. She used to be a sex worker who was in an abusive relationship. She was worried about what her kids were seeing in their home, so she took a class in martial arts."

"And now she's the teacher?" Angela said. "I'll think about it."

"Good," I said. I wrote down my phone number. Then I took out the cash card and held it out to her. "I wouldn't blame you for throwing this in my face, but I don't know what else to do."

Angela took the card and her mouth twisted in a wry smile. "I could use this to get myself some gym clothes so I could take that class," she said. "Or I could use it to buy Eddie a big-screen TV to replace the one he broke when he threw it at me. What do you think, Joanne?"

"Your choice," I said.

She shook her head. "Jesus, Joanne. You really are something else."

Angela watched as I went down the steps and picked up Willie's leash. "Are you going to see Nell?"

"I'm going to try."

"Do you know what sweetgrass is?" she said.

I nodded. "Sometimes the elders brought it to meetings when we were trying to get Racette-Hunter built. The opposition to building a training centre in North Central was fierce. We used to begin meetings with a smoke blessing to cleanse our thoughts."

"So you know how to smudge."

"I do."

"That's good," Angela said. "Nell believes someone put bad medicine on that house. She smudges to drive it out."

The new-mown-hay scent of sweetgrass did indeed meet me when Nell Standingready opened the door to Number 12 Rose Street. She was wearing a turquoise blouse, a long grey cotton skirt, and beaded moccasins. When I'd seen her previously, Nell's steel grey hair had been in a single braid that reached almost to her waist, but that morning her hair was loose. She did not greet me, nor did she invite me in.

I took the initiative. "I'm Joanne Shreve," I said. "I've come to ask you about your house."

"I don't talk about this house," she said and her lips set in a line.

"If you'd rather I just showed myself around, that's fine too."

She reached her arms out as if physically barring me from crossing the threshold. "Nobody comes in my house."

I took a step nearer her. I kept my voice gentle. "I know this is your home, and nobody wants to change that, but my husband and I now own this property and a number of other properties on Rose Street. I just want to see the house, so I'll know what repairs need to be made."

Nell Standingready's voice was a growl. "Get away," she said. "The house is fine."

"You don't have to let me in now," I said. "But if I send a written notice, I'll have the legal right to enter the house when I come back tomorrow."

Her eyes widened, and for the first time I saw fear. "Leave us alone. The house is fine. Just go."

"I'm sorry," I said. "But if you don't let me in, I'll come back tomorrow with the police."

"No," she wailed. Her body swayed, but when I reached out to steady her she backed into the hall, moved slowly towards the living room, and collapsed into an old armchair. She was breathing heavily. On the table beside her was a framed photograph of a child. A braid of sweetgrass smouldered in a bowl beside the photograph. The smell was overpowering.

"Just leave us alone. Please."

"I'll just have a quick look at the house, and I'll be gone."

"No . . . no . . ." She was keening.

"I won't be long," I said. I moved quickly. In the files, I had seen pictures of the other houses Cronus owned. Many of the photos were stomach-turning. I didn't remember seeing any of Number 12. The house was in good shape: no black mould, broken windows, or hanging screens; no holes in the plaster, blistering paint, or peeling wallpaper; no blood or feces on the walls. The place was shabby but neat as a new pin. Between them, Nell and SPOT-LESS did a good job. The appliances in the kitchen were decades old, but they shone. The counter was clean and the deep red linoleum floor was swept. The bathroom on the main floor was small but immaculate. Upstairs there were three bedrooms with mirrored ceilings. As Angus said, each bedroom had its own bathroom.

The door to the basement was just off the kitchen. The steps were steep, and I was grateful for the railing. The space I came into felt small and crowded. In addition to the furnace, a washing machine, two laundry tubs, and a dryer were jammed together strangely close to the stairs. For a moment I looked around, confused. Then I realized that the rear half of the cellar – the space Angus said might have been a recreation room – was walled off. I could see no door in the blank wall.

Nell Standingready's voice from the top of the stairs was a wail. "Now you've seen it. Go."

"What's in there?" I said.

When she didn't answer, I came up the stairs and faced her. "Nell, you have to help me. Bad things have happened, I know. But more bad things are happening, and I think somehow they're connected to this house. Why did you attend Cronus's funeral?" Nell didn't answer, only retreated into the kitchen. I followed her. "When we looked at the deeds for all the property he owned, there were list prices for all the properties except this one. 12 Rose Street was marked 'Not For Sale at Any Price.' Do you have any idea why?"

She teetered and then sat heavily on a kitchen chair. I feared I'd pushed too hard. I went into the living room and picked up the photo of the little girl. The child wasn't smiling, but her black hair was neatly cut in a Dutch bob, and her eyes were bright with intelligence and life. When I sensed that Nell Standingready had come into the room, I put the photo back down beside the smouldering sweetgrass.

"Do you know how to smudge?" Nell asked.

"Yes," I said.

Nell picked up the braid of sweetgrass and an eagle feather and fanned the smoke. I swept my hands through the smoke, touched my hair, my eyes, my ears, my heart, and my body – purifying myself. Nell put down the bowl with the sweetgrass and picked up the photograph of the child.

"Your granddaughter?" I said.

Nell nodded.

"She's lovely," I said.

"She's dead." Nell gazed at the picture for a very long time. Finally, she placed it back on the table. "Her name was Ellen," she said, and the agony in her voice knifed my heart.

When I got back in the Volvo, I had to rest my head on the steering wheel and take some deep breaths before I felt ready to drive. I checked Canada 411 for the address of SPOT-LESS. Their office was at Winnipeg and 8th – not far at all. Within ten minutes I was climbing the stairs that led to a warren of offices over Simply Pho You, a Vietnamese restaurant that promised the most savoury pho in the city.

The smells of the restaurant followed me as I peered at the names on the frosted-glass windows of the dingy offices, searching for SPOT-LESS. It was at the end of the hall and it was a compelling advertisement for the calibre of the services it offered. The paint on the company's door was fresh; the frosted-glass windows were bright, and the brass doorknob gleamed. The office itself was tiny. Seemingly, SPOT-LESS didn't encourage walk-in customers. The single welcoming note in the space was a flourishing salmon geranium on the counter that separated visitors from employees. There was no chair for those of us on the wrong side of the counter.

When I'd entered the office, the bell over the door tinkled, and a man who looked to be in his eighties appeared. Age had whittled him down. He was no taller than five feet, but he was dapper: his thinning white hair was neatly combed; his black turtleneck and slacks were nicely fitted to show off his trim physique, and he had splashed on the Old Spice lavishly. His old blue eyes were quick to take my measure, and when he spoke, his voice was high and querulous. "State your business," he said. "I'm a busy man."

"Actually, my business is your business," I said. "My name's Joanne Shreve. My husband and I inherited Cronus's properties in North Central. We'd like SPOT-LESS to give all the houses a thorough cleaning. Thirty-six properties in all. I'll send you the addresses this afternoon. It's a large job. Can you handle it?"

He turned on the charm. "You bet your sweet bippy we can," he said. He reached his arm across the counter for a handshake. The counter was high, so it was a stretch. "The name's Harold Haney, Mrs. Shreve. I'll have to hire some casuals, but we can be on the job by the end of the day. Time and half for my people if they work the weekend."

"That won't be a problem," I said. "We want the job done quickly, and I was impressed by your work at 12 Rose Street."

He sniffed the air. "Sweetgrass," he said. "You were at the house."

"I just came from there. I met Nell Standingready."

Harold Haney narrowed his eyes. "She let you inside?"

"I needed to get an idea about what repairs were necessary," I said. "But the fact that I was inside her home upset Nell so I just went through the house quickly and left."

"Did you see the entire house?"

"Yes, and I saw how the basement was blocked off. Mr. Haney, before I left Nell smudged me with sweetgrass. I'm familiar with the ceremony. Nell was purifying me, cleansing me of something bad in the house."

Harold Haney nodded. "She does that every time the wife and me finish cleaning," he said.

"When did Cronus block off the basement?" I asked. "I have his records, so I can find out when the construction took place, but you could save me some time."

Harold Haney's face pinched. He took his time deliberating. It was clear he didn't want to disclose anything, but I was now a client and a major one. In the end he decided to open up. "The work was done about ten years ago," he said. "I don't remember the date, but I remember the company had to rush to beat the snow."

"Thanks," I said. "I'll go through the file and find the exact date. Mr. Haney, there were no structural repairs on any of the other houses. From what I can see most of them are in far worse shape than 12 Rose Street. Why was Number 12 the house that was 'improved'?"

"Because that was the party house." He spat out the words.

"A lot of Cronus's houses are party houses," I said.

"Not like that one was," he said. "12 Rose Street was for perverts – rich perverts. They could do whatever they wanted there. It was a private house with thick doors and a bouncer. You couldn't get in unless you knew someone."

"A sex club," I said.

"Yes."

"And SPOT-LESS did the cleaning."

"My wife and me did the cleaning," he said. "Cronus and I went way back. SPOT-LESS did a lot of work for Cronus's father. He was a piece of work – deacon in the church but meaner than a junkyard dog. When Ron Jr. was in high school, Ron Sr. started sending him to collect rent money from delinquent tenants. If Ron Jr. didn't come back with the money, the old man would beat the hide off him. By the time he started buying houses in North Central, Ron Jr. had learned the business. When the opportunity to screw Ron Sr. came, Ron Jr. didn't hesitate. He cleaned the old man out, changed his name from Ronald Mewhort Junior to Cronus, and never looked back.

"Over the years, Cronus was generous in sending jobs our way. The woman who ran the sex club paid Cronus a bundle to renovate and rent the house at 12 Rose Street and Cronus paid SPOT-LESS a lot of money to the keep it clean. Everything had to be confidential and Cronus didn't trust anybody else to keep their mouth shut." Harold Haney shuddered. "My wife and I saw some terrible things. We never spoke of it. Not even to each other."

"But the club closed."

"Yes."

"When did it close?"

His mouth hardened. "I don't remember. It was a while back."

"But you still clean the house every two weeks. Why?"

"Because that's the way Cronus wanted it."

"Tomorrow, I want you to start on Number 15 Rose Street. After the house has been cleaned, I want you to make a list of everything that has to be done to make it safe and warm."

"Consider it done," he said, and he gave me a smart military salute. "I'll need your address for the billing," he said. I gave it to him and started to leave, but Mr. Haney stopped me. "One more thing," he said. "Was there a good turnout at the funeral?"

"No," I said. "Just six people."

"I should have been there," he said. "Cronus was always decent to the wife and me. But I'm a coward. I'm afraid of death."

"Most of us are," I said. "But Cronus wasn't. I don't think he had any regrets at the end, and he died bravely."

When I reached the door to Simply Pho You, I went in. Zack once told me about a former Supreme Court Justice who said practising trial law was like skating. The secret to skating was finding the balance between pushing and gliding; the secret to trial law was finding the balance between action and reflection. Lately, all I'd been doing was pushing. The prospect of reflecting over a bowl of the best spicy beef pho in the city was seductive.

The pho *was* excellent: the vegetables and the noodles had crunch, the beef slivers were tender, and the broth, redolent of cinnamon, star anise, basil, and red chilies, was comforting. It was restorative. So was the chance simply to sit and reflect. That morning had convinced me that Cronus had died because of something that had happened at 12 Rose Street. A private sex club where any fantasy could be fulfilled was fertile ground for tragedy. Slater Doyle's panicked call on his cell after Zack's reference to foundations was a slender reed to cling to, but I had an idea about how I could use it.

I'd scheduled a press conference the next morning for Zack and Brock to talk about Peggy Kreviazuk's allegations that the city's affordable housing allotment had ended up in Lancaster's bank account. Our original choice of venue for the press conference was Racette-Hunter. Zack and Brock had spent over a year wheedling, cajoling, appealing, and pressuring the public and private partners that had to come together to make the community centre a reality. They had succeeded, and the financial records of Racette-Hunter were available to anyone who cared to see them. The contrast between the transparency of Racette-Hunter's bookkeeping and the murky accounting practices at City Hall would have been dramatic.

But I couldn't shake the image of Slater Doyle's discomfort when Zack assured Nell Standingready that her house would have a firm foundation. I took a toonie from my change purse. It was time for a coin toss. Heads was Rose Street; tails was Racette-Hunter. When I saw the Queen's profile, I phoned Milo and asked him to move Brock's Wednesday morning press conference to the sidewalk outside Number 12 Rose Street. One of Milo's many strengths was that once a decision was made, he never questioned it. That day, he simply said, "Got it," and broke the connection.

I'd just finished paying my bill and picking up Simply Pho You's takeout menu to add to our family's collection when Peggy Kreviazuk called me. Her voice was controlled, but I could hear the tension. "Joanne, I've called the police, but I thought you and Zack should know I've been the victim of a home invasion."

"My God, Peggy, are you all right?"

"Shaken, but I'm fine. It all happened so quickly. The doorbell rang. I answered it and four men wearing ski masks pushed into the house and began wrecking things. When one of them picked up that photograph of Tommy Douglas on the mantle, I grabbed it out of his hand. He raised his arm. He was going to hit me. One of the other men stopped him. He said, 'Don't hurt her.' Then the first man said, "We were supposed to beat the crap out of her, remember?" Then the man who saved me said, "Fuck that. Let's get out of here." And as quickly as they'd come, they were gone."

"I'll be right there," I said. I stepped outside. I had two calls to make. Zack's phone went straight to voicemail, so I left a message. Jill Oziowy answered on the first ring. Clearly she was anxious to talk, but I didn't give her a chance. "I've got a story for you," I said. "Some goons just broke into Peggy Kreviazuk's house. They smashed her furniture and threatened her. Peggy told me you were at her house this morning trying to find out the name of her source about taxpayer money going to Lancaster."

"Peggy didn't tell me the name."

"That's because Peggy's an honourable person. She protected a friend. But you told Graham Meighen that Peggy wouldn't reveal her source, didn't you?"

"Jo, I never meant for anything like this to happen. You have to believe me."

"Why? Why do I have to believe you about anything? Just get a crew from NationTV to Peggy's house ASAP. You know the address, and I'm sure that, thanks to you, Graham does too. Show the world what your new beau is capable of when he doesn't get his way." As I ended the call, I was shaking with fury.

A police car was already parked in front of Peggy's when I arrived. It wasn't long before the NationTV truck rolled up; it was followed shortly by two media vans and a car with a reporter and photographer from our local paper. All journalists are aware of the first principle of tabloid reporting: "If it bleeds, it leads." There had been no bloodshed at Peggy's, but the destruction wrought on her pretty home was sobering, and Peggy's account of how one of her assailants said they had been instructed to "beat the crap out of her" was chilling.

Despite her ordeal, Peggy was careful to position herself so that during her interviews the camera caught her flanked by the portraits of Tommy Douglas and Woodrow Lloyd on her mantle. Peggy had been involved in politics long enough to understand the usefulness of the soundbite, so she answered questions succinctly. Her message was simple: "People in this city should be able to ask questions about where their taxes are going without being physically attacked."

After the police and the media left, I stayed with Peggy to wait for the insurance adjuster. She seemed fine, but I was relieved that I was able to convince her to join us for dinner that night. When the insurance man arrived, Peggy walked me to the door. "The struggle continues," she said. As I always did, I replied, "And so do we." Over the years, we'd said the words a thousand times, but standing in the rubble of Peggy's living room, the exchange had a special resonance. Peggy felt the intensity too. She embraced me. "We can't let them intimidate us, Joanne. If we back down, they win, and nothing changes."

"I know," I said. "We can't allow that to happen."

As I started down Peggy's walk, I felt strong and determined, and then I saw Jill. She was coming towards Peggy's, but as soon as she spotted me, she turned. Her cowardice unleashed something ugly in me. I ran to her and grabbed her arm roughly. "Those thugs threatened her, you know. Peggy heard one of them say their orders were to 'beat the crap out of her.'"

Jill was very pale. "But she's all right. Our reporter said Peggy's fine."

I was livid. "How the hell could she be 'fine'? She's eighty-two years old, Jill. She was sitting on her sofa listening to the news when goons broke in and tore her house apart. And they would have torn her apart too."

"Jo, you have to believe me, I didn't know there would be retaliation against Peggy."

"That's because you never thought about Peggy at all. She was just a tool to set the wheels in motion so you could get a story."

"Jo, please. Peggy's a friend. I would never sacrifice a friend—"

I cut her off. "You'd never sacrifice a friend to get what you wanted? Have you forgotten who you're talking to? I was your friend, but that didn't keep you away from my husband." I tightened my grip on her arm. "And while we're on the subject of my husband. Was the baby that you aborted Ian's?"

She crumpled. When she responded, her voice was a whisper. "Of course. From the moment I met Ian there was never anyone else."

"That's a coincidence," I said. "Because that's the way it was for me too."

Except for the morning after the abortion, I had never seen Jill cry, but she was crying now. "Jo, you're not the only one who suffered. After the abortion, Ian was very tender with me, but we never had vaginal intercourse again. He said he didn't want to put me through the pain of another unwanted pregnancy."

I was incredulous. "Jill, have you lost your mind? I don't want to hear how tender my husband was with you. And I don't want to hear that, out of concern for you, he denied himself the pleasures of vaginal sex. Actually, Ian and I conceived two children during that period, so obviously he didn't deny himself totally."

Jill hung her head like a whipped dog. "I've never known you to be cruel."

"Then get away from me. Go back to Toronto."

I was relieved Zack wasn't there when I got home. He was always sensitive to my emotional temperature and I was feverish with anger. I stripped off my clothes, turned the shower on hot and high, and tried to wash away the last two hours.

I had limited success. I'd arranged with my new best friend, Harold Haney, to have a SPOT-LESS crew clean up Peggy's house as soon as the police and the insurance company gave the go ahead. The house could be restored, but I wasn't so sure about me. After I towelled off, I wiped the steam from the mirror and looked at my reflection. Jill was right. I had never been a cruel person, but when she told me about Ian's tenderness to her after the abortion I wanted to hurt her and I wanted to hurt him. Ian was beyond pain, but Jill wasn't, and remembering the pleasure I felt in wounding her, I was sick at heart.

Until that morning, I'd handled the situation as well as anyone could have. When Slater Doyle broke the news, my first thoughts were about how I could lessen the blow for Mieka and her brothers. I had laid out the facts as I knew them, without embellishment and without anger. It appeared to have worked. I had vowed that I was not going to let a past betrayal ruin future happiness, and that appeared to be working too.

Incredible as it now seemed, I had never once pictured Jill and Ian tangling limbs and exchanging juices in the act of love. Jill's admission that in the years after the abortion she and Ian never had vaginal sex changed all that. Now my mind was filled with a kaleidoscope of images of the two of them engaged in discovering all the strokings and penetrations that aroused their lover: Ian tonguing Jill's clitoris until she climaxed; Jill sucking Ian's nipples as he moaned with pleasure; Ian sliding his erect penis into Jill's anus as she ecstatically urged him to go deeper.

I shook my head to clear my mind, then I dressed, dried my hair, and put on moisturizer and lipstick. I still had one photo of Ian. It was of the two of us the night our party won the unwinnable first election. I'd hung the picture in the corner of our family room that I used as an office. I went into the family room and took down the photo. It was a nice picture of a happy moment. I was nine months' pregnant with Mieka and I was beaming. Ian was beaming too. According to Valerie Smythe, Ian and Jill had begun their affair a few weeks before E-Day. I walked out into the hall, dropped the framed photograph down the chute our condo reserved for non-recyclable garbage, then went back inside, hung the portrait of Cronus in the place where the photo of Ian and I had been, and made myself tea and toast.

By the time Zack came home, I was on my second cup of Earl Grey and I was able to pass for sane. When I bent to embrace him, Zack drew a deep and appreciative breath. "You smell good."

"Thank Taylor," I said. "That's my birthday body lotion. How was your day?"

"Very informative. But you first. How's Peggy doing?"

"She's amazing," I said. "She was brilliant with the media. When I left, she was dealing with the insurance adjuster."

"How bad is the damage?"

"Bad enough," I said. "The dining room chairs and the end tables in the living room will have to be replaced, and they smashed the mirror over the mantle and Peggy's mother's collection of Royal Doulton figurines. Peggy was sanguine. She said that at her age she's learned to let go of things, but I'd like to keep an eye on her for a while. She agreed to come out for dinner with us, and I'm hoping I can convince her to stay in our guest room tonight."

"Good idea," Zack said. "Where do you want to eat?"

"Peggy told me she likes the new vegan place on Cornwall Street – the Wheat Grass Smoothie."

Zack grimaced. "Does she have a second choice?"

"Well, she raves about the black and bleu burger at Bushwakkers."

"Bushwakkers it is. It's close so nobody has to drive, and we can sample the brews to our hearts' content."

"Now tell me about your day."

"I spent most of it with developers and Chamber of Commerce types."

"Enemy territory," I said. "That can't have been much fun."

"Actually, it was. Peggy's revelation that large sums of city money have gone straight into the Lancaster bank account has really pissed them off. A lot of them are Lancaster's competitors. As long as the city threw them a meaty bone now and again they were fine, but learning that while they've been playing nice, Lancaster's been raking in the tax dollars has raised their ire. They won't vote for me, but they say they're not giving another cent to the Ridgeway campaign, and I believe them."

"And nobody from Ridgeway's campaign has approached them to discredit what Peggy said."

"Nope, apparently the information Peggy passed along was solid. Milo's getting one of our supporters to launch a social media campaign demanding a public investigation."

"So some good has come of Peggy's ordeal," I said. "She's certainly paid in hard coin for telling the truth. I ran into Jill outside Peggy's house this afternoon. She said she didn't know there would be retaliation against Peggy and that she would never sacrifice a friend."

Zack scowled. "I bet that went straight to the bone."

"It did." I took a deep breath. "I lashed out, and Jill said she'd suffered too. She told me that the baby she aborted was Ian's, and that after the abortion she and Ian never had vaginal sex again. Apparently, he wanted to spare Jill the pain of another unwanted pregnancy."

Zack was the master of the unreadable expression, but that afternoon he made no attempt to hide his disgust. "What a prick," he said.

"That's pretty much my take too," I said. "But Ian didn't renounce all sex with Jill – just vaginal. The affair didn't end. For the next fifteen years they were doing something to each other. Since I came home from Peggy's, visions of Jill and Ian in all one hundred positions of the *Kama Sutra* have been dancing in my head."

Zack wheeled over to me. "Let's sit down on the couch and neck." He squeezed my leg. "You do realize that you're smiling again."

"You always make life better."

"That works both ways," Zack said. "Let's not waste time fooling around on the couch. It's been years since I checked out the *Kama Sutra*. There must be a couple of positions we still haven't tried."

After we made love, I took my ceramic Ernest Lindner off the nightstand, balanced it on my chest, and looked at Ernie's face.

"Penny for your thoughts," Zack said.

"I was thinking that with both you and Ernie Linder on my side, I might just be able to make it through the rest of the day."

Zack reached over and tousled my hair. "This really has been rough on you, hasn't it?"

"It's been rough on all of us," I said. "And it's not going to get any better. Zack, I moved Brock's press conference tomorrow morning from the R-H Centre to 12 Rose Street, but now I'm getting cold feet."

"That doesn't sound catastrophic, but if you're worried, we can go back to the original plan."

I took a deep breath. "No. We have to stay the course. Ever since I saw Slater Doyle's reaction when you said we were going to make certain all the houses we own in North Central would meet the building code, I've had a gut feeling that somehow Cronus's murder and everything that's happened since is connected to 12 Rose Street."

Zack frowned. "All this because of Slater's reaction? Jo, I've learned to trust your instincts, but that's quite a leap."

"I'm hoping that changing the venue of the press conference will spook Ridgeway's people into making a move.

Something strange is going on with that house." As I related what I'd learned from Angus and Harold Haney, Zack was rapt, but when I told him that Nell Standingready constantly burns sweetgrass to try to rid her house of its bad medicine, he was incredulous.

"Bad medicine? Jesus, Jo, what are we talking about here?"

"I don't know. All I know is that Nell did not want me to see the house, but I insisted. She was beside herself. Zack, at least half of the basement is sealed off – enclosed by concrete walls. Harold Haney says that Number 12 was a sex club for 'rich perverts.' Admission was for members only. The door was always locked and the walls were thick."

Zack's eyes widened. "I heard about that club, though I didn't know exactly where it was. I was invited to go a few times, but it wasn't my scene. Apparently customers could get whatever they wanted there, but from what I heard the people who frequented that place were into seriously kinky stuff. A few years ago, the club suddenly closed."

"It was almost ten years ago," I said. "And that's when the room was sealed off. Mr. Haney couldn't remember the exact date, but he said the workers had to rush to beat the snow."

"So we're moving the press conference to make the Ridgeway camp believe we know something incriminating about the history of 12 Rose Street. You're really rolling the dice, Jo."

"I know I am," I said. "But Peggy's last words to me today were 'If we back down, they win, and nothing changes.' She's right. We'll be cautious until this blows over, but we can't back down. We have to keep the Ridgeway campaign's feet to the fire."

Zack moved to transfer his body to his chair. "Okay," he said. "Let's do it."

Zack and I showered, and then he made calls while I went downstairs to talk to Brock. The change of venue would be a gamble, and Brock would be at the centre of it. As I explained my reasons for the move, I watched for Brock's reaction. There was none. In fact, he was so preoccupied he didn't seem to be following what I said. Finally, I stopped in mid-sentence. "Brock, are you okay with all this?"

"Sure. I'll be there."

"If you don't like the idea, we can go back to the original plan."

Brock rubbed his temples as if to clear his head. "I get it, and I'm in. I'm having trouble processing something I just heard. Michael called me a few minutes ago to tell me he and Slater Doyle were married yesterday." Brock shook his head. "I still can't believe it. When Michael and I were together I was sure we'd both found what we wanted. Looking back, I guess Slater has always had a hold on Michael."

"But Michael left Slater for you."

"It wasn't that straightforward. Slater and Michael's affair was long-term but very private. Slater had a wife."

"I've met his daughter, Bridie. She's a beautiful child. Where is her mother in all this?"

"She died," Brock said. "It was very sudden. She seemed to be in perfect health. She was on the treadmill, and she collapsed. Apparently, it was a genetic problem with her heart. After she died, Michael assumed he and Slater could be open about their relationship, but Slater wasn't ready. They split up, and by the time I came along, Michael was willing to try again. It was the best time of my life, but in retrospect, I realize Michael never severed his ties with Slater."

"Were the ties personal?"

"I didn't think so. Michael and Slater were both close to Graham Meighen so it seemed natural enough for them to stay in touch. Apparently, the relationship was more complex than I thought." Brock's obsidian eyes were troubled. "Jo, I'm certain Michael doesn't love Slater Doyle. Since

Michael told me about the marriage I've been racking my brain trying to figure out why the man I love, a man whom I'm sure still loves me, just married someone else."

Brock joined us for dinner at Bushwakkers. A couple of hours with good food, good company, and a good band always lightens the burden. When the four of us left the restaurant, we were restored. Zack and I convinced Peggy to spend the night with us. The destruction of Peggy's house was the lead story on the late news on all three of our city's network outlets. Thankfully, we were beside Peggy when images of her home's slashed upholstery, broken furniture, and shattered keepsakes filled the screen. The reporters hinted at the possibility of a connection between Peggy's comments on *Quinlan Live* and the havoc that persons unknown had wreaked on her property, and then the cameras turned to Peggy for her reaction.

Shoulders squared, voice steady as she vowed to continue to speak the truth, she was an appealing figure. As much as I was sickened by the cruelty to which Peggy had been subjected, I knew her misfortune would bring us votes. I also knew E-Day was still twenty-three days away, and a great deal could happen in three weeks.

CHAPTER

12

Peggy once told me that the secret of not being a bore when you reach your eighties is realizing that the state of your bowels is of little or no interest to others. Wednesday morning when I came back from my run, she and Taylor were debating whether art that was created for a solely commercial purpose such as advertising or set design was still art.

Taylor's birth mother Sally Love's work continued to earn money through sales of posters, postcards, and the like, and Taylor herself had built a respectable savings account from her connection with Corydon. But in both cases, companies were still dealing with the rights to original pieces of art. Now Corydon had asked Taylor to create a series of paintings that featured beautiful young men searching for identity. The idea intrigued Taylor, but she was wary of becoming a commercial artist. The discussion she and Peggy were having was spirited and punctuated by laughter. I poured myself a cup of coffee and left them to it.

The press conference was scheduled for 10:00 a.m. Peggy was determined to go. I was apprehensive, but I knew once

Peggy made up her mind there was no way to dissuade her. Taylor had left for school, and I was checking Milo's latest figures on likely voters in Ward 6 when Margot brought Lexi over to show off the new baby tooth peeking through her gum. Peggy was fond of children and when she began playing ride-a-horsey with Lexi, Margot took my arm. "Let's take advantage of the lull in the action," she said. "We haven't had a chance to visit for a while and Lexi will play ride-a-horsey for hours or until Peggy's leg gives out."

I laughed. "Which will be never," I said. "Peggy is tireless, which is more than I can say for me."

"You do look a little weary," she said. "Why don't we book one of those spa treatments I gave you for your birthday?"

I rubbed my eyes. "God, that seems like a thousand years ago."

Margot raised an eyebrow. "It was less than a week." She leaned close to me. "Jo, what's the matter?"

"Too much to talk about now. Margot, are you planning to come to the press conference?"

"Do you want me to?"

"I'd appreciate it. Michael called Brock yesterday to announce that he and Slater Doyle had just been married."

Margot's brow furrowed. "How did Brock take it?"

"He's upset, but more than anything, he's baffled. He still loves Michael and he believes Michael still loves him."

"I'm baffled too," Margot said. "The three of us spent time together when Brock and I first began considering the intrauterine insemination. Brock wanted Michael to be part of the discussion and Michael was very supportive. All that ended when Brock told Michael we'd conceived a child through intercourse. According to Brock, Michael was beside himself with rage. I never said anything to Brock, but Michael's reaction didn't ring true to me. At first, I felt responsible, but now I'm not at all certain that the breakup was my fault."

"Whatever is going on with Michael, I'd appreciate it if you were there to support Brock," I said. "I wouldn't be surprised if Slater pulled some stunt to throw Brock off his game."

"I'll be watching," Margot said. "I've had some experience with boyish hijinks."

"Another favour," I said. "Could you bring Peggy with you? There may be some unpleasantness, and I'd be relieved to know you can spirit her away if there's trouble."

The pavement in front of 12 Rose Street was crowded with curious onlookers, and the media was out in full force. Slater Doyle was there, and surprise of surprises, he'd brought Dr. Michael Goetz along to keep him company. It was a cheap trick and when I pointed the two men out to Margot, she didn't miss a beat. Margot handed Lexi to me and walked over to where Brock was talking to some journalists, took his hand, and held it against her baby bump. I glanced at Michael Goetz. He looked as if he was about to spontaneously combust.

I had my own human drama with which to deal. Peggy and I had found a spot that was close to Zack and Brock but out of camera range. Peggy eyed the crowd. "Jill Oziowy's over there at the NationTV van. Shall we go over and say hello?"

"You go ahead."

"You two haven't resolved your problem?"

"No," I said.

"You and Jill will iron this out," she said. "You're both intelligent enough to realize that trustworthy friends should be cherished." I just nodded.

The press conference went well. Brock set the tone by saying our campaign did not have all the answers, but we had enough evidence to suggest that Scott Ridgeway and Lancaster owed the public some explanations. Zack then laid out exactly what we knew about taxpayer money going straight to Lancaster and suggested that it was time for serious investigative journalists to serve their community and start digging.

Jill was first off the mark with a question: "Is the Shreve campaign sending a message by deciding to stage a second press conference here on Rose Street?"

"We are," Zack said. 'To quote Edmund Burke, 'The only thing necessary for the triumph of evil is for good people to do nothing.'"

"And 12 Rose Street connects to that how?"

Zack half turned his chair so he could point to the mustard-yellow house. "Our campaign has some knowledge about what went on in that house, but we need more information. We believe that discovering the truth about the history of 12 Rose Street will shed light on what's been going on at City Hall.

"But we need help. Political campaigns are staffed largely by volunteers. If we're going to unearth the facts, journalists like you and your colleagues have to become part of the investigation. We're also asking Regina's citizens to accept the challenge and get involved."

Slater and Michael didn't stay till the end of the news conference, but when they left both men appeared dazed. After the press conference ended, Zack and Brock stayed behind to talk to some of the Rose Street neighbours. I was waiting with Peggy, Margot, and Lexi when Jill approached.

Part of Jill's charm had always been her immense vitality, but that day despite the makeup that had been skilfully applied for the television camera, she seemed spent. She touched my arm. "Can we talk for a minute?"

I stepped away. "There's nothing more to say."

"If you ever change your mind . . ."

"I'm not going to. The kids and I are finished with you, Jill."

"Message received," she said. "Will you tell Zack that I'm committed to this story, and I'm going to dig until I find something."

"I'll pass that along," I said.

———

Zack had half an hour till his next meeting so I spirited him off to the Noodle House to rev up the troops while I made yet another to-do list. As always there was music in our campaign headquarters. Zack knew many things, but he never had children growing up in the 1980s and 1990s. When he was greeted by a searing guitar solo, he frowned. "Can people actually think in here with all that noise?"

"That's not 'noise.' That's 'Today' by The Smashing Pumpkins," I said. "A seminal song."

"You know all that?"

"Milo knows all that. He was the one who figured out that a constant menu of classic rock would bring people into campaign headquarters. He was also the one who was smart enough to suggest that we call our headquarters 'the Noodle House' because it sounds cool."

Zack was thoughtful. "You're very fond of Milo, aren't you?"

"I am," I said. "I like people who commit to what they do. That's one of the many reasons I love you."

Zack wheeled over, put his arm around my legs, and squeezed. "That goes both ways, Jo. You're doing a helluva job with this campaign. Moving the press conference to Rose Street was a good call."

"The jury's still out on that," I said. "Incidentally, Jill asked me to tell you she's committed to this story and she's not going to quit until she knows the truth."

"That was the response I was hoping for," Zack said. "The more people who know about this, the less vulnerable we are." His cell beeped a reminder. "Time to head out. I'll just say a quick hello to everybody."

When I got back to my place by the door, my cell rang. I picked up. The urgent, imploring tone of the caller's voice was immediately recognizable. "Joanne, it's Liz Meighen. Are you free to talk?"

"Yes," I said. I walked outside. It was chilly, but the sun was warm and I was very eager to hear from Liz.

"I know I should have been in touch sooner. I should have called to explain why I didn't come that morning." Her voice faltered. "Suddenly my life is full of 'should haves.'"

"As long as you're all right."

"I'm not really," she said slowly. "I'm on a new medication and it's making me confused – but I think I already told you that – the night I forgot to put the white chocolate in the pots de crème."

"And the dessert turned out brilliantly. Liz, we're all getting older. These things happen."

"Not the kind of things that happen to me. One day – I'm not sure exactly which day it was – I drove to the drugstore. It was the same drugstore we've been going to for thirty years. It's six blocks from my house and I couldn't remember how to get home."

"Have you talked to your doctor?"

"I don't know where he is," she said.

"Are you at home now?"

"No. I'm in a safe place. When everything started spinning out of control, I knew I had to get away."

"Where are you?"

"It's better for you not to know. That way Graham can't put pressure on you. He can't be trusted, Joanne. I don't know who to trust any more. I thought my psychiatrist was on my side. He's always been supportive, but lately I've had the feeling he was undermining me. Working against me. Does that sound crazy? This new medication jumbles my thoughts."

"What you said doesn't sound crazy," I said. "Do you have any idea why your psychiatrist would decide to work against you?"

"Yes. The morning I was supposed to see you, I discovered that Dr. Goetz is one of them."

My veins tightened. "The psychiatrist you're seeing is Michael Goetz?"

"Do you know him?"

"We met briefly. Liz, when you said Dr. Goetz was 'one of them,' what did you mean?"

Suddenly, she was angry. "You don't believe me," she said.

"I do," I said quickly. "I just didn't understand what you meant."

She said the words slowly as if she were explaining something that was self-evident. "Dr. Goetz was one of the men in Graham's group. The morning I was supposed to see you, I overheard Graham talking to him on the phone. Graham was very angry. Of course, I couldn't hear Dr. Goetz's side of the conversation, but Graham wouldn't listen to him. He just kept shouting, 'You've got to do it. There's no other way.' Joanne, I know Graham is trying to convince Dr. Goetz to get me committed so he can get power of attorney and take over my money."

"Liz, I'm your friend, and I know what you've been going through, but for your own sake you have to be careful not to jump to conclusions."

"I'm not jumping to conclusions. Graham's having financial difficulties. The night before I was supposed to meet you, he asked me for money and I turned him down. When I overheard him talking to Michael Goetz, I was sure I knew exactly what was happening. I confronted Graham. He said he'd been trying to convince Dr. Goetz to change my medication because the medication I was on was scrambling my mind and he was afraid I'd say something – something – something – I can't remember the word. It's a word I used to know, but I can't remember it any more." There was an edge of hysteria in her voice. "I've always been able to remember words. I'm losing my words, Joanne. I'm losing myself."

"Liz, you need help. Is there someone there I can talk to?"

She lowered her voice to a whisper. "I'm not sure if there's anyone I can trust here."

"You told me you were in a safe place."

"I thought I was, but now . . ." Her voice rose till it was almost a shout. "Don't trust anybody. Do you hear what I'm saying, Joanne? Do not trust anybody." Liz had trouble hanging up the phone. It sounded as if she'd dropped it. There was background noise – another voice – someone offering to help. Then, finally the phone was back in its cradle and there was silence.

I tried *69 to check the number of the last call I'd received, but it was blocked. I left a message at the Meighen house asking Graham to call me. Then I called Michael Goetz's office. His nurse said he was in a therapy session. I told her I had concerns about one of Dr. Goetz's patients, and I left my name and number. I was not optimistic that either Graham Meighen or Michael Goetz would get back to me.

It had been a disquieting morning, and the prospect of being alone with my thoughts in an empty condo was not appealing. Besides, I had information about Michael Goetz that would interest Margot. When I got off the elevator in our building, I went straight to her place.

She beamed when she opened the door and saw me. "I was just thinking about you," she said. "The press conference went well, didn't it?"

"Yes," I said. "Did you notice that Slater and Michael beat a hasty retreat?"

Margot nodded. "I wondered about that," she said. "Come on in. Lexi's down for a nap. Stay and have lunch with me. Jasmina made cabbage soup and I have some very nice rye bread."

"Do you happen to have some very nice rye whisky to go with it?"

Margot raised an eyebrow. "I take it that the morning took a nose-dive after the press conference. Lucky for you Leland always made sure we had a bottle of Crown Royal in the house. I've been pregnant or nursing forever, so it's all yours."

Margot put the soup on to warm; I made myself a drink, and we sat down at the kitchen table.

"About twenty minutes ago, I had a call from Liz Meighen," I said.

"Graham's wife? What's up with her?"

"I wish I knew. She wouldn't tell me where she was. To be honest, I'm not certain she knew that herself. She's been pretty unstable for a while now."

"I remember hearing that she and Graham lost their daughter last year."

"And the loss was devastating, but Liz seemed to be getting better. Then, out of nowhere, she started falling apart."

"Grief has no timetable," Margot said. "I've been learning that myself."

I reached across the table and touched Margot's hand. "I know how difficult it's been for you since Leland died. But I think the root of Liz's problems may be more sinister than grief."

Margot frowned. "That sounds ominous."

"If what Liz Meighen told me is true, she's being victimized. But I honestly don't know if I can trust what she says." I sipped my drink and felt the warmth spread through my veins. "Margot, do you know anything about Graham's current financial status?"

"Nothing definite, but there's been a fair amount of buzz about the subject lately. Apparently, Graham is suddenly afflicted with the reverse Midas touch. Everything he touches turns to ashes. He's made some lousy decisions, and rumour has it that he's gambling."

"That would lend credence to what Liz told me on the phone. She believes Graham and her psychiatrist are conspiring to have her declared *non compos mentis*."

"So Graham can get at her money?"

"Presumably," I said. "Now take a wild guess at the identity of Liz's psychiatrist."

Margot's eyes widened. "Michael Goetz. Wow. If Michael *is* conspiring with Graham Meighen to get Liz's money, he's in deep doo-doo – legally, and with the College of Physicians and Surgeons."

"That might explain why Michael was so eager to distance himself from Brock."

"You think he's protecting Brock?"

"I don't know. Margot, I don't even know if what Liz told me is true. Given what you said about Graham's financial problems, it makes sense, but when Liz talked about Michael Goetz being 'one of them,' she did sound delusional. And her reaction when she thought I didn't believe her was erratic. She was furious and then she just seemed to lapse into despair."

"So are you going to the police with this?"

"I don't know. We can't ignore the fact that Michael Goetz is married to Slater Doyle and Slater works for Graham. But if we're wrong and Liz is having some sort of psychotic episode, a false charge could derail Michael's life. He's not my favourite person, but Brock is a good man, and he loves Michael. I don't think we can take a chance."

"So we shouldn't tell Brock."

"We have to tread lightly. There's been enough damage, and there's more to come. Liz left town on Saturday and Sunday night, Zack and I saw Graham and Jill having what had all the earmarks of a romantic dinner."

Margot raised an eyebrow. "Did somebody forget to tell Graham he's married?"

"That doesn't seem to be an issue," I said. "Of course, it never was for Jill either. Zack said he told you about Jill's affair with Ian."

"He did," Margot said. "I was waiting for you to bring up the subject. I'm sorry, Jo. I really am. You deserved better."

"Ultimately, I got the best," I said. "And Jill is getting involved with another man who will just be using her. Zack says Graham's a sociopath."

"That's interesting. More than once, Leland told me Graham was a man without a conscience." She cocked her head. "So are you going to warn Jill about the new man in her life?"

"I don't know," I said. "I'm certain Graham's sudden interest in Jill stems from the fact that he needs money."

"I didn't realize there was big money in journalism," Margot said.

"There isn't," I said. "A few years back, Jill was married. The marriage didn't last long, but when her husband died, Jill inherited a very healthy investment portfolio."

"Money is a powerful aphrodisiac," Margot said. She stretched lazily. "Soup's ready. Do you want a refill for that drink?"

"No, that hit the spot, but I trust Jasmina's cabbage soup to do the rest."

I always enjoyed Margot's company and the food was comforting. As I was leaving Lexi awakened, so I managed to work in a snuggle and a gummy grin. My hour at Margot's had been a happy one, but my concern about Liz nagged at me, and despite everything, I was worried about Jill. By the time I walked across the hall to our condo, I'd decided to call her.

When I picked up the phone, my nerve failed, so I took the coward's way out and sent Jill a text. "Disturbing rumours about Graham Meighen. Don't get involved with him." I hadn't expected to hear from Jill, and by six o'clock when she hadn't acknowledged receipt of the text, I assumed her silence was my answer.

CHAPTER

13

Howard Dowhanuik buzzed from our lobby early Thursday morning. It was chilly, and when Howard arrived on the doorstep his cheeks were still rosy. Howard was a political animal, and the campaign had reinvigorated him. He was wearing a black cable-knit crewneck sweater and the red toque with a pom-pom that one of his daughters had knit for him. "You look like an ad for one of those enriched living retirement homes," I said.

"Still sassy after all these years," Howard said. "How about a cup of coffee? It's cold out there."

I poured Howard's coffee and we sat together at the butcher-block table. "I'm glad you're here," I said. "I heard some disturbing news about Graham Meighen yesterday, and I sent Jill a text warning her about him. Since the last time I encountered her, I told her that I wanted her out of our lives, I understand why she's ignoring the messenger, but I need to make certain she's paying attention to the message. Could you talk to her?"

Howard's head-shake was vehement. "She wouldn't listen to me, but, Jo, she would listen to you." Howard's gaze could still pierce. "If Jill thought you cared enough about her to deliver the message in person, she'd take it seriously."

"It's not happening, Howard."

He sipped his coffee. His eyes hadn't left my face. "Why not? Jill's staying at the Hotel Saskatchewan, Suite 806. Just knock on her door and tell her. You don't even have to go inside."

"Howard, these days, I don't like the person I become when I'm around Jill."

"Then don't be that person," Howard said. "I won't minimize what Jill and Ian did, but you and the kids survived. You have a future. Ian's dead and Jill wishes she was dead. She called me last night. She knows you'll never forgive her, but she's hoping that if she gets the inside story on Graham Meighen's role in the Ridgeway campaign she can help Zack get elected."

"And in the process she'll get a story that will be a poke in the eye to the young turks at NationTV. Howard, Jill is not involving herself with Graham Meighen so she can get Zack elected. She's after a story, and she's prepared to do what it takes to get what she wants."

"But you think she'll get more than she bargained for with Graham Meighen."

"I do."

"Then tell her. Jo, I know you, and if anything happened to Jill because you hadn't warned her, you'd never forgive yourself." Howard was still wearing his red knit toque, and the combination of his hangdog look and the pom-pom defeated me.

"All right, I'll go," I said.

Suddenly, Howard was all brisk efficiency. "I'll get your jacket. You've always believed in getting the tough stuff out of way early in the day."

I was at the hotel by nine o'clock. Howard was right. I'd always believed in getting the tough stuff out of the way early, and facing Jill would be tough. As I walked across the blue and gold carpet of the hotel lobby, I was tense. When Graham Meighen stepped out of the elevator not ten feet from where I was standing, his focus was wholly on his phone, but I didn't want to risk being seen so I stepped into Coco's, the patisserie that faced the elevators and watched him.

Graham was elegant. As always, he was deeply tanned; his silver hair was artfully tousled, his dusky blue-striped tie complemented his grey three-piece suit. He was the image of success, but he was scowling. Clearly, the information he was getting was not to his liking.

When Graham disappeared down the stairs that led to the hotel exit, I turned my attention to the patisserie's offerings. Thanksgiving was approaching and the shop was redolent of the spices of autumn. In addition to the usual trays of macaroons, profiteroles, croissants, éclairs, and cookies, the display cases were bright with tarts filled with fresh-picked fall fruit: cherries, apples, blackberries, and peaches. A three-tier stand on the counter held pumpkin cupcakes, each topped with a buttercream rose. Jill loved anything pumpkin, and without thinking I gestured to the woman behind the counter and told her I was ready to order. Then the image of Jill with Ian flashed through my mind. I waved off the woman behind the counter and walked out of Coco's empty-handed.

I hesitated in front of the door to Suite 806. My impulse was to retrace my steps, press the call button for the elevator, and escape. But I knew I'd regret turning away. I knocked. Jill answered almost immediately. She opened the door wide. She was clearly expecting someone, but it wasn't me. She was wearing a filmy ecru negligee; her makeup was fresh and her hair was carefully styled. She pulled the door half shut behind her. "I thought you were someone else."

"Graham," I said. "I saw him cross the lobby while I was waiting for the elevator. He didn't see me. May I come in?"

Jill stood aside and gestured towards two flowered couches that faced each other in front of the window. The remains of a room service breakfast for two were on the table between the couches. "Would you like to sit down?"

"I won't stay. Jill, I sent you a text last night."

"I received it. I appreciate your concern. I really do, Jo, but I know what I'm doing."

"Do you? I glanced at the dishes on the room service tray. I assume you and Graham are sleeping together?"

Jill didn't flinch. "There's no reason not to. You made it clear that there's no place for me in your family's life, and Graham wants me to be part of his."

"So it's serious."

"Graham says his marriage is over," she said. "We're attracted to each other. He needs me, Jo. People are turning away from him."

"Follow their example," I said. "Graham Meighen is dangerous. Zack believes he's a sociopath. Leland Hunter said he lacks a conscience. And Liz Meighen thinks Graham is working with her doctor to convince her that she's losing her mind so he can get control of her money—"

Jill cut me off. "Don't believe everything you hear, Jo."

Despite her long affair with Ian, I was afraid for her. "Be careful," I said. "You're playing with fire."

She shrugged. "When you have nothing left to lose, playing with fire is no big deal."

The ad agency had assembled a rough cut of the commercial they'd made of Zack and Brock's press conference. They delivered it to our place around four. Zack phoned Brock and invited him to come upstairs and check out the ad, and I asked Margot and Lexi to join us.

The ad was eye-catching and powerful: shots of Brock touring the slum houses juxtaposed with shots of one of the houses Peyben workers were making habitable for winter. The ad closed with Zack standing in front of I2 Rose Street answering Jill's question about the choice of venue for the press conference, delivering his challenge about getting involved, and quoting Edmund Burke.

When the screen went blank, Margot leapt to her feet, raised Lexi in her arms, and twirled. "We're giving you a standing ovation," Margot said. "And Lexi and I do not hand these out indiscriminately."

Zack whipped out his phone to capture the moment, and we were all still smiling when the landline rang. I was closest.

It was Jill. Her voice was strained. "I have bad news," she said. "Liz Meighen committed suicide this morning. Graham asked me to call you. He knew how fond you were of Liz."

Suddenly I was very cold. "What happened?"

"A drug overdose," Jill said. "Graham's devastated. He's been afraid of this for weeks. Liz called sometime after midnight. Graham was on the phone with her for close to an hour. When he came back to bed, he said he tried to convince Liz that she had everything to live for, but she was so confused and depressed that he couldn't get through to her. Finally, she hung up on him."

"Did he try to get help for her?"

"He didn't know where she was. Graham asked Liz to let him talk to someone at the place where she was staying, but she refused."

"Jill, did you actually hear Graham's side of the conversation?"

"No. He took the phone in the other room because he didn't want to awaken me. I know what you're getting at, Jo, but you couldn't be more wrong. Graham is in shock. His marriage to Liz might have been over, but she was part of his life for thirty-eight years, and he's determined to do the right thing. He's already on his way to Calgary to bring Liz home."

I could feel the anger rise in my throat. "That's very high-minded of him, especially since he was in bed with you when Liz made that desperate call."

Jill didn't bother responding. She just hung up.

While I was talking to Jill, Zack, Margot, and Brock had fallen silent. They were looking at me expectantly.

"Liz Meighen committed suicide this morning," I said, then I turned to Brock and told him what I knew about Michael's involvement.

Brock stood abruptly. "Why didn't you tell me about this before?"

"Because I didn't know whether Liz was delusional. I still don't. But she's dead now. Brock, I have to pass along what I know to the police."

"If Michael did what Liz suspected he did, he could lose his licence," Brock said.

Margot was curt. "If Michael did what Liz suspected he did, he *should* lose his licence."

Taylor had come from school and gone straight to her studio to work, so only Zack and I were at the condo when Debbie arrived. She looked exhausted. It had been a month to the day since Cronus was murdered. The police had followed every lead and gotten nowhere. The black SUV that had forced me off the road and presumably followed Brock the night before had been found. It was stolen and whoever had been driving it knew a thing or two about DNA because the forensics team reported that the car was clean as a whistle. The police were still investigating the home invasion at Peggy's. And now Liz Meighen was dead – an apparent suicide but certainly a lucky spin of the wheel of fortune for her husband.

I brought Debbie coffee and told her that I'd learned about Liz's death from Jill Oziowy, and that Jill was now Graham Meighen's girlfriend. Then I told her everything I knew about Liz. Debbie's pencil was flying. When I was through, Debbie closed her notebook and picked up her coffee cup. "Jo, do you believe Liz Meighen committed suicide?"

Zack moved his chair closer to me and took my hand. "I do," I said. "But something happened to Liz between the luncheon on September 2 and yesterday afternoon when she called me. At the luncheon, people were sharing their memories of Beverly. Bev was Liz's only child, and as the program went on, Liz was clearly suffering, but she was in control. Yesterday she was disintegrating. She alluded to problems with the medication she was taking. She said it made her confused and anxious. Liz was extraordinarily articulate, but when she was trying to relate something Graham had told her she forgot a simple word and she crumbled. It was heartbreaking. She said, 'I'm losing my words. I'm losing myself.' Then she said. 'Don't trust anybody,' and hung up."

Debbie had picked up her notepad again. "What do you think changed between September 2 and this morning?"

"I think Michael Goetz prescribed medication that interfered with Liz's thought processes, and that Graham pushed her into a state where she saw suicide as the only option."

Debbie turned the page in her notebook. "So you think I should interview Dr. Goetz and Mr. Meighen."

"I do," I said.

"Do you have any idea where Meighen is?"

"Jill Oziowy told me he's already in Calgary. According to her, he wants 'to bring Liz home.'"

Zack raised his eyebrows. "The grieving widower isn't wasting any time."

Debbie was acerbic. "I hope the Calgary police aren't wasting any time getting to Meighen and keeping him away from the scene of the suicide."

Zack and I moved into the living room while Debbie made her calls. It was nearly ten minutes before she joined us. "We're finally getting somewhere," she said. "Mrs. Meighen was staying at a retreat house about forty-five minutes from Calgary. When she didn't show up for breakfast, one of the staff checked her room and found her body. It was 8:30 a.m. Calgary time."

"I saw Graham Meighen leaving the hotel where his girlfriend was staying at 9:00. He seemed preoccupied. I guess he was getting the news about Liz."

"But the staff at the retreat house *did* call the police," Zack said.

Debbie shook her head. "No, apparently, they're kind of otherworldly. They called the next of kin, and then they waited for the universe to unfold. And it did." Debbie consulted her notes. "Mr. Meighen caught the 10:30 flight from Regina and was in Calgary by 12:00 their time. It took him an hour to get to Bragg Creek. So he was alone with the body from, say, one to three o'clock when he decided the police should be called in."

"Two hours," Zack said. "Plenty of time to get rid of anything of evidentiary value."

"The RCMP are on the case now. They do the policing in the Bragg Creek area, and they'll be doing exactly what they should do in the case of a suicide. From now on, it's by the book. They'll determine the victim's identity, the cause of death, and the approximate time and date of death. They'll do a preliminary examination of the body. They'll examine the scene for consistency or inconsistency of facts. They'll interview the other people at the retreat house. They'll seize items of value: jewellery, money, et cetera, and they'll look for the suicide note, pills, pill bottles with the names of the victim and the prescribing physician. And that's where the fun will begin. Because Zack's right: Meighen had two hours in which to get rid of anything of evidentiary value."

"And no one would have stopped a grieving widower pleading for time alone with his dead wife."

"I'm going back to the station," Debbie said. "Let me know if you hear anything."

After Debbie left, Zack made martinis and I rummaged through the fridge and the freezer for something for supper. The larder was bare. I turned to Zack. "There's enough frozen spaghetti sauce for two. We are three. There's also a meatloaf that's been in the freezer way too long. Order in?"

Zack reached into our "order in" drawer of menus. "What are you in the mood for?"

"Fish and chips," I said.

"Fish and chips it is." Zack handed me my martini, picked up his phone, hit speed-dial, and ordered. "Dinner will be here at 6:30," he said. He raised his glass. "To Liz Meighen."

"May she find peace at last," I said. "Zack, the hours before her death must have been excruciating for her. Jill said Liz called Graham some time after midnight. She was despondent and incoherent. According to Jill, Graham tried strenuously to convince Liz that life was worth living."

"And he failed," Zack said. "Jo, I think we've come to the end of the road with this."

"If Debbie checks the phone records, I'm certain she'll find out that Graham was the one who made the call."

"And that will make no difference whatsoever," Zack said. "Meighen will say it was the middle of the night and he was groggy. He'll admit that he could be mistaken about who called whom, but he'll be clear about what was said. Graham's holding all the cards. Liz is no longer alive to tell her side of the story. Even if emotional abuse was the root cause for Liz's suicide, emotional abuse is not a crime; it's just a reason to leave a relationship."

"And so Graham Meighen gets away with it," I said.

"The only way the prosecution could successfully argue that Meighen's abusive behaviour somehow constituted criminal negligence would be if they had proof that Michael Goetz and Graham conspired to drive Liz to the brink. That would mean proving that Michael Goetz knowingly pre-scribed medication that would harm Liz."

"And Graham will have disposed of any pills or pill bot-tles that would link Michael Goetz to the drugs Liz was taking," I said. "But, Zack, they were prescription drugs; the pharmacist would have records."

"How many free pharmaceuticals do you think come into a psychiatrist's office? Doctors always have a drawer full of freebies. As you know only too well, all sorts of aggrava-tions come with paraplegia. When I'm in Henry Chan's office because something's gone wrong for me, more often than not Henry just hands me some samples and says 'Let's see if these work.'"

"And there's no record of those samples," I said. "So Michael Goetz and Graham Meighen get away scot-free."

"The justice system is not always just, Jo. That's still hard for me to accept, but it's a fact of life."

CHAPTER

14

Liz Meighen's funeral was scheduled for 10:30 a.m. on Thursday, October 9, a day before the Thanksgiving long weekend. Zack and I had gone back and forth about the propriety of him attending the funeral of Graham Meighen's wife, knowing that the whole Ridgeway team would be there. But Zack knew it would be a difficult morning for me, and for him, that was all that mattered.

The service was being held at St. Paul's Cathedral, our church. After Bev's death, Liz had apparently become a regular worshiper at St. Paul's nine o'clock Sunday service and at the Wednesday morning service as well. She was also a regular attendant at the monthly Eucharists in the columbarium beneath the church. Bev Levy's ashes were there, and Liz's will stipulated that the urn with her ashes be placed in the same case as her daughter's.

Zack was meeting me at the Cathedral. Warren Weber had invited Zack to have breakfast at the Scarth Club with Warren and some of his old friends. It was a command performance. Warren and his pals were high rollers and Zack was wearing one of his slick lawyer suits and a Countess

Mara tie that I particularly liked. When I bent to kiss him goodbye, I whispered, "You look good enough to eat."

He drew me close. "Promises, promises," he growled.

Zack and I had arranged to meet at the area at the front of the nave that was set aside for people in wheelchairs. The handicapped area had the added advantage of giving us a good view of the family of the deceased, and Zack was interested in watching Graham Meighen's behaviour during the service.

Zack had already pulled a chair into the place beside him, so I sat, said a brief prayer for Liz, and took Zack's hand. The organist began to play "Jesu, Joy of Man's Desiring." Zack breathed deeply and for a few moments we simply allowed Bach to soothe us. When I glanced at the back of the church, I saw that the family was coming in. I rose and Zack turned his chair towards the centre aisle.

Zack and his law partners always entered together at the funeral of a partner or a partner's spouse. Graham Meighen and his associates apparently followed the same practice. Margot had told me that the men accompanying Meighen were known in development circles simply as "the Seven Brothers." The sobriquet was not affectionate. The strategic planners, construction company owners, and commercial real estate dealers to whom the name referred were related by entitlement, not blood. The equation was simple. Lancaster had a pipeline to the city's plans for development, and as soon as they knew where the city had encouraged the building of a big-box store, the Seven Brothers took over – getting corporate funding, buying land, choosing the sweetest properties for development, building overpriced houses, and then getting the city to advertise the desirability of the housing in the new development. The equation had worked for years, but if Zack won the election, the Seven Brothers would have to take their place in line with their competitors.

The men had followed Graham down the aisle, but he lingered, so they filed into the front pew. He was carrying the silver urn that contained Liz's ashes. He paused before he mounted the three steps to the chancel. After he'd placed the urn on a low table near the steps, he allowed his hand to rest on the urn just long enough to suggest pain at parting.

The form of the Anglican Funeral Liturgy is clearly set out. Readings, prayers, psalms – even anthems and hymns – are suggested, but despite the guidelines, the funeral of a suicide is always difficult.

When it came to the eulogy, Dean Mike met the difficulty head on. He talked about Liz's search for comfort in faith after her daughter's death, and how she had found solace in two verses from Psalm 139: "All the days for me were written in your book before one of them came to be." Mike said that Liz interpreted those lines as meaning that God is present in all our circumstances. He said that until very recently, he and Liz both believed she'd found solid footing, but even the strongest have a breaking point.

As the dean talked about how God had worked through Liz during her lifetime, I looked over at Graham Meighen, the man who had married Liz thirty-eight years ago. He had raised a child with her. They had lost that child and seemingly, somewhere along the way, they had lost each other. I wondered what he was feeling. His expression was unreadable.

After Eucharist, the service moved inexorably towards a close. The dean said that Liz had been fond of the Evensong Prayer, so we read it in unison:

Support us, O Lord,
All the day long of this troublesome life,
Until the shadows lengthen and the evening comes,
The busy world is hushed,
The fever of life is over
And our work is done.
Then, Lord, in your mercy grant us a safe lodging,
A holy rest, and peace at the last.

The organist struck the opening notes of the hymn "Holy, Holy, Holy" and the service was over. Across the aisle from us, Graham and his colleagues rose to leave.

I slid out of the pew and stood beside Zack. The two of us watched as Graham and the Seven Brothers moved towards the back of the church.

Zack flexed his shoulders the way athletes do after a strenuous event.

I stepped behind him and rubbed his neck. "If you and I go to the reception at Graham Meighen's, we'll be the proverbial skunks at the garden party," I said. "Why don't we just head home?"

"You read my mind," Zack said, wheeling towards the door. "As far as I'm concerned, the sooner we start the weekend, the better."

When we got off the elevator in our building, I saw that Declan and Taylor had been busy. Twenty of us would be sitting down to Thanksgiving dinner, and laundry hampers filled with food, wine, fresh fruit, juice, and soft drinks lined the hall. The kids came out of Margot's, each carrying a hamper of produce. "The turkeys are still in the refrigerator," Declan said, "but everything else is out here. We're ready to load up."

"Great," I said. "Have you guys had lunch?"

"Taylor made sandwiches. She made some for you and Zack too," Declan said, and the look he gave our daughter would have melted a harder heart than mine.

"Good," I said. "As soon as we've eaten, we can take off. In the meantime, would you two start putting the hampers in the cars? The dogs will be in the station wagon, so no food there. Pantera eats anything that's not nailed down."

"Last night, he ate a bag of Granny Smith apples," Taylor said. She grinned at Declan. "That was pretty much a disaster."

"I don't need that image in my head," Declan said. "Let's load up."

Some of the happiest times of my life were spent at Lawyers' Bay. The horseshoe-shaped piece of land surrounding the bay had been owned by the family of Zack's partner Kevin Hynd, and when the firm of Falconer, Shreve, Altieri, Wainberg, and Hynd began to show a profit, the young partners built cottages on the land. Years later, after Chris Altieri died and Zack and I were together, Zack bought Chris's cottage to use when our family joined us at the lake. For me, it was the best of family arrangements – we were together but we were separate.

Our grown children and their guests were responsible for getting their own breakfast and lunch, but every night we all sat down for dinner together in the sunroom overlooking the lake. Zack had given his decorator carte blanche to furnish the house, and the decorator had found a cheap treasure at a country auction: a partners' table from a long-defunct law firm. Twenty-four chairs had come with the table, and Zack was never happier than when every place at the table was filled. That Thanksgiving we were going to come close.

The rain started as soon as we got to Lawyers' Bay and continued pretty much unabated throughout the weekend, but we were unstoppable. We had raingear, and Zack had his all-terrain wheelchair, so we carried on with our usual activities: walks around the bay; touch football in the mud; movie marathons, board games and card games with the kids. Candyland had lost its charm for Madeleine and Lena, but Zack had taught them blackjack as a preparation for a Grade One curriculum that called for mastering "the skills necessary for numerical literacy." Both girls were quick studies when it came to Monopoly, a game Howard Dowhanuik never tired of. He had played endless games with his son, Charlie, and Mieka, Peter, and Angus when they were children, and the years had not dimmed his enthusiasm. Once they settled around the board and Madeleine got the bank in order, she, Howard, and Lena were incommunicado for at least two hours.

Our usual plan when we were at the lake was to make Saturday "Cook's Night Out" and eat at Magoos, a hamburger joint that, in addition to its signature loaded burgers, made transcendent onion rings, savoury coleslaw, perfectly seasoned shoestring fries, and milkshakes so thick that patrons had to use spoons to get every last drop of shake from the old-fashioned metal containers.

Magoos was across the lake from us, and part of the fun of the adventure was getting there by boat. As the time for dinner approached and the rain continued, we were all eyeing the sky anxiously. The clouds hovered, but just as we'd agreed the prudent course was to drive, the skies cleared. It was the last Saturday Magoos would be open until the May long weekend, so we decided to take a chance.

Getting twenty people into boats when four of the twenty are children is complex, but we managed. Zack, Noah Wainberg, and Brock each drove a boat, and the rest of us found a place, shrugged into our life jackets, helped the kids into their life jackets, and waited for the fun to begin.

It was always a joy bringing new people to Magoos. Two years earlier on a sultry summer evening, Zack and I had introduced Margot and her fiancé, Leland Hunter, to the restaurant. In addition to the great food, Magoos boasted a solid dance floor and a vintage Wurlitzer jukebox that played nothing that had been written after 1970. That July night, after we had passed the midpoint of the lake, we had heard Buddy Holly singing "Oh Boy." Margot joined in immediately. She hadn't missed a single "Dum dee dum dum," and as Leland watched his fiancée, his love for her was palpable. Not long after that, he was dead.

This was a very different night, chilly and damp. Margot and I were sitting next to each other behind Zack. Lexi was on Margot's knee, delighting in everything. When we heard the late, great Ritchie Valens singing "La Bamba," Margot drew Lexi close. "I wish your dad was here," she whispered. I squeezed Margot's arm.

Herb McFaull, who owned Magoos, welcomed us at the door. Because we had small children in tow, we'd arrived early, but except for us the place was deserted. Herb's smile was welcoming. "I was afraid I was going to have to dance with myself tonight," he said.

"There are twenty of us – all ages and stages," Zack said. "And all enthusiastic dancers. You will not dance alone, Herb."

Husky servers pulled three long tables together in front of the windows that looked out on the lake. We took our places and began to check out the menus. The evening was about to begin.

It was a happy meal. The Wainbergs were raising Jacob with all organic, healthful foods, but he was two and half and when he spied a plate with French fries and a burger it was love at first sight. Inspired and emboldened, Lexi shoved aside her Dora the Explorer plate of spinach, rice, and

slivered chicken breast and grabbed a fistful of fries from
Margot's plate.

As he always did, Zack unloaded his onions onto Taylor's
burger because she loved onions, and she never remembered
to order extra. When Declan gave Taylor his onions too,
Margot whispered, "I told you it was serious." We took turns
feeding loonies to the Wurlitzer. For a magical couple of
hours, all the greats were alive again: Bill Haley and the
Comets, Buddy Holly, Chubby Checker, Elvis, Little Richard,
The Four Lads, Jerry Lee Lewis, and the Big Bopper.

Everyone danced, and because there was no one but us in
the restaurant, we were uninhibited. Delia Wainberg, the most
disciplined person I'd ever known, did a down-and-dirty twist
with her husband, Noah. Mieka and Maisie taught Madeleine
and Lena a wild Watusi. We all took a turn on the dance floor
with Jacob and Lexi. Zack made some deadly moves with his
chair as Buddy Holly sang "That'll Be the Day."

Taylor, Isobel Wainberg, and Gracie Falconer had been
besties since the first summer my family spent at Lawyers'
Bay. I had watched with my heart in my mouth as the three
of them learned to dive off the high board, and that night it
was fun to hear the three of them urging Declan to join
them in putting a little hip-hop into the sock hop. Margot
seemed contented to stay on the sidelines. Despite offers
from Noah, Blake Falconer, Zack, and Declan, she didn't
venture onto the dance floor.

After Lexi and I had finished bopping to Paul Anka, we
went back to Margot's table. She was looking meditative
and fingering a loonie. "All night I've been trying to decide
whether I'm brave enough to play C-5," she said.

I didn't need an explanation. The night Zack and I brought
Margot and Leland to Magoos, Margot had played C-5 – Slim
Whitman's "I Remember You." For both Margot and Leland,
the road to a deep and loving partnership had been rocky,

but as they danced to Slim Whitman, it was clear that the journey was over, and the future was bright. They had chosen "I Remember You" as the bride-and-groom dance for their old-fashioned small-town Saskatchewan wedding. The reception had been on the greens of the town golf course. Everyone in Wadena was there, and as Leland and Margot moved gracefully across the grass, there was a hush. It seemed that nothing could ever part them.

Lexi was in my arms, drifting towards sleep. I smiled at Margot. "Memories," I whispered.

"But they were good ones," Margot said. She stood, walked over to the Wurlitzer, and suddenly the room was filled with Slim Whitman's soaring falsetto. When Margot started back to our table, Brock held out his arms. "May I have this dance?" he said. Margot frowned and said, "I don't think . . ." and then wordlessly, she moved into his embrace.

Zack was wheeling towards me, but he didn't miss the action on the dance floor. "What's going on there?" he said.

"I'm not sure," I said. "But whatever it is, it's a good thing. Margot and Brock's new baby and Lexi will have two very fine parents in their lives." Margot and Brock consulted over the next two jukebox selections – both tunes they chose were slow and they danced easily and well together. When they ceded the jukebox to the younger generation, Margot and Brock walked off the dance floor hand in hand.

Lexi was deep in sleep. "I think it's time we headed home," Margot said. "But you guys stay. I can get Declan to take us."

"We should all get going," Zack said. "I just checked the weather and the reprieve from the rain is about to end."

"That's good enough for me," Margot said. "But first I'm visiting the ladies' room."

"Me too," I said. I handed Lexi to Zack.

He drew her close. "She always smells so good," he said.

"Not always," Margot said.

The women's bathroom at Magoos was a trip down memory lane. There were Hollywood-style makeup mirrors and the walls featured photographs of Mr. Magoo, the cranky, myopic, misanthropic cartoon character ogling the silver screen beauties of the day: Jane Russell, Marilyn Monroe, Audrey Hepburn, Debbie Reynolds, and Elizabeth Taylor.

Two years earlier when Margot and I had stood in front of adjacent mirrors repairing our makeup in the ladies' room at Magoos, I had guessed correctly that she was pregnant. This Thanksgiving weekend, she was five months into her second pregnancy. Margot was a woman who bloomed with pregnancy: her skin and hair glowed, but as she stared at her reflection, she looked close to tears.

"Bad night?" I said.

"No," she said. Then she laughed. "Actually, no and yes. Jo, my brain knows that Brock's gay, but my body hasn't seemed to pick up on that. When he and I were dancing I was feeling urges that a pregnant woman should not be feeling."

"You're pregnant, you're not dead," I said. "Gay or straight, Brock's a very attractive man. When I was pregnant, my hormones were in overdrive."

Margot raised an eyebrow. "Somehow I can't imagine you in overdrive."

"I was, especially when I was pregnant with the boys. Ian loved it. He said half the time he couldn't even get out of his coat before I was ripping off his pants." Suddenly I remembered that even during my pregnancies, Jill had been in the picture. "Screw Ian," I said. "Brock's a nice guy who happens to be very hot; you're a healthy woman who, at the moment, has raging hormones. What you're feeling is perfectly normal."

The party was breaking up when we got back. Gracie and Isobel had zipped up their windbreakers and were helping Jacob with his. Madeleine and Lena and Taylor and Declan were having one last dance. Mieka, her brothers, and Maisie were chatting. Lexi had awakened and was playing with one of the ornamental gourds that had been in a basket on our table.

Margot scooped up her daughter. "That's a gourd," she said. "The wartiest gourd in the basket– good choice."

Brock was at Margot's elbow. "Allow me to carry the owner of the warty gourd to the boat. When we came, I noticed the ground was getting slippery." Lexi held her arms out to Brock, and the matter was settled.

The evening was our treat, so Zack and I were the last to leave the restaurant. As we started down the hill, he said, "So what were you and Margot doing in the women's bathroom all that time?"

"Kissing," I said.

He chortled. "You always say that."

"And every time I say it, you and I end up with some very pleasant midnight groping."

It was drizzling Sunday morning when I put the leashes on Pantera and Willie. The night before, Howard had announced that he was coming with me on the morning walk, and I should rap on his door before I got ready. Howard was not a fan of physical activity, nor was he an early riser, so I assumed he had an agenda. He was dressed when I knocked on his door, and it didn't take him long to get to the point. We had just started down the hill to the beach when he said, "I want to talk about Jill."

"Go for it," I said.

Howard grunted. "You always surprise me. I figured the minute I mentioned Jill's name, you'd shut me down."

"It's 5:45 a.m., it's raining, and you're out for a walk," I said. "You've earned a hearing. Say what you want to say."

"It's Thanksgiving," he said. "I was hoping you might give Jill another chance."

"At what?" I said. "Being my friend? Howard, I loved Jill, and I trusted her. So did the kids. From the time they were babies, Auntie Jill was always the fun aunt. The one who never tired of playing ride-a-horsey with them; the one who took them to the Ex and gave them money for the midway; the one who took them to the rock concerts and bought them overpriced T-shirts. Even after Jill moved to Toronto, she stayed in touch with the kids. She was as much a part of their lives as you are. But the other day Mieka told me that when she packed Jill's bag, it made her sick to touch Jill's clothes. I've tried to talk to Peter and Angus about the situation, but as soon as I mention Jill's name, they freeze. And it makes me crazy because I know they're hurting."

"Do you want me to talk to them?"

"What would you say? Howard, you're good at spin, but even you couldn't spin Ian's affair with Jill in a way that would make my kids feel less betrayed or make me feel less inadequate."

Howard slapped his forehead. "Jesus, Jo, you don't often misread a situation, but you're way out in left field with this. It was *Ian* who felt inadequate. That's why he turned to Jill. That's why he stayed with her."

"And what sent you leaping to that conclusion?"

"Ian did. I told you I talked to him a hundred times about ending it with Jill. In addition to everything else, he was jeopardizing his future. One night we had a few drinks together, and I revisited the subject. I told him that he had to choose: he could either end the affair with Jill or he could kiss his future political aspirations goodbye."

"And he chose Jill."

"He didn't have to choose. He said that Jill loved you and the kids. She knew you and the children would always be part of Ian's life and that's the way she wanted it."

"Howard, that is just bizarre."

"Maybe so, but I'd worked myself into a corner where the bizarre was acceptable. I had a huge personal investment in Ian. I'd brought him along; I'd groomed him; I'd made him deputy premier and I'd made certain there was nobody else waiting in the wings. Ian was performing brilliantly. You and he were an extraordinary team: young, smart, and blessed with an appealing family. I knew that if we kept it together, Ian could become federal leader, and as federal leader, he could open up a whole new area of possibilities for us."

"So where did Jill fit in?

"Ian said he couldn't function without her. When I pressed him, he said he needed Jill because he needed someone who looked up to him."

"And I didn't look up to him."

Howard's voice was husky. "You remember how it was. Ian had shortcomings and you filled the gaps."

"Isn't that what people do in a healthy relationship? That's the way it is for Zack and me."

"Ian wasn't Zack. Zack is comfortable in his own skin. He knows how good he is. The fact that you're good at what you do isn't a threat to him."

"And it was to Ian?"

"Yeah. You were smarter than Ian was and that galled him. The speeches he gave that really inspired people were the ones you wrote. And you were better with people than he was. When Ian's arrogance pissed people off, you smoothed the ruffled feathers. When he blew up at members of his staff, you talked them into staying with him."

"Howard, I never made a big deal about anything I did."

"I know you didn't. But Ian knew how much he needed you, and he resented it."

Suddenly I was livid. "Let me see if I've got this straight. Ian needed me to keep his political career on track. His need

made him resentful, so he worked off his resentment by
having sex with Jill."

"I'm sorry, Jo."

"So am I," I said. "Give me a break, Howard. You've just
destroyed whatever shreds of respect I had left for Ian."

"Ian was a good man," Howard said. "He simply made an
error in judgment. Can't you accept that?"

"Why should I accept that?" I said. "When a good man
makes an error in judgment, he atones for it. Ian just kept
right on banging Jill."

"Jo, you're breaking her heart."

"I'm not a saint, Howard."

"Agreed. But you *are* a woman who has a houseful of
people who love her waiting to celebrate Thanksgiving with
her. Jill doesn't have that. She doesn't have anybody but a
bottom feeder who's after her money and a future that
sucks. You won, Jo. Do the right thing."

When we got back from our walk, Zack met me at the door
with a lapful of old beach towels. The beach had been
muddy. Our hose was still hooked up, so I hosed Pantera and
Willie down, gave them a preliminary rub, and sent them
inside to shake off the excess water on Zack.

After the dogs had wandered into the sunroom, Zack
poured us both a cup of coffee. "Jill called," he said.

"Speak of the devil," I said.

Zack's head snapped up. "Whoa. Where did that come
from?"

"Howard just finished explaining to me that Ian banged
Jill because I made him feel inadequate."

"I'm not going to touch that with a ten-foot pole," Zack
said.

"Very wise," I said. "Did Jill say what she wanted?"

"She wanted you. She's going to call back."

"Swell." Right on cue, my cell rang.

Jill's tone was urgent. "I have to see you, Jo."

"It's Thanksgiving," I said. "We're at the lake."

"I'm at the lake too. More accurately, I'm at the Dairy Queen at the turnoff to your place. Can you meet me here?"

"What's this about, Jill?"

"You were right about Graham," she said, and her voice was dead.

"I just got back from taking the dogs for a run," I said. "I need to shower and change. I'll be there in twenty minutes."

I was dressed and my hair was combed but still wet when I came out of our bedroom. Zack was waiting for me. "What's up?"

"Jill wants to see me. I'm meeting her at the DQ on the highway."

Zack wheeled over to the closet where we hung our jackets. He handed me mine and then took down his. "I'm coming with you. Whatever's going on, you shouldn't be alone."

I kissed the top of Zack's head. "I'm glad I have you," I said.

"And I'm glad I have you," he said. "Jo, do you ever have second thoughts about this mayoralty thing?"

"Constantly," I said. "But we can't turn back. That quote from Edmund Burke you've been using puts steel in my spine. Now we'd better make tracks. We're eating at six, and there's a lot to do before you sharpen your trusty Henckel and call us to the table."

Jill was sitting by the window when we got to the Dairy Queen. The rain was falling steadily. It was a gloomy morning and somehow the fluorescent lights of the DQ only deepened the gloom. When we pulled into the parking lot, Zack opened the door on the passenger side and reached into the back seat for his chair. I didn't move.

"Aren't you coming?" Zack said.

"I am. I just need a minute. I'm still smarting from Howard's insight." I opened the car door and stepped out into the rain. "Okay. I'm ready, but let's make it quick."

When she saw us, Jill gave a brief wave. I joined her, and Zack took a place at a table across the room where he could keep me in view.

Like me, Jill hadn't bothered with makeup, and the scattering of freckles on her pale skin brought back memories of the fresh-faced girl I'd once known.

"Thanks for coming," she said. "Does Zack really believe he needs to protect you from me?"

"He doesn't want me to be alone."

"It's probably just as well Zack came. He should hear this too." When Jill reached into her bag and took out her phone, I motioned to Zack to join us. He and Jill exchanged greetings and then Jill turned her attention to her phone. "Slater called Graham early this morning. Graham thought I was still sleeping, so he took the call in the living room. I went over to the bedroom door and opened it a crack. I thought if Graham caught me, I'd just say I'd heard the phone and wondered if everything was all right."

"But he didn't catch you," Zack said.

"I guess it was my lucky day," Jill said. She tapped her phone and I heard Graham Meighen's voice, loud and furious: "Slater, the media are going to be out in full force, to see if Ridgeway shows. He has to be at St. Joseph's Hall by noon today. It's a tradition. The mayor and city council always serve dinner to the homeless at Thanksgiving. Ridgeway doesn't have to say a goddamned thing. All he has to do is show up, throw a slice of turkey on a fucking plate, and not look like a zombie.

"Put him on. I'll tell him myself." There was a pause, then Meighen said, "Scott, Slater tells me you're not feeling well enough to go to dish out the turkey today. People are already asking questions about what the hell's going on with you. If you don't show up today, people are going to continue asking questions and sooner or later they're going to stumble on things we don't want them to stumble on. Then we'll lose the election and the ground will open up and swallow us all.

"It's up to you to keep that from happening. Scott, we're in the clear. Cronus is out of the picture, so the four of us are the only ones who can connect us with that night, and none of us are going to talk."

The tape clicked off. "Graham didn't catch you?" I said.

Jill picked up her paper napkin and began pleating it into accordion folds. "No, he went to the bathroom. By the time he came back to bed I was there pretending to be asleep."

"Do you have any idea about the night Graham was talking about?" Zack asked

"No," Jill said. "But I'm going to find out. Graham and I are through, but he doesn't know that."

"What happened?"

Jill focused on pleating her napkin. "He was cheating on me. Jo, I realize the irony of me talking about betrayal with you, but if you can get past that, I'm in a position now to get my story and to help your campaign. Graham is flailing. He was counting on Liz's money to get him out of the hole he's dug himself, but recently Liz changed her will and left everything to the Beverly Levy Scholarship Fund."

I whistled. "Whoa."

Jill was cool. "Whoa, indeed. Anyway, Graham's desperate, and desperate people make mistakes. Graham may not trust me completely, but he needs my money. Last night he asked me for $500,000."

I touched her arm. "Be careful, Jill."

Before we pulled out of the parking lot, I looked back at the restaurant. Jill was standing by the window. Backlit by

the harsh fluorescent lights, she looked frail and alone. I had
to swallow hard to keep the tears back.

Zack and I came back to a house warm with the promise of
Thanksgiving. Angus greeted us at the door. I stood on the
threshold for moment, overwhelmed by memories. In profile,
Angus looked exactly as Ian had when I met him. I remem-
bered how intensely I had loved Ian at the beginning, then
Zack turned to me and grinned and the memory of Ian passed.

Angus pushed back his unruly forelock. "Glad you're
home. Mieka says French chefs say a turkey should rest for
the same amount of time as it was cooked, so we have to get
the birds in the oven. I've chopped the onions and the celery,
but nobody knows your stuffing recipe."

"There is no recipe," I said. "But you can watch and learn
if you want."

"Actually, I do," Angus said. "Leah's moving back to
Regina and one of her 'concerns' about me when we broke
up was that I was immature."

"And stuffing a turkey is proof of maturity?" I said.

"It's a step," Angus said.

Our rule for family dinners is simple: everybody who doesn't
bring a dish has to pitch in with the cooking. Most of us do
both. Angus stuffed one of the turkeys and Mieka taught
him a dynamite recipe for Brussels sprouts. Peter and Maisie
brought a sweet potato casserole and made a fire. Zack
played the piano, and the little kids played with the piano
pedals. Taylor, Isobel, and Gracie set the table and exchanged
whispered confidences. It was the kind of mellow day we'd
shared dozens of times, but since Labour Day our lives had
been short of mellow days and I treasured this one.

As the smell of turkey drifted through the house, I was
content. Zack poured us both a martini. When he handed

me my drink, he said, "You look more at peace than you have in a long time."

"I am more at peace," I said.

"One last job," Zack said. "Mieka says she thinks that everything's ready, but she wants you to check to see if anything's missing." I followed Zack into the sunroom. The old partners' table was set for twenty. I'd invited Milo, but he'd declined, so there were four extra chairs pulled to the side. The pies and dessert plates were on the sideboard. Angus and I had each cooked a twenty-five-pound turkey and the birds were sitting on the kitchen workspace, wrapped in parchment paper and kitchen towels, waiting to be carved. The side dishes were being kept warm in the oven and the gravy was simmering.

"Perfect," I said, and it was.

I couldn't have asked for a better Thanksgiving, but my eyes kept being drawn to the four empty chairs that had been pulled aside. I found myself wishing that circumstances had been different and that Jill had been in one of them.

Finally, the last sliver of pumpkin pie was eaten, and we cleaned up and went our separate ways. Everybody seven and over and under the age of forty went to the guest cottage to watch movies. The rest of us stayed behind to play with Jacob and Lexi and chat. It was a perfect post-Thanksgiving evening, but Howard was in a brown study. Finally, he pushed himself out of his chair. "This has been great," he said. "But I think I'll drive back to town tonight."

"Everything okay?" Zack said.

"Yeah, I thought I'd check on Jill, if you're okay with that, Jo."

"I'm okay with that," I said. "Jill's been on my mind too."

"Can I tell her you're thinking of her?"

"Yes," I said. "Howard, I'm doing my best, but this is terra incognita for me. I've lost friends to death, but in some ways this situation with Jill is worse. When friends die, you mourn, but you know they're not suffering and you have memories that make you smile. Everything's jumbled for Jill and me. I know she's suffering, but every memory I have of our time together is shadowed by what she and Ian did."

Howard gave me an avuncular hug. "You'll work it out, Jo. You always do."

CHAPTER

15

The long weekend had been idyllic, but all good things come to an end. We'd driven back to the city after supper Monday night, and Tuesday-morning reality hit. Howard and Milo, the odd couple, arrived bright and early with the polling results. I topped off Zack's coffee and poured Howard a cup. Milo unwrapped a fresh Crispy Crunch bar. Howard plopped his ancient briefcase on the table and waded right in. "Milo tells me our numbers aren't good," he said. "We're still four points ahead, but the momentum we had before Thanksgiving has gone up in smoke."

"The fucking perp ads are killing us," Milo said. "Those clips of Zack on the courthouse steps yucking it up with his thug-clients are cutting us off at the knees. No offence, Zack."

"None taken," Zack said. "Okay. So Ridgeway's ads are working. How do we make them stop working?"

"Jo told me about the recording you heard of Graham Meighen's conversation with Slater Doyle," Milo said. "That's a starting point."

The penny dropped. "It may be enough," I said. "Ridgeway's perp ads are fact-free. There's nothing there but juxtaposition and innuendo, but they're killing us. So lesson learned. We'll use juxtaposition and innuendo. Jill's determined to discover the truth about the Ridgeway campaign. If she can get us footage of Graham Meighen yucking it up with Scott Ridgeway and Slater, we can run it with a voice-over: *'They have secrets – things they don't want you to know.'* It's ugly, but it should drive the snakes out from under the rocks."

Milo jumped off his stool. "Welcome to the world of gutter politics, Jo," he said. "And how about this lick – we can finish the ads with a set up like Crime Stoppers. *'If you have information about why Lancaster Development is pulling the strings at City Hall, call us. We'll follow through and we guarantee all callers anonymity.'*"

Zack shot me a look of concern. "Are sure you're okay with this, Jo?"

"I am. We know Ridgeway is in Graham Meighen's pocket, but we don't know why. It's just a matter of time till we discover what Graham has on Scott Ridgeway. I don't want to find the smoking gun the day after we've lost the election."

Milo's long fingers beat a tattoo on the table. "Time to go for the gonads." He glanced at me. "Last chance," he said.

"It's my fault we didn't go negative sooner," I said. "Let's do what we have to do and deal with our consciences later. Zack, try to come home for lunch. We should have something concrete blocked out by then."

After Zack left, we divvied up the tasks. Milo called the ad agency and ran the new idea past them. The conversation was lengthy – at least lengthy for Milo. When he broke the connection, he was upbeat. "Here's where we are. The agency loves the *'They've got secrets'* angle, but they think we should lawyer up."

"We already have," I said. "Zack's a lawyer and when we

ran this by him, he didn't blink an eye. Why would he? The Ridgeway campaign does have secrets. If they want to take us to court, let them try."

"That's the spirit," Milo said. "And the agency likes the Crime Stoppers shtick. I like it because it's punchy, but the agency thinks it might actually cause an informant to step forth. And one last piece of good news. We've already bought a substantial number of thirty-second spots in the time leading up to E-Day, so we've got the air time."

"And the bad news . . . ?" I said.

Milo started to unwrap a fresh Crispy Crunch bar and then stuck it back in his jeans pocket. He'd never mentioned it, but I had a sense he was trying to cut back. He patted his jeans pocket longingly and then soldiered on. "The bad news is that the agency says there's no way they can get three new commercials in shape to air by the weekend."

"They don't have an option," I said. "If we don't counter the perp ads, we'll lose, and we all agree that the '*They have secrets*' campaign will work. We have four days. The agency people will have to pull all-nighters, but the Shreve campaign has enough money in the bank to pay overtime."

Milo didn't dawdle. He pulled out his Crispy Crunch, said, "Later," and took off.

Howard and I exchanged headshakes. "Milo's an original," I said. "Anyway, I'll begin drafting copy for the ads. You call Jill and ask if she can get us footage of Ridgeway and company cozying up to Meighen."

Howard trained his crafty old eagle's eyes on me. "I'll take a shot at the copy, Jo. You should be the one to see Jill."

I groaned. "Howard, no matter how many times you throw Jill and me together, nothing is going to change. Sometimes we reap what we sow," I said. "And sometimes other people have to reap what we sow. That's one of life's crueller lessons." I picked up my bag. "But I will go and see Jill. She should know we'll be grateful for her help."

A large ceramic bowl filled with the fruits of the season welcomed guests at the Hotel Saskatchewan reception desk. When I passed by on my way to the elevators, one of the clerks noticed me eyeing the bowl. "Take a piece of fruit," he said. "That's what they're there for." I chose a rosy red apple and I was still holding it when I knocked on the door to Jill's suite.

She opened the door immediately. She was wearing jeans, a white turtleneck, and a silver pendant engraved with a stylized wheat sheaf that the kids and I had given her for Christmas the year before. When she saw me, her face lit up. "Jo. I thought it was room service. I suddenly realized I hadn't eaten today, so I ordered something."

I handed her the apple. "Here," I said. "This will tide you over till room service arrives."

"Thanks," she said. She stood aside. "Come in."

"I'm here to ask a favour," I said. "Ridgeway's ads with Zack and his criminal clients are killing us. We're going to make some new ads based on the information in that tape you made of Graham talking to Scott Ridgeway."

"There's not much there," she said.

"There's enough, or there will be after we do a little doctoring. Jill, NationTV must have footage of Ridgeway and the members of city council cozying up to Graham and his associates. I know there are legal hoops to jump through before we can use the footage, but is there a way we could expedite the process?"

"When do you need it?"

"This afternoon."

Jill's laugh was brief. "Jo, if I follow protocol, that's impossible."

"What if you don't follow protocol?"

"The file will be on your computer by three o'clock."

"Thanks. We're really up against it."

Jill lowered her gaze. "If there's anything more I can do, I'm available."

I paused before I answered. "I could use your help getting the commercial to air," I said. "We can't blow this."

"Then it's a done deal." There was a knock at the door. "Room service," Jill said. "Just in the nick of time to keep you from changing your mind."

"I'm not going to change my mind," I said. "I'll call you after we have a chance to check out the footage."

When I left the hotel, the bands that had been tight around my chest since Slater Doyle broke the news about Ian's infidelity had begun to loosen. I called Howard to tell him that Jill was staying in Regina to help the campaign. His relief was palpable. "If I believed in God, I'd be down on my knees," he said.

"It wouldn't hurt you to get down on your knees once in a while," I said. "You never know."

"You're right about that," he said. "You never know."

Brock hadn't mentioned Michael Goetz since the day we heard that Liz Meighen had committed suicide. At the lake Brock had been an ideal guest – warm and unobtrusively helpful, but since we'd come back to the city, he'd kept to himself. That Wednesday morning as we did our pre-run stretches, his mind was clearly elsewhere.

"Penny for your thoughts," I said.

Brock tried a smile. "We don't use pennies any more, remember?"

"I remember. Brock, is something wrong?"

"Michael isn't answering my calls. I left a voicemail telling him that if he wanted to talk, I was available."

"And he didn't get back to you?"

"No, and he hasn't responded to my texts. I don't know what else I can do. Michael obviously doesn't want me in his life."

"Or someone else doesn't want you in his life," I said.

"That thought has occurred to me," Brock said. "And it scares me. Jo, I can't stop thinking about what happened to Liz Meighen. The Michael I know would never have compromised the well-being of a patient. The possibility that he played a role in Liz Meighen's suicide is making me sick."

"Let's hit the pavement," I said. "At his last checkup Pantera weighed in at one hundred and seventy-five pounds. He needs a workout."

We ran farther and harder than usual, and when we returned to Halifax Street we were sweat-soaked and panting almost as hard as the dogs. Brock did a couple of stretches before we got on the elevator. "That helped," he said.

I squeezed his arm. "Let's hear it for endorphins." As soon as I came in the door, I filled the dogs' water dishes and Zack poured me a glass of filtered water from the jug in the fridge. "I see you turned your run up a notch," he said.

I held the glass of cool water against my forehead before taking a sip. "Brock's an athlete. They're trained to play through pain, and Brock is suffering. He wants to help Michael, but Michael's not answering his phone calls or texts."

Zack sighed. "Tough on Brock, but legally, this might be the proverbial silver lining. If the police have cause to believe that Michael Goetz is responsible for Liz Meighen's death, the less Brock knows, the better."

I kissed Zack on the top of the head. "Ever the optimist," I said. "I'm going upstairs to shower."

"Make it a quick one," Zack said. "Milo's on his way over with what he says is a very rough rough cut of the first of the new ads."

"That was speedy."

"Wait till you see the bill for the whole team at the agency working overtime, but Milo likes the ad. He says it'll blow Ridgeway and his crew out of the water."

"Let's hope," I said. "Why don't you call Howard and Brock and ask them to come over and watch the new ad with us?"

"What about Jill?"

"I'll call her. I don't think she'd feel comfortable coming here, but she should have the option."

Over the years, Jill and I had worked together frequently. It was proving surprisingly easy to slip into the old grooves professionally. Re-establishing a personal relationship was another matter, but at the moment Jill and I had a common goal, and I knew she deserved to see the ad.

Jill picked up on the first ring. "How's it going?" she said.

"There's a rough cut of the new ad on its way here, and I thought you might want to see it."

"Thanks," she said. "It's probably best if I keep my distance for a while, but I appreciate the offer, Jo. I really do."

"We couldn't have made the ad without you," I said. "And according to Milo, it's dynamite. I'm girding my loins for retribution."

For a beat there was silence, then Jill said, "Jo, don't put yourself in a position where you're alone with Graham."

I felt a chill. "Was he violent with you?"

Jill hesitated before answering. "Yes. Thanksgiving night. We just started the evening when he got a phone call. He said it was urgent, but he'd be right back. The call had come in on Graham's landline, so I checked to see the identity of the last caller. It was Slater Doyle. When Graham didn't come home, I did a little judicious snooping. I photographed a few things on his desk that seemed provocative, and I discovered a safe behind the painting over the bed in the master bedroom. It's probably just for jewellery, but there could be something of interest in there.

"Anyway, he called at ten to tell me to take a cab back to the hotel and he'd meet me there. He arrived at eleven. He told me he wanted to make love to me on our first Thanksgiving together. He started to push me towards the bedroom. He smelled of liquor and sex. He hadn't even bothered showering before he came to the hotel. That tore it for me. I told him I was through with him, and I was going back to Toronto. He called me a cunt, and then he reached out and tried to throttle me."

"He did what?"

"He put his hands around my throat and pressed his thumbs on my trachea. Graham works out every morning at a gym. He's strong. If he had been sober, he would have killed me. Luckily, he was far from sober. I was able to pull back enough to knee him in the groin. That was it."

"And you didn't you go to the police?"

"Graham has powerful friends. It would have been a he said–she said situation. Graham's the grieving widower. I'm the big-city slut who's been putting out for him. He would have said he was trying to end the relationship and I was just a woman scorned."

"Jill, you have to press charges. Graham Meighen is dangerous. He shouldn't be walking around."

"I know that, but I want to crucify Graham Meighen, and I can't crucify him till I have the nails."

Howard, Milo, Brock, Zack, and I watched the ad three times before any of us said anything.

"That oughta do it," Zack said finally. "It may not be a knockout punch, but they'll be on the ropes."

The thirty-second ad had been shot in black and white. It was technically brilliant, morally reprehensible, and politically devastating. Footage of Scott Ridgeway handing Graham Meighen an envelope and the two men shaking hands was followed by a close-up of a man's hand opening the envelope and withdrawing a blank cheque made out to Lancaster Development and signed "The Taxpayers of Regina." The final footage was of Graham Meighen whispering in Scott Ridgeway's ear and Scott nodding understanding and approval. The camera froze on Graham Meighen whispering in the mayor's ear. A woman's voice, soft and insinuating, said, *"They have secrets they don't want you to know."* Then another voice, male and authoritative, delivered the Crime Stoppers tag. Our campaign's contact information was on the screen.

"They really knocked it out of the park," I said. "Milo, see if you can get your friends at Orange Smile to push it through post-production. We'll pay what it takes. We've bought time on *Canada's Future Stars* tomorrow night, and that ad is perfect for their audience."

"Done," Milo said. He leapt up and started for the door.

"And," I said. "Before you leave, could you send a copy to Jill and one to me."

Milo opened his laptop and tapped away. "Also done," he said.

Zack frowned. "Probably best not to show this around. We can deal with Meighen's lawyers after it gets on the air, but we don't want them to scare off the broadcaster."

"I'll be careful," I said. The grandmother clock struck the quarter hour. "Guess what?" I said. "You're supposed to be spending recess with the teachers at Riffel High."

"Shit," Zack said. "When's recess?"

"In fifteen minutes. If you hit the lights, you'll make it."

The first of the ads highlighting the close relationship between Scott Ridgeway and Graham Meighen aired on Friday, October 17, five days before E-Day. We were all running on fumes, but we were resolute. We had two goals in mind: capturing swing voters and blowing the Ridgeway campaign out of the water. Getting all four ads to air by the weekend was imperative. Orange Smile had already completed post-production on the second ad and was working on the third. Getting the fourth to air on Sunday night would be a nail-biter, but we were optimistic.

Declan had come home for the weekend, so when we sat down to watch *Canada's Future Stars*, the show on which the first ad would air, the atmosphere was reassuringly homelike. Margot and Lexi were there. So were Brock, Howard, and Milo. For reasons that were beyond me, *Canada's Future Stars* was wildly popular, with special appeal for the twenty-eight to forty-nine demographic, where Zack's numbers had been eroded by the perp ads. We had bought ten spots on the show – our "Secrets" ad would appear every six minutes. Saturation. Uncommitted voters would remember the drumbeat of the ads; more significantly, the Ridgeway campaign would know we were in this to win.

The "Secrets" ad appeared just after the host introduced the show. My cellphone was ringing before the ad was finished. My caller was Slater Doyle, and he was foaming at the mouth. "Where did you get that material?"

"From a supporter."

"Where did he get it?"

"I didn't ask. Slater, you should probably take a few deep breaths. We have a lot more information and we've made a substantial media buy to make sure voters understand the connection between Graham Meighen and your candidate before they mark their ballots."

"We'll get an injunction."

"Better find a lawyer who's licensed to practise in Saskatchewan first. You've been disbarred, remember?"

"You really are a bitch," Slater said, then he slammed down the phone.

On the weekend before E-Day, all of our extended family were out door-knocking. I spent most of my time at the Noodle House. The last days of any campaign are filled with rumours, endless cycles of hope and despair and manic energy desperately in need of channelling. My job that weekend was to quell the rumours, bring hope and despair into some sort of realistic confluence, and put the manic energy that bounced around the Noodle House to good use.

Zack and I were both sleeping an average of four hours a night – not enough – but Zack's store of energy was endless, and it was impossible to be in the Noodle House without getting a contact adrenaline high from the volunteers. I'd been in politics long enough to know that that crazy energy is what gets a campaign across the finish line, so I kept the pizza and soft drinks coming and cheered on the troops.

I was sitting at a desk near the front door checking volunteer reports and humming along with Stevie Nicks when a young man with the physique of a bodybuilder and a heartbreaking case of acne came in.

"I need to talk to Zack Shreve," he said.

"You just missed him," I said. "He's pretty well tied up for the afternoon, but I'm his campaign manager, so I might be able to help."

The young man eyed me and apparently decided to go for it. "I saw your ad on *Canada's Future Stars* Friday night. I have information," he said, "but it has to be kept confidential."

The woman at the next desk swivelled her chair to face us. "If you need to talk privately," she said, "the back room is free."

I stood. I'm five-foot-eight, but the bodybuilder's bulk dwarfed me. "I didn't catch your name," I said.

"It's Eli," he said.

"I'm Joanne," I said. "Let's go to the back, so we don't get interrupted."

As always the Noodle House was packed with volunteers – most of them sitting on their exercise balls, texting, tweeting, or working on their laptops. Eli and I threaded our way among the bodies and went into the room where three weeks earlier Slater Doyle had dropped a grenade into my life.

When we were inside, I shut the door. Under the harsh overhead light, it was difficult to get past the inflamed pustules on Eli's face and neck and upper trunk, but I managed. Except for his skin, he was a good-looking young man, probably in his early twenties. He was fine-featured and had beautiful eyes and enviable eyelashes. "Okay, Eli," I said. "What kind of information do you have?"

"Information about Graham Meighen. I don't know what he has on the mayor, but I know that Meighen's behind a lot of the stuff that's been going down lately. He hired the guys who trashed that lady's house."

"Peggy Kreviazuk," I said. "She's a friend. She told us that the men had been instructed to give her a beating she'd never forget, but the leader stopped them."

Eli looked down at his feet for what seemed like a very long time. Finally, he raised his head and met my eyes. "I wish I'd never got involved."

"You mean with Graham Meighen?"

"He has this system."

"What kind of system?"

Eli shook his head vehemently. "No, I've already said too much. I just wanted to warn you."

I glanced at my watch. "I can get Zack back here in twenty minutes. We can help you deal with Graham Meighen."

"You don't understand what he's capable of."

"Then tell me," I said.

Eli's eyes were filled with misery. "Anything," he said. He raised a hand to his ravaged face. "He's capable of anything and everything."

Angus had suffered from acne. He had always been a confident kid, but when the acne became serious, he began to withdraw. I'd made an appointment with a dermatologist. Angus responded well to the medication. His skin cleared up and his confidence returned. I found myself wishing that there was someone in Eli's life who would steer him to a dermatologist.

I found a piece of paper on the desk, wrote my name and the numbers for my cell and my landline, and handed the paper to Eli. His body was powerful, but there was vulnerability in his face. I touched his arm. "You don't have to handle this alone," I said.

"I don't want anybody else to get hurt," he said.

"Eli, is there somewhere I can get in touch with you?"

He struck a mocking muscleman pose. "At the gym," he said. Then he walked out the door, leaving behind more than a few troubling questions. I was optimistic that I could find the answer to at least one of them. I picked up the phone and dialed Jill's number.

She answered on the first ring. "What's up?"

"Just a question," I said. "You mentioned that Graham works out regularly. Does he always go to the same gym?"

"Yes," she said. "Da Silva's on 13th. What's this about?"

"I'll tell you later. I have a theory. If I can prove it, we'll have another nail for Graham's coffin. When's a good time to call you?"

"It's probably best if I call you," she said. "Does three o'clock work for you?"

"Yes, and call my cell," I said. "I have some errands to run."

Someone had donated two ancient TVs to the campaign. Both were on constantly, and it seemed every time I glanced toward a screen, one of our ads was running. Saturation. I remembered the old movie *The Hucksters*, where Sydney Greenstreet says the secret of advertising is to repeat the slogan until people say it in their sleep. The secret to selling soap, Greenstreet's character said, is "Irritate. Irritate. Irritate."

That afternoon as I picked up Zack from a meeting at Warren Weber's, our "Secrets" ad was playing on the radio. After Zack transferred his body from his chair to the car, snapped his chair apart, and stowed it in the back seat, he leaned over and turned off the radio.

"Hey, we're paying a lot of money for that," I said.

Zack rolled his eyes. "Don't I know it, and the ads seem to be having an effect – at least among Warren's crowd. That ad on *Canada's Future Stars* was all they could talk about."

"I wouldn't have thought Warren's crowd would be fans of *Canada's Future Stars*."

"I'm sure they're not, but word about the ad is getting around."

"Are they going to vote for you?"

"Warren's trying to push them in that direction, but our agenda is to change the way this city is run and they don't want change. Why would they? The system works for them. Just between us, Ms. Shreve, I think that no matter how many dark innuendos and examples of civic malfeasance we pull out of the hat, Warren's friends will hold their noses and vote for Ridgeway."

"That's what Howard and Milo are afraid will happen in parts of the east end too."

"So what are the odds?"

"Fifty–fifty?"

"I've faced worse," Zack said. "Anyway, enough of this. Let's go home. I need a couple of hours to get caught up on messages." He squeezed my thigh. "You and I could do a little catching up too."

"I wish," I said. "There's something I have to take care of. I'll call you when I'm done."

There are some upscale gyms in our city. Da Silva's on 13th is not among them. The building was freshly painted – black with yellow trim. Bright as a bumblebee, but there was a FOR SALE sign on the patch of lawn in front of the building; the front door sagged, and the path leading to it was seriously in need of repair. The morning was bright, but when I stepped into Da Silva's I entered a place that seemed to exist outside of time, weather, and the events of the world.

A customer was checking in at the front counter. I stood behind him and waited as a grizzled man wearing a windbreaker with the name "Sarge" stitched over the breast pocket stamped the newcomer in and handed him a small, worn towel. When the client disappeared, Sarge turned a rheumy eye to me. "Well?" he said. His tone was neither friendly nor unfriendly.

"I'm looking for a young man named Eli," I said. "I think he might work out here."

Sarge kept his eye fixed on me, waiting for further information. "I don't know his last name," I said. "He's a bodybuilder, about my height. He's nice-looking but he has a serious case of acne." Sarge continued to stare. "Bad skin," I explained.

Sarge cleared his throat. "I know what acne is." His voice was rusty, as if he seldom used it. "Pimples," he added.

I nodded. "Can you help me?"

His gaze hadn't wavered. He was waiting me out. I reached into my bag for my wallet, found a twenty, and lay it on the counter.

Sarge was quick. He slapped his hand over the twenty, drew it to the edge of the counter, and pocketed it. "Eli hasn't been in for a while," he said.

"Has he been in since Labour Day weekend?" I asked.

"One day's pretty much the same as the next around here."

I pulled out another twenty. "I failed to pay Eli for a job he did. I want to give him what I owe him. Can I leave you my name and number?" Sarge took my twenty and pushed a pad across the counter towards me. When I'd written my contact information, I pushed the pad back. He looked at what I'd written without interest. "Somebody told me Eli's working at a garage out of town," he said. I put another twenty on the counter. "The garage is in Southey."

"Got it," I said. "If Eli comes in here, please let him know I can help him."

For the first time, Sarge looked at me with interest. "Why do you want to help him?"

I met his eyes. "Eli came to me. He believes in justice. So do I."

Southey was a town fifty-five kilometres north of Regina on Highway 6. The population was a shade over seven hundred, so finding the A-1 gas station wasn't difficult. A-1 was painted the same black with yellow trim as Da Silva's gym. It wasn't much of a stretch to surmise that the gym and the gas station had the same owner. I put my money on Sarge. Eli was in the bay hunched over the engine of a Honda. His one-piece uniform was black and his name was stitched in yellow over the breast pocket. The owner of Da Silva's and A-1 clearly believed in one-stop shopping.

When Eli realized I was behind him, he turned, raised his hand reflexively to cover his cheek. "My uncle called. He said he thought you'd come. He says I should talk to you because we need help."

"We?"

"My uncle and me both. Graham Meighen is ruining my uncle's business. Da Silva's has always been an ordinary gym. A place where guys – mostly bodybuilders and guys interested in boxing – can work out without paying a lot. We don't have fancy equipment – just the basics, dumbbells, barbells, weight-lifting benches, some punching bags. Nothing to attract ladies like you." He gave me a shy smile. "Anyway, Da Silva's has always been a gym for guys who live paycheque to paycheque and everybody was as happy as guys like us ever are. And then Graham Meighen came along. He's rich. Nobody could figure out why he was training in a gym like ours. After a while everybody got used to him being there. That's when he started offering some of us jobs."

"What kind of jobs?"

Eli raised his arm and wiped his forehead with his sleeve. "Grey area jobs – the kind where you get paid under the table. At first there was nothing illegal, but when the jobs started to get iffy, some of us tried to turn him down. That's when Meighen told us he'd been keeping track. He had recordings of us agreeing to do jobs. He said he'd send them to the police."

"So people went along with what he suggested."

"Mrs. Shreve . . ."

"Joanne . . ." I said.

Eli nodded. "Joanne, most of the guys who come to Da Silva's didn't finish high school. And here's Graham Meighen, a pal of the mayor and everybody else who's important in this city, asking us to do jobs that we're nervous about. One of our guys who'd done work for Meighen in the past tried to stand up to him about a job he was offering that definitely did not pass the smell test. Meighen started spouting a bunch of legal mumbo-jumbo and convinced our guy that if he didn't do the job, Meighen would turn over evidence to the police that would land the guy in jail."

"And so your friend did what he was told," I said.

Eli nodded. "He did and after that, everyone fell into line. None of us wanted to do the stomping, but Meighen said the man was already dead and he was a thug who deserved what he got. Then he waved what he called our 'rap sheets' at us and told us our choices were to stomp on the dead guy and get paid two grand apiece or refuse and end up in jail. We didn't think we had a choice." Eli's eyes were downcast. "The man *was* dead when we did it, but I don't think he'd been dead long. After it was over, I went home and checked online. Wikipedia says rigor mortis starts about three to four hours after death."

"And Cronus didn't show any signs of rigor mortis?"

Eli shook his head. "No."

"Did Meighen give you the red kerchief?"

"He said the dead guy had gang connections and that if we did it right, the cops would assume it was gang-related."

"And you did it," I said.

Eli nodded miserably.

"You have to go to the police, Eli, but for the time being just sit tight. Graham Meighen is dangerous. I don't want you or your friends getting hurt. I'll talk to Zack about your legal position, but I think if you cooperate with the police, we can sort this out. If Graham Meighen gets in touch with you about another job, tell him no. If he tries to coerce you into doing whatever he wants done, tell him you have a lawyer, and he should talk to her."

"Do I have a lawyer?"

"Well, in about twenty minutes you will. Her name is Maisie Crawford. You'll like her. She plays lacrosse."

CHAPTER

16

It was past four when I left Southey. Jill was supposed to have called me at three, but there was no message on my phone. I'd tried her cell before I left, but there was no answer. Forgetting a promised phone call wasn't like Jill, and the vision of Graham Meighen's hands on her throat frightened me. When I got back to Regina just after five, I drove straight to the Hotel Saskatchewan.

As I walked down the hall towards Jill's suite, I passed a woman with a housekeeping cart. When she noticed that I'd stopped in front of Jill's door, she joined me. "Would you mind asking Ms. Oziowy if she wants me to do her room? I've knocked on the door, but she's not answering. I heard voices in her room earlier – loud voices. And then that man she's seeing came out. His hair was messed up and his face was very angry. When he ran past me, he knocked me over. He didn't stop. He just kept running till he got to the elevator. Ms. Oziowy's a nice woman. She always gives me something extra for taking good care of her. I called hotel security but nobody's answering."

I felt a chill. I knocked and called Jill's name, but there was no response. "I have a key," the woman from house-keeping said.

"Use it," I said.

The housekeeper opened the door. Jill had never been tidy, and the living room looked much like every other room Jill had occupied: coffee cups on the windowsill; sections of the morning paper dropped as she had read them on the floor; a blanket, a pillow, and a tin of olive body butter on one of the loveseats; and on the matching loveseat a room service tray holding the remains of a Greek salad and an empty wine glass. Standard Jill.

But when I walked into the bedroom, my heart clenched. She was lying on her back on the bed. It had been years since I'd seen Jill naked. When we were changing into our swim-suits with the kids, they were always were fascinated by Jill's freckles. Jill told them that the Freckle Fairy usually just scatters a few adorable freckles across a child's nose, but that she had been chosen to be "the lavishly freckled one," so the Fairy had dumped a whole basket of freckles on her.

I ran to the bed. "Call 911," I said to the housekeeper. I felt for a pulse in Jill's neck. The pulse was thready, but it was there. Suddenly, I was very cool. I knew what had happened, and I knew what I had to do. Graham Meighen had tried to kill Jill, and my job now was to make sure he paid for what he'd done. I longed to cover Jill's broken body, but this was a crime scene and I knew enough about the chain of evidence to know how easily it can be contaminated and dismissed in court. I couldn't let that happen.

I had to make certain the case against Graham Meighen was airtight. I took out my phone and snapped a dozen pic-tures of Jill from every angle and then I photographed the bedroom and the bathroom. I didn't know what was impor-tant so I just kept taking photos.

As the EMT crew was securing Jill on the stretcher, the woman from housekeeping took a rosary from her uniform pocket and placed it in Jill's hands. The crew was carrying the stretcher out when Debbie and her colleagues arrived. I bent and kissed Jill's forehead, then turned to Debbie. I didn't waste time on preamble. "Arrest Graham Meighen," I said. "Find him and lock him up."

Debbie's eyes locked on mine. "You're sure he did this."

"Absolutely." I turned to the woman from housekeeping. "Could you tell Inspector Haczkewicz what happened here this afternoon?"

The housekeeper had been stunned by the violence that had been done to Jill, but her account of what she had heard and seen was clear and her description of Graham Meighen was dead on. When she was finished, she told Debbie her name was Annetta Kopchek and gave her contact information. Debbie thanked her and said that she could get on with her day but that the police would be in touch.

I walked Annetta to the door. "Thank you for your help," I said. "And thank you for giving Jill the rosary."

"I always carry an extra one," she said. "I see many sad things in my work."

When I went back to the bedroom, Debbie was staring at the tangled sheets of the bed.

"What Meighen did to Jill was inhuman," I said. "I could see the marks of his fingers on her throat. His teethmarks were on her breasts. Her vagina was bleeding and her face was broken. He must have kicked it after he finished raping her."

"Jesus," Debbie breathed. She spoke to a young constable standing by the door. "Get out an APB on Graham Meighen." The constable nodded and hit speed-dial on his cell.

"Now, Jo, tell me what you're doing here."

The police team was moving purposefully through the hotel suite, dusting for fingerprints and bagging evidence. As a female constable began taking photographs, I remembered my own pictures. I took out my phone and handed it to Debbie. "I knew the EMT would want to get Jill to the hospital, so I took these before they came."

Debbie's face hardened as she scrolled through the photos. "You're right," she said. "Meighen's an animal." She pulled out her paper notebook and pen. "We need to talk, but let's get out of here. We'll just be in the way."

There was a small couch against the wall facing the elevators, and Debbie and I sank into it. "Zack's expecting me any minute. I'd better let him know what's happening." Zack offered to meet me at Regina General, and I didn't dissuade him. When I got to the Emergency Room, Zack was there with a takeout bag from Orange Izakaya. "I'm guessing you're not in the mood for eating, but I know you get wonky when you're hungry, so do your best. Taylor made us a thermos of Japanese tea."

The food from Orange Izakaya was always good, but that night my stomach was heaving. Taylor's thermos of tea helped and I was able to eat enough to feel my strength returning.

We'd just finished when a doctor came in. He was young, as increasingly all doctors seemed to be, and nerdy in a very winning way. He looked as bushed as I felt. "I'm Mitch Nagel-Zeller, Jill Oziowy's doctor," he said. "You must be her friend, Joanne."

I nodded. "How did you know my name?"

"You were the only person Jill wanted us to call," he said.

Relief washed over me. "She's able to speak?" I said.

He nodded. "She's very lucky. Her attacker choked her, and choking can have devastating results. We don't know how long Jill was without oxygen, but she doesn't appear to have suffered brain damage. Her speech is clear; she's lucid.

Her coordination is fine. There's no numbness in her extremities. That's the good news."

"And the bad news?"

"The rape was brutal. Her vagina is badly torn up. Her assailant must have raped her with some kind of metal instrument. Given the nature of her injuries and the fact that the assault took place in a hotel room, my guess is that he used the ice tongs from the bar."

My intake of breath was audible. Zack clutched my hand and held it tight. The doctor continued. "Mercifully, for the moment, Jill doesn't remember what happened," he said. "She remembers the choke hold. After that, nothing."

"The physical harm is treatable?" I said.

"Yes, we've patched her up. Joanne, the problem will come when she starts to remember what happened – and she will remember. She'll need someone to keep an eye on her. Ideally, it would be us, but we haven't got the space or the personnel to spend 24/7 with a patient who's not in any imminent physical danger. Does Jill have family?"

"A stepdaughter, but she's in New York City, and she and Jill aren't close."

"Then arrangements will have to be made," the doctor said.

Zack held out his hand. "I'm Zack Shreve – Joanne's husband. We'll take care of it, doctor." I shot him an anxious look. I wasn't ready to have Jill in our home, but Zack had a better plan. "We've used the services of a company that provides nurses for people who need short-term but focused nursing care. It's called Whitman Convalescent."

Dr. Nagel-Zeller checked his phone. His decision wasn't hasty. When he looked up, his expression revealed nothing. "Whitman appears to be excellent, except their nursing staff is largely male. Given Jill's recent experience, she might not be comfortable with a male nurse."

I stood. "May I ask her?"

"Of course. She's eager to talk to you too," he said. "Don't stay long. We've given her something for pain and she's starting to drift a little. Joanne, if she brings up the rape, let her talk about it."

Jill was still in one of the curtained-off cubicles in emergency. It was painful to look at her. She was in a hospital gown. Her nose was swollen, and the harsh overhead lights threw every bruise and abrasion into sharp relief. It was impossible to ignore the marks Graham Meighen's hands had left around her neck.

When she saw me, she tried a smile. "Am I going to live?"

"You're going to live," I said.

Her smile became tentative. "Are you glad?"

I covered her hand with my own. "Very glad," I said.

She closed her eyes and for a few seconds, I thought she was asleep. "I hurt," she said. "He raped me, didn't he?"

"Yes," I said. "Zack and I talked to your doctor. I know it doesn't feel that way now, but you were very lucky. They don't know how long you were unconscious, but your brain is working, and your other wounds will heal. Dr. Nagel-Zeller's concern, and ours, is how best to help you deal with what happened. The doctor feels that for the next few days at least, there should be someone with you all the time."

"To make sure I don't kill myself?"

"No, to be there to let you talk when you're ready. I'd sign on, but there are only two days before the election . . ."

Jill raised her hand to wave off my explanation. "I understand. I'll be all right."

"We're getting a nurse to stay here with you tonight. A couple of years ago Zack had a bout with a pressure ulcer and the flu. I needed help, and we hired a nurse from a company called Whitman Convalescent. He was excellent and the company has a very good reputation, but their staff is mostly male. Dr. Nagel-Zeller wondered if you might prefer a female nurse."

She shook her head wearily. "No. Anybody they send will be fine." She closed her eyes again. "Jo, why are you doing this for me?'

"Because you'd do it for me," I said. "See you in the morning."

Taylor and Declan were on the couch when we got home. They sprang apart as soon as they heard us come in the door. Both were both fully clothed, but their hair was mussed and their faces were rosy with joy and guilt.

"How's everything with Jill?" Declan asked.

"She'll be all right," I said. "But it's going to take a while."

"Is there anything we can do?" Taylor said.

"Thanks, but no. Your dad and I are going to bed. It's been a long day."

Taylor frowned. "It's not even eight-thirty."

Zack looked at his watch. "You're right. And Declan's going back to Toronto tomorrow. Since it's still early, let's have a visit. What can I get everybody to drink?"

"V-8," Taylor said.

"A healthful choice," Zack said. "But I'm in the mood for a beer."

"Beer sounds good to me," I said.

Declan leaped up. "I'm all over it," he said. And he was. When Zack suggested that we stay downstairs to talk to the kids, I'd been less than enthusiastic, but sipping a Corona and feeling the electricity between our daughter and Declan as they talked about classes and friends and jointly hosting a party for Taylor's sixteenth birthday was tonic. That night I was badly in need of an infusion of belief in the future. Taylor and Declan gave me that, and when Zack and I said our goodnights and promised to call Declan with the election results, we were all smiling.

Two calls came before we finally turned out the lights. In very different ways, both turned out to be reassuring. The first was from Luke Forbes, the nurse who'd been assigned to Jill's case. Jill was sleeping now, but they'd talked briefly. She didn't want to go back to the hotel, so he suggested that when she was released from the hospital she spend a few days at the rest and rehab facility that Whitman Nursing ran. Luke and Dr. Nagel-Zeller had agreed that if Jill seemed ready, she could be moved to Whitman Convalescent late the next day.

Our second call was from Debbie. Graham Meighen had been arrested at the airport, on his way to Belize. It turned out that the Meighens owned a winter home there. Graham was carrying a significant amount of cash, and he put up a fight when the officers approached him at the airport. Debbie said that the arresting officers were surprised at Meighen's physical strength and at the level of violence he exhibited. They suspected he was using anabolic steroids. He was being held in the Provincial Correctional Centre, just east of the city limits, and as a danger to others and a flight risk, it seemed unlikely that Meighen would be granted bail. Debbie assured us he would be there for a while.

Zack immediately called Maisie Crawford to tell her that it was now safe for Eli to go the police. Maisie had arranged for legal representation for the other young men who'd been involved with Graham Meighen. Eli and his friends could supply key pieces to solving two crimes. Now that Meighen was locked up, they could be open about how he had used them to do his dirty work. It had been seven weeks since Cronus's death. Debbie needed an arrest, and Zack was hopeful she'd go easy on the people who could put Graham Meighen where he belonged.

Zack turned out his light. "Score one for the good guys," he said. "If that woman from housekeeping . . ."

"Annetta Kopchek," I said.

"If Annetta Kopchek hadn't been in the hall when you went to Jill's suite . . ."

My throat closed. "Life really does turn on a dime, doesn't it?"

"I imagine Graham Meighen's contemplating that fact at this very moment. If you and Annetta Kopchek hadn't opened the door to Jill's suite, he would have caught his flight and right about now he'd be on his way to paradise."

"The authorities in Belize would have sent him back, wouldn't they?"

"Eventually. But Belize doesn't have an extradition treaty with Canada. Justice would have been slow in coming. And in the meantime, Graham would have been lolling on the beach, working on his suntan, drinking salty dogs, and munching conch fritters."

"Thank God for Annetta Kopchek," I said. "When I saw Jill today, she was still holding the rosary Annetta gave her. Jill had been clutching it so tightly, the cross had made a mark on her palm."

Zack shook his head. "The mark of the cross on Jill's palm and the marks of Graham Meighen's hands on her neck. I wonder how Jill is interpreting those images tonight."

I reached over and turned out the light on my nightstand. "There's an old Russian proverb," I said. "'The morning is wiser than the evening.' Let's save the existential questions till after we've had our first cup of coffee."

CHAPTER

17

Zack was making porridge when I got back from my run with Brock and the dogs. I leaned over and gave him a sweaty kiss. "I've decided that if we're going to get everything done we need to do between now and E-Day, we should make lists of our priorities."

Zack took down the magnetized pad we kept on the refrigerator door for grocery lists, ripped off a page, and handed the rest of the pad to me.

"A man of action," I said. "Can I shower first?"

"Nope! No time to screw around," Zack said. He'd already wheeled over to the kitchen table and taken out his pen. When we were both finished our lists, I said, "Okay, let's trade."

Zack slipped on his reading glasses and read my list out loud:

> "1. Get Jill settled ASAP at Whitman's Convalescent.
> 2. Deal with the fallout from Graham Meighen's arrest – Z to give statement to press.
> 3. Tell Debbie everything. Make certain the lawyers protect Eli and friends.

4. Meet with all poll captains – go over voter lists –
make sure there are enough runners for election day.
If possible send volunteers to wavering voters.
5. Make sure pizza money's in petty cash at the
Noodle House.
6. Don't panic.
N.B. Don't forget Madeleine's basketball game at St.
Pius 3:45 Monday.

Zack removed his glasses. "Commendably thorough," he said. "Now it's your turn."

I read Zack's priority list out loud:

"1. Joanne and Taylor
2. Jill
3. Madeleine's basketball game at Pius – 3:45 TODAY!
4. Everything else."

"You put us first," I said.

"You and Taylor always come first. That's why I made sure there are cashews, dried cranberries, *and* candied ginger in the porridge."

"Time to call Taylor?" I asked.

"Yep. Breakfast is ready."

We were just sitting down when Milo buzzed from the lobby. As always, he entered bopping, baseball hat turned backward, fingers tapping.

"How about some porridge?" Zack said. "Start your day off right."

"Thanks, big man, but my day is already aces." Milo took his laptop from his backpack. "Check this out."

It took a moment to grasp what was on the screen. It was a melee – a violent free-for-all, the purpose of which was not immediately clear. When Graham Meighen hove into view, I realized that I was watching the scene at the airport when Graham had been arrested. At one point his face was pushed towards the camera and I was gratified to see that

Graham Meighen looked both vicious and desperate. Meighen was on the second floor of the terminal and about to go through security when the police caught up to him. We watched the video to the end when Graham Meighen was subdued, cuffed, and led into an elevator by two brawny cops, both female.

"Want to see it again?" Milo asked.

"Once was enough," I said. "Graham's luck appears to have turned."

Zack grinned. "Yep, as one of my former clients would say, 'If luck were shit, that guy is no longer getting a sniff.'"

Taylor chortled. "Good one, Dad."

I laughed too. "That life lesson aside, our campaign did just catch a break. If this footage has already been shown on the news . . ."

"And it has," Milo said.

"Then we don't have to do a thing," I said. "No more oblique references to Graham Meighen's character. That video at the airport shows the kind of man Meighen is, and our latest ad makes it clear that he and Scott Ridgeway are joined at the hip. The media will be all over the mayor for a response to Meighen's arrest. All Zack has to do is say is that Graham Meighen is the subject of a number of ongoing investigations and it would be inappropriate for him to comment at this time."

Milo dropped his iPad into his backpack and pulled out a Crispy Crunch. He flipped it to Taylor. "For recess," he said, and with that, he was gone.

Jill was having breakfast when I got to the hospital. Luke was familiar with hospital food, so he'd brought Jill a brown bag breakfast from Whitman Convalescent: fresh-baked bran muffins, a sliced peach, a container of milk, and a thermos of real coffee. Jill was in a great deal of pain, but she was doing her best to eat, and despite the bruising and swelling on her face she was looking better.

"We're pushing to get Jill moved out of here today," Luke said, then left us alone.

"Welcoming as this place is," Jill said, "I'm ready to move along." She shifted her body a little and grimaced in pain.

"Are you all right?" I said.

"Stitches," she said tightly. "Did they catch him?"

"Yes," I said. "How much do you want to know?"

"Everything."

"He was at the airport. He had a ticket to Belize."

Jill's smile was ironic. "Graham invited me to join him there. He made the offer tempting. He was eloquent about the joys of lovemaking on the white sands, but I wasn't convinced. That particular trip to paradise would have cost me half a million dollars."

"Graham won't be going anywhere for a long time," I said. "You could probably pick up Graham's Belize property for $500,000 and it wouldn't come with a sociopath for a lover."

"Do the police have enough evidence to charge him?"

"Yes. And not just for what he did to you." I lowered my voice. "I'm sure they'll be able to prove that he killed Cronus. Cronus died from manual strangulation, and Meighen attempted to strangle you – the same modus operandi. Meighen coerced some young men from his gym into stomping on Cronus's body, and the men are ready to talk."

"Graham really is a monster."

"He is," I agreed. "And I'm certain that the police will discover that Graham was responsible for Liz Meighen's suicide. He set out to destroy the mind of his dead daughter's mother, and he succeeded. There has to be a special place in hell for someone capable of that kind of calculated cruelty."

Jill hands were trembling. "Had enough?" I said.

"For now, yes. But, Jo, as soon as I'm well, I'm going to go after this story. There are big questions that haven't been answered. Why did Graham kill Cronus? Why was Scott Ridgeway funnelling money to Graham's company? And why was Graham so desperate for money that he drove Liz to suicide?"

"Exactly the same questions that have been plaguing me," I said. "And, Jill, I know the answer is in plain sight. Everything is connected to that house at Number 12 Rose Street, where Zack held his press conference. I just can't see the connections yet."

Jill leaned forward. The life had come back into her eyes. "Tell me what you know," she said.

And I did.

The meeting between Maisie Crawford, her client Eli Wishlow, and Debbie Haczkewicz was being held in the boardroom at Falconer Shreve. It was an imposing space, but we wanted Eli to feel that he had the weight of the law behind him. Among her many talents, Norine MacDonald knew how to dress and groom clients for court and for meetings that would have a significant impact on their future. Zack said once that Norine could make Hannibal Lecter look like a guy who deserved a second chance, and when I checked out Eli, it seemed Zack was right on the money. Eli was freshly shaven and barbered, and he was wearing a business suit and shoes with a hard shine. He looked like a young man on his way to meet his girl-friend's parents.

Maisie and Eli had already talked several times, and they had a natural rapport. The three other young men Meighen had coerced were represented by lawyers from other firms, and Eli assured me that they were all prepared for what lay ahead. When I left Falconer Shreve, I headed for the Noodle

House, optimistic that at long last the pieces were beginning to fall into place.

Zack and I pulled into the St. Pius X parking lot at exactly the same time. I waited while he got out of his car. He gave me the once-over. "You look frisky," he said. "Good day?"

"I may still be on a sugar high," I said. "I spent the afternoon at the Noodle House. My lunch was three jelly doughnuts."

"That should get you through," Zack said. "How did the meeting between Debbie and Eli go?"

"All right, I think. Of course, I was just there to wish Eli luck, but he called me after he had talked to Debbie. Apparently, she was frank about needing their help to nail Cronus, and she seemed open to cutting a deal. Eli said he trusted Debbie, but he was glad Maisie Crawford had been with him."

"We lawyers have our uses," Zack said. "Anything else?"

"One more thing," I said. "I gave Eli the name of the dermatologist Angus went to here in the city when he had acne. Eli said he'd been on the list for a while. Could we find a dermatologist out of province whom he could see immediately?"

Zack pulled out his phone and hit speed-dial. He talked for a minute, then broke the connection. "All will be well. Norine is on the case. Now, let's get to the gym before all the courtside seats are taken."

"Okay. Now remember, no gloating, and if Madeleine gets a bad call or is on the end of cheap shot, we'll say nothing."

"Not a word," Zack said. "Madeleine herself has spoken to me about grandparental etiquette at games."

Grades Three and Four basketball was apparently not a high-interest sport. Zack's concern that there wouldn't be room for us courtside proved to be groundless. There were only a scattering of parents and family members present.

There is no private time in politics, and a few people came over to ask Zack questions or to wish him well. Just as the game was about to begin, a man with a blond crewcut and a bristling attitude approached us. "I'm a friend of Graham Meighen's and I wanted you to know you're going to pay for what you did to him."

Zack was sanguine. "And now I know. Let's just enjoy the game."

"I'm not through," the man said.

"I think you are," Zack said.

The man was quick. He reached down, grabbed the twin vertical tubes that attached the armrests to the side frame of Zack's wheelchair, and flipped the chair backward. I heard Zack's head hit the floor. The incident was over in seconds. Lena and I dropped to our knees and knelt beside Zack, and Madeleine ran across the court. The blond crewcut flashed a triumphant smile. "It is such a rush to see you helpless, Shreve," he said. I was aware of someone behind me taking pictures, but when I turned, whoever it was had disappeared through the exit.

Mo St. Amand, the principal of Pius, appeared out of nowhere, spoke firmly but quietly to the blond crewcut, then escorted him out of the gym. We righted the wheelchair. Zack said his head was hard and he was none the worse for wear, so, heart pounding, I sat back to watch the game.

Zack and I had been at many Pius functions, and we knew and liked Mo St. Amand. When Mo came to check on Zack, his concern was palpable. Zack waved him off. "I'm fine. But did you know the guy?"

Mo cracked an odd smile. "Oh yeah. His name is Hank Brodner. He's a pillar of the community, an ardent supporter of what he believes are all the right causes. Zack, if I'd seen him come in, I would have headed him off. Believe it or not, he can be a decent guy, but this election is making him crazy."

Zack shook his head. "This election is making a lot of people crazy, Mo. Don't give it a second thought."

St. Pius X won by two points. Madeleine scored two points – not the winning two, but as Zack pointed out if it hadn't been for Madeleine's two points, the game would have been a tie. Persuaded by Zack's argument, the four of us went to Dessart on 13th for celebratory ice-cream cones. A day in the life.

The front page of the next morning's paper featured the photo of Zack sprawled on the gym floor with the grand-daughters and me hovering. I was furious – at the fact that Zack had been made to look helpless and at the fact that the photographer had captured the children's fear so com-pletely. The kids at school would tease the girls. Madeleine would be stoic; Lena would be fiery, but they would both be wounded.

I showed Zack. "Why the hell would they do that?" he fumed.

"It's the day before the election," I said. "And that's a dramatic photo."

Zack drained his coffee, wheeled over to the hall closet, and took down his jacket.

"Where are you going?" I said.

"To Mieka's – to talk to our granddaughters."

When Mieka answered the door, she seemed harried, but she managed a smile. "Don't waste your time here," she said. "You already have my vote. But I think my next-door neighbours are wavering."

"I'll work on them after I talk to the girls," Zack said.

"They're upstairs getting ready for school," Mieka said. "What's up?"

"Have you seen the morning paper?"

Mieka smiled. "Zack, I haven't subscribed to a newspaper in years. I get all my news online."

Zack took out his iPad and fiddled with it till he had the front page of the *Leader-Post*.

"How did that happen?" she said quietly.

"A guy who does not wish me well tipped my wheel-chair," Zack said. "The girls and your mother came running. One of the parents at the game must have decided to immortalize the moment."

Mieka's brow was furrowed. "But you're okay?" she said.

"I'm fine," Zack said. "I'm just worried that Madeleine and Lena will get hassled at school, so I'm here to apologize."

"No need," Mieka said. "The girls understand elections. They've had a few dustups at school already."

I touched her arm. "You never said anything."

"I didn't want to worry you. I talked to Mo and he spoke to the kids involved. It's all good now."

"What happened when it wasn't 'all good'?" Zack said.

"Some kids made some nasty comments about you. Madeleine told them to stop, and things got out of hand."

Zack continued to press. "How out of hand?" he said.

Mieka's tone was resigned. "One of the girls shoved Madeleine. Maddy shoved back and they were going at it until the teacher separated them."

"That doesn't sound like Madeleine," Zack said.

"It isn't like Madeleine," Mieka said. "But she loves you, Zack. She's not going to stand by and let another kid say cruel things about you."

"Were there any repercussions?"

"Madeleine was uninvited to a sleepover. The parents are Ridgeway supporters and friends of the parents of the girl who started the shoving. The mother called me and told me that it would be best if Maddy didn't come to the party."

Zack closed his eyes and pinched the bridge of his nose.

"I'd do anything to keep those girls from being hurt," he said. "I hope you know that, Mieka."

"I do," she said. "And it's not as if the Kilbourns haven't been down this road before. Elections were always tough for my brothers and me, but we survived. Madeleine and Lena will too."

"What can I do to help?" Zack asked.

"Just do what Mum always did with Pete and Angus and me. Tell the girls you love them, you're proud of them, and that they should hang on to what J.S. Woodsworth said. 'What we desire for ourselves, we wish for all.'"

"You remember," I said.

For the first time that morning, Mieka's smile was unforced. "Mum, it's not as if we didn't hear it a million times. Plus we had Woodsworth's 'Prayer Before Meat' on all those paper placemats that sweet lady at party office ordered before someone told her that paper placemats were not environmentally friendly."

I laughed. "But our family used them. Three times a day for God knows how long, and we never even made a dent in the supply."

"There are still boxes of them in my basement," Mieka said. "Somehow it didn't seem environmentally friendly to throw them out."

"If they're not mouldy, bring them along to the victory party tomorrow night," I said. "They'll be a nice souvenir."

"More importantly, they'll finally be out of my house," Mieka said. My daughter was rarely physically demonstrative with Zack, but she could feel his misery about the girls and bent to embrace him. "The girls will be fine," she said. "So will I. Everybody will be fine."

When we left Mieka's, Zack was quiet and clearly troubled.

I slid into the driver's seat, but I didn't put the keys into the ignition. "We knew this wouldn't be easy," I said.

"Yeah," Zack said, "but I assumed the hits would be aimed at me. Knowing that our grandkids and our kids are being hurt by this makes me sick. Ridgeway's people haven't laid a hand on me. They've been content to go after the people around me. And all I can do is stand by and watch you take the blows."

Zack's face was grey and his eyes were deeply shadowed. "We have an hour before we start making the rounds to cheer on the volunteers," I said. "Let's take a walk along the levee and see if we can find our old pals the beavers. We both deserve time off."

"Sold," Zack said. He took his chair out of the back seat and began assembling it again. When he'd transferred his weight from the car to the chair, we moved towards the levee that the city built on both sides of the creek to protect us from floods during spring runoff.

For a body of water in a residential area ten minutes from downtown, Wascana Creek is large, about twenty-five metres across. As a further flood precaution, the banks have been planted with indigenous bushes. In spring and summer their leaves rustle musically in the wind, but on that late October morning only a few leaves clung to their branches. The morning sunshine was pale, and the creek was silent. As we walked down the levee towards our old house, Zack and I were silent too.

I found the flat rock I used to sit on in early mornings when the dogs and I had finished our run, and Zack moved his chair close to me. "It's so peaceful here," he said.

"Taylor says that at this time of year, the creek is like a Japanese etching. Earth, tree, and sky – the lines are simple, but every stroke is right."

Zack's voice was low. "Do you miss living close to the creek?"

"I do. For years, the creek was part of my life. When you

and I found our house and I realized it was just across the creek from where I'd lived with Ian and the kids, I felt as if I'd been predestined to live here. Kismet."

"Do you wish we'd moved back into our house after we had it rebuilt?"

I picked up a shiny stone and examined it. "Too late now," I said. "A nice doctor and her family are living there. I'll bet the first thing they did was change that Lavendre de Provence paint you and Taylor and I spent so much time choosing."

Zack didn't smile. "Jo, do you regret marrying me?"

"God, no. Never. Not for a single second."

He took my hand. "You have no idea how relieved I am to hear that."

I leaned towards him. "Whatever made you think that I've had second thoughts about us?"

Zack gazed across the creek. "Our lives haven't been exactly sunshine and lollipops lately."

"But we've been together," I said. "That's all that matters to me."

"That's all that matters to me too," Zack said. "My greatest fear is losing you."

"It will never happen," I said. "The day after Cronus died, I had a dream. I was at a lake and I was on one of those old inner tubes that kids used to inflate so they could lie on them and hang on to a rope attached to a motorboat. The motors were always outboards – with just enough horsepower to give kids a thrill. In my dream, I was being towed by a red speedboat that had real power. I could see people on the shoreline waving and shouting. I was moving so fast I couldn't make out what they were saying, but I knew they were telling me to let go. I ignored them. Then the driver of the red speedboat opened the motor full throttle and headed for the centre of the lake. The water there was

black, deep, and weedy. I knew the weeds could catch a
swimmer's legs and pull her under. I was terrified so I let go
of the rope. I watched until the red speedboat disappeared.
I was safe, but I was numb with grief. I knew I'd lost something I could never recover." I took Zack's hand. "That
something was life with you."

Zack's voice was rough with emotion. "Do we have time
to go home and make love?"

"We'll make time," I said.

A former client of Zack's claimed that "a heavy-duty love
sesh" cleansed the body, freed the mind, and increased efficiency. Zack's and my lovemaking that morning cut into our
time to visit poll captains and tweak our E-Day prepara-
tions, but later, as I roamed the Noodle House, reviewing
lists, bucking up the discouraged, and checking the cartons
of "Thank You, Regina" banners we planned to staple to
our lawn signs if we won, I felt better than I had in weeks.

Zack came home and had dinner with Taylor and me but
left for some last-minute meetings before dessert. Taylor and
I were just cleaning up the dishes when the phone rang. It
was Luke, letting me know that Jill had moved to Whitman
Convalescent and she would welcome company.

"How's she doing?" I said.

"The stitches are still giving her a lot of pain."

"I remember that from the episiotomies I had when the
kids were born."

"At least you ended up with a child," Luke said.

Remembering the onesies and the baby sweater with the
pattern of ducks I'd seen in Jill's dresser drawer, I was swept
with a wave of sadness. "How are her spirits?" I asked.

"Not great," Luke said. "She's relieved to be out of the
hospital, of course, but the rape and what comes next are
weighing heavily on her mind."

"Do you think I should come by?"

"Yes. So does Jill, but she was afraid to ask. Joanne, Jill told me that she and your first husband had an affair. She thought it was important for me to understand why you might not want to visit her."

"I'll be there in half an hour," I said.

After Falconer Shreve outgrew the twin heritage houses in the city centre that had served as their offices, Whitman Convalescent purchased the buildings and renovated them to meet the needs of their clientele.

That October night, I was impressed by how faithfully the owners of Whitman had preserved the houses' starchy charm. The lawns were raked and the round iron planters filled with jumbo gold and rust chrysanthemums were in place. The discreet brass plates on the front doors that once bore the firm's name now read simply, South House or North House. Jill was in North House, reserved for patients who were fully ambulatory.

Luke met me at the door. The first thing that struck me about the interior of North House was its simple, uncluttered beauty. The lighting was muted and the place was blessedly silent. I instinctively lowered my voice. "How is she tonight?" I said.

"Looking forward to seeing you," Luke said. He half turned and gestured towards the hallway. "And here she is."

Jill's walk was shuffling. She had always been proud of her body and had favoured outfits that showcased it. That night, for the first time in my memory, she was wearing sweatpants.

She reached out to embrace me, then thought better of it and dropped her arms to her sides. "I'm glad you're here," she said. "Can I get you something to drink – tea or something stronger?"

"I'm fine," I said. "But I'd like to see your new digs."

I followed her down the hall to her room. Like the rest of the facility, Jill's room was plain and welcoming: a double bed covered with a handsome quilt, brass lamps that pooled warm light on the night tables, a chaise longue, and, by the window, a table and two chairs.

I gestured to the chaise longue. "Why don't you stretch out there?"

"Thanks," Jill said. "I'm still a little unsteady. She lowered herself carefully onto the chaise longue and sighed. "That's better," she said. "How's the election going?"

"We'll know tomorrow night," I said. "I'll be glad when it's over."

"Subject closed?"

"Subject closed," I said. "Let's talk about you. Whitman's seems like a good place to get your life back on an even keel."

Jill's laugh was short and sharp. "I'm not sure that's possible. You're right about this being a great haven, but at some point I'm going to have to rejoin the world."

"Take your time," I said. "When you're ready, there are many possibilities awaiting you. The Graham Meighen story is going to be huge, especially because Debbie now has information that will tie Meighen to Cronus's murder. When that story goes to air, you'll show that little putz at NationTV what real journalism is. And there are all those questions about 12 Rose Street that are still to be answered. You can have a good life, Jill."

"But it will be a life without you and your kids. Because of me, they lost their father for the second time. I'll never forgive myself for that."

"They'll be all right. They *were* hurt, but they're adults. They have lives of their own. Ultimately, I think Ian will just become a distant memory for them."

"Is that how it will be for you?"

I shrugged. "I'm working on it. For the first few days after Slater broke the news, I felt like the walking dead. I went through the motions, but I was in a daze. Finally, I realized that people counted on me. I had to smarten up, so I threw out the one picture I had kept of Ian and me."

"Goodbye to all that?" Jill said.

"Yes, and so far, it seems to be working."

Jill's face was ineffably sad. "I'll never be able to say goodbye."

"You have to," I said. "Ian never deserved a woman as fine as you."

"How can you say that after everything I did?"

"I can say it because it's true." I leaned down and kissed her forehead. "Don't get up. I can see myself out. We'll have more time to talk after the election's over."

The first thing I did on E-Day after peeing, splashing my face, brushing my teeth, and kissing my husband was to go out on our terrace and check the weather. After that I rummaged through my closet till I found my favourite running pants and the T-shirt I was wearing the day I met Zack. When I was dressed, I read Zack's, Brock's, and my horoscopes. If the entrails of a sacrificed animal had been handy, I would have attempted to divine the state of its liver.

Brock was already waiting when the dogs and I reached the stoop of our building. I stepped out into a perfect October day – still, sunny, blue-skied, and crisp but not cold. Brock took both dogs' leashes so I could stretch to get the tightness out of my calves and Achilles tendons. After I'd bounced on my toes a few times, Brock handed me Willie's leash. That's when I noticed Brock was wearing a black braided leather necklace.

"I like the leather," I said.

"I've had it since high school. It's always brought me luck when I wrote exams."

I unzipped my jacket and pointed to my T-shirt. "I was wearing this the first time I met Zack. I'd say that was lucky."

"So would I." Brock laughed. "Here we are, two rational human beings with our talismans."

"It's E-Day. Everybody's superstitious," I said. "Let's go."

No black cats crossed our path and no ladders blocked our way. It was a good run. My cell was vibrating when we got back at the condo. There was a text from Zack: *Ask Brock to come up with you.*

I handed Brock my cell so he could read the message. "What's up?" he said.

"Beats me," I said. "Let's hope Zack didn't break a mirror."

When we came into the condo, Zack was sitting at the butcher-block table; the dogs' water dishes were filled, and there was a pitcher of water from the refrigerator on the counter for Brock and me. I poured us each a glass, then Brock and I joined Zack. "So what's the big news," I said.

"Graham Meighen is dead," Zack said.

"Suicide?" Brock asked.

"Apparently natural causes," Zack said. "Debbie called about ten minutes ago. According to Debbie, Meighen had a heart attack last night. The police were nearing the end of another round of interrogation when it happened. They were pressing Meighen hard on the Cronus case. They'd caught him in some inconsistencies, and Meighen was in the process of reaming them out when he collapsed. The cops rushed him to the hospital. The medical people did what they could, but Meighen died about an hour ago."

Brock drained his water glass. "It's hard to know how to react."

I thought of what Meighen had to done to Jill's body. "It's not hard for me," I said. "Zack, did Debbie tell you when the police will be releasing the news about Meighen's death to the media?"

"No, but it'll be soon. Are you concerned about Jill?"

"Yes. She shouldn't get this from the media," I said. "I'll call Luke and tell him I'm on my way."

Jill was waiting in the living room for me. She was on the couch talking with a man who looked to be in his early eighties. A copy of Colm Tóibín's *The Master* was on the end table beside him. He and Jill were having coffee and talking about Tóibín and Henry James. Jill introduced us. His name was Russell Exton. Jill promised him she'd be back to discuss the novel later, and then the two of us walked down the hall to her room.

She closed the door but stood with her back against it, facing me. "Something's happened," she said.

"Graham Meighen died this morning," I said. "It was a heart attack."

Her skin paled. "You'd better sit down," I said. I helped her to the chaise longue.

"I'm all right. It's just a shock." Her voice was flat. "I've had a few of those lately."

"Take some deep breaths," I said.

Before long, the colour began to return to Jill's cheeks. "Did he suffer?" she asked finally.

"I don't know," I said.

For a moment we were both silent and then I asked the question that had been dogging me. "Jill, you knew the kind of man Graham Meighen was. Why did you get involved with him?"

Her tone was sardonic. "Why did I get involved with any of the men I've been with? When my one and only marriage ended, I went to a shrink. I wanted to know why, when I finally decided to marry, I chose a man whom I knew was incapable of love. She told me I was punishing myself for my affair with Ian. And, Jo, she told me something else. She told me that the reason I was so obsessed with having Bryn as my daughter was because of my guilt about the abortion."

"Did you buy that?"

"I don't know. I may be a fallen-away Catholic, but I've always had an endless supply of guilt." Jill flexed her long, freckled, ringless fingers. "Do you want to hear something weird?" she said. "There was a point in my relationship with Graham when I really believed he was Mr. Right."

I was incredulous. "How could that happen?"

"As soon as you told me that Slater Doyle had played you the tape of Ian and me, I knew the shining new life I was planning to build with you and your family would never happen. I've never felt so alone. But Graham was there, attentive, flattering, and apparently willing to pick up the pieces." Jill closed her eyes. "And you know the rest. My knight in shining armour turned out to be a monster who tried to kill me."

"Because he realized you'd given me the information about his phone call with Slater Doyle."

Jill frowned. "That's what I thought at first. Everything happened so fast, but I've had time to think since I got here. Jo, Graham never even mentioned his phone call with Slater Doyle. All he cared about was getting my phone itself. I didn't have it. After I talked to you I went for a run in Victoria Park. When I couldn't find the phone in my hotel room, I assumed I'd lost it on my run. I was on my way out the door to retrace my steps when Graham burst in demanding that I hand over my phone. I told him I didn't have it, and I was just about to go looking for it. That's when he went crazy. He said he knew I'd taken pictures. Apparently there's a surveillance camera in the master bedroom and he'd seen me taking pictures of the safe and of the papers on his desk. At that point, he was raving, and I just wanted to get away from him. I apologized. I told him he could come with me to the park and when I found my camera, I'd hand it over to him. That's when he began choking me.

"I was sure I was dying. I must have passed out. When I regained consciousness, I was naked, and he was raping me. He'd removed his hands from my throat. I was starved for oxygen. When he saw I was able to gasp for air, he choked me again. I don't know how long it went on. Finally, I just slid into unconsciousness. That's when he must have . . . done whatever he did to me."

Jill was shaking violently. I put my arms around her shoulders and held her until her body calmed. "It's over," I said finally. "Graham Meighen will never hurt you or anyone else again. You won't have to testify because there won't be a trial. What Graham Meighen did to you is proof that he was a very sick man who killed once and tried to kill again. He had to be stopped. You have your story, Jill."

"The story isn't finished," Jill said. "Jo, my phone's over on the nightstand. Someone found it in Vic Park. The phone wasn't locked so they checked my email address and got in touch with NationTV. Luke picked the phone up for me this afternoon. Until now, I didn't want to look at it – too many memories."

"But you're ready now," I said.

Jill nodded, then, heads touching, she and I looked through the pictures she'd taken at Graham's home on Thanksgiving night. Several photos were of slips of paper she'd taken from a drawer in Graham's desk. She said they didn't make any sense – they were just numbers jotted down. But she'd noticed that one of the number sequences was repeated many times.

Jill indicated it with her fingertip. "Obviously those numbers were much on Graham's mind. Can you see any significance there?"

"Yes," I said. "These are the numbers Cronus sent with the photo of him, Zack and Brock. The afternoon before he died, Cronus asked me to take a buddy shot of him with Zack and Brock. I have no idea to whom he sent the picture, but when he tapped out the message he said a series of numbers out loud: "2-5-1-0-0-6. I assumed it was all one number, but Graham's written the figures so they're spaced. 25 10 06. Jill, we have to call Debbie Haczkewicz with this."

"Give me one day," Jill said. "This is my story. Let me try to work it out. Besides, it's E-Day. You have a thousand things to do, and Graham's dead. The police won't be able to move as quickly on this as I can, and if I can get solid proof of what was really going on between Graham and Ridgeway, we might be able to sway some late voters. Give me one day to help before you go to the police."

I stood. "All right, but first thing tomorrow morning, we're going to Debbie."

CHAPTER

18

On E-Day, time stands still. After months in which every minute is accounted for, there is suddenly nothing to do but wait. When I got back to the condo, I was dreading the long day ahead, but Zack and Taylor were at the breakfast table, seemingly oblivious to the larger world.

"Dad just made the best breakfast," Taylor said. "I love Boursin au poivre in anything, but it is soooooo good in scrambled eggs."

Zack pushed his chair back from the table. "I can make you some eggs," he said.

"Thanks, but my stomach's a little queasy. I'll just have tea and toast."

Zack frowned. "Are you coming down with something?"

"No. Telling Jill about Graham was rough, and the news seemed to jolt her memory about the assault. Anyway, I'm not sick. It's just nerves."

"After you have your toast, let's go for a swim. That always relaxes you."

"This really is a banner day," I said. "That's the first time you've ever actually volunteered to go for a swim."

"I just want to watch you get into your bathing suit."

Taylor coughed theatrically. "I'm still here, you know."

"Duly noted," Zack said. "Do you want a ride to school?"

Taylor's lips twitched with mischief. "Are you trying to get me out of the way?"

"No flies on you," Zack said. "But the drive to school is a time-sensitive offer, and the clock is ticking."

Zack and I were in our robes and ready to go down to the pool when Milo called from downstairs.

Zack uttered his favourite expletive, but he buzzed Milo in. As always, Milo came in drumming, but when he saw that we were in our swimming gear, he stopped in his tracks. "You guys are going swimming," he said.

"If you want to talk, we can wait," Zack said amiably.

"Actually, what I'd like to do is have a swim," Milo said. "I don't suppose you have a spare suit around here."

Zack shot me a warning look, but I ignored him. "I'll get you one of Angus's," I said.

I found Milo a suit, a robe, and a towel, and told him the pool was in the basement, and we'd meet him there. When we got into the elevator Zack was still grumbling. "This swim was supposed to relax you," he said. "Nobody can relax around Milo."

"Tomorrow Milo will be gone," I said. "It'll be nice to have a little private time with him today. He's been terrific, Zack."

"I know," Zack said. "He's taken a lot of the burden off you, and for that I am very grateful. Where's Milo going anyway?"

"To the next campaign," I said. "It's a congressional seat in Alabama. The current congressman got caught with his pecker in the pickle barrel, so there's a special election. Milo's candidate is slightly to the right of Genghis Khan."

"That'll be a one-eighty for him. Our campaign was pretty progressive."

"Milo won't miss a beat," I said. "He's a professional. He doesn't have principles, he has very specialized skills. He'll give his new candidate exactly the kind of loyalty and commitment he gave you."

Zack's smile was sheepish. "Kind of like a lawyer," he said.

"Exactly," I said.

Milo's swimming was a surprise. He knifed into the pool, barely rippling the surface. Water was clearly Milo's element. Swimming gave his wild, kinetic energy a conduit, and he moved with grace and power. For twenty minutes, side-by-side, the three of us did laps. Enveloped in our watery tranquil world, no one said a word. When we pulled ourselves out of the pool, the bond was still there. Then Milo shook the water from his head and turned to Zack and me. "That fucking fucker Meighen may have finally fucked us," he said.

"How so?" Zack said.

Milo wrapped his thin body in his towel. "Meighen's death gives Ridgeway a free pass for the day. Slater Doyle's a douchebag, but he's not stupid. By now he will have a called a press conference and he'll be coaching his candidate, the homeroom monitor, on what he should say."

"The homeroom monitor should be able to handle this assignment," Zack said. All he needs to say is that people should remember that Meighen was innocent until proven guilty, and since nothing had been proven when he died, Meighen died an innocent man. As long as no one challenges him, he'll be fine. And if he gets a tough question, he can always just choke up and run."

Milo spent the rest of the morning at the Noodle House tweeting and checking voter turnout. Zack didn't want to comment on the Meighen situation until after Scott Ridgeway's press conference, so he and I kept a low profile, moving from poll to poll and thanking poll captains and volunteers. We were home in time for the noon news. Zack's prediction that the mayor would crumble at the first probing question was prescient.

As he stepped before the microphones in his black suit, white shirt, and navy tie, the mayor was red-eyed, wan, and sombre. He read a prepared statement that was almost word for word what Zack had reeled off by the swimming pool. When he turned to leave, the media began to shout questions. Ridgeway looked startled, but he walked back to the microphones. A rangy young woman with a ponytail asked whether the Meighen case would remain on the books as still open.

The question seemed to stun Ridgeway. "But Graham's dead," he said.

The young woman had clearly done her homework. "My information is that the evidence the police have amassed against Graham Meighen points to 'beyond a reasonable doubt' proof of his guilt in at least two major crimes."

The mayor was exasperated. "Didn't you hear me? Graham's dead. Why would there be a trial?"

"So even though the evidence against Meighen hasn't been tested before the courts, you're in favour of putting the investigation to bed."

The mayor's eyes darted towards Slater Doyle. The intent of Doyle's subtle headshake was clear. He was urging the mayor to say no, but Scott Ridgeway didn't get the message. "I don't know what I think," he said. "All I know is that my friend is dead." Then Ridgeway teared up and fled.

Milo had alerted the media that Zack and I would be voting in one of the gymnasia at Racette-Hunter at one o'clock, so they were ready with cameras and questions when we arrived. After we'd smiled for the obligatory "candidate and spouse entering the voting booth" photos, the questions began. Once again, the rangy young woman took the lead: "Did you see the mayor's news conference?"

"I did," Zack said.

"Any thoughts about why the mayor left the room rather than face questions about Graham Meighen's activities since Labour Day?"

Zack shrugged. "The mayor's campaign manager used to be a lawyer. I'm sure by now he's reminded the mayor that depending on the evidence, the police might decide to push ahead with the investigation into Cronus's murder, despite Mr. Meighen's death. I'm sure Mr. Doyle has also reminded the mayor that if the case is still open, he shouldn't comment on it. I'm a lawyer, so I won't be commenting either. Thank you for coming out today. The photos of Joanne and me voting will be a nice souvenir."

And with that, we went home to wait. The latest Insightrix Poll had Zack at 52 per cent of likely voters and Scott Ridgeway at 48 per cent. Way too close to call.

Margot had invited Brock, us, the kids, and the grandkids to eat and watch the results at her house. Margot's caterer of choice was Evolution, and Aimee had outdone herself with the buffet. But the children were the only ones who had an appetite. Even Taylor, who was normally a trencherwoman, picked at her food and watched the clock, waiting for the polls to close.

Not long after eight, the numbers started to come in. The first results were from the south end, an area that was supposedly solid for Ridgeway, but Zack was doing surprisingly well. The east end was a disappointment. We thought we'd made real inroads, but apparently dog whistle politics had triumphed, and while Zack's numbers there improved, they never surged. After the first half-hour the numbers came so quickly, we didn't even bother writing them down.

Zack was getting the figures directly from Milo on Twitter. Hunched over his phone, peering through his reading glasses at the screen, Zack was a solitary figure. Several times I went over to massage his shoulders. He smiled absently and kept his eyes on the numbers.

At 9:25, with thirty-two of the thirty-two precincts reporting, Zack was ahead by 251 votes. Margot had muted the sound on the television. For a few minutes, we all just stared at the screen, but no matter how hard we stared, the numbers didn't change.

Finally, Taylor walked over to Zack, kissed him, and said the unsayable. "It looks like you won, Dad."

Zack took off his glasses and turned to me. "So now we wait for Ridgeway to concede."

"And he may not," I said. "Slater may want a recount."

"Do you think he will?"

"I don't, but what does Milo say?"

Zack checked Twitter. "There were 58,395 accepted votes. Milo thinks a lead of 251 should be enough."

"I think so too," I said. "But it's their move. If I were Slater, I'd concede. If they want a recount, they'll have to go to court. The process will drag on for days, and in the end, nothing will change. The count Milo gave us was of *accepted* votes. That means those 58,395 votes have already passed the smell test. Concession will give Ridgeway a dignified exit, and after a dirty campaign they could use a grace note."

As always on election nights, Howard had been quiet, watching the numbers, assessing the possibilities. I turned to him. "What do you think?"

He didn't hesitate. As Howard had reminded me during a sharp exchange about strategy during Zack's campaign, he had been to the rodeo many times before. "They'll concede," he said. "Every sitting member of city council was defeated tonight. Scott Ridgeway was a puppet. He doesn't have the brains or the stomach to deal with a council that will oppose him, even if the count did somehow prove to be wrong. And the money boys won't be encouraging him to stay. They need a winner and Ridgeway lost." Howard checked his watch. "9:45," he said. "Jo, I'll bet you a bottle of Crown Royal, Ridgeway will be onstage at the Travelodge within half an hour giving his concession speech."

"You're on," I said. "Except we're betting for a dozen Black and White cookies. Do you really think they'll concede within half an hour?"

"Slater Doyle will be writing the speech, and it's his last chance to fuck with our minds," Howard said. "But he's not stupid. He knows it's over."

At 10:10, Scott Ridgeway entered the convention room of the Travelodge to give his concession speech. The mayor appeared dazed. Slater Doyle came onstage with him and stood less than a metre away. As Ridgeway spoke, his eyes kept seeking Slater's. The speech was good, but the sparse audience's response was tepid. Howard had won his cookies.

When they left the stage, I turned off my phone. "That's it," I said. "Time to move."

Zack wheeled towards the door. "I'll get our jackets."

Taylor leapt up. "I'll help you, Dad."

I looked around the room. Everyone was still awake. "Who's up for the Pile O' Bones?" I said.

Madeleine and Lena were the first to volunteer. "Tomorrow's a school day," Mieka said. The girls groaned. "Okay, this is a special occasion. Grab your coats."

It was almost impossible to find parking around the club. I dropped Zack and Taylor off and began searching for a spot. After my third tour of the neighbourhood, I dug the

handicapped sign out of the glove compartment, went back
to the Pile O' Bones, and nosed into a spot near the entrance.

Inside, Zack and Taylor were still attempting to navigate
through the crowd. Brock had joined them, but they weren't
having much success. People were hugging them and some
were crying. It seemed everyone wanted to talk to the newly
elected mayor and councillor. I was relieved when Howard,
who had driven over in his own car, steered them purposefully towards the ramp that led to the stage.

It was already close to eleven and the next day was a workday. The sooner the speeches were over, the better. I saw that
our family and Margot's had gathered on the left side of the
hall. I managed to push through the well-wishers to join
them. When we were together, I gave Howard the high sign
to get the evening underway.

Howard introduced Brock as the new councillor from
Ward 6, and the crowd erupted. Brock's speech was brief and
gracious, then he introduced Zack. When the applause and
whoops and hollers died down, Zack began by congratulat-
ing Scott Ridgeway for a spirited campaign. Predictably,
there were boos and catcalls. Equally predictably, Zack qui-
eted the grumbling and began.

"Tonight when we finally knew the election results, our
seven-year-old granddaughter, Lena, said, 'Well I'm glad
that's over.'" There was laughter. Zack joined in, then he
continued. "I understand how she felt. I imagine you do
too. It's been a long, hard campaign. When we began, everybody wrote us off. The idea that a slate of populists could
defeat an entrenched mayor and council seemed ludicrous.
But we did it.

"And in the process, we reminded the citizens of Regina
that rich or poor, Canadian-born or born elsewhere; Muslim,
Hindu, Jew, Christian, agnostic or atheist; male or female;
gay, straight, bi, or questioning, we are all in this together.

"Almost a hundred years ago, a man who was as wise as he was humane said, 'What we desire for ourselves we wish for all.' His words still resonate. We are a wealthy city that truly does have enough for all – enough money, enough food, enough work, enough challenges. And it seems we're finally accepting the truth of that old adage: 'My neighbour's strength is my strength.'

"Lena was right. Part of our job *is* over. You were the reason we won tonight. You were our ground game. Day after day, you went door to door, talked to your neighbours, phoned radio shows, worked social media, made personal phone calls. You identified the voters who supported us and today you mobilized them.

"What we've accomplished together is nothing short of miraculous. But we've just begun. So go home. Get a good night's sleep. Dream big dreams and tomorrow we'll get to work."

Our family joined Zack and Brock on stage. We smiled, waved, grouped, and regrouped. When the last picture was snapped, Taylor went home with Margot and Lexi, and Zack and I began wading through the crowd towards the exit. It was slow going, but it was good to see so many of the people I'd come to know at the Noodle House. Zack hadn't exaggerated the importance of our ground game. These volunteers had been the key to our success, and they deserved a personal thank you. I was especially pleased to see Elder Ernest Beauvais, who had gathered together the corps of Aboriginal and Métis workers who got out the vote in our ward. Ernest was six-foot-six – easy to spot in a crowd. He was shepherding Peggy Kreviazuk, and they were both beaming. Peggy had worked in elections since she was a teenager. Like Ernest, she had lost more battles than she'd won, and they were both clearly relishing this win.

———

I was pleasantly surprised to bump into my good Samaritan, Boomer, who was there with his lady. Her name was Kelly, and they had both worked hard to get their fellow bikers to the polls. When Warren and Annie Weber approached Boomer and Kelly, it was old-home week. Before she married her millionaire, Annie had worked at the biker bar on Winnipeg Street and she, Boomer, and Kelly had obviously shared some great times. As the bikers reminisced, Zack and Warren had a confab. That left me free to seek out the person I most wanted to see that night.

I knew where to find him. Like all political pros, Milo would be at the back of the hall, near the exit. When he saw me he gave me the thumbs-up.

"Nice work," I said.

"It turned out," he said laconically.

I moved closer to him. "Milo, when are you through in Alabama?"

"December 4."

"Have you got anything after that?"

He shrugged. "It's a last-minute business. What's up?"

"How would you feel about coming back here and working for Zack and me?"

"The election's over. I'm a one-trick pony."

"Maybe, but it's a useful trick. Lancaster Development is not going to sit back and let us govern for three years. They won't even give us three weeks. My guess is they're already strategizing about how to defeat every initiative Zack and the new council bring forward. At the end of Ridgeway's campaign, the Lancaster people held back their money, so they already have a war chest, and they have deep pockets. They can buy 'experts' who will shoot holes in everything we propose, and they can blanket the media with ads targeting their supporters and urging them to bombard Zack and the new council with hate mail.

"We only won by 251 votes," I continued. "Dog whistle politics almost worked for the Lancaster group today. They're going to be pushing and we have to push back – hard. We need to keep our volunteers active. We need to poll. We need to figure out how to tell our story and sell our vision. We need you to mobilize our ground game again. I can do some of this now, and Christmas will give us breathing space, but by January we have to be ready to go on the attack."

"Got it," Milo said. "I'm in."

"Aren't you going to ask about salary?"

"I never care about that shit," he said. "I'm just in it for the rush."

I thought about my life since Labour Day and laughed. "Yeah, me too," I said.

Milo handed me a Crispy Crunch bar. "See you around," he said.

When Zack joined me, he looked around quizzically. "Where's Milo?"

"On his way to Alabama. But he's coming back in December to work for us. We'll talk about it in the car."

Zack raised an eyebrow when he saw that we were parked in the handicapped zone. "It was either here or six blocks away," I said. "And I don't know about you, but I'm not up to a midnight jaunt."

"No. As usual, you made the right call, Ms. Shreve. Want me to drive?"

"Yes. I don't think I'm too sharp."

"You were sharp enough to find and hire Milo in the five minutes I was talking to Warren."

We snapped on our seatbelts and Zack pulled out of the parking lot.

"I had to move fast," I said. "As soon as I realized we'd won, I knew exactly what we needed."

"Milo?" Zack said.

"A goalie," I said. "A lot of people are going to be taking shots at us. Ken Dryden always said the goalie's job is to know what's coming next and insert himself like a stick into the spokes of a bike and stop the action. Milo's job will be to know what's coming next so we can stop it."

"Maggie Muggins could have used Milo," Zack said.

I laughed. "The truth is that for all her wondering about what would happen tomorrow, nothing much ever happened to Maggie. Every day she'd skip over to Mr. McGarrity's garden, chat with Fitzgerald Fieldmouse and Grandmother Frog, solve a very small problem, and then skip home."

"The road we're going to be travelling will be a lot rockier than Maggie's," Zack said. For a few minutes he was silent. Then he turned to me. "Jo, did you think we were going to win?"

"No," I said. "Did you?"

"No." Then he took me in his arms. "What a long, strange journey it's been," he said.

CHAPTER

19

It was a little after five the next morning when Jill called, sounding like her old self. "I've got something," she said. "I couldn't get to sleep last night. Congratulations about the election, incidentally."

"Thanks," I said. "But I take it this isn't just a courtesy call."

"No. As I was tossing and turning, I kept asking myself why Graham would have repeatedly written down the numbers Cronus sent with his photo. Finally I got up, plugged the numbers and Scott Ridgeway's name into Google, and voila – Scott Ridgeway was first elected mayor of Regina on October 25, 2006."

"Wow," I said. "That's major."

"I think you're right," Jill said. "Now we just have to figure out what to do with the information."

Zack was still sleeping when the dogs and I left for our run. It had been a long night, and as excited as I was about Jill's news, I didn't want to awaken him. I was eager to tell Brock, but when he got on the elevator he was sombre and preoccupied. He hesitated before pressing the Down button.

"Something you want to talk about?" I said.

"Michael and I spent the night together," he said.

"To the victor go the spoils," I said.

"You're angry," Brock said.

"Just upset. Brock, getting involved with Michael again would be a terrible mistake."

"Michael knows what he did was wrong," Brock said. "He admits he was guilty of a terrible lapse of judgment with Liz Meighen."

The memory of the agony in Liz's voice when she told me she'd lost her words was fresh. "What Michael did goes well beyond 'a lapse of judgment,'" I said. "He's a physician and Liz was his patient. At the very least his actions were unethical."

Brock lowered his eyes. "He never intended for Liz Meighen to die," he said softly. "The plan was to give Liz prescription drugs that would confuse her enough so that she would hand over power of attorney to Graham. Once Graham had access to Liz's money, Michael would scale back on the drugs, and Liz would be fine."

I tried to keep my temper in check. "But she's not fine, Brock. Liz is dead. And Michael is responsible. Did he explain to you why he went along with Graham's plan?"

Brock rubbed Pantera's neck. "No. Last night we were as close as two people could be, but Michael refused to talk about his relationship with Meighen. I thought Meighen's death would mean the end of whatever hold he had over Michael, but Michael is still afraid. I know he's in serious trouble, but I'd be prepared to stick it out if I was the only one involved."

"But you're not the only one involved," I said. "Brock, we won last night. We have an obligation to the people who voted for Zack and you and the rest of the slate. We made promises, and we have to honour them."

"So you think I should tell Michael he's on his own?"

"I think you need to know the whole story before you make a decision," I said.

"Is Michael still at your place?"

Brock nodded.

"I have a question that might be the key to getting him to open up to you. Are you willing to let me try?"

"At this point, I'll try anything," Brock said. "Let's go."

Michael was dressed and in the living room checking his phone when we came in. Seeing me must have been a shock, but he kept his greeting neutral.

I came straight to the point: "Brock told me about your part in Graham's plan to convince Liz Meighen she should entrust her affairs to him. Michael, it's only a matter of time before the truth about everything Graham Meighen did comes out. Your best option now is just to tell the truth."

Brock put his arm around Michael's shoulder. "You're not alone," he said. "But I can't help you until I know what's going on."

"I don't know where to start," Michael said

"Let me tell you what we know," I said. "On the afternoon he died, Cronus sent out a photo of himself with the message 25, 10, 06. Graham Meighen doodled those same numbers repeatedly on papers that were found on his desk. Scott Ridgeway was elected mayor for the first time on October 25, 2006. What's the significance of that date?"

The blood drained from Michael's face. "It was the worst night of my life," he said, "but when it began I was on the cusp of the life I'd always wanted. Slater had managed Scott Ridgeway's campaign and he'd promised me that as soon as the election was over he'd tell his wife that he was gay, and we could be together. Slater had introduced me to Graham Meighen, and Graham had been like a father to me. I'd never been interested in politics, but Graham had shown me the importance of having a mayor and a city council that would make our city a magnet for excellence. For two years, Graham and his cohorts at Lancaster Development had groomed men and women who shared their vision. When the results came in that night, Graham said this was just the beginning and that from now on everything would come our way.

"A group of us went to a hotel room to celebrate. We had a lot to drink and we dropped ecstasy. People drifted off. Finally there were just four of us: Slater, Scott, Graham, and me. Graham said he'd been to a club on Rose Street that specialized in what he called 'designer sex.' We just had to call ahead and tell them what we wanted. The sex workers were both male and female. They were young and medically certified as clean – no protection necessary, and they would do whatever we asked. Cronus owned the house at 12 Rose Street. Graham called him and he said he'd set it all up with the woman who ran the sex club. Slater wanted a foursome with me and two twinks – really young guys, blond, slender, no body hair. We went upstairs and the boys came in. They were gorgeous and they were willing. The four of us went at it. Molly has a way of making time disappear. I don't know how much time passed before I realized someone was knocking at the door. We ignored it, but they got frantic. Finally, Slater pulled on his pants and unlocked the door. Scott was standing in the hall, naked, covered in blood, and hysterical. He said, 'She needs a doctor, Michael. You've got to help me.'

"Slater went to find Graham, and I followed Scott downstairs into a bedroom in the basement. The door was open, but there were no lights on. I hit the switch for the overhead light. The first thing that struck me was how small the girl was. The second was the amount of blood. I said, 'My God, what did you do to her?'

"Scott was barely coherent. Finally he said, 'I said I wanted to have sex with a virgin. This is the girl they sent.'

"I remember saying, 'She's just a child. What were you thinking?' Then I turned my attention to the girl. I knelt beside her. I knew she was dying. There were some flashes of light behind me. I turned and saw Graham in the doorway taking pictures. I told him to stop and call an ambulance because the girl was bleeding out.

"I remember he was very calm. He said, 'I'll take care of it. Just get everybody out of here. The escorts have been paid. Tell Slater to go home to his wife and take Scott to your place. He's babbling about calling the police and that can't happen. Give him a shot to knock him out.'

"I told Graham I didn't want any part of what was going on. He just laughed and held up his camera. 'You are a part of what's going on," he said. 'I have pictures.'

"I took Scott home with me, put him in the shower, gave him something to calm him down, got rid of his clothes, and went to bed. The next morning I called the hospitals – no girl had been admitted. When I called Graham and asked him where the girl was, he said she'd been taken care of. I said I was going to the police and Graham told me to take a drive by 12 Rose Street before I did anything.

"I told Scott to stay at my place and I drove to Rose Street. There were trucks from one of Lancaster's construction companies there. The workers had taken down the back fence and driven the trucks right into the yard. There were already huge mounds of earth, but they were still digging. A cement truck was there to pour concrete when the time was right. I knew the girl would be under that concrete, and I knew that I would never draw another free breath."

"Graham Meighen used the pictures he took that night to keep you in line," I said.

Michael appeared to be on the verge of collapse. Brock tightened his hold on Michael's shoulders. "Maybe you should lie down," he said.

"No," I said. "Keep him here." I was angrier than I could ever remember being. "There's something he needs to know." I stepped closer to Michael. "Her name was Ellen," I said.

He looked at me without comprehension.

"The girl you let bleed to death – the girl buried under the concrete at 12 Rose Street – she had a name. Her name was Ellen."

Zack wasn't there when I came in. There was a note on the kitchen table. "Driving Taylor to school and then doing an interview on NationTV. Back in an hour." He'd signed his note "Zachary Davis Shreve, Mayor Elect, City of Regina."

For the only time I could remember, I was grateful to be alone in the condo. As I texted Brock the contact info for Asia Libke, a lawyer Zack often recommended, I couldn't stop trembling. I went into the bedroom, put on my bathing suit, and took the elevator down to the pool. I swam until I was able to control my breathing and my body. Controlling my mind would be less easy. I knew the image of Ellen, the girl with the shining eyes who died because she was a virgin, would stay with me forever.

Zack was buoyant when he came back. He wheeled over to me and held out his arms. "You have no idea how many people just confided in me that they were with me all along."

"Victory has a thousand fathers," I said.

"Lots of congratulatory calls, lots of back slaps, and attaboys at NationTV, and there's a great picture of you, Taylor, and me on the front page of the paper."

"A banner day," I said.

"You bet," Zack said. "And right now, I'm in the mood for one of those Bull Durham kisses – the long, slow, deep soft ones that last three days."

"So am I," I said. "But we're going to have to start that kiss this afternoon. Zack, I know why Cronus died, and you need to be out of the city today. I want you to drive out to Lawyers' Bay. Don't answer the phone, and don't check your email or your texts until I get there. Taylor has a spare last period, so with luck, we should be at the lake by four."

"And you can't tell me what this is about?"

"No," I said. "I can't, and you really should get on the highway ASAP."

Jill was in the living room reading the morning paper when I arrived. She was clearly surprised to see me. When she rose to her feet, she was a little unsteady. I held her arm and helped her back to her room. "Are you ready for an outing?" I asked.

"Sure. Where are we going?"

"The police station."

As we drove downtown I filled Jill in on Michael Goetz's account of the events of October 25, 2006.

When I was through, Jill looked as miserable as I felt. "That poor child. So Zack's first day as mayor-elect is going to be a gong show."

"No," I said. "It's going to be tranquil. I packed him off to the lake half an hour ago and told him not to answer his phone or read his email or texts. There'll be a lot of confusion in the next few days – outside media, rumours, crazy stuff. Zack and Taylor and I will come back to the city Monday morning. By then, the facts will have come to the surface, and Zack can say something that pours oil on the roiling waters."

———

The interview with Debbie Hackewicz took a little over half an hour. When Jill and I left, Michael Goetz and his lawyer, Asia Libke, were waiting in the outer office.

Jill insisted on walking back to my car. The nearest parking place was a block and half from the police station and as she snapped on her seatbelt she was clearly in pain. "Was this too much for you?" I said.

"No. It needed to be done. Jo, could we drive by the house on Rose Street."

"Of course. It's not far from here." The rain was coming down hard as we pulled up in front of Number 12. Oblivious, a drunk did his lumbering dance along the sidewalk towards us. A whip-thin dog nosed a greasy fast-food wrapper in the gutter. The windows of Number 12 were squares of light in the dark afternoon.

"Ellen's grandmother lives in that house."

"Was she connected with the sex club?"

"No. Cronus kept records of the tenants in each of his houses. During the period when 12 Rose Street housed the sex club, no one lived there. The owner of the club had a lease. Nell Standingready moved in the week after that terrible night and she's lived there rent-free ever since. She had lived in one of the other houses Cronus owned. My guess is Cronus needed an ideal tenant who wouldn't do anything to cause the authorities to visit 12 Rose Street. Nell Standingready has made the house a shrine to that child."

"By this time tomorrow, the police will be destroying the shrine," I said. "And they will have found the child who died because Scott Ridgeway wanted to have sex with a virgin. I don't know about you, but I've had enough."

I speeded up and started down the street. A sex worker wearing thigh-high boots, a micro mini, and an animal-print jacket stood under a streetlight at the intersection of Rose and 7th Avenue. It was a high-traffic area. She was carrying an umbrella, and as we passed, she waved at us with her free hand. I kept on driving.

Jill glanced back at the intersection. "She's flagging you down, Jo."

I made a U-turn, drove back towards the intersection, and pulled over. The woman ran across the street and approached the driver's side of the Volvo. When I opened my window, the woman moved her umbrella back so I could see her face.

It was Angela. She was heavily made up and her hair was elaborately curled. She was breathless from the effort of running. "Joanne, I've been trying to get the nerve to call you, and here you are. I'm taking that martial arts class, and I've thrown Eddie out. I thought you'd like to know that."

"That's the best news I've had in a long time," I said. "How are your children doing?"

"They're good. Nell Standingready's watching them when I'm at work." Angela's laugh was rough-edged. "Yeah, this is still what I do for a living." She met my eyes. "It pays the bills, Joanne."

"Got it," I said. "Angela, if I came by the R-H Centre one day next week after your class, could we have coffee?"

This time there was no mistaking the derision in her laughter. "Like girlfriends," she said. "I don't see that happening, Joanne."

Before I could respond, she ran back across the street.

Jill and I were both quiet as we drove to Whitman Convalescent. Jill broke the silence. "What are you going to do about your friend back there?"

"Angela?" I said. "I'm going to keep showing up at the R-H Centre after her martial arts class until she agrees to have coffee with me."

"Are you bucking for sainthood?"

"Nope. My mother used to say I never knew when to leave well enough alone. She also told me at least once a day that I was a pain in the ass. How are you doing?"

"I'm okay. Jo, do you think your children will ever forgive me?"

"It'll take time, but they'll come around."

"Have you forgiven me?"

"Yes," I said.

Jill reached in her bag and took out the rosary Anneta Kopchek had given her. "Good," she said. "Because I've just about worn this thing out praying."

It was a chilly evening. Zack had the fire roaring when Taylor and I arrived at the lake. There were steaks on a plate on the kitchen counter and the table was set.

Taylor took a cup of tea to her studio. Zack poured us both a martini, and we settled in on the couch in front of the fireplace. "So are you going to fill me in on what's happened?" he said.

"Not yet," I said. "Not until that fire has warmed my bones, we've had our drinks and our steaks, and we've devoted some serious time to that long, slow, deep, soft, wet kiss."

"The one that last three days?"

"We're going to have to settle for the abbreviated version tonight," I said. "The enormity of what's ahead is starting to sink in. I saw Angela this afternoon, Zack. She's back working the streets."

"So the struggle continues," Zack said. "But now we have a chance to do our part. You did a hell of a job managing the campaign, Jo. You totally outkicked your coverage."

I put my head on Zack's shoulder. Our bodies were close and I could feel his warmth. "At times like this I really believe that there's nothing we can't do," I said.

Zack sipped his drink. "Keep believing," he said. "Keep believing, and we may just make it happen."

ACKNOWLEDGEMENTS

Thanks to:

Hildy Bowen, Brett Bell, Max Bowen, Carrie Renner Bowen, and Nathaniel Bowen for sharing their knowledge about the many things I don't know and for their love and laughter.

Kai Langen, Madeleine Bowen-Diaz, Lena Bowen-Diaz, Chesney Langen Bell, Ben Bowen-Bell, Peyton Bowen, and Lexi Kate Bowen for being the light of our lives.

Rick Mitchell, retired Staff Sergeant in Charge of Major Crimes Section, Regina Police Service, for reading the manuscript of *12 Rose Street* twice and for his incisive comments.

Najma Kazmi, M.D., for seeing her patients as people and meeting their needs with grace and skill.

Ryan B. Eidness, M.D., for his excellent diagnostic and surgical skills and his gentle manner.

Lara Hinchberger, my editor, and her associate, Kendra Ward, for editorial work that was nothing short of brilliant.

Heather Sangster, extraordinary copy editor and sister dog lover.

Ashley Dunn, for being Ashley Dunn – perfect in every way.

Mark Summers (Cap'n Slappy) and John Baur (Ol' Chumbucket), the Pirate Guys, for generosity and good cheer.

Finally, thanks once again to the City of Regina, which continues to allow me and my family to live rich and meaningful lives. J.S. Woodsworth once said, "What we desire for ourselves we wish for all." Those words were never far from my mind when I wrote *12 Rose Street*. Regina is a great city, but there is work to be done.

I have tried to portray our city truthfully, but my novels are fiction. In *12 Rose Street*, I have created a mayor and city council who serve my narrative purposes but who bear no resemblance to our real mayor and city council. The mandate of Regina's real mayor and city council is to make this a great city for all its citizens. It's a big job, but they are working tirelessly to make J.S. Woodsworth's ideal a reality.